Jenna took Blue's hand. "Will you walk me out to my truck? I really have to go or Uncle Ron will be calling Nate to round up a search party."

Jenna led Blue out into the cold night air and down the steps to where her truck was parked. He let her lead, which was a first, and stopped obediently beside her as she went to open the door.

"Thanks for a great—"

The rest of what she had been going to say was devoured by his kiss, which tasted of peaches and hot man— a combination that was rapidly becoming her all-time favorite. Her back was against the truck and his body covered her completely, one of his hands anchored around her hips and the other tangled in her hair.

She fought to free one hand from between them and wrapped it around his neck, holding on to all that lean-muscled power for dear life. God, he was beautiful. It was like petting a jaguar. There was nothing else in her vision than Blue's face and the feel of his mouth moving over hers. Eventually, even she had to breathe and she broke off the kiss and buried her face in the crook of his neck . . .

Books by Kate Pearce

The House of Pleasure Series
SIMPLY SEXUAL
SIMPLY SINFUL
SIMPLY SHAMELESS
SIMPLY WICKED
SIMPLY INSATIABLE
SIMPLY FORBIDDEN
SIMPLY CARNAL
SIMPLY VORACIOUS
SIMPLY SCANDALOUS
SIMPLY PLEASURE (e-novella)
SIMPLY IRRESISTIBLE (e-novella)

The Sinners Club Series
THE SINNERS CLUB
TEMPTING A SINNER
MASTERING A SINNER
THE FIRST SINNERS (e-novella)

Single Titles
RAW DESIRE

The Morgan Brothers Ranch
THE RELUCTANT COWBOY
THE MAVERICK COWBOY

Anthologies
SOME LIKE IT ROUGH
LORDS OF PASSION

Published by Kensington Publishing Corporation

THE
MAVERICK COWBOY

KATE PEARCE

ZEBRA BOOKS
KENSINGTON PUBLISHING CORP.
http://www.kensingtonbooks.com

ZEBRA BOOKS are published by

Kensington Publishing Corp.
119 West 40th Street
New York, NY 10018

All Kensington titles, imprints, and distributed lines are available at special quantity discounts for bulk purchases for sales promotion, premiums, fund-raising, educational, or institutional use.

Special book excerpts or customized printings can also be created to fit specific needs. For details, write or phone the office of the Kensington Sales Manager: Attn.: Sales Department. Kensington Publishing Corp., 119 West 40th Street, New York, NY 10018. Phone: 1-800-221-2647.

Zebra and the Z logo Reg. U.S. Pat. & TM Off.

First Printing: February 2017
ISBN-13: 978-1-4201-4002-6
ISBN-10: 1-4201-4002-7

eISBN-13: 978-1-4201-4003-3
eISBN-10: 1-4201-4003-5

10 9 8 7 6 5 4 3 2 1

Printed in the United States of America

ACKNOWLEDGMENTS

A big thank you to husband and wife team Sam and Kat for helping me out with all things Marine. (Any mistakes are definitely my own.) And thanks to my trusty beta readers: Sidney Bristol, Genevieve Turner and Zara Keane.

Chapter One

Humboldt-Toiyabe National Forest, California
Marine Corps Mountain Warfare Training Center

"Holy shit!"

The sight of a one-hundred-and-thirty-pound Marine flailing around like a chicken—a Marine Blue Morgan was tethered to on the side of a sheer cliff face—was not good. With a yell, the idiot lost his grip, and his booted feet scrabbled for purchase, narrowly missing Blue's head. The only thing keeping them from plummeting to the bottom of the canyon was the steel pin driven into the rock. It still meant Fielding swung out on his rope like a pendulum, jerking his unfortunate instructor up to meet him.

Blue barely had time to brace himself before he smashed into the other man. His head did a weird flick-flack and then mercifully everything went black.

"Gunny? You okay?"

Blue opened one eye and saw two versions of Mel, his

fellow instructor, dancing against the bright Californian sky. He winced and retreated back into the darkness.

"Gunnery Sergeant Morgan?"

"Yeah." He managed to croak. "Is Fielding okay?"

"He's fine. Blubbing like a baby, but nothing broken. You took the hit for him."

"Tell me about it." Blue attempted to roll onto his side and broke out into a sweat as nausea engulfed him.

"Take it easy. The corpsman's coming." Mel patted Blue's shoulder. "I got you down. You two were unconscious for a while and swinging back and forth like a brace of pheasant."

"Funny," Blue muttered. "It wasn't Fielding's fault. He startled some kind of bird."

"He still panicked, though."

"Which is why this is called Basic Cliff Assault Training, so he'll learn not to do it somewhere important."

A shadow came over his other side and someone touched his shoulder. The smell of antiseptic swept over Blue, making him shudder.

"It's Ives. Do you know where you are?"

"Still in the Marines?"

Ives chuckled. "Specifically at this moment."

"Flat on my back with the headache from hell."

"What's your name and rank?"

"Gunnery Sergeant Morgan."

"What day is it?"

"Tuesday."

"Good. I'm going to check you over and take you back to the hospital, okay?"

Hospital.

Blue had seen quite enough of them to last a lifetime. He only had six months left in the military. He'd hoped to see it out peacefully in his home state. This was his last training course. He'd managed to complete his final deployment in the sandbox, without a scratch, and now this.

Sometimes life sucked.

Ives placed a collar around his neck and Blue was gently lifted onto a board. He assumed the other six guys who had been climbing with their group had already been taken back to base. He was loaded into a vehicle and Ives got in behind him. Two others followed and the doors were shut.

Blue tried to relax, but the pain behind his eyes kept growing.

"Sorry, Gunny."

That was definitely Fielding, the little shit. Blue didn't have the ability to reply as his head started to pound and he literally saw stars. He set his jaw, aware that if he puked he was strapped to a board and couldn't even turn his head. He'd been in far worse situations than this. There was nothing left to do but hang on and hang in there.

"Concussion, whiplash, two broken ribs, and a black eye." The doc shook his head. "The newbie boot got a little graze on his widdle nose when he collided with your helmet."

"Figures," Blue muttered. "When can I leave?"

"You'll need to stay overnight so we can check on that concussion. You've had a couple in the last few years, so we've got to be extra careful. We'll see how you're feeling in the morning, okay?"

The doc was way too cheerful and loud for Blue's liking, but that might be his headache talking. Pretty much everything was too much at this point.

"Can I sit up?"

"In an hour or so we'll raise the head of the bed."

"Do I have to keep the collar on?"

"For a couple of weeks minimum. We called your grandmother."

"God, no," Blue groaned.

"She says to give you her love, and she'll see you soon. Command are working on a security pass for her."

"Great."

The thought of Ruth descending on him was half-comforting and half-terrifying. She'd never been one to let her grandkids sleep in and was highly suspicious of any attempt to get out of chores. On the other hand, if you were really hurt she would coddle you like a newborn calf . . .

Blue drifted off to sleep again, only to be woken up by a nurse because—concussion. He'd been there before and wasn't looking forward to a night filled with fitful sleep and wake-up calls. He longed for the peace and quiet of his bed at the ranch where the only sounds were the livestock, his grandma's TV, and his brother and January getting too loud in their bedroom.

He could do without the last one. But Chase only grinned when Blue reminded him to keep it down and suggested he was jealous. Blue thought about that. Was he jealous that Chase had found the right woman?

Nah.

He liked his life just as it was. He was in control, and no one was ever going to take that away from him. Twelve years in the Marines had made him a man to be reckoned with. It hadn't been easy. When he'd enlisted he'd been something of a hothead, and soon learned that didn't work in the Corps. They'd knocked him into shape and taught him everything he needed to know about how to survive.

But he had a new purpose now—to save Morgan Ranch

and make it profitable again. Ruth and Chase were relying on him, and he was looking forward to the challenge.

"Blue, darling?"

The smell of apples and cinnamon drifted over him and he opened his eyes to see his grandmother sitting beside his bed. The lights were still too bright and it was now dusk outside.

"Ruth. You smell like pie."

"That's because I was making them when the call came through."

The nurse raised his bed so he could see his grandma's worried face. She had the same blue eyes as him and Chase, and her lined skin was baked brown by the harsh sun. She barely topped five feet, but she was still formidable.

"You look terrible, BB."

"Thanks."

She patted his hand. "What were you doing dangling off a cliff? Didn't I teach you not to do stupid stuff? I would've thought the military would have drummed that into you by now."

Jardin, his nurse, gave a snort of laughter and winked at him as she arranged his pillows.

"It's my job, Ruth. I was trying to teach some idiot how to climb."

"Well, stop doing it."

Blue raised an eyebrow, and even that hurt. "I can't just stop when I feel like it—although I'm pretty much done here anyway."

"Why?" Her sharp gaze moved over him. "Is there something they didn't tell me?"

"Nope, I'm good. It was my last training exercise."

A voice came from the bottom of the bed. "Mrs. Morgan? I'm Blue's physician. He's going to be just fine, but he will be on light duty. Best guess, his command will probably just put him behind a desk until he separates."

"Might as well shoot me now," Blue groaned.

"Can I take him home?" Ruth asked.

"Not yet. We have to keep him here because of the concussion, but I'm sure he'll be able to come visit you soon. It's nice that you're so close."

Ruth sighed. "Well, that's a pity. I brought Chase's big truck so I could put him in the back."

Blue tensed. "Wait a minute. You didn't drive that monster all the way up here, did you?"

She fixed him with a quelling look. "I'm quite capable of driving anything I want, young man. I brought January with me. She's waiting in the truck."

"Okay, then." Blue subsided back onto the pillow, which suddenly seemed very welcoming. Holding his head up was hard work. "I don't suppose you brought some of that pie?"

"There's a hamper beside your bed with three different kinds of pie in it. I knew you'd be asking." She stood up and gently kissed his forehead. "Now you take care of yourself, BB, and no more getting into trouble, you hear me?"

"Yes, Grandma," Blue murmured as she smoothed a hand through his short hair as if he was five again. "Tell January to drive carefully."

She kissed him one last time and then went off chatting to his doctor. He closed his eyes and heard a scraping noise, which brought him instantly alert.

"What are you doing with my pies, Jardin?"

The nurse patted his knee. "I'm just going to put them in a safe place until you are allowed to eat solid food."

"Like the staff refrigerator?" He snorted. "They're fine right there."

"Sorry, the cooler's a fire hazard sticking out like that. Don't worry, I'll save you a piece."

He already knew that Ruth would've brought enough pie to feed fifty, so he didn't really mind the hijack.

"Peach," he murmured as he started to fall asleep again. "That's my favorite."

"You've got it." Jardin's voice faded and he let himself fall into the blackness.

"Well, this isn't good."

Blue rubbed his aching temple and studied his desk, which in his five-day absence had acquired about ten two-foot-high stacks of paper. He'd been released from the hospital, his ribs were taped up, and it hurt when he breathed too hard. His black eye was determined to capture every color of the rainbow, and he had at least another week in the neck brace. He was going to ditch that sucker as soon as no one was around to see him do it.

Carly Hughes, his liaison from admin, smiled sympathetically. "The separation process for leaving the service is paved with more paperwork than a very messy celebrity divorce." She moved one stack closer to another. "And while you're doing all that you'll be attending classes to prepare you for reentry into civilian life and help to find you a new career."

"I already know what I'm doing next."

She glanced at him. "Really?"

"Yeah. My family owns a cattle ranch near here."

"So you're a *cowboy*?"

He shrugged. "More of a rancher, but I can ride a horse."

"And you rope cattle and all that kind of dirty, messy manly stuff?"

She sounded all kinds of *breathy*. Was she one of those women who thought cowboys were romantic? Blue put more space between them. "I do what needs to be done."

She sat down on the corner of his desk and studied him carefully. "That's good to know."

He picked up the nearest folder and looked inside. There were about ten forms in there alone. He hastily put it back on the stack.

"As I can't climb and I'm on my way out, I've also got to help the other instructors with scheduling and lesson plans." Which was about as exciting as it sounded. The other guys had been delighted to pass all the shit jobs over to him.

"Then you're going to be a busy man." She stood up and brushed down her skirt. "Let me know if you need any extra help."

"Will do."

She waited a second longer than necessary, but he slid into his chair and started firing up his laptop. Carly was a great-looking woman, but he'd already set his sights on the next phase of his life, and getting involved with someone still in the service wasn't going to work out. Getting involved with someone *period* was going to have to wait a few years until he'd established himself at the ranch.

He had a plan, and nothing was going to stop him from making Morgan Ranch the best historical dude ranch in the state of California, if not the world. He was a Marine. When he set his mind to something, he never failed.

Taking a deep breath, Blue took another file, scanned the contents, got a pen and started to fill in the blanks.

* * *

"Mom . . ." Jenna McDonald sighed and held the phone farther away from her ear as her mother started in on an all-too familiar theme. "Let's not do this right now, okay? I just called to wish you happy birthday."

She closed her eyes. "Yeah, I wish I was with you, too. No, I don't want you to look for a safer job for me where you live. I'm really happy here with Uncle Ron and Aunt Amy. Yeah. I also know that when Faith gets back, I might be out of work."

Her mom kept talking and eventually Jenna just let it flow over her. It was almost three and afternoon clinic was due to start, which meant she needed to move things along. Adopting her most cheerful, nonaggressive, super-validating tone—the one she'd learned in family therapy—she cut across what her mom was saying.

"I know you worry because you care, Mom. I understand your position *perfectly*, and I will think about every single thing you have said to me today. Now why don't you go and have a nice dinner with Dad? Call me tomorrow and tell me all about it, okay?"

She barely waited for her mom to make some kind of agreeing noise before she said an airy good-bye and put the phone down. She loved her mom, but sometimes it was like trying to stop a river in flood. Not that her dad was any better, but at least he tried to listen to her occasionally and had been instrumental in finding her the job with his brother at the most northern end of California, far from her mother and hypersuccessful sisters.

"Jenna?" Meg, one of the veterinary techs put her head around the door. She was an older woman who'd been with the practice for years and had saved Jenna's ass on several occasions already. "You okay to start seeing folks? You're the only one here."

"Sure." She grabbed her white coat and slid her reading glasses on top of her head. "Do we have many waiting?"

Unlike most modern veterinary practices, her uncle preferred to let the afternoon clinic remain a free-for-all, which meant sometimes there were twenty people crammed into the small waiting room and other days it was crickets. Jenna didn't mind. It was all new to her, and every appointment helped her gain valuable knowledge. Most large animal veterinary practices didn't deal with the smaller pet stuff, but they were the only clinic for forty miles, so they happily coped with everything.

"Only three so far. I've put Monica Flaherty in exam room one, so you can start there. Files on the outside of the door."

"Got it."

Jenna went into the exam room, closing the door quickly behind her because she never knew exactly what she'd be facing. There were many desperate escapees who didn't want to be there—and that was just the humans.

Ha.

"Hey, Monica. What's up?"

The teenager frowned. "Where's Dave?"

"He's out on a call." Inwardly Jenna sighed. Her cousin was thirty-one and single and the cause of intense local feminine interest. "Do you want to go back to the front desk and make an appointment to see him specifically?"

Monica's sigh was almost loud enough to rattle the window glass. "No. It's okay. I found this by the side of the highway." She pointed at a box on the metal exam table.

Jenna cautiously opened the lid and peered inside. There was a towel covering the bottom of the box, and coiled within it was a large white and brown patterned snake.

"Did you find this guy in the actual box, or on the road?"

"On the road. I put him on the damp towel and sat him on top of the water heater last night."

"Great idea. He was probably way too cold out there to survive." Jenna checked over what she could see of the snake's lean coils.

Monica came to look over her shoulder. "What kind is it?"

"It's a California king snake, I think. He's not poisonous or anything, but he is a powerful constrictor." Jenna glanced at Monica. "You probably know that, seeing as you picked him up."

"I made Finn do it. He thought it was a rattlesnake."

"They sometimes rattle their tails to scare predators into thinking they *are* rattlesnakes." Jenna closed the lid of the box. "I assume you don't want to keep him?"

"I'd like to, but my mom said no." Monica pouted. "Can you find him a good home?"

"I can certainly ask around, but he could survive in the wild. He's native to California and he's not called the king for nothing."

Monica fiddled with the box. "Dave knows a lot about snakes, doesn't he?"

Which was probably why Monica had made her boyfriend pick the snake up in the first place. The poor guy. "He sure does. I'll check in with him when he comes back. Do you want me to call and let you know what happens?"

"When you talk to Dave?" Monica perked up. "Maybe he could call me himself?"

"Someone will definitely call you when we've made a decision." Jenna hid a smile as she washed her hands. "Thanks for bringing the big guy in."

"Okay."

Jenna patted the teen's shoulder as she left the exam

room and belatedly picked up the chart Meg had left in a slot by the door. She wrote a quick summary of the visit. It was weird going back to writing notes with a real pen after the tablets at her last job. Attempting to decipher her colleagues' handwriting was another head-numbing task altogether.

Meg came out of the second exam room and Jenna handed her the file. "Monica found a California king snake by the side of the road. I don't know enough about them to tell if it's injured or not. Can we put it out back in the heated terrarium until Dave comes in?"

"Sure." Meg nodded. "I'll take it right out and then come back to assist you. Pet rabbit in two."

"Got it." This time Jenna remembered to pick up the clipboard and went into the room. She found one of the Hayes family that ran the local hotel clutching a large black and white rabbit to his chest. "Hey, Wade, who's this?"

The boy cuddled the rabbit even closer. He was the youngest boy in the big Hayes family and Jenna reckoned he was around twelve. "Duke."

"That's a great name." Jenna perched on the edge of the table and gently stroked Duke's nose. "So what's up with him?"

"He's been, like, acting really strange."

"In what way?"

"Getting cranky with me, trying to dig his way out of the cage and, like, moving stuff around the place into big piles in the corners."

"Weird," Jenna said. "Can I take a good look at him?"

"He's like real grumpy at the moment."

"I'll be careful," Jenna promised as she set the rabbit on the exam table. She kept petting him with one hand as she palpated his abdomen with the other. "Do you have any other rabbits?"

"Yeah, one more called Stan, short for Stanford."

"Do they share a cage?"

"Yeah, why?"

Jenna looked at Wade over Duke's head. "Is your mom here with you?"

To her dismay, the boy's eyes teared up. "Duke's going to die, isn't he? You can tell me. I don't need my mom here. I'm almost twelve."

"He's not going to die." Jenna held his gaze. "Duke's going to be a mother."

"What?"

"He's female and he's pregnant."

A dull red color rose from Wade's neck to cover his face. "He's a . . . *girl*? Do you mean, like that he and Stan . . . ?"

Jenna nodded. "Yeah, I think they did, and judging from the size of Duke's belly, she's going to give birth fairly soon."

Almost before the words left her mouth, Wade was running for the door. Jenna waited for a minute and then started to smile. Meg came in and raised her eyebrows.

"What did you say to Wade? He ran past me like he was being chased by something with teeth. Is there something wrong with Duke?"

"Duke's a girl and she's pregnant," Jenna said, patting the rabbit. "Wade was horrified by every single word in that sentence." She grinned at Meg, and they both burst out laughing.

"The poor kid." Jenna eventually recollected herself. "Can you see if Mrs. Hayes is out there so I can talk to her?"

"Will do," Meg said.

While Jenna waited for Mrs. Hayes, her thoughts flew back to her parents. They would probably never understand how a day like today could make her love her job even more. They thrived on order, and the life Jenna had chosen wasn't like that at all. To say that she loved a challenge was an understatement. After years of knowing exactly what was expected and obeying every demand made on her, surely she was entitled to enjoy a little bit of chaos?

Much later she was sitting in the back office writing notes about the cases she'd seen when the back door banged and opened to admit her cousin Dave. He stomped in looking tired and rumpled. The veterinary offices were housed in the original McDonald homestead, and the family had moved up the hill into a larger, more convenient house. It made the commute to work fairly straightforward, although they spent most of their time on the road visiting the various ranches around Morgantown.

Uncle Ron kept saying he was going to rebuild the clinic, but he'd never gotten around to it and Jenna doubted he ever would. Which meant that they all put up with the inconvenient old ranch house and made the best of the space available.

Jenna wrinkled her nose. "What did you fall into?"

"Pig shit. I did shower."

"Still eew."

"I was on a call near Morgan Ranch, so I went to check out the new arrivals." Dave dumped his bag on the table and turned to take off his coat and wash his hands. He'd already removed his boots in the mudroom and wore mismatched socks. "The darling little piggies tripped me, and the mama pig sat on me when I was down."

"I don't suppose Roy got that on camera?"

"I hope not. I think he was laughing too hard." With a groan, Dave sat down and shoved his hands through his spiky black hair. "Sometimes I wonder why I do this job."

Jenna patted his shoulder. "Because you love it?"

"There is that."

"I didn't know Ruth was thinking of keeping pigs," Jenna said as she got up to make some more coffee.

"She wasn't. It's all Roy's idea. Apparently, he's always wanted to keep pigs, and Ruth decided it would add authenticity to the idea of a self-sufficient historical ranch."

Jenna tended to the old coffee percolator, which needed a firm hand, and got out two clean mugs. "Do you think the Morgans are going to make that idea work?"

"The historical dude ranch guest house thing?"

"Yes."

"I don't see why not. With Chase Morgan's financial connections, and Ruth and Roy's experience, it could work out really well."

Jenna put one of the mugs in front of Dave, who added three spoonfuls of sugar. "And don't forget January and the Morgantown Historical Society."

"How could I when my parents are on the board?" Dave groaned. "Next thing you know I'll be dressed up like a cowboy and be expected to fake being an old-fashioned veterinarian or some such crap."

"Ruth would probably love that." Jenna took a sip of her coffee. "Was January back or was she still in San Francisco with Chase?"

"She's back, but she and Ruth had to dash off to the Marine place near Bridgeport. Apparently, BB was in an accident."

"Blue Morgan? Oh wow, what happened?" Jenna hadn't taken to the arrogant Marine when she'd met him at spring branding, but she still hoped he was okay.

"BB was in the base hospital with concussion after a fall from a cliff or something. Ruth was going to go by herself, but January offered to drive her."

"Why do you call him BB rather than Blue?"

"It's his name."

Jenna raised her eyebrows. "His actual name?"

"His initials are BB. His full name is Blue Boy."

"You're kidding me, right?" Jenna started to grin. "The big tough Marine is little boy blue?"

Dave shuddered. "We stopped saying that around second grade after he'd beaten the crap out of us a few times. His dad named him after a TV cowboy show, I think. You'll have to ask him which one. I'm not doing it."

The Marine did have very blue eyes. She remembered that. She also remembered his Internet-derived assumptions about her profession. She hated being talked down to. But he had at least tried to apologize before she'd brushed him off. She'd appreciated the gesture, which had taken her by surprise.

"Monica Flaherty brought in a snake for you."

Dave perked up. "What kind?"

"California king, I think. I'm not sure if there's something wrong with it or if Monica just saw the darn thing and wanted an excuse to come in and see you."

"Where's the snake?"

"In the terrarium next to the vaccine refrigerator. Where else would it be?"

Dave was already moving, his mug gripped in his hand. Jenna sensed he got tired of dealing with horses, cattle, and various large animals sometimes. She followed him into the other room and waited as he took his first gander at the snake.

"Looks in pretty good shape to me," Dave commented.

"I couldn't see any obvious injuries, but I don't know a lot about snakes," Jenna confessed. "She did find him out at night, so he might have gotten cold."

"True." Dave opened the terrarium and ran his fingertip

over the coils of the snake. "We can keep an eye on him for a day or two. If he's capable of eating live food, we can probably release him back into the wild." He replaced the lid and washed his hands.

"Do you want to call Monica and tell her?" Jenna asked.

"No thanks." Dave mock frowned at her. "There's no need to encourage her."

Jenna snorted. "From what I've seen, you don't need to do anything to encourage them. They all just fall in love with you at first sight."

Dave refilled his coffee mug. "God knows why. Vets aren't exactly a catch. We're usually covered in shit, un-available at the weekends, and always in debt."

"They should go after the Morgans," Jenna said. "Local gossip says they have all the money."

"Well, Chase does. But he's engaged to January, BB's in the military, and the twins haven't been back for years and are pretty wild." Dave lingered by the door. "Are you coming up to the main house?"

Jenna looked at her pile of paper. "I'm just about done, so I should go and eat. Amy said something about a nut casserole."

"Then you've got to come right now. Ma makes a really good one." Dave held open the door. "And I want to talk to you about Morgan Ranch."

"You want me to do what?" Jenna asked.

Dave sat back in his chair and let out a loud and very indiscreet belch. They'd eaten dinner together in the large pine kitchen and taken themselves into the den. There was no sign of Amy and Ron, who tended to go to bed early and watch TV until they fell asleep. If Dave's groupies could see him in his natural habitat, smelly socks and all, Jenna doubted they'd be quite so infatuated with him.

"Horses are your area of expertise, right?"

"They're supposed to be, but—"

"Then you are the perfect person to help the Morgans out. Firstly, they need to assemble a stable of rideable horses for the guests, and then they need to keep them healthy. You can start by helping them select good stock."

"I suppose I could," Jenna said doubtfully. "But won't it take up a lot of my time?"

"Look, I know Dad's stepping back, but—" Dave sat up, dislodging his huge feet from the coffee table. "If you want to stay and Faith decides she wants to practice here when she graduates, we're going to need all the work we can get to justify employing three vets. Don't get me wrong, we *want* you to stay, we love you, but if it comes down to it and we don't have enough clients, Dad's going to pick his own daughter over you."

Jenna nodded. One thing she really liked about Dave was his honesty. "Do you think Morgan Ranch could end up being a really lucrative client?"

"Yeah, with the grass-fed cattle and the dude ranch? Definitely."

"Then I'd be happy to do whatever needs doing."

Dave winked at her. "Good girl. I'm not kidding, it could become a full-time job if the ranch does well."

Jenna clinked her mug against his. "As long as the younger Morgan brothers keep away, I think I'll do just fine."

Chapter Two

Blue sucked in a great big lung full of Morgan Ranch air. Home.

The place that had kept him sane through all the years of deployments and the terror and boredom of modern warfare. Whenever it had gotten too much for him, he would let his mind wander to the lush green pastures, the craggy heights of the Sierra mountain range, and the crisp bite of the morning air.

His still-healing ribs gave a twinge of warning, and he carefully exhaled. Sure he'd thought he was leaving it all behind forever when he'd left to join the Marines, but all he'd done was make the place more vivid in his memories. The bad times were almost forgotten, and the good ones replayed endlessly when he needed a boost.

Separating from the military was even harder than leaving home. He'd accumulated a lot of leave because for some reason Uncle Sam didn't like soldiers taking a few days off in the middle of a war zone. He'd got five days at the ranch now, and then he had to go back to his desk for another week. He hated that desk so much he was thinking of setting it on fire on his last day.

Sitting around on his ass had never worked well for him. He got up to mischief.

He took a turn around the wooden porch, checking the dainty Victorian railings as he passed. On his last leave he'd repaired and painted the deck. Now he needed to start on the rest of it. Chase had offered to pay for a crew to come in and fix everything, but Blue preferred to do it himself. He needed to be busy, and he'd always found working with his hands very soothing.

Ruth said the saying "the devil finds work for idle hands" had been written with Blue in mind. Even as a kid he'd always wanted to know how everything worked, a curiosity he'd taken with him into the Marines, which had gotten him into and out of some fairly hairy situations.

"BB?"

He turned to see Ruth at the kitchen door.

"You want some bacon?"

He grinned at her. "Roy's pigs are already producing?"

"Not yet. They need some fattening up first. Jenna says it will take a while."

Blue followed his grandmother inside the homely kitchen, where nothing much had changed since he was a kid. "Jenna McDonald's taking care of the pigs?"

"She's taking care of most of the stock these days since Big Mac decided to retire. Although as Ron's only in his late fifties, I don't know what he plans to do with the rest of his life. Golf, I suppose. He and Amy love doing that. I've never fancied it myself. Walking around hitting a little ball with a stick into a hole." Ruth went back to flipping bacon in the cast iron skillet. "Want some eggs?"

"Three would be good, please. I know Big Mac is semi-retiring, but what about Dave?"

"He still comes out occasionally."

Blue got himself some coffee and sat back down at the scarred kitchen table. "How's Jenna doing?"

Ruth turned to look at him. "In herself or with the workload?"

Blue narrowed his eyes. "With the work. From what I remember, she's a slip of a thing."

"She's taller than me, and I've never met a cow or a horse I couldn't master," Ruth retorted. "Why don't you come out and say that you don't think she's up to the job?"

"I didn't say that. I was just asking how she was coping. She's only just qualified, right?"

Ruth put a plate with six pieces of bacon, three eggs, and four pieces of toast on the side in front of him.

"She was working for a couple of years at some horse racing stables near Sacramento."

Blue dug into the plate of food. "So what made her come out here?"

"When Ron had his knee replacement surgery she came to help Dave, and she fit right in. I like her. She's good with the animals and she listens to her elders and betters." Ruth pointed the spatula at him. "Some people could learn a lot from her."

"I've been listening to officers for years, and I can't say it did much for me." Blue chugged down some coffee and then attacked his second egg. "But I promise I'll be nice to her, okay?"

"You'd better be. She's going to be helping you choose the horses for the guests."

Blue hastily swallowed his mouthful of food. "She is?"

"Can't think of anyone better." Ruth turned back to the stove. "You want more eggs?"

Blue eyed his plate. "Nah, I think I'm done. Thanks, Ruth. Where's January this morning?"

"She's around here somewhere. She was talking to Roy

about where we're going to put all these guests who'll be turning up in a year or so."

"Where are you thinking?"

"There are the old bunkhouses, for a start."

"Hardly luxury accommodation."

"That's what January said, but they would work if we did school trips and for volunteers. She's thinking about detached log cabins or something fancier for the real paying guests."

"Sounds expensive."

"Chase can afford it." Ruth wiped out the cast iron pan and left it sitting on the back of the stove to cool down.

"So you're happy to take his money now?"

Ruth winked at him. "Sure, it's for a good cause— Morgan Ranch." She looked past Blue to the door. "Morning, Billy."

Blue tensed and stayed where he was as his father made his quiet way into the kitchen. After twenty years away, Billy's sudden reappearance at the ranch still set Blue's teeth on edge. Walking out on four young sons after confessing to murdering your wife and baby made one hell of a mess of your kid's head. Sure, the murder was unproven and there was renewed hope that his mother and sister were actually alive, but still . . .

"Morning, BB."

Blue briefly met his dad's eyes as Billy sat opposite him and then rose to his feet.

"I've got to get on." He picked up his plate and mug. "I'm still catching up on Chase's chores."

"I could do those for you, son," Billy offered.

"It's okay." Blue rinsed his plate under the faucet and put it in the dishwasher. "I've got it covered."

"You be careful now," Ruth warned. "That nice doctor said your ribs still weren't healed."

Billy half rose from his seat. "Are you sure—?"

"I'm good." Blue kissed Ruth's cheek and headed for the door. "I'll be down in the barn if anyone wants me."

Apart from my father, who I'd rather not see at all.

He put his boots on in the mudroom and walked across the wide circle and down to the barn on the opposite side. With his newly approved budget from Chase he'd already started adding new horses to the old twelve-stall barn, which was now filling up nicely. January said they'd probably need to build another smaller, family barn at some point, but until things got off the ground the original would have to do.

His ancestor, William Morgan, the original landowner, had built the barn in the 1850s. Blue loved it in there. The slightly lopsided hand-sawed beams, the birds nesting in every tiny crevice swooping down to grab corn or nest-building material from the unsuspecting horses below. The chicken coop was at one end and the manure heap on the continuing slope that made things a lot easier to dispose of.

On the far side of the barn, January, his brother's fiancée, was standing with Roy, the ranch foreman. She had a clipboard in one hand and was gesticulating wildly with the other. Blue fought a grin. It had taken him very little time to decide he liked January and that she was perfect for his nerdy older brother. She was as straight as they came and had no compunction in telling him and Chase where they were going wrong. She was also as passionate about the ranch as he was.

"Hey," she called out to him and beckoned him over. The humongous engagement ring Chase had given her caught the sun and almost blinded him.

He pretended to stagger and shielded his eyes. "Damn, that diamond's big."

"It's obscene," January said proudly. "I told Chase to take it back."

"And?"

"He said it was ethically sourced and that if I gave it back I'd be depriving a village in Africa of a new school."

"That's remarkably specific."

"That's Chase for you." January shrugged. "You know what he's like. He probably flew out there, mined the diamond, and built the school himself." She said it with such goofy fondness that he had to grin back at her.

"Yeah, knowing my bro, he probably did." Blue gestured at the clipboard. "What are you planning now?"

"Where to put the guest cabins." She pointed down the slope. "We've got to keep them away from the pigs and the manure heap, but close enough to the barn and house for the guests to easily get up here to eat and ride. I was thinking the natural slope down toward the creek would work well."

Behind him he heard the sound of an approaching truck and instinctively turned toward the noise, seeking the nearest shelter. Old habits died hard. He wasn't sure if he'd ever be able to walk down a street without expecting the worst.

"How many cabins are you planning to build?" He forced himself to act like a normal person having a normal conversation while still hating having his back turned to the approaching visitor.

"Half a dozen at first. Two bedrooms and a shared bath in between them."

"Sounds good." Blue fought not to turn his head as a prickle of awareness crept up his spine. "So basic, but not too basic."

"Exactly." January looked up from her clipboard. "Hey."

"Hey, January."

Roy touched the brim of his cowboy hat. "Morning, Miss Jenna. Have you come to see the pigs?"

Blue turned then and looked down at the diminutive new vet he'd last seen at the spring branding. She wore a blue hoodie, jeans, and big work boots. Her reddish brown hair was pulled back into a ponytail, making her look about twelve, although local rumor had it she was in her mid twenties.

"Hey."

She briefly met his gaze. "Hi." And then she looked over at Roy. "I'd be happy to see the pigs if they need me. I actually came out to talk about the horses. Do you have time to do that?"

Roy pointed at Blue. "Talk to this guy. He's going to be dealing with most of new horse stuff. I'm going to concentrate on the ranch hands and all the 'magic'"—Roy made bunny ears with his index fingers—"that happens in the background to keep everything rolling along."

Blue nodded at Jenna. "I've got plenty of time to talk."

She looked him up and down as though he was a less-than-satisfactory specimen. It didn't faze him. He'd been stared at by the best the Marines had to offer, and he'd never backed down from a challenge.

"Are you sure you're okay?" Jenna asked. "Ruth said you had a concussion."

"I did. I'm fine now." He wasn't, but he was tired of being asked about it and more than ready to just get on with the job of separating from the military and moving forward with his plans for the ranch.

"He's not fine," January chimed in. "He's got busted ribs, but he's too much of a hero to mention them."

Blue gave her his death glare but she just grinned. She really was becoming like a sister to him.

"Roy and I are going back to the house to show Ruth

the potential location for the cabins. I'm sure you and Jenna can deal with the horse thing?" January looked expectantly at him.

"Sure. Where do you want to talk?" Blue gave his attention back to Jenna. "We can go back up to the house, or you can check out the horses I've already added to the string."

"I'd like to see the horses first." Jenna picked up her medical bag, which was almost as big as she was. Blue instinctively went to take it from her, but she stepped swiftly out of his reach. "I've got this."

He held up both hands in mock surrender, which she didn't notice because she was already moving ahead of him. January snagged the hem of his T-shirt, holding him still.

"Be nice to her, okay?"

"I wasn't planning on being anything else," Blue muttered. "She's the one with the problem. Not me."

"She's just new here and shy. Give her a break."

"As I said, not a problem for me." He detached her fingers from his dark blue T-shirt and returned them to her. "I'll be as sweet as sugar."

January snorted. "I'd like to see that." To his relief, she winked at him and started back up the slight slope to the house with Roy, leaving him with nothing to do but follow the new vet into the barn.

She was standing in the center aisle, her bag at her feet.

"I see Sugar Lump, Sunflower, Messi, and Nolly, so who's new?"

Blue pointed at the three stalls farthest away. "I put them over here so you could check them out before I let them mingle with the others."

"Cool." She stripped off her gloves and tucked them in the back pocket of her jeans. "Where shall we start?"

* * *

A while later, Jenna put down the horse's rear left foot and straightened up.

"There's a stone in there."

"Do you want me to get it out?" Blue produced a wicked-looking knife. He'd spent the last hour or so propping up the wall, answering her questions and obviously keeping an eye on her. He wasn't openly *keeping* a score sheet, but she was pretty darned sure that she was being judged.

"It's okay. I've got it." She readjusted her grip, picked up the affected foot, and used the tip of her hoof pick to ease out the small pebble wedged between the metal shoe and the hoof. "That's it. I'd get her reshod if I were you. That gap's going to cause problems."

"Good catch," Blue said as she wiped her hand on her jeans. "I'll get that done as soon as possible."

The sun had risen overhead, and inside the stable it had gotten warm enough for her to start sweating. Apparently Marines didn't sweat, and the dark blue T-shirt stretched across Blue's muscled chest looked remarkably wrinkle free.

Jenna straightened her spine and waited as Blue made a note on the horse's chart.

He looked up. "Are we finished here?"

"I've just got to draw some blood." Jenna reached for her bag only to have Blue get there faster and offer her the sealed sampling kit.

"Here you go."

"Thanks."

She concentrated on her task, all too aware of Blue's assessing gaze on her. She swabbed the horse's neck. "I'm quite competent, you know."

"So I've been told."

She looked over at him. "Then you don't have to watch me all the time."

He raised an eyebrow. "I'm watching because I like to learn new things. If I was caught out here on my own with an emergency, I'd like to be able to handle it."

Now she felt like a heel. "You can do the last blood test if you like. It's not hard, and it is a good skill for a rancher to have."

"Sure."

He eased away from the wall and came to stand beside her, bringing the scent of warm man and citrus to add to the peppery smell of the horse.

She finished capping the blood sample. "I meant for the next horse."

"Ah, okay." He didn't retreat, but began to stroke the horse's neck. "Everything looking good so far?"

"Yes."

Her gaze followed the rhythmic stroke of his long, scarred fingers, and she almost dropped the tube.

She cleared her throat. "I think we're done with this one."

"Only one more to go, then."

"You can take the blood sample first if you like and then leave me to it," Jenna said quickly.

His hand went still. "As I said, I'd rather stick around, if that's okay with you."

She stowed the sample in her bag and picked it up. "I just meant—"

"That you don't like me hanging around. I get it. But I'm the one who is ultimately responsible for these horses, and I want to make sure I picked good ones."

"I understand that."

"Then what's the problem?"

She met his gaze. "It feels more like you're waiting for me to mess up."

His frown deepened. "I have a right to expect the best veterinary care for my animals."

"And you don't think I'm good enough, right? Let me guess. You'd prefer a man."

"I have no problem with you being a woman. But I guess I'd prefer someone with more experience." He didn't look away his blue gaze cool.

Wow, well, that was direct. She raised her chin. "I spent two years dealing specifically with horses at a racing stables after I left college. I'm knowledgeable about all the latest treatments and I graduated first in my class with honors. Would you like to see my references?"

"Yeah, actually I would."

She blinked at him. Her uncle hadn't asked to see anything. "Then I'll look them up for you. Would you prefer Dave to come up here until you're satisfied I'm competent?"

"No, we're good." He gave the horse one final pat and walked toward the door. "Ready for the next one?"

She hastily closed her mouth, picked up her bag, and followed him into the end stall. He certainly didn't believe in beating around the bush.

"This one's my favorite." Blue rubbed his knuckles over the quarter horse's brown nose and was almost knocked over as the horse responded with a head but. "He's a sweetheart."

"Geldings usually are," Jenna murmured as she found her stethoscope. "There's a lesson in there for mankind, don't you think?"

His crack of laughter surprised her. "So it's not just me? You're just generally down on all males?"

"I'm . . . not down on you."

"Right, you haven't forgiven me for telling you how to do your job at the spring branding yet, have you?"

"That's not true. You apologized and—"

"You blew me off."

Jenna sighed. "Look, you have no idea how hard it's been for me the last six months. Every time I go out on a call I'm asked when Uncle Ron or Dave will be coming out to give their seal of approval to my silly newbie *feminine* medical decisions. I'm getting kind of tired of it."

"It's hardly my fault if most ranchers are idiots."

"They aren't idiots."

"You're defending them now?" Blue asked.

"I'm trying not to whine and think the whole world is out to get me."

"Out here it takes a while for people to accept new things."

"So I've noticed."

"Which means you have two choices. Stick it out and prove them wrong, or run back home. Where is home, by the way?"

"Los Angeles." She shuddered. "I don't want to go back there."

This time his smile held more than a hint of a challenge. "Then you're going to have to man up and show everyone what you're worth."

"Woman up, you mean?"

He shrugged his broad shoulders. "Whatever works for you."

"You're giving *me* advice now?"

"Just passing on the benefit of my experience."

"Like you ever had a problem fitting in here. Your family founded the darn town."

He handed her the blood testing kit. "Which means I went into the Marines thinking I was special. I had to make a quick decision about whether I was willing to do what it took to stay in the Corps or drop out whining like a little kid."

"You stayed."

"I manned up. Hence my giving you advice." He met her gaze. "Now show me how to do the blood test, and I'll leave you to finish up alone."

Prickly.

Yeah. That about summed up Jenna McDonald. Like one of those little hedgehogs he'd seen on the Internet. Cute, but deadly. He liked her determination and the way she went about her work. It didn't mean he wouldn't check out her references, though. He'd bet the ranch that her uncle hadn't bothered to call them himself.

Not that she wasn't competent from what he'd seen. He also understood her current prickliness because most of the ranchers around Morgantown had dealt with Big Mac for forty years and didn't like change. They'd only accepted Dave because he was Mac's son, and Jenna was something else altogether. He didn't have a problem with her being female. He'd learned during his military service that women were just as capable as men.

"Blue?"

He looked up to see Jenna emerging from the barn. He'd gone to check on the feed bins and traps set out for the various vermin that liked a free meal.

"I'm in here."

She came over to him lugging her bag, strands of her hair stuck to her cheek and her long-sleeved T-shirt clinging to her curves. Blue made himself look her in the eye.

"You're finished?"

"For now." She actually smiled at him.

"Then come up to the house and have something cool to drink before Roy gets you out looking at those pigs again."

"Sure."

This time he didn't even try and take charge of her bag and just started walking. Three of the dogs from the barn came along with him, running in circles and jumping like they were a circus act. Behind him, Jenna started to puff as the incline increased.

He glanced back at her. "Why don't you have a special truck like Big Mac for all your equipment?"

"Because Dave inherited the truck, and there isn't enough money to buy another one."

"Bummer."

He reached the porch, climbed the steps, and held open the screen door, which thanks to him no longer squeaked. "You can leave your boots in the mudroom if you like. It's on the left next to the small bathroom."

"Thanks."

He turned right and went into the kitchen, where the heavenly smell of bacon still lingered. Roy and Ruth sat at the table with January. The three of them were making enough noise for a town meeting.

He washed up and poured himself a cup of coffee and listened to the arguments, which were for the most part amicable. Despite the noise he didn't think he was going to have to intervene and play peacekeeper. Not a natural role for him anyway. He'd always preferred to be the one causing the trouble.

He spotted Jenna hovering in the doorway and held up his mug of coffee.

"You want coffee or something colder?"

Ruth looked around. "There's lemonade in the refrigerator. Help yourself, Jenna, dear."

"Thanks, Ruth."

Blue pointed at the nearest chair. "Sit down. I'll get it for you."

For a second he thought she might start arguing, but she nodded instead. "Thanks, that would be great."

The lemonade looked so good that he took a glass for himself and sat opposite Jenna at the table. Ruth pushed a plate of oatmeal cookies down toward Jenna and continued her animated discussion with Roy. Blue ate a cookie and reached for another one at the same time as Jenna did, resulting in a tangle of fingers and an unintentional fist bump.

January looked over at him and pulled a face, rolling her eyes at Ruth, who was now having a long discussion about what the proposed site for the cabins had been used for back in the dark ages or something.

Just as Blue was about to intervene and get the discussion back on track, Jenna cleared her throat.

"I hate to be rude, Roy, but I have to get back before three to help with afternoon clinic, so if there is anything you want to ask me about the pigs, go right ahead."

Roy looked up, his gaze taking in Blue and Jenna.

"Horses okay?"

"Yes. Blue chose very well."

"Knew he would. I taught him." Roy grinned, showing the crooked line of his teeth, which had come off the worst in a couple of bucking incidents. "The pigs are good. I was just wondering when their next round of shots is due."

Jenna frowned. "I'll have to check with Dave. He was here last, right?"

"Don't you guys keep everything online now?" Blue had to ask. "It would make sharing information a lot easier."

"I know. It's something I'd like to do, but Uncle Ron

isn't keen on keeping anything on the Internet in case it gets taken over by hostile forces or something."

Roy nodded. "Well, I can see his point. I don't understand all that googling nonsense myself."

Jenna finished her lemonade and rose to her feet, wiping cookie crumbs from her lips. "I'd better be going." She focused on Blue. "Unless there's anything else?"

"I'm good. I'll give you a call when I'm planning on seeing some new horses. Maybe you could come out with me?"

She blinked at him. "I'd like that."

Ruth gave him a pointed look, so he followed Jenna out to her truck, which he thought had once belonged to Dave and was perfectly suited to the rough terrain of the local ranches. He waited as she stowed her bag and got into the driver's seat.

She lowered the window and looked down at him consideringly.

"What?" he asked.

"You're really okay about me coming out with you, or did you just say that to keep Ruth and Roy happy?"

"I don't say what I don't mean."

"Then I'd love to come." This time her smile transformed her face and left him staring at her mouth before she blew him a kiss and drove away.

Chapter Three

Blue braced himself and took the seat opposite his father at the table. Roy and Ruth had gone to check out the pigs, January was working on her thesis, and for once the ranch was quiet.

"Can I talk to you about something?" Blue asked.

"Sure." Billy sat back, a wary expression in his blue eyes, which wasn't surprising seeing as Blue spent most of his time trying to avoid acknowledging his father's existence. "What can I do for you?"

Blue opened the speckled black composition notebook he'd bought in Maureen's store and uncapped his pen. "I've got a few questions for you about the night Mom and Rachel disappeared."

Billy frowned. "I thought Chase was setting some private detectives to finding out what happened to them?"

"He will be once I get all the facts from you." Blue wrote the date on the top line and underlined it hard. If he handled this like a military investigation, he wouldn't need to get emotional about shit. "So let's go over this again. The last time you saw Mom was in this kitchen when she attacked you with a butcher's knife."

"That's right."

"But you didn't see her leave."

"During the struggle I fell against the wall and was knocked out for a minute or so. By the time I opened my eyes, she was gone."

"And you didn't realize she'd taken Rachel with her."

"No, I came to and ran straight out into the yard to see if Annie's truck was still there. When I came back inside, Chase had come downstairs and I told him to call nine-one-one while I went and searched for your mom. I didn't even think about Rachel sleeping in the crib by the fire." Billy hesitated. "Do you remember much about that night yourself, BB?"

"I remember the screaming and yelling and trying to distract the twins, who were getting upset, yeah." Blue forced himself to meet his father's gaze. He didn't want to talk about himself in relation to anything. "It's not one of the best memories of my life."

Billy briefly closed his eyes. "I'm sorry, son."

"So you said. Shall we move on? You'd already decided to take the blame, saying you attacked her, and made Chase lie to the cops for you."

Billy swallowed hard. "I thought it would give Annie the chance to be free of me and the ranch. I thought she was leaving by herself, you see."

"When did you realize Rachel was missing as well?"

"Not until the sheriff started questioning me at the jail. And then I kind of lost my goddamned mind trying to get out of there . . ." Billy swallowed hard. "When I calmed down a bit I realized that if she'd taken Rachel, she probably hadn't killed herself. She loved that little girl so much."

Blue wrote another note. "Eventually, after the seventy-two-hour mandatory hold the sheriff let you go due to lack of evidence of a crime."

"That's right."

"So whatever happened—if you had murdered them—you would've gotten away with it."

Billy raised his chin. "I didn't, BB. I loved them."

There were a million things Blue wanted to say to that, but he squashed the emotions down and concentrated on the cold, hard facts.

"If you didn't kill her and she didn't kill herself, where did she go?" Blue tapped his pen against the paper. "She didn't take her truck, so she must have walked off the ranch, which would have been difficult with a young baby in her arms, or she had help from someone here."

Billy nodded. "The sheriff's men and the county rescue team searched the area pretty thoroughly, and there was no sign of her or any tracks."

"Then someone gave her a ride. How many hands did you have working on the ranch back then?"

"About a dozen."

"And they all knew Mom, right?"

"Yeah, because back in those days, we used to cook for the hands and the family three times a day, so they'd all come up to the house in shifts to eat."

"Ruth and Mom handled that, right?"

"Mostly. It was a lot of work."

"I bet it was."

Blue wrote a note. *Ask Ruth about the hands who came up to eat in the house.*

"Who did Mom talk to most?"

"She was nice to everyone when she was in one of her good moods. After Rachel's birth she got a lot quieter."

"But she must have talked to someone because he or she helped her leave you. If you had to take a guess, who do you think that was?"

Billy rubbed a hand over his beard. "As I mentioned before, she liked Big Mike."

"Anyone else?"

"Larry Paquino and Red Williams."

Blue wrote the names down. "Roy has all the old ranch records at his place, doesn't he?"

"I think so."

"I'll start there." Blue closed his notebook and stashed his pen in his shirt pocket. "Anything else you can think of?"

"Not right at this moment."

Blue half rose and then paused. "Did she take her purse with her?"

"I don't know."

"Ruth will." He nodded brusquely at his father. "I'll come and find you if I have any more questions."

Billy remained seated, his head lowered toward his clasped hands. "You can ask me anything you like, son. That's why I'm here. To try and help."

"Until you disappear back to San Francisco?"

"I'm not planning on going back there for a while," Billy said quietly.

"Why not? I'm sure if you asked him nicely, Chase would set you up in an apartment."

There was a long tick of silence. "I don't want to be financially beholden to him."

There was a stubborn note in Billy's voice that Blue recognized all too well.

"So you'd rather hang out here. It's certainly cheaper."

Billy looked up. "BB, I know you're angry with me, and I know I deserve it, but this was my home, too. I grew up here just like you did, and I missed it more than I could ever have imagined."

"It's always been here. You were the one who walked away from it, or should I say crawled?" Blue headed for the door. "You were probably too drunk to remember much about that." *Or about deserting your kids, letting four boys grow up without a mother or a father.*

He slammed the door like a teenager, marched over to the barn, and saddled up Messi with quick jerky movements. This was why he didn't talk to his dad. It made him want to let all the rage out, and he was too old for that now. He'd learned to live with the betrayal and moved on with his life to become a strong and balanced individual. He rested his forehead against Messi's rough neck and breathed in the reassuring scent of horse.

The quicker he worked out whether there was a chance his mother and sister were alive, the sooner his father would be gone.

That was one hell of an incentive to get the matter cleared up once and for all.

Jenna patted the mama pig on her ample backside and reversed out of the pigsty, her hands held high like she was in a hostage situation. The thing was, mama sows were super protective of their young, and this one had about twenty little piglets to keep an eye on. She'd grudgingly accepted Jenna in her space, but it wasn't worth pushing her luck. Better vets than Jenna had ended up on the wrong side of a pig.

"She's doing great." Jenna disposed of the syringes in the hazard waste receptacle and washed up in the bucket of hot water Roy put beside her. "And so are the little guys."

"She's a good mother, that one," Roy commented, leaning over the wall to contemplate his charge with some satisfaction. "I picked a fine-looking pig."

Jenna had nothing to say to that as she located her bag and looked for the paperwork that accompanied the shots.

"Have you named her yet?"

"I can't decide whether she's a Bertha or a Martha. Time will tell."

Jenna studied the pig. "She looks more like a Peggy to me, but I'm not sure I'd feel right naming my food."

"Vegetarians." Roy chuckled. "Come out of the sun while you do all that necessary stuff," Roy said as he walked upslope to his modest foreman's cottage. "I've got iced tea."

"Sold," Jenna called out as she followed him. In the distance there was a small cloud of dust getting bigger by the second. Squinting into the sun, Jenna tried to recognize the horse and rider.

"BB's coming." Roy didn't even need to look. "Not sure why."

"If you're busy, I could just go home and do the paperwork there," Jenna offered.

"No need. I'd much rather look at your pretty face than BB's. So come on in and take the weight off."

Jenna went into the kitchen diner, which comprised a third of Roy's living space. It smelled of horse, leather, and wet dog, which was pretty much the same as the man himself. Jenna parked herself and her bag at the scarred oak table and got out her pen, trying not to listen as Blue and Roy had a low-voiced conversation outside, which resulted in both men coming through the door into the kitchen.

"Hey." Jenna smiled at Blue, who was wearing a green checked shirt and faded jeans that fit him like a glove. "I'm just finishing up some paperwork, and I'll be on my way."

"Jenna."

He didn't look particularly happy to see her, and her

heart sank. She hated people who couldn't make up their minds about how to treat a person and changed direction like a squally sea breeze. It made her uncomfortable.

Roy slapped Blue on the back and propelled him farther into the room. "You want the ranch records from when your mom vanished, right? Are you trying to work out whom she might have taken off with?"

Blue raised an eyebrow. "I see Ruth's keeping you up to date on our family business, then."

"Course she is. I *am* practically family. Been here longer than you, your brothers, and your grandma."

"True," Blue conceded with a nod. "But I'm sure Jenna doesn't need to hear our sordid family history."

Jenna met his gaze. "I know that your mother and baby sister disappeared, which must've been awful for you all. I'm quite happy to leave if it makes you uncomfortable talking about it in front of me."

Blue sighed and took off his Stetson, running his fingers through his military short brown hair. "It's not a problem. I had to talk to Billy about what he remembers, and I'm in a foul mood. It's not your fault."

Roy handed Jenna a glass of iced tea and offered one to Blue. "BB's looking to see who was employed at the ranch back then because someone must have helped Annie to leave."

"If she did leave," Blue murmured.

Roy set the iced tea down on the counter in front of him. "I agree with your daddy on this one. If she'd meant to kill herself, she would never have taken the baby. She loved that little girl something fierce."

"I thought so, too." Blue's smile was strained. "She still could've been murdered."

"But they never found her body."

"Plenty of places to hide a body out here, Roy, when we have our own fricking mine on the premises."

Roy patted Blue's arm. "Don't give up hope, son."

Jenna had to look away from the sudden flare of emotion in Blue's eyes. He might claim to be unaffected by what had happened, but it obviously wasn't true. Perhaps the big bad Marine really did have a softer side.

"Let me find those records for you," Roy offered. "I keep them in my office."

"You have an office here?" Jenna couldn't help but ask.

Roy shrugged. "Laundry room, office, feed store. It's all the same to me. I use all the space I can find. It might take a while."

Jenna focused on her paperwork as Blue paced the small living space, snapping his hat against his thigh. It was kind of distracting, but it wasn't her house and she was pretty sure he was too agitated to even realize he was doing it. Years of being her family's peacemaker made her speak up.

"Is your father going to stay on the ranch now?"

He stopped pacing to look at her, his blue gaze assessing.

"Technically, it's his place."

"I thought Chase was in charge."

"Well, he is and he isn't. Chase has the money and Ruth has the know-how to run the ranch, but I suppose my dad inherited the place from his father."

Jenna swung around in her seat. "Does that mean he gets a say in the future plans?"

The dawning horror on Blue's face made her wish she hadn't started the conversation.

"Holy crap. I hadn't thought of that." Blue rubbed a hand over his stubbled chin. "I'm going to have to talk to our family lawyer."

"I don't get the sense that he'd want to interfere," Jenna said quickly. "He seems like such a nice, quiet guy."

"You think so?"

She regarded him warily. "You don't like him, do you?"

A muscle flicked in his jaw. "I find it hard to forgive him for falling into a bottle and walking out on his four kids who had just lost their mother as well."

"How long was it before you saw him again?"

"He turned up about two months ago. Chase said he knew where Billy was all the time, but this was his first visit back to the ranch in twenty years."

"Wow, that's a long time to be gone." Jenna put down her pen. "Why do you think he came back? Did he find out about Chase's plans for the ranch?"

"Nah, it was kind of a coincidence." Blue came to lean against the edge of the countertop and picked up his glass of iced tea. "Sort of a collection of things that ended up making him come home twenty years too late to 'make amends.'"

The sarcasm in his voice was edged with anger—something Jenna understood all too well.

"Do you think he really wants to make things right with you?"

"I don't know." Blue was back to pacing again. He had way too much energy to be confined in such a small space. "He's definitely changed and he says he's given up drinking."

"That's good," Jenna said cautiously.

"I suppose so." Blue half smiled. "I'm just all out of group hugs and family reconciliation moments right now. If he wants my trust, he'll have to earn it."

"Here you go, BB." Roy came through the door with a couple of cardboard boxes covered in cobwebs. "I got you the payroll and the daily ledger for the whole year."

"Thanks, Roy."

Blue put them on the table next to Jenna, who kept a wary eye out for spiders. When Blue wasn't looking, she quickly used her tissue to clean them up a little. He perched on the edge of the table, reached past her shoulder, and opened the first box. Inside was a bundle of correspondence and bills and several notebooks.

"Jeez, this is going to take forever."

"Get January to help you. She's a historian. She loves poking around in old documents," Roy advised. "Or I bet if Miss Jenna can read Big Mac's handwriting, she can read anything."

"Jenna has a full-time job." Blue talked over her head as he took several payroll books out of the box and flipped through them. "She's not going to want to get involved in this clusterfuck."

"I wouldn't mind helping." Jenna spoke before she could talk herself out of it. "I quite like deciphering puzzles and I'm used to research work."

Blue looked down at her. "I've got it."

"But I really wouldn't mind—"

"Seriously, I've got it."

Jenna picked up her completed paperwork and put it neatly in the folder. "Not a problem."

She'd forgotten he was rather like her sister Lily—a type A personality who could do anything she set her mind to. Funny how she felt like she'd been firmly set in her place and how much it stung.

"I'd better be off, then." She smiled at Roy as she put her things away in her bag. "Let me know if you see any side effects from the vaccinations."

"Will do, Miss Jenna, and thanks for coming out here."

With a brief nod in Blue's direction, Jenna headed out the door and lugged her bag over to her truck.

"Hey."

She looked behind her to see that Blue had followed her out. He jogged to a stop right in front of her.

"I didn't mean to imply that your help wouldn't be useful."

"I didn't think that you did. You just assumed that you could do it better." She inclined her head an inch. "And, hey, you're probably right."

"Roy said—"

"If Roy told you to come out here and smooth down my ruffled feathers, that was very sweet of him, but I'm a big girl."

"Hell, I was going to come after you anyway."

Jenna blinked at him. "You were?"

"When I turned down your offer of help, you looked like I'd kicked your favorite puppy."

"I did *not*."

He shrugged. "Well, your least favorite puppy, then."

She stepped into his space, the toes of her boots touching his. "If you kicked a single puppy anywhere near me, I'd shoot you."

"You'd shoot *me*?"

"Yes, Mr. Marine Officer and a Gentleman or whatever you are."

His mouth quirked up at the corner. "I enlisted. If we're going to be formal here, I'm Gunnery Sergeant Morgan."

"That makes perfect sense. Aren't sergeants the ones who shout at everyone?"

"I'm not shouting, and I think you mean drill sergeants. I'm better at the more technical aspects of warfare."

"Like bossing people around and assuming you know better than everyone else?" she said sweetly. "I noticed that."

He sighed. "Look, all I wanted to say was I'm sorry

if I was abrupt with you back there. I have a tendency to forget I'm no longer supposed to be—"

"Bossing everyone around," she finished for him.

"Yeah. The thing is . . ." He hesitated. "This business with my mom? It's kind of a sensitive issue for me."

"Don't tell me, you have *feelings*?" Jenna asked.

He nodded. "Yeah. Sensitive ones."

She held his gaze and slowly exhaled. "I'm the one who should be apologizing. Your family business is nothing to do with me, and I let my own personal issues dictate how I responded to your perfectly reasonable decision not to involve me."

"You what?" He angled his head to one side. "Can you run that by me again in English?"

She glared at him. "My sister does everything so perfectly that I spent my entire childhood being told to butt out because I wasn't good enough. *Okay?* I obviously have a residual issue about it."

"Ah, now I totally get it. Imagine what it was like growing up with Mr. Perfect Chase Morgan as an older brother."

"Your brother is lovely."

"Exactly."

"And you're—"

"Not." He held her gaze. "I'm used to giving and receiving orders. Hell, I'm used to orders period, and after twelve years in the military, I'm just starting to come back into the real world. So if I'm being overbearing just tell me, okay?"

Jenna stared at him. "Just tell you."

He nodded. "You have a problem with that?"

"I just don't believe you mean it. You can't change who you are at your core."

"And as far as you are concerned, I'll always be a dictatorial dumbass?"

"I didn't call you a dumb anything," she protested.

"I'm just paraphrasing here. You'd probably put it more nicely." He took a step back and touched the brim of his Stetson. "So we're good?"

She nodded, and after a quick smile he turned and went back into the house, leaving her standing there like a fool.

No one was that direct.

Were they?

She got into the truck, made sure her bag was closed tight, and started the engine. As she bumped down the uneven drive away from the ranch, she tried to imagine Blue in one of the innumerable family therapy meetings her parents had considered mandatory when she was growing up.

They'd insisted that a healthy family dynamic needed to be worked upon, and to be fair, in Jenna's family there had been a lot of passive-aggressive shit going on. She bet Blue Morgan didn't do passive anything. He just told you how it was going to be and expected you to go along with it. Her parents would hate him.

She was still smiling as she pulled into a parking space in Morgantown and found her small purse. There was at least half an hour before clinic hours, and after dealing with the Marine, she needed coffee and chocolate to make it through the rest of the day. The dark aroma of roasting coffee led her toward Yvonne's café on Main Street, where she managed to find a small vacant corner table and settled into the comfortable chair.

The small space was done up to resemble a Parisian coffee shop, with outside tables shaded with umbrellas and an opulent interior décor that mirrored the richness of the cakes and coffee the proprietor Yvonne produced. It also had excellent Wi-Fi, which made both the passing tourists and the locals very happy.

"Jenna!"

She looked up to see Yvonne waving at her. Yvonne wore her usual black dress with a prim white collar that made her look vaguely French maid-ish, which Jenna knew was the exact effect she was going for,

"I wasn't expecting you in today. Didn't you have to go and see some pigs?"

Jenna hastily withdrew her muddy feet from sight. "I did, but I had some time before surgery. Can I have a triple-shot cappuccino and a chocolate muffin, please?"

"Of course you can," Yvonne said. "I'll be right back."

Jenna filled her lungs with the soothing smell of coffee and melted chocolate and slowly relaxed. She was the calm one in her family. The one who stepped between her parents and siblings and offered solutions and practical advice and . . . Blue Morgan made her want to forget all about peace and just argue right back.

But hadn't she learned through all those years of enforced family therapy that arguing was the worst way to solve anything? Reasonable discussion, validating someone else's point of view, and compromise were surely the ways to go?

Did the Marine even have those words in his vocabulary? Somehow she doubted it. But then he'd probably argue that compromise had no place in the military. He'd probably argue about all of it. She just knew it.

Yvonne slid into the seat beside her.

"Hey, stranger."

"I was here three days ago."

"Exactly. With January all engrossed with that man of hers, I've missed talking to you."

Jenna grabbed her cappuccino and took a huge gulp. Luckily, Yvonne knew her well enough to make it super milky and cool enough to drink right away.

"That's really good, thank you. I'm sorry I haven't been around much. I've been busy as hell helping out the Morgans."

Yvonne handed her a napkin and gestured at Jenna's mouth. "You've got a foam mustache. It's very fetching, but you might want to wipe it off before you go back to work."

Jenna mopped her top lip and then set about unwrapping the muffin and dividing it carefully into eight sections. She always ate the bottom four parts first, followed by the top.

"Were you up at Morgan Ranch this morning?"

"Yes." Jenna crammed a piece of muffin in her mouth and chewed fast. "I had to vaccinate some pigs."

"Did you see January?"

"Nope. She was busy writing her thesis or something."

Yvonne patted her upswept hair. "Was beautiful Blue Morgan there?"

Jenna paused with a chunk of muffin halfway to her mouth. "*Beautiful?* Blue Morgan is pretty average-looking, in my opinion."

"You're kidding, right?" Yvonne was staring at her. "He's totally . . . fit."

Jenna shrugged. "He's a Marine. I'd expect him to be fit."

Yvonne gave a delicious shudder. "I bet that man can go for hours."

"Talking? Yeah. He does love telling everyone what to do."

"That wasn't quite what I meant, but I can't say I mind a man who likes to order me around in bed." Yvonne gave her a lascivious wink.

"Then you're probably a match made in heaven because that particular man *loves* to speak his mind."

Yvonne sat back. "You don't like him?"

"He's . . . okay."

"Hang on, you like *everyone*." Yvonne lowered her voice. "So what has Blue Morgan done to get you all in a fidget?"

"He's bossy and opinionated."

"And?" Yvonne made an encouraging gesture with her elegant, long-fingered, perfectly manicured hand.

"And what? I don't like being bossed around." Jenna tidied the crumbs on her plate into a pattern with her finger. "Not that he'd ever try that with you."

Yvonne gave a happy sigh. "I think he likes me."

"Who doesn't? You're gorgeous."

Jenna said it without any rancor. Not only was Yvonne her friend, but it was obvious to anyone with a brain that Blue would want to date the tall, slender cake maker with the mysterious French accent. Jenna still couldn't understand why Yvonne's previous boyfriend had walked out and returned to France.

"Blue has come in to see me a couple of times," Yvonne admitted. "And he's always been charming."

"Because he's flirting with you." Jenna ate another section of muffin. "He doesn't flirt with me. I'm just the newbie vet he doesn't quite trust to keep an eye on his horses."

"I'm sure he trusts you." Yvonne patted her hand. "Did he happen to mention when he's returning to the ranch full-time?"

"I think Roy said it was officially another month or so, but Blue said it might be sooner because of accumulated leave."

"It will be nice to see him settled back at the ranch."

"'Settled' isn't a word I'd ever use to describe that man. He literally hums with pent-up energy."

Yvonne rose to her feet. "As I said, I can't wait to find out what he can do with all that energy."

Jenna met Yvonne's gaze. "You really like him, then?"

"Only if you're okay with it." Yvonne stopped smiling, her expression serious. "I'm not one of those women who thinks it's okay to steal her friends' boyfriends."

"Well, don't worry. I don't want him." Jenna shuddered. "Much too high maintenance."

"Then as January has already snagged the town's only multimillionaire, it's only fair that I get a chance at his brother, right?" Yvonne winked as she picked up the empty plate. "Poor man won't know what's hit him."

"Go for it. If you can bring him to his knees and take his mind off the ranch a bit, I'd be extremely grateful." Jenna finished up her coffee and put the cup down in the saucer. "I've got to run. Clinic starts soon."

"Then I'll put this on your tab." Yvonne waved her away. "Have fun!"

Chapter Four

"I'm trying to get in touch with Red Williams. Have you heard from him lately, ma'am?"

Blue held the phone away from his ear as the enraged female on the other end said a few things about Red that weren't at all complimentary. When she paused for breath, Blue tried again.

"Do you have a forwarding address or phone number for him?"

Another rant followed and then the call was cut off, leaving Blue in blessed silence. Red Williams had obviously been leading an exciting life since leaving the ranch. That was the third woman Blue had spoken to who had nothing nice to say about the man who was apparently a liar, a thief, and a two-timing bastard.

Blue stared down at his notes. Red sounded just like the sort of man who might have done more than offer the owner of the ranch's wife an appreciative smile. Had he charmed Annie into leaving with him and then dumped her as soon as she got tiresome? It would follow his usual pattern. Would he have wanted a baby around? Blue couldn't imagine that.

He crossed another name from the list of Red's contacts and contemplated the last one left. The number had been given to him by the first of Red's ex-wives, who had gotten over Red's adultery and had kicked him out twenty-five years ago. He glanced at the kitchen clock and calculated the time difference to the East Coast. If the number really did belong to Red's mother, she might well have gone to bed by now.

Heaving a sigh, Blue pushed away from the table, stretched out his spine, and got himself more coffee from the old metal pot sitting on the range. It was strong enough to take the enamel off his teeth, but he needed the energy. He much preferred dealing with horses than with people. His phone vibrated as a text came in, and he glanced down at it.

Are you home?

He frowned at the unexpected message from Jenna and typed an affirmative.

Can you meet me at the south boundary of Lymond Ranch?

He didn't bother to do more than type another yes before he was out of the house and saddling up Messi. The Lymond boundary ran alongside theirs for a mile or so. After about fifteen minutes riding cross-country to where the two properties met by the road proper, he spotted Jenna's truck parked up in the shade and headed toward her.

She waved as he approached and beckoned him to dismount.

"Thanks for coming."

"What's up?" Blue asked. After two weeks working together they'd gotten far more comfortable with each other. "Did your truck break down?"

"No." She swallowed hard. "I wanted you to see this."

She headed for the copse of trees that shaded both the narrow track and the wire fencing that enclosed the ranchlands.

Blue automatically felt for his weapon and realized he had nothing more threatening than his phone. With a soft curse, he followed Jenna, treading as quietly as he could over the uneven surface. Jenna stopped at the fence and was staring out at something.

"Look," she whispered as he came level with her.

There were four horses in the field, which contained nothing else except a rusted bucket by the far gate. Blue narrowed his gaze on the foremost gelding.

"What the hell's going on? They look like they haven't been properly fed for weeks."

"And there's no shelter or any obvious food for them apart from the grass." Jenna turned to face him. "Will you come up to the Lymonds' with me and find out what's going on?"

"Sure."

"Thanks so much." She patted his arm. "I didn't know who else to call. Mark Lymond doesn't like me very much."

"He's an old grouch. Ruth's had plenty of run-ins with him over the years."

"Uncle Ron said he was difficult, but lately he's seemed a lot worse."

Blue had started walking toward the truck but stopped to look back at Jenna.

"In what way worse?"

She sighed. "Losing his temper over the slightest problem, threatening to sue us, you know the kind of thing."

"And Big Mac let you come up here alone?"

She looked down at her boots. "Well, I haven't actually told him what Mr. Lymond has been saying. I didn't want to worry him and I didn't want him thinking I couldn't cope."

"Then I'm glad you called me. Come on. We'll take your truck and leave Messi here."

"Will he be okay?" Jenna asked.

"He's trained to stand for as long as necessary. I'll make sure he can't trip over the reins."

"I can't see Nolly doing that," Jenna said.

"Nolly's a nightmare. He'd be following us up the drive and poking his nose into everything. I have no idea why Chase puts up with him."

Blue checked Messi over and made sure he was in the shade before getting into the passenger seat of the truck. Jenna backed up and turned to face the driveway to the Lymond ranch house. Her grip on the steering wheel tightened as they approached the final gate.

"Were you due to visit the ranch today?" Blue asked.

"I've already been there."

"So Mark won't be expecting a return visit."

"Actually, I forgot to get him to fill in one of the forms for the Department of Agriculture, so I stopped on the road to get it done and heard the horses neighing to each other." Jenna took a deep breath. "The thing is—when I asked him earlier, Mr. Lymond told me he'd sold off most of his horses, not left them in a field and seemingly forgotten about them." She glanced over at Blue, her brown eyes troubled. "Why would he do that?"

"Maybe he couldn't afford to pay for their upkeep or veterinary fees and decided to let them live off the land for a bit." Blue shrugged. "He wouldn't be the first rancher to do that when times are hard. He's never had a lot of spare cash."

"But why didn't he just sell them on like he said he did?"

"I don't know. Perhaps he didn't want to admit he was short of money."

Blue got out to open the gate and closed it behind them. Two dogs ran out barking as they came to a stop in front of the ranch house. It was an unappealing square box with gray textured walls and a shingle roof that was in desperate need of repair.

In fact, the whole place looked like it was suffering from neglect. Blue's tension level rose as no one came out of the house to greet them.

"How do you want to handle this?" he asked Jenna softly.

"I'm not sure." She hesitated. "Although maybe I could tell him that I didn't get his signature on that form, and while he's fixing that, I could just casually ask about the horses."

"It's a plan," Blue said dubiously. "I'll just follow along behind you."

He wanted to do a lot more than that, but over the years he'd learned that the diplomatic approach was always the first thing to try. If Mark got in Jenna's face about anything, he'd be dealing with Blue instead, and screw diplomacy.

Jenna got out of the truck and patted the two dogs that had come around to investigate her arrival. Blue noted the dogs were on the thin side, too. Whatever was going on at Lymond Ranch was affecting all the livestock. He'd hardly seen any young cattle out in the pasturelands as they'd driven up to the house. If Mark didn't have cattle, he wouldn't need ranch hands and they wouldn't need horses.

Blue walked up to the door of the house and banged the

knocker, the sound echoing through the quiet house. There was only one vehicle parked nearby that he knew belonged to Mark and no others, which accounted for the silence. A ranch couldn't operate with just one man running it.

Blue gave up on the house and directed his attention to the barn.

"Let's try down there."

Jenna nodded and set off, her bag in her hand and her chin set at a determined angle that didn't quite disguise her nervousness. Mark Lymond was a big man and probably a foot taller than Jenna. The thought of her confronting him by herself made Blue want to curse like a sailor. She didn't lack for guts, though. That was one thing he'd already learned about her.

"Mr. Lymond?" Jenna called out.

A shadow detached itself from the innards of the barn and moved toward them.

"I'm so sorry to bother you again, but I forgot to get your signature on one of the forms," Jenna said.

"Damn stupid woman," Mark Lymond muttered as he threw his shovel to the ground. "Shouldn't be allowed to do work that's beyond their understanding."

Blue stepped up until his shoulder touched Jenna's.

"Morning, Mark."

The old rancher stopped moving, his gaze flicking between Jenna and Blue.

"BB Morgan. I heard that you and your father were back in town."

Blue nodded. "I'm due to leave the Marines this summer. I'll be living on the ranch full-time and helping Ruth run the place."

"Good luck getting her to listen to a damned thing you have to say."

Blue's smile wasn't friendly. "She's the expert. I'm the

one who's learning, so I'll be doing the listening." He glanced down at Jenna. "Have you got that paper for Mark to sign?"

"It's here." Jenna took out the form and found a pen. "There always seems to be one more form than I'm expecting, so I apologize for missing this one."

Mark grunted and moved across to take the form from Jenna's outstretched hand. "As I said, send Dave next time. He never messes up."

"I'll certainly bear that in mind." Despite the fact that Mark was looming over her, Jenna certainly didn't seem intimidated. "I noticed you had some horses down at the far end of your property. Did you want me to check them over for you while I'm here?"

Mark slowly straightened, the pen clenched in his fist like a weapon. "You spying on me, little girl?"

Blue cleared his throat. "I saw the horses when I was riding the fence line and I asked the vet what she knew about them."

"What's it got to do with you, Morgan?"

Blue met Mark's furious glare. "I'm looking to buy some more horses for our new program at the ranch. I was wondering whether those four were for sale."

Some of the anger leeched out of the old rancher's face. "They might be."

"Then you won't mind if Ms. Jenna checks them over, will you? If they are sound, I can make you a cash offer and you can take it or leave it." Blue shrugged. "It's way cheaper for me to source my horses locally than have them transported here, so you'd be doing me a favor."

Mark held Blue's gaze for a long moment. "She can look at them."

"'She' has a name. Use it."

"I don't hold with female veterinarians," Mark snapped. "They don't have the strength or the brains to work with large animals."

Blue stepped back. "Then we'll be on our way. I don't deal with misogynists."

"Miss so jar whats?" Mark scratched his head.

Blue picked up Jenna's bag. "You ready to go, Ms. Jenna? We've got a lot to do this afternoon."

"Wait." Mark spoke from behind them, but Blue didn't turn around. "The veterinarian can look at the horses."

"Thank you." Blue nodded at Jenna. Mark must really need the cash. "Do you have time to do that right now, or do you need to schedule a new appointment?"

"I think I can fit it in if I skip lunch," Jenna said. "I'll call the clinic and make sure they know where I am. Thank you, Mr. Lymond."

Mark couldn't quite force out a "you're welcome," but at least he kept his mouth shut as Jenna walked to the truck. Blue waited a beat and then turned to the surly rancher, lowering his voice.

"If I ever hear that you have disrespected one hair on that woman's head, I will come over here and beat the shit out of you. Understood?"

Mark dropped his gaze, but not before Blue had seen the flash of rage residing there.

"And if those horses don't make it because you couldn't be bothered to take care of them, *I'll* make sure you face every charge I can pin on you for animal cruelty." Blue touched the brim of his Stetson. "I'll be in touch about purchasing the horses. Have a nice day."

He hefted Jenna's bag into the truck and got in beside her as she started the engine and drove off.

* * *

"What were you saying to him?"

"Nothing much. Just making arrangements for potentially buying the horses."

"Yeah right, that's why he changed color." Jenna gave Blue the side eye. He looked like some dangerously smug predator sitting beside her. "Did you threaten him?"

"I might have suggested some consequences for his actions that he wouldn't like if he messed up."

"I just bet you did." She focused on the road for a moment. "My parents always told me that violence wasn't the answer, but sometimes, when I see animals that have been neglected or mistreated, I wish I had a gun." She bit her lip. "You probably think that's appalling, right?"

"Nah. I'd be the one giving you the weapon."

She fought a smile. "You'd have to teach me how to use it first. My parents—"

"Don't approve of guns."

"How did you know?"

He shrugged. "Just a wild guess."

"Thanks for helping out." She shivered. "He kind of scares me."

"I'm not surprised." The smile was gone from his face. "I know it's got nothing to do with me, but I'd suggest you get Dave to go up there for a while until Mark gets over his temper tantrum. I didn't see his wife's car there. I wonder if she's still around? He's definitely struggling, and for some reason he's decided to take it out on you."

"It's okay. I'm not one of those TSTL females."

"TSTL?"

"You know, the kind who knows there's a serial killer at large, hears a noise in the basement, and goes down the stairs to see what's going on with nothing more than a brave smile and a candle clutched in her hand? Too stupid to live."

His chuckle surprised her. "I like that."

"And I'm glad you were with me today."

"Any time." He pointed out of the side window. "You should pull in here so we can get into that field."

Jenna got out of the truck and almost fell over, her knees were trembling so much.

"You okay?" Blue moved so fast he was right beside her, one hand under her elbow.

Jenna took a deep shuddering breath.

"I *hate* violence."

"Hey, it's okay."

A second later she was turned against the solid wall of his chest, her head neatly under his chin and one of his arms around her shoulders. She should step back, but there was something so appealing about leaning her forehead against him that she let it happen. He smelled of leather and horse and some kind of manly shower gel.

"I wouldn't have let him touch you."

"I know that." She took a big gulp of air, which only meant she inhaled more of him. He smelled good.

His fingers smoothed over her hair as if he was petting her. "I don't suppose you'd believe me if I told you that even if he had tried anything, you could've taken him down."

This time she did raise her head. "Me? He's about a foot taller and built like a brick house."

"Everyone except Ruth is probably taller than you." His stare became assessing. "Did you ever take a self-defense class?"

"No, it's not usually one they recommend at veterinary school."

"Well, they should. Everyone needs to know how to defend themselves."

There was an implacable note in his voice that Jenna had come to know rather well.

"Maybe I'll teach you the basics while I'm teaching you how to fire a gun." Blue nodded as if it was a done deal. "Yeah, I'll talk to Roy and—"

"Hang on, who appointed you my teacher?"

He raised an eyebrow. "I did. If we're going to be working together, you don't want a big old war-toughened Marine deciding to defend you. It could get nasty real quick. You'd be much better learning to do it for yourself."

Jenna found herself nodding.

"Great." He took charge of her bag and opened the gate into the field. "I'll set it up."

By the time she'd finished checking the horses, the sun was right overhead and the temperature had escalated from fine to blistering hot. Blue had taken her truck and gone for water, seeing as there was none in the ancient horse trough and the water feed pipe had rusted through.

He'd been really helpful, catching the horses and keeping them calm while she got the basic examinations done. None of the animals showed signs of serious ill treatment and had come willingly to hand. They were just thin and probably dehydrated. If Mark Lymond really couldn't afford to keep them, Jenna wished he'd just told her. She was in contact with several equine rescue foundations and might have been able to place the horses elsewhere for him.

But he'd made his opinion about her interference clear enough and, like a lot of the local ranchers, obviously didn't reckon she was up to the job. She sighed so hard that the gelding she was working on turned to nuzzle her hair.

The sound of her truck returning made her look toward

the edge of the field where Blue was now manhandling a large plastic drum out of the open back of the vehicle. Even he staggered a bit as he rolled the drum toward the field and then picked it up and dumped it inside the old trough. Sunlight glinted on the blade of his knife as he efficiently cut a third of the plastic away to reveal the fresh water within.

"This should hold them until tomorrow."

Jenna released the fourth horse with a pat and strolled toward him. "Gosh, that thing must weigh a ton."

"It sure felt like it."

He wiped a hand over his brow and then brought his T-shirt up to mop his face. Jenna almost stopped breathing at her first in-person view of six-pack abs. Sure, she'd heard about them, seen them on TV and read about them, but this was her first experience of real abs out in the wild. If she wasn't mistaken, there were also beads of sweat rolling down *over* his abs in beautiful slow motion toward his lats.

"Latissimus dorsi," she murmured. "Oh yeah."

"What's up?"

He'd lowered his T-shirt and was looking at her strangely. Was her mouth open? Was she actually drooling?

"It's hot, isn't it?" Was that her squeaky voice?

"Yeah."

He was still watching her as though she was an unexploded bomb he might have to deal with. She'd been pressed up against that chest and those abs earlier. She hadn't appreciated what lay beneath his boring T-shirt.

"You look a bit flushed yourself," Blue said. "Do you have sunscreen on?"

"Yeah. But I left my hat in the truck." She flapped her hand in a wide circle. Great, she was babbling *and* pointing now.

"Would you like me to get your hat for you, or are you finished here?"

"I'm done. The horses are all in good shape."

"Good. I'll talk to Chase tonight and make sure we have the cash available at the bank in town to give to Mark." He put away his knife.

"You're going to take them?"

"Sure." He paused. "Unless you have any objections. They seem pretty well-trained and even-tempered to me."

"I agree."

She picked up her bag and walked toward her truck while Blue gave Messi a turn at the water trough before mounting up. He rode alongside her truck and looked down at her, his face shadowed beneath the brim of his hat.

"Will you come back to the ranch?"

"Do you need me to?"

His smile made her want to smile back and maybe twirl her hair and giggle. "It's lunchtime, and Ruth would never forgive me if I didn't invite you. You can tell her and Roy what happened today at Lymond's place."

"Do you think I should?"

"Yeah." He nodded. "I'll see you back there, then."

With a click to Messi, Blue took off cross-country, leaving Jenna staring at a cloud of dust. What was it about Blue Morgan that made her nod and follow along so obediently? He just made huge assumptions about *everything*, and she seemed incapable of stopping him.

And she'd practically slavered over his abs after assuring Yvonne that she didn't think he was all that.

And he'd held her close and not made fun of her when she'd had a delayed reaction to the stress of dealing with Mr. Lymond. In fact, he'd offered to teach her how to defend herself.

Jenna jammed her hat on her head and started the engine. Actually, he hadn't offered, he'd basically told her he was going to teach her some moves. How would it feel getting up close and personal with a muscular Marine with the reflexes of a cat?

She realized she was making a moaning breathy sound and hastily shut her mouth as she turned into the long drive up to Morgan Ranch. She didn't have to do anything he suggested.

She could just say no.

Not that it would make any difference. She had a sense that when he made a decision, he wouldn't let little things like her halfhearted objections get in the way. He wasn't so much bossy as formidable. Yet he'd suggested she could learn to take care of *herself* rather than assuming she was just a weak and feeble female who needed a strong man to defend her. That was . . . encouraging. Because she could take care of herself. She'd already learned that the hard way.

Chapter Five

"So you and Blue seem to be getting along well," January said as she licked cream out of her chocolate éclair.

The three of them were sharing a table at the coffee shop for a quick lunch and catch-up session before January got back into writing her thesis about the origins of Morgan Ranch and Jenna returned to the clinic. Morgantown might not be a metropolis, but it had everything Jenna needed to survive as well as two good friends who didn't know her family, which was a definite bonus.

Jenna tried for an indifferent shrug. "He's okay."

"Okay?" Yvonne asked. "Three weeks ago you said he was bossy and opinionated and that I could have him. So what's changed?"

"Abs." Jenna took a hasty gulp of her cappuccino.

"You saw his *abs*?" Yvonne leaned closer. "Were they as fine as I imagined they would be?"

"Finer," Jenna admitted. "When I saw them I kind of lost the power of speech for a moment."

January cleared her throat. "Are you two objectifying my future brother-in-law here?"

"It depends on what you mean by objectifying," Jenna said. "I certainly didn't touch anything."

Yvonne snorted. "But you wanted to, didn't you? I can see it in your eyes."

Jenna sighed. "There was this bead of sweat just traveling downward I couldn't stop staring at."

"You *like* him." January nudged her. "You wanted to lick him like a Popsicle, didn't you?"

"I did not!" Jenna looked up to see both of her friends shaking their heads. *"What?"*

"You are a terrible liar," Yvonne pronounced. "But it's okay. If I'd seen Blue Morgan without his shirt on, I would probably have thrown myself at him and licked him all over."

Jenna held Yvonne's gaze. "And you should, because he likes you."

"I'm not getting in the way of true lust, girlfriend." Yvonne held out her hand palm up. "You go for it."

"I'm not going to do anything. We get along fine now, but our relationship is purely professional," Jenna said. "He doesn't think of me like that, anyway. I'm just the annoying new vet."

"You see, there's your problem. You need to *make* him think of you like that," Yvonne said, and January nodded. "She's right."

"How? By accidentally falling out of the hayloft into his arms? I'd probably break my neck."

"He'd catch you." January and Yvonne spoke in unison. "You know he would."

"If he was around, maybe, but knowing my luck I'd fall on Roy and kill him."

"You've got to get rid of the negative attitude, and there's no need to be so dramatic." Yvonne pointed one long finger at Jenna. "All you have to do is pay him some genuine attention. You know, really listen to him when he talks, make eye contact, touch him in little ways, you know, like owning him, right?"

Jenna stared at Yvonne. "I have no idea what you're talking about. I don't do that stuff and Blue's not stupid. He'd know that something was up."

"He'd know that you were interested in him." Yvonne sipped her coffee. "And if you really *are* interested, then you'll do those things naturally."

Jenna sat back, her arms folded across her chest. "Which makes no sense because I'm not doing them, so I'm obviously not that keen on him after all."

"Stop." Yvonne rubbed her forehead. "You're giving me frown lines. Sometimes a man needs a little nudge to stop seeing you as one thing and see you as another, okay? So maybe Blue sees you as the veterinarian, so if you want to change that dynamic you need to help him see you as a woman."

"A woman who wants him," January added helpfully.

"I don't—" Jenna sighed. "Okay, maybe I do, but he's not interested in me. I get nothing back from him at all."

"That's not true," January said. "He definitely notices you, and he always says very positive things about you when you're not there."

"He does?" For a moment Jenna perked up. "I mean, he *did* offer to teach me self-defense techniques, one-on-one, which was super nice of him . . ."

"Nice?" Yvonne sighed dramatically. "I would've demanded my first lesson immediately, and preferably naked." Yvonne's cell buzzed and she put down her cup. "I've got to get back to work. Think about what I said, Jenna, and try and use some of those feminine wiles God gifted you with."

January stood up, too, brushing crumbs off her boobs. "Do you want me to put a good word in for you?"

"God no. This isn't high school." Jenna buried her face in her hands. "I wish I'd just kept my big mouth shut about those abs."

"From the sound of it, they are a thing of awe and beauty that should be shared with the female population." January winked at her. "Maybe I'll just slip Blue a note under the table at dinner tonight saying 'do you like Jenna, check box yes or box no.'"

"I need to get back to work," Jenna muttered. "And stop thinking about abs."

Blue finished his turkey sandwich and took a long slug of iced tea.

"Thanks for lunch, Ruth."

"You're welcome. No Jenna today, then?"

"She had other stuff to do."

Ruth was peeling apples, which probably meant pie, which made Blue very happy.

"You seem to be getting on great with her now."

"She's good at her job. I like that." Blue took another sip of tea and tasted the mint Ruth liked to infuse in it. "I like her. She's good company."

"Pretty, too."

Blue eyed his grandmother over the top of his glass. "I hadn't noticed."

"Hard to miss." Ruth cut an apple into quarters and placed it in the bowl.

"You matchmaking here?"

"I wouldn't dare." Ruth started peeling another apple. "Just pointing out the obvious."

Blue thought about Jenna's big brown eyes and the

way her hair glinted red in the sunlight. Her smile was nice, too. They'd been getting on great for the past few weeks. If he'd been in the market for a real long-term relationship, she was just the sort of woman he'd want. Smart, hardworking, and able to stand toe to toe with him and argue her point.

But he wasn't ready to settle down yet, and she wasn't the sort of woman who would be happy with the short-term sexual relationships he specialized in when both parties knew what they were getting into and how to get out. She deserved the whole package, the white picket fence, two kids, and all that implied. He wasn't sure if he'd ever be the man to deliver *that* little fantasy.

"Anyone home?"

Ruth looked up. "Is that you, Chase?"

"Yup." Blue's older brother came through the kitchen door and enveloped his grandmother in a hug. "How are you doing?"

"I'm good." Ruth kissed his cheek. "Come and sit down and have something to eat."

Chase obediently sat and nodded at Blue. "You still here?"

"I'm due back on base in two days." Blue grimaced. "I can't wait to see how much more paperwork I've got to complete to finally be free."

Chase took some iced tea. "Any idea about the actual end date yet?"

"Not quite. There are all kinds of algorithms to be worked through before we can arrive at anything that straightforward. But I'm hoping it's less than a month away now."

"Good. I'd like you to be here as we move forward."

"Trust me, I'm working on it, bro."

Ruth placed a grilled cheese sandwich in front of Chase and patted his shoulder. "Eat it while it's hot."

Chase sank his teeth into the golden bread, and strands of cheese dripped down from his chin onto the plate. "Damn, that's good."

Before Blue could even articulate the thought, Ruth put another sandwich in front of him.

He grinned at her. "How did you know?"

"Because you've always wanted what your older brother had."

"Apart from his stressful tech job and his fiancée?" Blue added. "I'd like his millions, though."

"Wouldn't we all?" Ruth agreed.

Chase finished his sandwich and wiped his chin. "Where's January?"

"She's in town with Yvonne and Jenna." Blue answered him through a mouthful of cheese. "They're having lunch and talking shit about you. She said she'd be back around three."

"Cool. That gives us time to go over a few things." Chase retrieved his laptop from his bag and fired it up. "I've done a new cost analysis on the overall financial upkeep of the barn and other elements involved in the wear and tear of running a string of horses for guests."

"Great," Blue groaned. "Just how I wanted to spend my afternoon, being lectured by you."

"I bet you'd rather be out with Jenna, wouldn't you, Blue?" Ruth put two mugs on the table and filled them with coffee.

"Jenna McDonald?" Chase looked up from his spread-sheet. "You're seeing her?"

"We're working together on the horses." Blue gave Ruth a "quit meddling" look. "She's doing a great job."

"I know January speaks very highly of her." Chase's

interest returned to the financials. "I'm thinking we might need a vet permanently on staff if we do this thing right. Do you think Jenna would be interested?"

"I have no idea." Blue considered the notion of Jenna being at the ranch all the time, and it didn't scare him one bit. "But I wouldn't mind if she took the job."

Then maybe in ten or twenty years' time, when he'd matured into the kind of man who was ready to settle down, she'd be ready to settle down with him. Blue snorted. Like she'd still be around. She was way too cute and intelligent to be without a man if she wanted one. But he'd started to enjoy her company and looked forward to spending time with her, which was a first for him.

"BB?"

He looked up to find Chase staring at him. "What?"

"You're not concentrating." His brother shut his laptop. "How about we take a ride into town, pick up the mail, and meet up with January for lunch?"

"Sounds way better than looking at spreadsheets with you." Blue stood up and gathered up the plates and mugs. Thank God for Chase's all-consuming interest in his fiancée. "I wanted to talk to Yvonne about an idea I had anyway."

Jenna finished her cappuccino and surreptitiously ate the remains of January's second chocolate muffin before finally standing up to leave. To her surprise, January was walking back toward her, a huge smile on her face and a tall, dark, and handsome cowboy behind her.

"Hey. Don't go just yet! Chase is here."

"I'm sure he'd much rather see you than me," Jenna said even as Chase Morgan, who had the same bright blue eyes as his brother, took her hand in a firm grasp and shook it.

"Nice to see you again, Jenna. I hear you've been doing sterling work at the ranch."

"I've just been helping Blue with the horses."

"So he said and doing a great job, too." Chase smiled down at her. He was slightly taller than Blue and his muscles were less well defined, but the resemblance between them was obvious. "Once the ranch is up and running, I might want to talk to you about signing on as the vet on staff."

"For the whole of Morgan Ranch?"

"Yeah." He considered her for a long moment. "We'd pay you and everything."

She grinned. "Pay? Wow, that would be a novelty. My uncle makes me work for nothing."

He gestured at her vacated seat. "Have you got five minutes?"

She checked her cell and messages and there was nothing urgent. "Sure. As long as I'm back by three I'm good."

January sat down, too, and Chase hooked an arm out to snag another chair. "Blue's around here somewhere."

Jenna looked toward the door and saw Blue talking to Yvonne, his face relaxed, his body language leaning toward her friend as though he was listening intently. Her earlier faint spark of hope that he might be persuaded to become interested in her died. Yvonne was definitely his type—sophisticated, educated, and way more sexually experienced than Jenna would ever be.

Blue patted Yvonne on the shoulder and stood back to allow her to precede him into the shop. She went into the kitchen and he strolled over to their table with his usual smooth grace. He nodded at January and Jenna as he sat down.

"Yvonne's going to try and join us in a minute as well."

"Why, what's up?" January asked.

"Just something I thought of doing that might benefit the community," Blue said. "Actually, Jenna gave me the idea."

"To do what?" Judging by the way his eyebrows went up, Jenna thought she might have sounded a bit snappy.

"Self-defense classes."

"Oh." So much for her getting some one-on-one time with him. He'd obviously decided to go far wider with his act of generosity.

"I thought we could hold them here one evening a week." Blue blithely continued as if oblivious to the fact that he needed to shut up right now. "Yvonne thinks it might work really well."

"What a great idea!" January said. "I'd love to learn how to take a man down, wouldn't you, Jenna?"

"Oh yes, I'd like that a lot," Jenna replied. "I'm sure there are a lot of folks here who would benefit from that kind of knowledge. Maybe you could include instructions on how to kill a man." She grabbed her bag. "Sorry, I have to go. I forgot I promised to help Uncle Ron clip his cat's claws."

Blue and Chase automatically rose to their feet and then she had to practically clamber over Blue's knees to escape. Yvonne was coming toward her, a pot of coffee in one hand.

"Where are you going? What do you think of Blue's idea?"

Jenna smiled. "It's great. Hey, you can offer to be his class model or something. Gotta run!"

Yvonne frowned at her. "What about those feminine wiles I mentioned you using? Running away isn't going to help your cause."

Jenna executed a slick move worthy of a quarterback stepping outside his box and managed to get past Yvonne and out into the fresh air. Blue's idea *was* awesome, and her disappointment that he'd decided to make his abs and strength available to *all* the females in Morgantown— and she would bet her last dollar that the class would be full—was negligible.

Hadn't she learned early on in life that there was always someone more interesting and attractive than her around and that stepping back into the shadows was for the best? At least he had no idea that she'd been building some pretty darn unrealistic daydreams around him during the last month or so. She was *so* glad she'd kept those to herself.

Blue turned from watching Jenna exit the coffee shop to find Chase shaking his head at him.

"I don't know exactly what you did, BB, but *something* made Jenna rush off."

"Why does it have to be because of me? Maybe she got scared off by one of your stupid spreadsheets or something."

"Jenna mentioned Blue had offered to give her self-defense lessons." January squeezed Chase's hand.

Blue frowned. "That's right, I did."

"And now he's offering to teach every female in the town and surrounding area."

"So?"

Chase nodded at January. "Jenna probably feels bad about that."

"Why?"

January sighed as if he was a super-slow learner. "Because you asked her *first*."

"Because she inspired the idea. I mentioned that. Are

you saying Jenna thinks I'd rather teach a class load of women than her?"

Yvonne had come up behind him and set the coffeepot on the table. "Yes."

"But the two things have nothing to do with each other."

"Yes, they do," January and Yvonne chorused.

Blue rubbed the back of his neck. "I still don't get it."

"Abs," January said, nodding cryptically at Yvonne.

"Yeah, I have abs." Blue patted his flat stomach. "I also have the ability to teach proper self-defense techniques—something I think everyone should know."

"So would you expect Jenna to come to this class?"

Blue shrugged. "If she wants to, sure."

"So your offer to teach her by herself is no longer on the table?"

Blue stared from January to Yvonne and then looked at Chase. "Have you any idea what they are getting at?"

"I *think* they are saying that Jenna might feel hurt that you enlarged on your original proposal to teach her to include the entire female population of Morgantown."

"You nailed it." January kissed Chase's cheek. "I'm so proud of you right now."

Chase smiled complacently at Blue.

"But that would imply that Jenna . . ." Blue stopped speaking.

"That Jenna?" Chase repeated. "What?"

Blue stood up. "Can you get a ride back with January, Chase?"

"Why, where are you going?"

January grinned up at Blue. "Don't worry about your brother. I'll make sure he gets home safely. You go and do what you have to do."

Blue nodded, made sure he had the keys to his truck, and went out the door.

"Stupid, stupid," Jenna muttered to herself as she sat down in the back office to catch up on some paperwork. It was quiet for once, as most of the staff was at lunch or on call. She'd flat out lied to Chase and wasn't needed for at least an hour.

The back door opened, and assuming it was Dave, she didn't bother to look up until a large shape sat opposite her at the table.

"Big Mac doesn't own a cat."

Her head came up and she locked gazes with Blue.

"Did I say cat? I meant rat, his pet ornamental rat."

His eyebrow went up. "I think you just wanted to get away."

"Now why on earth would you think that?"

"Because I put my big foot in it."

She shrugged. "I didn't notice. I just assumed you wanted to talk to Yvonne about your idea and that my presence was superfluous."

"And superfluous means?"

"Redundant, unnecessary."

"So you wouldn't join my self-defense class?"

"Whatever gave you that idea? I think it's a great thing to do for the town."

"So you'd come?"

"Sure!" She picked up her pen again. "You didn't come all the way over here just to clear that up, did you?"

He was watching her intently. "I got the impression that I might have offended you in some way."

"You didn't."

"Okay." He hesitated. "Just because I suggested running a class doesn't mean I don't want to teach you one-on-one."

A tingling awareness of dread coalesced in her gut. "Have you been talking to January?"

Now he looked downright uncomfortable. "She and Chase might have mentioned that I *might* have screwed up here."

"Did she send you?"

"No, I came by myself once I realized that you might have read more into my offer of teaching you than I'd meant. I like you, Jenna, but—"

She held up her hand. "Stop right there."

"Before I say what?"

"Before you totally humiliate me and give me your little speech about how you *like* me and all that, but the thought of anything more makes you break out in hives, or that you're already married, or you're off to explore the Antarctic or any of those million and one excuses a person uses when they think someone else likes them a little *too* much."

She almost ran out of breath completing her way-too-complicated sentence. "I don't need to hear it because I'm not stupid, and I'm not interested in you like that, okay? So maybe you should just go."

Yeah, like he would move before he'd said his piece. He was nothing but direct.

"Jenna, I do like you."

"We've already established that. We make a great professional team." She shot to her feet and headed for the door. "Can I show you out? I'm sure you've got way better things to do than sit here chatting with me."

He carried on speaking. "The thing is, I'm not in the

right frame of mind to consider a serious relationship with anyone at this moment."

She turned to stare at him. His gaze was directed downward to his clasped hands.

"It's not on my schedule. I'm separating from the military and starting a new career at the ranch. I have to focus on those two goals before I even think about anything more personal." He looked up, his blue eyes serious. "I'm not even sure I'm capable of having a long-term relationship. I've never been around long enough in one place to ever try one out."

He slowly rose to his feet and strolled toward her.

"If I was the kind of man who wanted that—" He came even closer and she flattened herself against the door as he stopped right in front of her. "You'd be just the kind of woman I'd want."

Her breath hissed out as he cupped her chin and gently dropped a kiss on her lips.

"Okay," she muttered.

His thumb smoothed over her jawline. "So, we're good?"

"Yes."

He stepped back. "Cool. I'll see you tomorrow, then."

"Bye."

He was leaving and she didn't think she'd ever be able to peel herself off the door again. Part of her wanted to run after him and ask him to repeat everything he'd just said. The rest of her would remember his words forever. With a soft sound she slid down the door and stared at the wall opposite.

He liked her, and if he were in the mood for a permanent relationship he would be thinking about her . . .

Jenna's smile died. "The conceited ass! Why does everything have to be on his agenda? What about what *I* want? Maybe I don't want him at all! What about if I want a relationship *right now*?"

No one answered her, but one of the dogs out the back started to howl. She felt like joining in.

How typical of Blue to have his "own schedule" and to kindly tell her he wasn't ready, but that she would've qualified if he had been. He might as well have patted her on the head instead of kissing her. Now she'd be wondering things—like about how he'd kiss her properly and other more intimate hot, sweaty, *naked* things.

"Hey. What are you doing down there?"

She looked up to see Dave towering over her.

"I'm thinking."

"Well, think somewhere else or we'll be tripping over you all day."

Jenna took his proffered hand and was hauled to her feet.

"Dave, do you have any friends who are single?"

He put his bag down on the table and eyed her suspiciously. "Sure. All of them. Why do you want to know?"

"Do you think one of them would be willing to take me out on a date?"

"Well, a couple of them have asked me if you are available, but I've been telling them to back off."

"Thanks."

"You're family. I don't want any of those idiots messing with your head. And if you fell out with them, I'd have to stop being their friend, and that would suck."

"Nice logic."

"Makes sense to me." Dave studied her. "You serious about this?"

"Totally."

"How about Nate?"

"Nate the deputy sheriff guy?"

"Yeah. He's the best of the bunch." He took his cell out of his pocket. "Do you want me to call him?"

"Not when I'm standing right here! What if he says no?"

"He won't. He's desperate."

"Wow. Thanks."

"I meant he's desperate to settle down and have a family. I have no idea why, but he's boring the pants off the rest of us down at the Red Dragon every Friday night moaning about finding the right woman."

"He *wants* to settle down?"

"Yeah." Dave shook his head. "Poor fool. He's obviously deranged."

"No, he's *perfect*."

Dave held up his hand. "Hold on, cos, don't crowd your fences. You haven't even met him yet."

"Do you think he might be persuaded to swing by Morgan Ranch tomorrow, pick me up, and take me out for a drink?"

"Tomorrow?"

She smiled sweetly at her oblivious cousin. "Will you just ask him if he'd be willing to do that for me?"

"Sure."

Jenna sat back down at the table and picked up her pen. She couldn't wait to see how Blue Morgan would react to finding out she had an agenda all of her very own.

Chapter Six

"What's Nate doing here?" Blue adjusted his grip on Messi's halter and craned his neck to see outside the barn where a truck had just pulled up.

"Nate Turner?" Jenna asked.

"Yeah, the deputy sheriff. I hope there's nothing wrong." Blue led Messi back in his stall and slid the lock in place. "I'll go see what he wants."

"Chase is at the house and so is Ruth. I'm sure they can take care of him."

Blue paused to look more carefully at his companion, who had been acting strange all day. He guessed she felt a little awkward around him after their conversation the day before, but he hadn't called her out on it. In fact, she'd taken what he'd said right on the chin, which had relieved him greatly. He didn't want her to stop coming to the ranch or not be his friend.

She was already walking away from him, her bag in one hand, the other patting at her hair, which had been well mussed up by Nolly, who seemed to think it was edible.

"Hey, wait up."

Jenna kept going so he increased his speed, jogged past her, and went up the porch steps to open the door for her.

"Ma'am."

"Show-off." She gave him a look. "And don't call me that."

He grinned back at her. "Just being polite."

Ruth had Nate sitting at the table drinking iced tea while she grilled him about his family, who had lived in Morgantown for almost as long as the Morgans. Blue had gone to school with Nate and his brother Matt and had always liked him.

"Hey." Blue nodded at Nate. "What's up?"

Nate rose to his feet and shook Blue's proffered hand.

"Great to see you back at the ranch, BB."

"Hopefully for good this time." Blue sat down. "You here on official business?"

"Not this time. Thank the Lord." Nate's gaze shifted past Blue and came to rest on Jenna. "You ready, Ms. Jenna?"

She smiled at him. "I just need to wash up and brush my hair and I'll be right with you."

Nate sat back down. "Take your time. I'll just be here catching up with Ruth and BB."

Blue looked from Jenna to Nate. "You two know each other?"

"Yes, Dave introduced us quite a while ago," Jenna said. "I won't be long, Nate, I promise."

Ruth passed Blue a glass of iced tea and he automatically sipped at it. "Jenna's not in trouble, is she?"

Nate chuckled. "Not as far as I know, but I'll see how our date goes."

"You two are dating?"

"That is why I'm here, BB. I'm taking her out for lunch today." Nate glanced from him to Ruth. "It's hard to align our schedules sometimes, so this was the best I could do this week."

Ruth patted his shoulder. "That's very sweet of you, Nate. Where are you going to take her?"

"Just to the hotel. They do a really nice soup and salad lunch buffet there now. Mrs. Hayes says it goes down a treat with the tourists."

"So I hear. I'll have to get Chase to take me one day."

"I'll take you today, if you like, Ruth," Blue offered. "We could all go together."

"And spoil Jenna's date?" Ruth shook her head. "We'll go another day."

"Sure," Blue murmured as Jenna came back down the stairs and into the kitchen. She'd obviously availed herself of January's makeup because her hair was glossy, her lips red, and her eyes rimmed with some kind of black goo.

Nate shot to his feet. "You look great, Ms. Jenna."

"Thank you." Jenna smiled. "Shall we go? I have to be back at three to talk to Chase."

Nate practically ran to her side and Blue couldn't blame him. She looked good enough to eat.

"Is it okay if I leave the truck here?" Jenna asked him.

"Not a problem." Blue held her gaze for just a bit too long. "Have a good time."

"I'm sure I will."

They walked out chatting, and Ruth topped up his iced tea. "They make a lovely couple, don't they?"

"Some couple," Blue muttered. "I bet this is their first date."

"I don't think so, dear, they looked very comfortable with each other. I *thought* January said Jenna was seeing someone, but I wasn't exactly sure whom. But Nate is a very nice young man. He's ready to settle down."

"How do you know?"

"You can see it in his eyes."

Blue snorted. "Yeah right."

"Yes, you can. I always think men are like taxicabs, they drive around picking up passengers until one day for no apparent reason at all they pick up their last one and the light stays on."

"What the hell is that supposed to mean?"

"You know."

"But you forgot to add that there's always another one along in a minute." Blue stretched out his legs and contemplated his feet. "I suppose I'm still cruising the streets, then."

"Seems like it." Ruth put the jug of iced tea back in the refrigerator. "Although if you keep it up, all the good ones will be gone. You're thirty now. Thirty's a good age to settle down. I'd been married twelve years by then, and had a son."

"It's different now, Ruth. Look at Chase. He's only just met January and he's older than me."

"Chase felt obliged to look after all of you instead of finding the right woman."

"And make millions of dollars. Don't forget that. He's like me. The idea of having a family scared the crap out of him."

Ruth sat opposite him. "Mind your language."

"Sorry, but come on, Ruth. Why would any of us want to get hitched when we lived through the clusterfuck of our parents' marriage?"

"It wasn't all bad, BB, and don't use that word again or I'll wash your mouth out with soap."

"It wasn't good, either." Blue stood up.

"Chase seems to have gotten over it."

"That's because he's the eldest and the perfect child."

"Or because he decided to let go of the past and move forward."

"And allow our father to hang around this place like some kind of ghoul?" A movement in the doorway made him look over his shoulder to see his father standing there. "Great. Perfect timing as always. Excuse me, Ruth."

He pushed past Billy and was halfway to the barn before he realized he'd forgotten to put his boots back on. Muttering a blistering curse that would've made Ruth give him a clout round the ear, he retraced his steps, opened the screen door, and turned toward the mudroom.

"He's right, Mama. I am just hanging around here."

Blue froze in the hallway as his father spoke from inside the kitchen.

"It's your home, too, Billy. Don't ever forget that," Ruth reminded him. "BB will come around."

"No, he won't. He's not like Chase. BB sees everything as black or white. I used to be the same way." Billy sighed. "Roy's been letting me help out on the ranch and Chase has *tried* to get along with me, but it's hard for everyone, and that's my fault. Maybe I should go back to San Francisco."

"And give up on your sons again?" Ruth sounded fierce.

"The twins won't even come and visit while I'm here."

"They'll be here for the wedding. Promise me you'll stay until then, Billy."

There was a long silence broken only by the hiss of coffee percolating. Even Blue held his breath.

"Okay. I'll do that," Billy finally said. "Should I go and talk to BB?"

"I'd leave him be right now. You know what he's like."

At that point Blue crept toward the mudroom and put on his boots before escaping through the other door that led into the kitchen garden. It would take him a moment longer to walk around to the barn, but it was worth it to avoid his father and grandmother.

Was he really so inflexible? He had goals and he worked toward them with single-minded purpose. No one criticized Chase for doing the same thing. Order was important in *anyone's* life. It didn't take a session with a therapist to work out that he sought order and structure because of the chaos surrounding his mother and sister's disappearance during his childhood.

"And what the hell is wrong with that?" he demanded of the mountain range. "Should I have let the rage out and become a drunk like my dad?"

He'd tried it. Had spent his first few months in the Marines acting like a fool in the local bars and clubs, but he'd cleaned up his act because he hated the way he felt after a night screwing and boozing. *Hated* it.

So he wasn't sorry for the path he'd chosen even if he ended up alone. Blue opened the door into the feed store. *Jeez.* Ruth had made him feel like a loser. Or had that happened when he'd seen Jenna smiling at another man—a man who was ready to settle down, according to his grandma, who tended to be right about such things?

Blue unlocked the lid of the chicken feed and scooped out a bucketful to mix with the table scraps Ruth had left out in a covered bowl. He still wasn't buying the Jenna and Nate thing. It was way too convenient after his conversation with Jenna the day before. His hand stilled. Unless she really had taken his words to heart and moved on?

She was smart enough to do that, and she might have moved fast.

So, who exactly was the stupid one here?

* * *

"Thanks for coming to my rescue, Nate."

Jenna smiled at her dining companion as they settled back into their booth in the hotel dining room after getting their coffee and dessert. She'd spent the journey from the ranch into town telling him everything he needed to know about why he was taking her on a date. To her relief, he'd taken it so well she might have told him far more than she'd intended to.

"Just doing my job, ma'am." He handed her a new set of silverware wrapped in a napkin. "I'm not surprised BB's being a pain. He's usually the one overrun with choices."

"Exactly. Blue thinks I'm after him, and I just wanted to make it clear that I'm not."

"I get it—by pretending to go out with another man."

"No, by *really* going out with another man."

"Me?"

Jenna gave him an encouraging smile. "Why not?"

"Good question." He winked. "I am quite a nice guy."

"Dave said you were the best of the bunch."

Nate winced. "Which considering our friends doesn't mean much. But I'm glad he asked me. So what's the story? I got the impression that we're supposed to have known each other a while."

It was Jenna's turn to look sheepish. "I'm sorry I sprang that on you at the last minute."

"Seeing BB's face made it well worth it. He didn't look happy at all." Nate grinned. "He might say he's not interested in you, Jenna, but he sure didn't like me coming out to the ranch to take you out."

"Do you think so?" Jenna shook her head. "Hang on, Nate. We're not doing this for Blue's sake. We're doing it to see if we have anything in common and might want to start dating."

Nate sat back and considered her for a long moment. "I'm not feeling any spark between us. How about you?"

"Don't you think it's a bit early to tell? It's only our first date."

"Not for a Turner. We fall in love like that." He snapped his fingers. "When I meet The One, I'll just know."

"You really believe that?"

"Why not?"

"And it's definitely not me?"

"Nope, sorry." He raised his glass to her. "That doesn't mean we can't keep pretending to go out together. I'm more than happy to help the course of true love for someone else."

"That's really nice of you."

Nate shrugged. "Dave's my best bud, and BB's a conceited ass if he thinks he can keep you hanging until he's ready to make up his mind. I totally agree with your strategy."

"It's not really a strategy. I was just mad at him," Jenna confessed as she dug into her strawberry cheesecake. "He literally patted me on the head and told me not to waste my time pining after him."

"Idiot." Nate snorted. "But then he always was pretty definite about everything, even as a kid."

"He has an *agenda*, and falling in love and settling down isn't currently on it."

"You see, if he was a Turner? He wouldn't think like that. We know we have to be ready to find The One at any moment."

"Could be embarrassing if it was someone you were arresting."

"I have thought about that." Nate chuckled. "It would certainly be a great story for the grandkids."

Jenna finished her cheesecake and then drank her coffee. She'd asked Mrs. Hayes how Duke the rabbit was doing and heard she was the proud mother of six and that Mr. Hayes had made a new cage for Stan so there would be no more mishaps.

"So can we do this again?" Nate asked. "If you like I'll take you out to the Red Dragon on Friday for a drink."

"That would be awesome. January said she and Chase were going there on Friday night." Jenna hesitated. "Are you sure you're okay with this?"

"Definitely. One of the things I've noticed is that if a woman thinks a man is already taken, sometimes she'll be more relaxed and more her true self."

"That's certainly true for me." Jenna raised her cup and clinked it against Nate's. "To fake love and no happy ever after."

"Amen." Nate grinned at her. "And to making BB Morgan sweat."

"So basically Red Williams is a scumbag." Blue finished reading his notes out to Chase. "We can't rule him out because despite that he definitely had enough charm to convince a lot of women to step out with him."

"Do we know where he is right now?"

"I spoke to his mom, and she said he was in jail up in Sacramento penitentiary for nonpayment of child support, defrauding Social Security, and other small crimes."

Chase nodded. "We could probably visit him there. What about the other two guys?"

"Larry Paquino went back to Colombia a year after Mom and Rachel disappeared. I think he was here illegally, so he probably won't be coming back."

"Unlikely to be him, then, but I'll get the private investigators to check him out and make sure he traveled home alone. What about Big Mike?"

"He's living in San Diego."

"And?"

Blue shrugged. "That's as far as I've got."

"Well, it all helps." Chase tapped away at his keyboard and then stretched. "I'll send this along to Trevor and see what he makes of it."

"Cool."

Chase closed the lid of his laptop. "Is Jenna around?"

Blue tilted his chair back on two legs so he could look out of the window into the yard. "Her truck's still here, so she might not be back yet."

"That's right. Ruth said she went out with Nate for lunch."

"Did you know she was seeing him?"

Chase grinned. "Didn't everyone?"

Blue heard Nate's truck before he saw it and slipped out of the door and headed for the barn. He was just in time to see Nate get out and walk around to open the door for Jenna. The pair of them were laughing, and Nate wrapped a casual arm around Jenna's shoulders and hugged her. Jenna didn't seem to mind.

"That was fun." Nate's voice carried on the quiet afternoon breeze.

"It was awesome." Jenna looked up at him and he cupped her cheek. "See you Friday, then?"

"Definitely."

Nate dropped his head just as Jenna raised hers, and his kiss ended up on her chin, which made them both laugh even more, and attempt it again.

Blue stayed where he was until Nate got in his truck and drove away with one last wave to Jenna. She was still grinning like a loon when she came into the barn and saw him standing there.

"Hey, Blue. Is Chase around?"

He placed the coiled rope on the hook and wiped his hands on the back of his jeans. He'd done some thinking while she was away about Nate and the Turner clan in particular. "He's in the house."

"Cool."

"Did you have a nice lunch?"

She half turned toward him. "It was a really great meal. You should try it."

"I promised Ruth I'd take her some day."

"You should."

"You and Nate are definitely dating, then?"

"We have been for a while."

Blue shook his head. "You need to put in some work on that kissing, then. That looked really amateurish and more like a first date."

She stopped moving. "You were judging our *kissing*?"

"Couldn't help it when you were right in front of me."

Her hands went to her hips, which was never a good sign with a woman. "You're an expert about that as well, are you?"

He shrugged and closed the gap between them. "I'm not gonna lie. I'm pretty damn good at it."

She stayed put as he cupped her chin.

"First lesson is to make sure you have your woman just where you want her, like this." He leaned closer. "Second is to kiss her right on the lips."

"Wow, how profound."

Her words were sarcastic but the breathy delivery was a bit of a giveaway.

Blue smiled down into her eyes and licked a smooth line between her slightly parted lips until her mouth opened under his. He took advantage of that and then forgot all about strategy as the kiss turned crazy hot and all he could think about was never letting it end.

Her hand slid into his short hair, her fingernails scraping his scalp, and he just kept kissing her, one arm wrapped around her hips bringing her up close and personal with his extremely interested cock. She bucked her hips against him as if trying to get even closer, and he groaned into her mouth.

Within a second she eased away, leaving him feeling like a fish out of water gasping for breath. She wiped a hand over her mouth.

"Not bad. But Nate was definitely better. Not quite so *rehearsed*."

"What the hell is that supposed to mean?"

"As you said, you're the one with all the experience. Perhaps too *much* experience. Maybe I prefer to be kissed by someone who actually means it as opposed to someone who's just trying to prove a point." She gave him a sunny smile. "But hey, don't feel bad. I'm sure it works with most women."

Even as she was turning away, he reached for her, bringing her back against his body. Her breath exploded as he kissed her again. This time, he was the first to step away. He only did it out of pride because otherwise he would have thrown her over his shoulder, taken her into the nearest empty stall, and stripped her naked.

He didn't like feeling so out of control.

He didn't like it at all.

"That wasn't fair, Blue."

He inhaled a much-needed breath and let it out again. "Life's not fair. I'm not apologizing."

"I didn't expect you to. But you can't have it both ways.

You can't say a real relationship is not on your agenda and then kiss me like that."

He shrugged. "As you said, maybe I was just trying to prove a point."

Even as he said the words, he regretted it. The hurt that flashed in her eyes made it even worse.

"Then consider your point proved."

He shoved a hand through his hair. "Jenna . . ."

She walked away, leaving him standing by the barn wanting to slap himself silly. First for kissing her, second for enjoying it so much, and third—the worst sin of all— for panicking and hurting her feelings.

She didn't look back as she got in her truck and drove away.

Somehow, Blue couldn't blame her.

Chapter Seven

"He's an ass," Jenna repeated as she helped Chase carry the drinks back to their table at the Red Dragon. It was a typical noisy Friday night at the only bar in town with guys playing pool, watching the big TVs, and generally letting off steam before the upcoming weekend.

"Sure he is." Chase grinned. "But I think he knows that already. He's been in a foul mood all week. I was glad he went back to the base."

"So, what's your point?"

Chase considered her. "You unsettle him. I like that. He tends to get all caught up in his lists and schedules, and you put him off."

Nate clinked his beer bottle against hers. "Are we talking about BB?"

"Yup." Jenna sat and took a gulp of beer. "He's an idiot." Who kissed like a god, but Nate and Chase probably didn't need to know that. She might tell January later.

"He's just not used to having to do all the work. Women tend to fling themselves at him. God knows why." Chase set his beer on the table. "He's nowhere near as good-looking as I am."

January snorted. "Or half as conceited." She made up for the remark by kissing Chase's cheek. "He might not be as pretty as you, but he's damn fine all the same."

Jenna could only nod in agreement. To her secret relief, Blue had returned to the Marine base and wasn't expected home until late Friday or early Saturday morning. She'd gotten on with her work at the ranch and at the clinic without having to worry about bumping into the best kisser in the universe.

Not that she'd ever tell him that.

Nate's radio buzzed and he stood up. "Excuse me, guys, I'm on call this evening, so I've got to take this."

He made his way out of the bar, leaving Jenna to pick at her fried shrimp and beer-battered onion rings. Nate was good company, and seeing as he'd flat out decided she wasn't The One, she could have a good time and not worry about impressing him at all. It was quite relaxing.

He came back in and headed straight for Chase.

"We've got a situation over at Maureen's. Would you mind coming with me?"

Chase frowned. "What did I do?"

"I'm not sure." Nate was all business. "But I need a Morgan, and you're the only one around."

"Then I'll come, too." January rose and took Chase's hand.

"Seeing as you're taking me home, Nate, I suppose I'll need to tag along as well." Jenna finished her beer and stuffed the last of the shrimp in her mouth. The four of them left the bar to a chorus of good-byes and walked down Main Street to the general store, which sold everything and was always open until ten.

Light shone through the windows and the door was open, letting out all the air-conditioning.

"Hey, Maureen, what's up?" Chase called out a greeting

as he went through the door, nodding at Jill who was manning the checkout.

"Chase, darlin', is that you? Come out back!"

Nate and Chase went through to the private quarters of the store where the original owners had once lived, leaving Jenna and January to follow along behind. Jenna couldn't see much behind Nate's broad back and had to strain her ears to even hear what was going on.

"So, dear, is this who you expected to see?" Maureen was obviously talking to someone.

"I want to see Mr. Morgan."

Nate murmured to Chase. "She got off the bus and came into the store. That's when Maureen called me."

Chase crouched down in front of the girl and took off his hat. "I'm Chase Morgan. How can I help?"

"I'm Maria."

Chase held out his hand. "Nice to meet you, Maria. Are your parents around?"

The girl's lip trembled. "My mom's dead."

"I'm so sorry, honey. How about your dad?"

There was a long silence as Maria considered him. For the first time Jenna noticed what blue eyes she had.

"My real dad's last name is Morgan."

"Yeah?"

Beside Jenna, January stiffened, but Chase didn't seem too bothered.

"Do you remember what his first name is?" Chase's smile was sweet. "There are a lot of us Morgan brothers."

"I know he was in the military. That's where my mom met him."

"Okay, then I'll find him for you."

Chase slowly stood up and took out his cell, punching in a single number.

"BB? You'd better get your ass back here double quick."

* * *

Blue pulled into the parking lot that fronted the Morgantown Sheriff's Department and turned off the engine. He was already on his way home when Chase's call came through, so he'd just driven faster, his heart in his mouth as Chase had refused to elaborate on the phone. By the time he reached Morgantown, a thousand scenarios, each of them worse than the previous one, had crowded into his head.

He practically ran down the hallway into Nate's office and then pulled up short as he surveyed the unexpectedly peaceful scene in front of him. January and Jenna sat either side of a young girl, and Chase and Nate leaned against the desk talking intently on their cells.

"What's going on?" Blue said. "Is Ruth okay?"

Chase put his cell in his pocket. "She's good. I'll leave Nate to tell you what's going on."

Blue touched his brother's arm. "Chase, what's up?"

"Nate will explain. I'm not sure I have the words right now." He nodded at Blue. "We'll wait outside."

In fact they were all looking at him as if he'd done something heinous—except the child, and who the hell was she anyway?

January lingered, her anxious gaze moving between Chase and the girl. "Maybe I should stay—"

Jenna patted her arm. "I'll stay. Nate might need my help."

January and Chase went out, leaving Blue facing Nate. "What's up?"

"This is Maria. She just arrived on the last bus."

Blue nodded at the girl. "Hi, Maria."

Nate was watching him intently. "Do you know her?"

"Should I?"

Jenna cleared her throat. "Perhaps I should take Maria to sit outside as well."

"Hold up," Blue said. "Why should I know her?"

The girl pulled out of Jenna's grip and came over to Blue. "Because you're my father."

As if from a long way off, he became aware that he was shaking his head. "Hell, no."

"Yes, you are. My daddy, I mean the man I thought was my daddy told me."

"That can't be right."

She fixed him with a glare that reminded him forcefully of Ruth. "My mom was sick and my dad got sick, too, but his was because of drinking and he told me the truth." Her voice faltered. "He told me to get out."

Blue sank down onto his haunches in front of her. "Like out of the house?"

She nodded solemnly. She had very blue eyes. "He gave me some money and put me on the bus."

"That's . . . terrible."

She nodded again.

Blue stared at her. "What was your mom's name, sweetheart?"

"Angelina."

Blue stood up again and turned to Nate, lowering his voice. "I don't know what's going on here. I have no idea who or what she's talking about."

"Are you quite sure, BB?"

"Yes, I'm damned sure," Blue snapped and instantly reined in his temper. "I'm sorry, Nate. This is just a bit of a shock."

A yawn shuddered through Maria, and she raised her hand to cover her mouth.

"Do you have your dad's cell number, Maria?" Blue asked.

"He says he's not my dad, and I don't remember his number. He took my phone away from me before he put me on the bus."

Blue looked up at Nate, who shrugged. "So far I haven't been able to get any information out of her."

Jenna put her hand on Maria's shoulder. "She needs to get some sleep. Can Blue take her back to the ranch for the night so that Ruth can keep an eye on her?"

Blue stiffened. "I'm not sure if that's a good idea—"

The searing look Jenna gave him made him shut up real fast.

"CPS aren't going to be able to get back to me until tomorrow, so she needs a safe environment." Nate straightened up. "I'm quite happy for Ruth to take care of her if that's okay with you, BB?"

Blue looked at the forlorn figure and slowly nodded. "Sure. We can sort everything out in the morning. Shall we go?"

"Who's Ruth?"

Jenna answered before Blue. "She is Blue and Chase's grandmother. I bet she will be thrilled to meet you."

Maria didn't look convinced but she stood up, grabbing her backpack, which was covered in cartoon ponies with freakishly long manes and tails.

"I'll call Ruth and let her know you're on your way." Jenna nodded at Blue, her gaze distinctly unfriendly.

"Thanks." Blue didn't have time to sort out what was going on with Jenna; his attention was totally fixed on the little girl. He held out his hand to take the backpack, but instead she grabbed his fingers and squeezed hard. "Let's go and find Chase."

"I'll be round first thing, BB." Nate accompanied them to the door. "I'll talk to the bus company and to CPS."

"Cool." Blue saw Chase and January sitting in the front office. "We're taking Maria home for the night, okay?"

Chase frowned. "So you're admitting it now?"

Blue held his gaze. "She needs somewhere to sleep, Chase. That's it."

He looked down at Maria. "You're too old for a car seat, right?"

"Yes. I'm almost eleven."

Blue had thought her younger than that because she was quite petite. But then so was Ruth . . . He pushed that thought away.

"Maybe Maria would prefer to ride with me and January."

Blue slowly exhaled. What the hell was up with Chase? "Maria? Who do you want to go with?"

She tightened her grip on his hand. "You."

"Then that's settled." Blue gave his brother a short nod. "We'll see you at home."

Blue glanced over at his passenger as the ranch house came into view. "We're here."

Maria wrinkled her nose. "It smells bad."

"It's a ranch. You'll get used to it." He had no idea how to talk to kids. None of his friends were married, so he'd avoided having to deal with any ankle biters for years. He got out of the cab and came around to lift Maria down. "Come and meet Ruth."

His grandmother was already opening the door as they walked up the steps onto the porch. She flicked a glance at Blue and then smiled at Maria.

"Well, what a lovely surprise! Come on in, Maria, are you hungry?"

Maria allowed Ruth to lead her into the kitchen with Blue following along behind. Ruth helped Maria out of her bulky ski jacket and sat her at the table.

"You want something, BB?"

"I'll just have some coffee, thanks." His stomach was too knotted up to eat. The coffee would at least keep him awake while they attempted to get to the bottom of this world-class clusterfuck.

"You like grilled cheese, Maria?"

"Yes, please." Maria yawned again and politely covered her mouth. "Excuse me." Whoever had brought her up had done a good job on her manners.

Within a few minutes Ruth placed a sizzling sandwich in front of Maria and a tall glass of milk. "Eat your fill and then I'll take you up to bed. You look worn out. How long were you on that bus?"

"All day." Maria ate fast and then wiped her mouth with the paper towel Ruth had given her. "I had money to get food."

"How did you know when to get off?" Blue asked casually.

"My dad . . . asked the driver to let me off in Morgantown." She swallowed hard. "He said someone would be meeting me here."

Ruth came to sit by Maria. "You did the right thing going into the shop and asking Maureen for help. That was very sensible of you."

"I kind of knew there wouldn't be anyone waiting for me." Maria's tentative smile faded. "He just wanted me gone."

Ruth wrapped her arm around Maria's shoulders.

"You're safe with us now. We'll sort everything out in the morning."

She picked up Maria's backpack. "Say good night to BB."

Maria faced him, her expression solemn. "Good night."

Her eyes were exactly the same shade of blue as Ruth's.

"Night, Maria." He nodded and started to sit back down just as January and Chase came into the kitchen. January excused herself and went upstairs, leaving the two brothers alone in the kitchen. The comforting smell of grilled cheese and the soft lighting failed to soothe Blue's agitated nerves, and by the look on his face, Chase wasn't much happier either.

Chase poured himself a cup of coffee and took the seat Maria had vacated right opposite Blue. He looked all business.

"So are you going to tell me what's going on?"

"What do you want me to say?"

"Is she your daughter?"

"Hell, *no*! I haven't been hiding some dark secret for years—if that's what you're implying. Have a little faith, bro."

"Then how did she turn up here? She does have our blue eyes."

"So do a million other people." Blue scrubbed an unsteady hand over his unshaven jaw. "I have no idea who she is or where she came from. You've got to believe me."

Chase leaned back in his chair stretching out his long legs. "There's an easy way of proving you're not her father."

"DNA testing? Sure. I'm up for that. She said her mom's name was Angelina. I don't recall ever dating someone with that name, let alone creating a child with her."

"Is it possible Angelina didn't tell you about the child?"

Blue sat forward. "Chase, I haven't the faintest idea who Angelina *is*, so how do you expect me to answer that?"

"There's no need to get in my face. Let's approach this logically. Maria said she was almost eleven, so where were you twelve years ago?"

"Completing basic training and moving on to my first post."

"And did you have any sexual relationships around that time?"

"TC, I was eighteen and a cocky Marine, what do you think?"

"I think you might have slipped up."

"Thanks for the vote of confidence," Blue muttered.

"Can you put your hand on your heart and swear that you didn't have sex with some woman who might have had the ability to get pregnant?"

Blue sighed. "I suppose you have a point. I always tried to be careful and use protection. I'm not that dumb."

"I never said you were." Chase reached across the table and awkwardly patted Blue's hand. "It's okay. We'll sort this out."

"We'd better. I'm tired of everyone looking at me as if I'm something they need to scrape off their shoe."

Chase got up. "How about you make a list of all the women you did sleep with twelve years ago, and start working out how to contact them?"

"You're kidding, right?" Blue looked up at his brother. "I was *eighteen* and I screwed around like an idiot."

"Yeah, and now you might have a daughter." Chase pointed up the stairs. "Do your best, okay? Do it for her."

Blue shoved both hands in his hair and stared down at the table until Chase left. He'd gone to clubs and bars, gotten drunk and picked up women who liked a man in uniform. Sure, he'd heard the rumors about guys who'd gotten caught out by a pregnancy and ended up either married or supporting a kid. That's why he'd always tried to be careful.

But if he was going to be 100 percent honest with himself, there might have been a time or two when he'd been too damned drunk to know what the hell he was doing . . .

"BB."

He looked up as Ruth sat opposite him. He hated the fact that her face was creased with worry.

"She went straight to sleep. Poor girl doesn't know what's going to happen to her next. Fancy her father throwing her out like that."

"Do you think she's telling the truth?"

Ruth's blue gaze was steady on his. "Yes."

"I swear to you that I never knowingly left a child of mine behind, but I did some stupid stuff in my teens."

"I know you, BB." She took his hand between both of hers and held it tight. "That means I also know you'd never abandon your own child. If Maria is yours? Then we'll find out what happened and take it from there, okay?"

Blue nodded, which was about all he could manage. Ruth's calm acceptance of the predicament he found himself in was balm to his soul. If she'd started in on him, he didn't know what he would've done. Hightailed it out and left the mess behind him, maybe. But he was a better man than he'd been at eighteen. At least he was sure of that.

Whatever was going on, he would find a solution.

He had no choice.

Chapter Eight

"The bus driver said he picked her up in Sacramento and kept an eye on her for the whole journey." Nate checked his notes. "A dark-haired man in his mid thirties put her on the bus and asked the driver to let her off at Morgantown. Apparently he said there was a family emergency and that he couldn't accompany the girl as planned, but that she would be met at the bus stop."

The house was quiet. It was still early in the morning, and January had taken Maria down to the barn to meet the horses while Nate brought Blue, Chase, and Ruth up to speed.

Chase sipped his coffee. "Is it legal to put a kid on a long-distance bus without an adult?"

"Over the age of eight, yeah." Nate nodded. "The adult is supposed to fill out a form in advance with information about the child and the destination and all that stuff so the bus company knows who'll be picking up the kid."

"So we should be able to get all that information from the bus company, right?" Blue asked.

"Nope, because in this instance, the guy claimed it was an emergency situation and showed the driver he'd originally purchased two tickets. The driver felt sorry for him and let the girl on the bus. He shouldn't have done that."

"And he let her get off the bus without checking whether there was anyone to collect her?" Blue shook his head. "That's fucking criminal."

"BB, I know you are upset, but please don't use that language." Ruth frowned at him. "I guess I should mention that Maria told the driver she could see her aunt and just waved good-bye and went into the store."

"Why didn't she stay put and make a fuss?" Chase asked.

"Probably because she believed that son of a bitch who put her on the bus didn't want her anymore," Blue muttered.

"BB, that's enough." Ruth stuck a finger right in his face. "If you can't keep a civil tongue in your head, get out of my kitchen and go cool your heels in the barn with the other animals until you're ready to apologize."

"I'm sorry, Ruth." Blue rubbed an agitated hand over his short hair. "It's just what kind of father does that to his kid?"

"The kind who doesn't think he's her father anymore. Maria said he'd been drinking a lot since his wife died. Maybe he didn't know what he was doing."

Blue forced himself to calm down. "Okay, so what next, Nate?"

"I'd like to talk to Maria again." Nate looked at Ruth. "You can stay with her. Did she tell you her last name?"

"Lester."

"Wow, that's more than I got out of her. And what about her dad's first name?"

"Daniel, I think."

Lester . . .

Blue looked up. "I knew a Marine with that last name."

Nate turned to Blue. "Yeah?"

"Well, not exactly *knew* him well, but we were on the same base at the same time and I met his wife a couple of times . . ." Blue stopped speaking. "Her name wasn't Angelina, though, but it was something similar."

"Did you sleep with her?"

The question came from Chase, who never shied away from asking what no one else would dare.

"No." Blue met his brother's gaze. "I did not."

"But it might be a lead." Chase finished his coffee. "Are you still in contact with the guy?"

"I could probably find him if I tried."

"Then try." Chase nodded. "If you can't find him, let me know and I can have a look at it from my end." He stood up. "I have to get some work done. Thanks for everything, Nate. We really appreciate it."

Chase went out and Ruth took the opportunity to fill up Blue and Nate's coffee mugs and put a plate of cookies on the table.

"Can we keep Maria here until everything is sorted out?" Ruth handed Nate the sugar bowl and a spoon.

Nate dunked his cookie in his coffee. "I'll have to check in with CPS."

"I know Rebecca Smith, who manages this area. I'll give her a call so she knows we are more than willing to hold on to Maria."

"There might be paperwork involved," Nate warned.

"I'm good at that." Blue grimaced. "We can't in all conscience send her back to Sacramento and expect her to find her way home to a man who basically disowned her."

"We wouldn't do that, Blue. CPS would just find her a temporary home around here until we had everything sorted."

"Which might as well be here," Ruth declared. "I'll go

and call Rebecca right now and ask her what I need to do to meet their requirements. It wouldn't be the first time we've taken a child in on the ranch. Of course, back in the day no one remarked on it. It was just seen as doing the right thing."

"Thanks, Ruth." Nate closed his notebook and turned to Blue. "Do you think you could find Maria so that I can talk to her?"

"Sure." Blue pushed away from the table, put on his boots, and went down to the barn, where he found January, Maria, and Billy petting Nolly, who was loving all the attention.

"Hey," Blue called out to the little group. Billy was holding Maria up so that she could see into the stall and was nodding gravely at something she was telling him. Blue remembered being held by his father like that. The way Billy had really paid attention when any of his kids had spoken to him and had given his considered and thoughtful replies to the most outlandish of questions.

That had all gone south when the booze claimed him and he'd eventually just disappeared.

"What's up, January?"

January turned and smiled at Blue while Maria pressed closer against Billy's shoulder. Had he sounded too loud? She was probably hypersensitive to everything at the moment, especially if her dad was a drunk. Blue knew all about walking on eggshells around his dad's hangovers.

"Hey, Maria." He tried to sound nonthreatening and approachable. Difficult for a Marine. "Ruth's looking for you, so do you want to come back to the house?"

Billy lowered Maria to the ground, but kept a hand on her shoulder. She turned her face away from Blue.

"I'll walk her up there if you like, BB," Billy offered. "I see Nate's here as well."

Blue met his father's steady gaze. "Sure. Why don't you do that? Tell Ruth I'll be up in a minute."

He stayed beside January as Maria took Billy's hand and walked back up to the ranch.

"I think I scared her."

"You are a bit of a forceful personality." January gave him a sympathetic glance. "Don't worry, she'll come around."

"I doubt she'll be here long enough for that."

"Then you don't think she's your child?"

"I don't know, January. I'm still struggling to get my head round any of it." Blue took off his Stetson and slapped it against his thigh. "I feel like someone just threw a grenade in my face."

His acute hearing picked up the sound of an approaching truck, and he stayed where he was as Jenna pulled into the yard and parked alongside Nate. She wore her usual jeans, boots, and T-shirt combo but her smile was missing. She looked over toward the barn and went still when she saw him.

January patted his forearm. "I'm just going to find Chase, okay?"

"You do that, and ask him about getting that DNA sample going."

"Will do."

Jenna saw January going up to the house and spoke a few words to her before moving toward Blue, who didn't look particularly welcoming.

"Hey." He replaced his hat on his head, shading his expression. "Did you come to see Roy?"

"No. You and I were supposed to be going over to the

Membler spread to see some horses today. I tried to call you, but your cell's been off."

He patted the back pocket of his jeans. "Damn, I must've forgotten to charge my phone last night."

"Not surprising considering what's been going on." Jenna cleared her throat. "How's Maria doing this morning?"

"She's fine. Ruth is taking good care of her." Blue leaned back against the wall, his relaxed posture at odds with the storm in his eyes. "You might as well let it out."

"What?"

"Your question, or shall I just answer it for you? I haven't been concealing a daughter for the last eleven years."

"I didn't think you had, and anyway it's none of my business, is it?"

He raised an eyebrow. "Then why did you give me the stink eye yesterday night?"

"Because I felt sorry for Maria." She shifted her grip on her bag.

"Hell, *I* feel sorry for her, but I didn't create this mess."

"So you're one hundred percent certain that she couldn't be your daughter?"

"No, I'm not."

Unsurprised by his honesty, she waited him out until he exhaled and continued talking.

"I did some crazy things when I was a teenager. I'm not making any excuses for myself because there's no one else to blame but me. I was newly enlisted, away from the ranch for the first time in my life, and thought I was fricking *invincible*." His mouth twisted. "So, yeah, I can't say that I might not have made a mistake. All I can tell you is that I didn't walk away *knowing* I'd made a mistake."

"I'm glad to hear it." Jenna took an equally deep breath.

"I have a hard time sympathizing with men who walk away from their kids."

"Like my dad?"

"At least from what you told me, you had him for a few good years. I didn't even get that."

His blue gaze narrowed and focused entirely on her. "I thought you came from one of those well-to-do middle-class high-achieving families."

"Well, I do and I don't. I was adopted. Which probably explains why I got a bit defensive last night when I heard Maria's story. I was kind of reliving part of my own childhood." She half turned toward the house. "I assume we aren't going anywhere today? Is it okay if I just check in with Ruth to see if she has anything that needs looking at while I'm here?"

Blue moved to stand in front of her. "Jenna, you must know I'd never abandon my own kid."

She looked up into his clear eyes. "As I said, it's got nothing to do with me, but—"

"I'd *never* do what Billy did." Blue snatched a quick breath. "If she is my kid, I'll take care of her."

She couldn't help cupping his cheek and rubbing her thumb over his taut jawline. "You're a good man, Blue Morgan."

"I'm certainly more responsible than I was at eighteen, but what the hell am I supposed to do with a ten-year-old?"

"Ruth will help you." Her smile died as his hand closed gently around her wrist, keeping her palm against his face.

"How about you? If anyone knows how an abandoned kid might feel, it has to be you."

She shivered. "You have no idea."

His hand fell away and he opened his mouth, probably to ask even more questions, but she was done talking about her childhood. "Shall we go and see Ruth?"

"Okay." He held her gaze. "I know I have no right to ask for your help, but I'm still counting on it."

She rolled her eyes. "Instead of Boy, your middle name should really be Bossy."

He stiffened. "Who told you my real name?"

"Like I'd tell you. I hear you beat people up who call you Blue Boy."

"Not anymore, which means it must've been Dave, because I *did* thump him a couple of times back in elementary school when he tried it on."

"Which TV show?"

The look Blue gave her was resigned. "*The High Chaparral*. I checked it out once, and that character Blue Boy was a complete wuss."

"So, just like you, then."

He glanced down at her as they went up the steps into the house. "Is this your idea of cheering me up or something?"

"It might be."

He held the screen door open for her, but when she tried to duck under his arm, he trapped her against the door frame.

"Thank you, Jenna."

"For what?"

"For believing me and for trying to make me laugh. I needed that." He hesitated. "I just hate things being out of my control, you know?"

"I would never have guessed," she said solemnly. "You are normally such a free spirit—almost a hipster."

This time he actually did smile. While she watched that transform his face, he leaned in and kissed her mouth before letting her go.

She stumbled into the kitchen, her fingers on her lips, and sat down heavily on the nearest chair. God, he smelled so good up close, and the feel of his mouth on hers was way too exciting. For once she was glad that Ruth wasn't actually in the kitchen because she would've had a hard time explaining why she looked like a complete idiot.

"Ruth's in with Nate and Maria in the parlor. They should be done in a minute." Blue came in quietly without his boots and Jenna jumped. "Would you like some coffee?"

"Sure."

She needed something to do that didn't involve grabbing handfuls of Blue Morgan's T-shirt and ripping it off him. It was quite shocking that even when he was super worried and surly, she still couldn't stop lusting after him.

It was his fault for getting up close and kissing her. But she could hardly have stopped him, seeing as she was trying to cheer him up.

Yeah, right.

"You okay?" Blue slid a mug of coffee in front of her.

"I'm good. What did Nate want?"

"He's been following up with the bus company that dropped Maria off and dealing with the local CPS rep."

"They aren't going to put Maria in a temporary foster home, are they?" Jenna slammed her mug down so fast coffee went all over the table.

Without a word, Blue fetched a cloth and wiped up the flood of coffee. He refilled Jenna's mug and rinsed out the washcloth before sitting back down.

"You weren't adopted as a baby, I take it."

"No." She concentrated on sipping her coffee and avoiding his gaze. "I was about Maria's age when I was formally adopted."

"Not all foster homes are bad places," Blue said cautiously.

"That's true. The vast majority of them are excellent. My sister—" She swallowed down the rest of that sentence with some coffee. But of course he wouldn't let her get away with that.

"What's your sister's name?"

"I have two."

"The one who had a better experience in foster care than you did." He made it a statement rather than a question.

"That's Tessa. She was only in one place, so she transitioned into our permanent home really well."

"How many homes were you in?" Blue didn't look up as he traced the swirling pattern on the pine table with his spoon.

"A few." Jenna sighed. "My birth mom would occasionally get her act together and convince the authorities to let her have her children back." She attempted a smile. "It never lasted—especially if there was a man involved. So out we'd all go again."

"Until you were properly adopted, right?"

"Yeah. I was lucky. The McDonalds are such good people."

Blue nodded. "You certainly seemed to have turned out okay."

She managed to look up at him. "I'm the slacker in my family. Tessa's a surgeon and Lily went to MIT."

"Impressive."

"Yeah." She finished her coffee, her smile dying.

"I bet neither of them has ever held down a calf and castrated him, right?"

"I can't quite see either of them doing that, no."

He shrugged his powerful shoulders. "Then they aren't very useful around here, are they?"

She studied him over the rim of her coffee mug. "Are you trying to make *me* feel better now?"

"I'm just stating a fact." He held her gaze. "I'm going

to do my damndest to make sure Maria gets to stay here and not go into a foster home, okay?"

"That would be good."

The kitchen door opened and Maria came through with Ruth. She looked as if she had been crying, and Blue shot to his feet.

"Is everything okay?"

Ruth patted Maria's shoulder. "She's fine. A big glass of milk and a cookie will settle her down nicely while you go talk to Nate, Blue."

Blue went out and Jenna turned to the child, who had taken the seat beside her.

"Hi, Maria, I'm Jenna. I sort of met you last night."

"Hi." Maria's voice was barely audible. Her hands were clasped tightly together on the table and her shoulders were hunched almost up to her ears.

Jenna wanted to wrap an arm around the girl's shoulders and tell her that everything would be okay, but she also knew that sometimes it wasn't. Whatever had led up to Maria being kicked out of her home certainly hadn't happened overnight and must have left longstanding scars.

"It's kind of scary leaving all your stuff behind and moving to a different place super fast, isn't it?" Jenna glanced casually over at Maria. "I had to do it a couple of times when I was a kid. Is there anything you forgot to bring with you? Anything you need?"

Maria swallowed hard. "I got my ponies, my journal, and my plushies, so I'm good."

"Cool." Jenna smiled at her. "I used to keep a bag packed with all my special stuff just in case, you know?"

Maria nodded. "I started doing that a while ago because sometimes Dad didn't come home, and then I'd get worried, and I'd go sleep at my neighbor's house." She hesitated. "Did your family kick you out as well?"

"Yeah—well, my mom had some problems, and sometimes she couldn't cope with us being at home, so we went somewhere else for a while."

"So you went back?"

The hope in Maria's eyes made Jenna's stomach hurt.

"Not for long. She really couldn't handle dealing with us."

"Just like my dad."

Jenna patted her hand. "You never know. Maybe he'll work it out. Just remember you're in a good place here with people who want to take care of you, and if there's anything you need or want to talk about? You can always ask me."

Ruth placed a glass of milk in front of Maria and a plate of cherry and chocolate cookies.

"Now, don't you worry, my darling girl. Leave Nate and Blue to sort everything out."

"He won't want me back." Maria stared down at the table.

"Who won't?"

"My dad who says he's not my dad. He hates me."

Ruth sat opposite Maria, her gaze full of sympathy. "Nate is probably going to have to talk to him, Maria. He can't just abandon you."

"Yes, he can, if he's not my dad." Maria took a sip of milk. "He told me."

"It's not as simple as that," Ruth said firmly. "Is it, Jenna?"

"Um." She really wasn't the best person to ask about fatherly behavior, seeing as her biological father was a complete failure as a human being. "I don't suppose it is."

"He said I wasn't his child and that meant he had no responsibility for me." Maria's voice cracked.

"Then he's an idiot," Jenna said. "Don't you worry, Nate and Blue will set him straight." She looked up to see Nate waving at her in the doorway. "I'll be back in a minute."

Blue waited outside as Nate went to fetch Jenna. He wished he had his gun and something to kill. Even if Maria wasn't his kid, he still wanted to get hold of Daniel Lester and wring his neck. What kind of man did that to a child? Maria had believed that ass was her father for almost eleven years and had all that security and love ripped away in one day. He knew how that felt. What kind of selfish idiot put a ten-year-old on a bus to travel hundreds of miles by themselves?

Nate came and stood beside him. "I'll talk to the Sacramento Police Department. They might be able to find Daniel Lester's address."

"Cool, and I'll chase up the Lester I knew in the military."

"Is there a list you can consult or something?" Jenna had come out with Nate and stood listening quietly to them both.

"Not really an official one, but we had enough friends in common that I'll be sure to pick up his trail."

"Good to know." Nate put on his hat. "I'll keep in touch." He nodded at Blue and smiled at Jenna before giving her a peck on the cheek. "Bye, hon."

Blue wanted to roll his eyes, but just managed to restrain himself until Nate was in his vehicle.

"His kissing still needs work. He missed your mouth again."

"He was being polite in front of you."

"Yeah, right. I had to handle the screen door and stop you getting by me, and I still managed to find the right spot." He sighed as Nate pulled away with an airy wave. "I suppose I'd better get on with finding Jim Lester."

"And I'd better check in with Ruth about whether there are any jobs for me to do on the ranch."

Blue punched the number he'd jotted down in the back of his notebook into his cell and took a deep breath. He'd spent most of the afternoon chasing old Marine buddies on social media and had finally come up with a current cell phone number for the Lesters.

"Hello?"

It was a woman's voice.

"Hi, you might not remember me, Rosa, but it's Gunnery Sergeant Blue Morgan here, I—"

"I remember you. How are you *doing*? Did you want to speak to Jim?"

"Yeah, if I could. That would be great."

"He's at work and he can't take calls there. Do you want me to ask him to call you when he gets home?"

"Yes, please."

"Just let me get a pen and paper."

He waited as she bustled around banging drawers and heard a small yappy dog barking in the distance.

"Okay. Fire away."

He gave her his number and she repeated it back to him. "And what are you doing these days, Blue? Still barhopping and lady killing?"

Blue winced. "Nah, I've settled down. I'm too old for all that now. Once I get out of the military, I'm going to help run a cattle ranch."

"How cool is that?" She laughed. "Do you remember that night you took me and my sister-in-law out when she was visiting and Jim was still overseas? It was really kind of you. We had such a blast."

"That was Angelina, right?" Blue took a chance even as his stomach knotted up. "She was your sister-in-law? I thought she was your sister."

"She might as well have been. We practically grew up together." Her voice sobered. "She married Jim's brother."

"After I met her?"

"Well, when you met her they were going through a bad patch, and she'd kind of left him and wasn't acting like a married woman—if you know what I mean."

Yeah, he knew. Blue briefly closed his eyes. *Oh crap.*

"She did go back to him, though, and they were together until quite recently." The sadness was back in Rosa's voice. "She had cancer—the kind they can't cure, and she recently passed away. They have a daughter called Maria. I do hope she's okay. I'll have to call and see how she and Dan are doing."

Blue stared at the old green drapes in his bedroom and took a deep breath.

"I know where Maria is. That's why I called today."

There was silence filled only with yappy barks and then Rosa spoke again. "What on earth do you mean?"

"Apparently Dan decided that Maria wasn't his child and put her on a bus to me."

"Madre de Dios," Rosa whispered. "I thought no one was ever supposed to know."

Chapter Nine

After something of a search, Jenna finally found Blue out in the barn. She'd come back out to the ranch to attend to one of the piglets that had been badly bitten by a rat and walked into a Morgan family conference about where the hell had Blue gone? She'd offered to help look for him while Ruth got dinner and had started in the most obvious place. He was sitting in Messi's stall with his back against the wall. He didn't look up when she sat next to him and adopted the same pose.

Messi was finishing up his hay, and his long tail swung gently back and forth, providing some very basic air-conditioning as wisps of hay floated down to the floor to join the straw bedding. The heat coming off the horse suggested Blue had just returned from a long ride.

"Hey." Jenna kept her tone casual. "You know they are all worried about you up at the house, right?"

"Yeah."

"So, what's up?"

Blue sighed. "Just that I'm a complete bastard."

"I wouldn't say that." Jenna put a comforting hand on his denim-clad knee. "What happened?"

"I tracked down Jim Lester and spoke to his wife, Rosa."

"The military family you knew? What did she tell you?"

He stayed quiet for so long that she almost expired from holding her breath.

"I *did* meet Angelina Lester. I didn't know that was her name at the time. Back then she called herself Angel. I also didn't know she was married."

"Ah."

"I took Rosa and Angelina out as a favor to Jim when he was overseas. It was Rosa's birthday, and he didn't want her celebrating alone."

"You slept with Angelina?"

"Yeah." He groaned. "I was eighteen, she was gorgeous, and I was an idiot."

Jenna let that sink in. For some reason the thought of him with any other woman made her cross as crabs. But this wasn't about her. This was about Maria and the future.

"Why didn't Angelina tell you that she was pregnant?"

"Well, apparently having sex with a complete stranger was enough to send her running back home to make things right with her husband."

"Wow, you must've really sucked."

He turned to look at her. "Thanks."

"You're welcome." She hesitated. "But seriously, if she went back that quick and reconciled with him, she might not have realized the baby wasn't his."

"That's true."

"It also means that Maria might not actually be your child."

"But there is the faintest possibility that she could be."

"You only slept with her the once?"

"Yeah. I even used protection, I always do, but something went wrong, and I was too damned drunk to do much more than apologize and be glad when she said she was on the pill." He cleared his throat. "Sorry, that's probably more than you wanted to know."

"So what's the plan?"

"I dunno. Why do you think I'm sitting out here in the dark?"

"That's not like you."

"Hell, I know." He took a deep breath. "Okay. I think I'm over my pity party now. I need to get that DNA test done and talk to Dan Lester."

"Agreed." Jenna put her hand on his shoulder. "It's going to be okay."

"No, it's not, Jenna. Not for that little girl. You know that just as well as I do."

She rose to her knees, wrapped her hand around his neck, and got right in his face. "You'll do your best. I know *that*."

"Thanks," he murmured, his mouth so close to hers that she felt the vibration of the words rather than actually heard them. "Jenna—"

She closed the gap between them, and his mouth met hers, bringing them both into the kiss and enveloping them within it. He angled his head, slanting his lips over hers, and she leaned in even closer, allowing his arm to slide around her waist and practically drag her into his lap.

The kiss went on and on and she just let herself fall into it, the softness of her breasts now crushed against his chest, his big hand cupping her butt, pressing her closer and closer to the hard ridge of his jeans-covered cock. His fingers closed around her head and she moaned into his mouth, moving with him, wanting the intense waves of pleasure never to stop.

"Jenna—I'm so damn sorry about all this." He eased back a fraction so that he could see her face.

She gathered her wits and tried to smile. "It's okay, I

know this isn't what you want and that this is possibly the worst time in your personal universe to have a woman sitting in your lap making you kiss her."

He frowned. "You didn't make me kiss you."

"I definitely made the first move." She put her hand on his chest. "If you just let go of me, I'll get off you."

"And what if I don't want to let go?"

She gave him her best glare. "Your current schedule doesn't permit personal relationships. You know that."

"We're just kissing."

"And kissing leads to other things and . . ." She tried to ease away, but he held firm. "We can't do those things here—not that we would even want to do those things anywhere else, I mean."

He raised an eyebrow. "You've obviously never had sex in a barn before. We could do it right now. All you'd have to do was take off one boot and one leg of your jeans and I'd unzip and—"

She slapped her hand over his mouth. Why did he have to be so darned practical about everything? "We are *not* having sex, we are just kissing."

This time when she pushed on his chest, he let her go. She struggled to her feet, leaning against the wall for support as the rest of her felt like molasses. She made the mistake of looking down just as he curved a hand under the obvious length of his erection and ran his thumb along it.

"Unfair . . ." She breathed.

He looked up at her, his hand remaining in place. "Yeah. Bad timing in so many ways. I mean, why the hell would anyone want to get involved with me? I'm a bona fide loser."

"You are a good person."

He slowly rose to his feet and put his hand on the wall

beside her head. "I am *trying* to be a better person, which is why I'm not going to push this issue with you right now."

"What issue?"

"The us one."

"There is no 'us.' It's not on your timetable, remember? And I'm going out with Nate."

"Screw Nate." He kissed her until she stopped spluttering and just kissed him back. "Actually, rewind that. Don't screw Nate."

"Have you quite finished?" Jenna demanded.

"Apparently."

"Then shall we go back to the house?"

"If that's what you really want to do."

She wanted to strip him naked and lick him all over and then she wanted . . .

"Yes."

He straightened and then bent to pick up his hat. "Then after you, princess."

Jenna walked ahead of him up to the ranch house, which was now lit up like a Christmas tree. Had they really been worried about him? Blue wanted to kick himself for scaring Ruth. She'd had enough of waiting for her family to come home to last her a lifetime. Shame washed over him as he thought about what he had to tell them all. He'd always been so quick to judge everyone else, and now he was the one at fault, and it was entirely his own doing.

Jenna held open the outside door for him and he braced himself as he kicked off his boots and went into the kitchen. January and Chase sat together on one side of the table holding hands; Maria was between Ruth and Billy, who was talking quietly to her.

"Hey." Blue found a smile somewhere. "Sorry I was out in the barn for so long. One of the horses was limping."

"Which one?" Chase asked before January elbowed him hard in the side.

Blue held out a chair for Jenna. "Here you go." She'd remained by the door as she usually did, like she wasn't sure if she was wanted. He'd noticed that before. Now it kind of made more sense. "You can't leave. It's dinnertime. I'm sure Ruth has enough to feed you."

"I do." Ruth pointed at the table with her big spoon. "Sit down. I made mac and cheese for Maria, so you can share that while the rest of us dig into chicken and dumplings."

Blue waited until Jenna sat down before taking the seat beside her and opposite his father. "How's it going, Billy?"

"Good, son. I've been showing Maria around the ranch." Billy smiled down into Maria's apprehensive face. "I'm thinking you need to take her out on horseback to see the place more clearly."

"I can't ride," Maria said so quietly Blue almost couldn't hear her.

"Then we'll teach you." Billy patted her shoulder. "I taught Blue and his brothers when they were babies."

"Babies can't ride."

Billy chuckled. "They can if their daddy sits them up on a horse in front of them, can't they, boys?"

Chase passed down the iced tea. "Yeah. I remember watching Dad hold you just like that, Blue. It got a lot harder when the twins came along. They used to try and jump off."

"Like a pair of squabbling puppies." Billy's smile died. "I wish they'd come home soon."

"They are coming for the wedding." Ruth put the blue cast iron casserole dish on the table and the pan of macaroni and cheese, which was perfectly crisp and brown. "I heard from HW today, but Ry's coming, too."

Blue looked up at her. "Yeah? That's awesome." He focused on Maria. "Chase and I have two more brothers for you to meet. They're twins."

Maria nodded politely but didn't say anything else, so Blue helped himself to the casserole. He soon noticed she would chat away to Billy, of all people, and then shut down like a clam whenever he tried to speak to her directly. But how could he blame her? In her world he guessed that fathers were no longer to be trusted. He totally got that.

With everything that was going on, he'd also forgotten to check in with Chase about the search for their mother and sister. Wow, so much to feel guilty about and so little time.

Blue put down his silverware, his appetite gone, and rose swiftly to his feet.

"Excuse me, everyone. I have to make a phone call."

"Nothing's that important. You can at least finish your dinner." Ruth frowned at him. "I've got pie."

"That's awesome, but I have to do this. I'll come back as soon as I can, okay?"

His cell was practically burning a hole in his jeans pocket, the number Rosa had given him for Daniel Lester still on his screen. Blue went up to his bedroom and pressed to connect the call. It rang for a long time.

"Yeah, what?"

Daniel Lester's slurred tone was instantly recognizable to any son of a drunk.

"Is this Mr. Daniel Lester?"

"Yeah, what of it?"

"This is Gunnery Sergeant Blue Morgan."

Silence fell, broken only by Lester's hoarse breathing.

"I thought you might like to know that your daughter Maria got here safely. Not that you care, seeing as you put her on that bus alone to start with."

"She's not mine."

"Whatever, you still put a ten-year-old girl on a bus and took her phone away. What the hell were you thinking?"

"To get her away from me. To send her to her real father, which is apparently you."

"You don't know if that is true."

"Angelina fucking *lied* to me for years. She's a fucking unfaithful bitch—"

"Mr. Lester, if you want to have a discussion about this, may I suggest you refrain from speaking about your wife like that?"

"Why should I? Fucking bitch told me all about you when she was dying, Sergeant, how she deceived me for all those years, how she fucked me over—"

"As I said, your wife is dead. We need to work out how to proceed from here."

Lester laughed. "I've worked it out, dude. I sent her bastard to you. As far as I'm concerned, that's the end of that. Now fuck off and don't bother me again."

The phone went dead, leaving Blue staring out into the night sky, his jaw set so hard his teeth were hurting. He had to try to be charitable. Lester's wife had recently died way too young, leaving him alone with a young child. Maybe the drinking was a temporary thing and once he got his shit together he'd realize what a douchebag he'd been to his daughter.

"Yeah, right."

Blue spoke out loud as his cell screen went dead. There

was no point calling the man back. Lester was already well on his way to getting drunk out of his head, or maybe he was just drunk all the time now. Maybe when Blue turned the phone number over to Nate, Daniel Lester would change his tune when he had to deal with the authorities.

For Maria's sake, Blue hoped so.

There was a knock on his door.

"BB?"

"Come in, Chase."

His brother came in and closed the door behind him. He looked his usual calm self. "You okay?"

Blue rubbed his hand over his head. "Not really."

"Whom were you talking to?"

"Maria's father."

"You got his number. How did that go?"

"As you might expect when talking to a drunk." Blue appreciated Chase's lack of anxiety and matter-of-fact manner so much right now. "I want to tell you all what I found out today before I pass the information over to Nate."

"Cool." Chase dropped a packet on the bed. "I got this for you and Maria. It's a DNA kit that collects buccal cells from the inside of your cheek. You don't need the mother's DNA to get an accurate result. I know the guys who started the company, so you'll get priority."

Blue took the package and placed it on his old desk. "Thanks, Chase."

"You're welcome. It's prepaid for return, so just call them up and they'll get it back to the lab in California. I think it takes a minimum of five to ten days."

Blue nodded and Chase opened the door. "Now come on down, have some of your favorite pie, and we can talk it over after Ruth puts Maria to bed."

* * *

When Blue came back in with Chase, Jenna sent up a silent prayer of relief. He looked okay, a bit stern around the mouth, but she hadn't heard any shouting.

"Do you want some more pie, Jenna?" Ruth asked.

"No, thanks, I'm done." Jenna smiled as she pushed her bowl away. "That was awesome."

"You'll be coming back out here tomorrow to check on that piglet, won't you?" Ruth cut a piece of peach pie as big as Jenna's head and put it in a bowl for Blue with two scoops of ice cream.

"Yes, I told Roy I'd try to come out. I have to visit the Lymond place anyway."

Blue's gaze instantly came to her. "I thought you weren't going up there anymore."

"Dave's coming with me. One of Mark's horses is about to give birth."

"One of the two he has left?" Blue grimaced. "Just take care, won't you?"

"I will." She smiled at him and went to stand up. "Now, I'd better be going or my uncle will think I've been abducted by aliens."

Surprisingly it was Billy who laughed, making him look not only younger, but also very like Chase. "Ron's had a thing about aliens ever since he was a kid."

Blue put his hand on the back of her chair. "Then he won't mind if you stay a bit longer. I want you to hear what I've got to say as well."

She met his gaze. "Are you sure about that? I'm not really family."

"But I want you here. Is that okay?"

"If you're sure."

He nodded once and then turned back to the table, his expression resolute as Ruth returned from putting Maria to bed and brought Roy with her.

"Okay, Maria can't hear us talking, can she?"

Ruth shook her head. "No, she's the farthest away from the kitchen. I put her music on for her on her i-thing—well, Chase did, but it sure is loud for such a tiny little box."

Blue placed his hands flat down on the table. "I'm just going to tell it to you straight. I spoke to Dan Lester's wife Rosa, and found out I did actually spend a night with her sister-in-law Angelina Lester."

"And when you say spent the night," Chase said, "you mean you had unprotected sex with a married woman."

Jenna winced, but Blue didn't take offense.

"Number one, I didn't know she was married. I didn't even know until today that she was supposed to be separated at the time. Number two, something went wrong in the protection department, and I was too drunk to do much about it. She told me she was on the pill, and not to worry."

"Okay. So there is a possibility that Maria is your child."

"Yeah."

Silence fell around the table, and Jenna instinctively reached out and put her hand on Blue's knee. Despite his outwardly calm appearance, his muscles were so tense he was shaking.

"If it was a possibility, why didn't Angelina contact you before?" January leaned forward, her gaze sympathetic.

"I don't know." Blue shrugged. "Maybe she just wanted to forget what she'd done, pretend everything was normal and that any child was her husband's. I can understand that. What I don't understand is why she decided to confess what happened on that one solitary night to her husband just before she died."

"She *told* him Maria was your child?" Ruth demanded.

"She certainly implanted that suggestion at some point."

"How do you know?"

"Because when I spoke to Daniel Lester, he was drunk and abusive and told me he wanted nothing more to do with his wife's bastard."

"The horrible man!" Ruth muttered. "He doesn't deserve that sweet little girl."

"I agree. He sucks." Blue reached over to take Ruth's work-roughened hand. "The thing is—I wonder if Angelina knew anything more that would make even suggesting Maria isn't his kid make Dan think it was a done deal?"

"Like what?"

Chase stirred. "Maybe during her treatment, the blood work threw up some anomalies and made her think."

"It's possible, I suppose." Blue's shoulders relaxed a little bit. "Maybe they tested Maria to make sure she wasn't carrying the same genes and found out something else along the way."

"Unlikely if we're dealing with the maternal line, but there were probably a lot of tests." Chase frowned. "Did he sound one hundred percent convinced he wasn't her father?"

"Pretty much, but he was drunk, so you know what that's like."

Billy looked down at Blue's casual reference to his and Chase's shared past.

"I'm going to do the DNA tests that Chase got me. That will clear everything up once and for all." Blue looked around the table. "And if she's my daughter, I'll take care of her. I hope you all know that."

"Of course we do, BB," Ruth said. "I do have one favor to ask you. Can you do the test in a week or so when she's gotten more used to the place?"

"If we leave it that long, it will take another couple of weeks after that to get the results. Are you okay with *that*, Ruth?"

"She'll be fine here with us. She can treat it like a vacation and be our first guest at the new ranch."

Jenna smiled. "That's actually a good idea. She can try out the programs January and I have been working on for the kids. We can teach her how to ride."

Blue sat back. "You all sure about this? It's not like we're taking on a stray puppy here, and we won't be completely certain until we get the tests back whether she is my daughter or not."

"She sure looks like you, BB," Billy said quietly. "And Ruth."

Blue met his father's gaze. "She seems to like you a lot."

Billy shrugged. "I like kids."

"So—don't let her down, will you? Don't suddenly disappear on her or anything."

Billy swallowed hard, but he didn't look away. "I won't, BB. I promise."

"Don't promise." Blue stood up. "There's nothing worse for a kid than a broken promise from someone they care about."

"BB." Chase started to stand as well, his voice quiet. "Give him a chance, okay? We're all trying to help you out here."

Jenna took Blue's hand. "Will you walk me out to my

truck? I really have to go or Uncle Ron will be calling Nate to round up a search party."

January winked. "I'm sure Nate would be more than happy to come and find *you*, Jenna."

She grinned as Jenna led Blue out into the cold night air and down the steps to where her truck was parked. He let her lead, which was a first, and stopped obediently beside her as she went to open the door.

"Thanks for a great—"

The rest of what she had been going to say was devoured by his kiss, which tasted of peaches and hot man— a combination that was rapidly becoming her all-time favorite. Her back was against the truck and his body covered her completely, one of his hands anchored around her hips and the other tangled in her hair.

She fought to free one hand from between them and wrapped it around his neck, holding on to all that lean-muscled power for dear life. God, he was beautiful. It was like petting a jaguar. There was nothing else in her vision than Blue's face and the thrilling sensation of his mouth moving over hers. Eventually, even she had to breathe and she broke off the kiss and buried her face in the crook of his neck.

He held her close, his breathing slowing down along with hers, the tension in his body easing—apart from that one hard bit of him that she kind of longed to explore, but didn't quite have the nerve to attempt. In typical Blue fashion, he took her hand and solved that problem by guiding her fingers around him until he groaned.

"That was not a good idea," he breathed out hard against her forehead.

"You made me do it."

"I couldn't help myself."

She petted him just a little until his hips rolled against her, and he hissed a soft curse. Taking her hand, he placed it within his own and drew it down to her side.

"I want you." His blunt statement didn't surprise her. He was a man used to getting what he wanted when he wanted it. "But this really isn't good timing."

"So you said."

"I have to take care of Maria first."

"I know."

He searched her face. "You're making this very easy for me."

She attempted a shrug—difficult when your whole body was plastered over a man's hard unyielding torso. "It's all good. We're still only kissing, and I'm officially going out with Nate."

"No, you are not." His blue eyes struck sparks.

"I believe that is up to me, Blue Morgan."

He sighed. "Jeez, I can't believe I'm saying this, but he's a nice guy. You probably would be better off with him."

As her stomach dropped with disappointment, she gave him her sweetest smile. "I am. He's my only boyfriend, remember?"

"The way you just kissed me? I don't think so, sweetheart."

She shoved on his chest until he took an unwilling step back. There really was nothing left to lose, and she was determined that things wouldn't always run on his schedule. It was good for him to be thwarted occasionally.

"You can't have it both ways. You either stand aside and let me go out with Nate, or you ask me out yourself."

His jaw settled into a stubborn line she was becoming

way too familiar with. "I just explained why that can't happen right now, and you said you understood."

"I do understand."

"Then what exactly are we talking about?"

"It would be better for both of us if you focus on Maria and I focus on my job."

He cocked his head to one side and observed her. "So what you're saying is no more kissing unless we're a couple?"

"Exactly."

His slow grin held such a mixture of lust and devilry that she almost melted on the spot.

"Right. Got it."

"And you understand why I won't be kissing you anymore?"

"Totally." He nodded. "It's only fair."

"Then we're on the same page. Night then, Blue."

She nodded to him and went to get in her truck. Damn, she'd been way too confident, thinking he wouldn't want to stop kissing her just because she couldn't imagine not doing it anymore herself. She should know by now that she wasn't hard to give up. She'd never been special enough for anyone.

A tap on her window made her look up from fishing her keys out of her pocket to find Blue looking in on her. With a sigh, she rolled down the window. In her old truck, he was tall enough to be almost at her eye level.

"Drive safe and be careful at Mark Lymond's place tomorrow, okay?"

She managed a nod.

His smile disappeared. "Are you really okay?"

"Peachy."

He took her tightly clenched fist in his hand and

studied it. "You don't look it." He brought her fingers to his mouth and lightly kissed them. "Night, Jenna. Take care now."

She disengaged her hand and turned the wheel, reversing the truck in a wide arc around him, her lights sweeping over the slumbering barn and waking up the indignant chickens. He was still standing there as she bumped down the road, his gaze fixed on the departing truck.

She eased her fingers on the steering wheel, aware that somewhere inside her tears threatened. He'd told her the truth, which was more than most men did, and he had good, valid reasons why he couldn't currently get involved in a relationship with her. Was it too much to ask that one day, just *one* day, she would be the most important person in the world for someone?

"And why can't men be like women and multitask?" She asked the question to the still night air. "Why can't Blue do me and everything else at the same time?"

She didn't have the answer and was being *stupid*, and *unrealistic*, and *romantic*, and all those other things that had been pointed out to her countless times in family therapy sessions. She knew that she *did* have worth, that the fact that her birth parents hadn't wanted her, that her two sisters were way more intelligent than her, that she was smart, but not brilliant were all unimportant unless she believed at her core she had worth herself . . .

Like it was easy.

Maybe it was her fault. She seemed to be the only one in her adopted family who still struggled to feel accepted and loved. But then the others didn't really know what her earlier life had been like, and even worse, what had happened when she'd made the mistake of searching for her birth parents.

She stopped to open the final gate out onto the county road, drove through, and locked it behind her. None of this was Blue's fault. It really did come down to her and her stupid insecurities. One thing she did know was that Maria had to come first, and if that meant keeping away from the lure of Blue Morgan's kisses? She could do that.

Or at least she hoped she could.

Chapter Ten

"Billy . . ." Blue tried to catch his father's eye. "I think I can handle this."

To his surprise, Billy just kept right on walking down to the barn, his hand securely in Maria's. Normally, he would do whatever Blue said just to avoid an argument, so his championship of the little girl was as unexpected as it was unwelcome.

"Maria asked me to come along," Billy finally said over his shoulder.

"I bet she did." Blue ended up following meekly behind. "But I thought this would be a good way for her and me to spend some time together."

Billy patted Maria's shoulder. "Go ahead and find some of those old apples to feed the horses. I'll catch up with you in the barn. Don't go into any of the stalls, now."

After a quick anxious glance at Blue, Maria nodded and ran off, her pigtails bouncing.

Billy turned to Blue. "She's still a bit overwhelmed by all this."

"I get that. But I also want a chance to get to know her."

"I'm not stopping you doing that, BB." Billy held his gaze.

"You're—" Blue sighed. "Hell—you're better at it than I am. That's the God honest truth."

"I had five kids. I learned a lot before I shot myself in the foot and lost you all." Billy hesitated. "I think I spent more time with you boys than your mother did. It was hard for her. She hated the ranch. All I tried to do was show you what a great place it was to grow up—just like my father did to me."

Blue looked down at the ground, cleared his throat, and swallowed his pride. "Yeah, so how about we both teach her how to ride? It's the only way she's going to be willing to spend any time with me."

"She'll come around, BB. She's lost a lot in the last few weeks."

"I know how that feels."

They had reached the barn, and he could see Maria feeding Nolly an apple and talking away in the horse's ear. At least she wasn't scared of the horses anymore. Billy had already coaxed her out of that.

"Which horse do you think, Billy?"

"Sugar Lump. She's old and reliable."

"Just like Ruth."

Billy chuckled. "Don't let your grandma hear you say that." He raised his voice. "Hey, Maria, are you ready for your first lesson? Me and BB are going to turn you into a real cowgirl."

Hearing voices, Jenna walked through the barn and out into the fenced pasture beyond, where she could see Maria sitting in front of Blue on Sugar Lump, walking slowly around the inside of the white fence. Both of them were smiling, and if she'd been asked to put money on the fact that they were related she would've paid up immediately.

Billy was leaning against the fence, watching, and he winked at her as she came alongside.

"Morning, Jenna."

"Morning, Billy. How's the lesson going?"

"Great. He's not a bad teacher." Billy nodded at Blue, who had brought the horse to a stop by the gate. "Once I reminded him that she wasn't a new recruit and that shouting wasn't an option."

"You're funny, Billy."

Blue kicked his booted feet out of the stirrups and handed Maria down to Billy before he dismounted. After a quick smile at Jenna, he crouched in front of Maria and gave her his full attention.

"You're doing good. Time to try it for yourself, okay?"

She huddled closer to Billy, who patted her shoulder. "You can do it. Blue's going to lead you around. All you have to do is sit tight and hold on to the reins, okay?"

"Okay."

Billy met Blue's questioning gaze and nodded. "Put her up there."

Within a second, Maria was swept up into Blue's arms and settled in the big old saddle. She clutched at the pommel with both hands.

"I want to get down."

Blue put his hand on her ankle. "You're going to be okay. I promise you. I won't let you fall."

She looked down at him, her blue gaze doubtful, and Jenna held her breath.

"Please?" He coaxed her. "You're going to rock this so hard. I just know it." He gathered the reins and held them out to her. "Remember how to hold these? Like an ice cream cone?"

She took the reins in her right hand, the other still clinging onto the pommel.

"Okay, then." Blue moved to stand by Sugar Lump's head. "Ready?"

Apart from a small squeak of alarm as they moved off, Maria stayed put in the saddle as Blue led Sugar Lump forward. As he clicked to the horse, Jenna let out her breath.

"She looks okay up there."

"Yeah." Billy angled his head against the encroaching sun. "She's a brave little girl."

Blue had already started in a loop back toward the fence. He was talking away to Maria, who was beginning to sit tall and looking around her. Jenna smiled at the picture they made together. She couldn't imagine her birth father ever relating to her like that. Blue might not think he'd gotten much from Billy, but he'd obviously learned how to be a father from someone.

Billy sighed as if echoing her thoughts. "I hope he is her dad. She deserves the best."

"I hope so, too. Once he takes her on, she'll never doubt she's loved, will she?"

Billy glanced at her. "Yeah. He's black and white, that one."

She wanted that. She wanted someone so on her team that she'd never feel alone again.

"Good job, Maria!" Billy clapped and called out as they approached the fence. Blue was smiling as he turned to lift Maria down. Before he could say anything to her, she'd run over to Billy and was hugging him hard.

"I did it!"

Blue's smile died as he coiled the reins in his fingers.

"Why don't you take Maria back up to the house, Billy, while I put Sugar away?"

Billy turned Maria to face Blue. "Say thank you, darlin'."

"Thank you," Maria whispered.

"You're welcome." Blue tipped his hat and turned back to the horse. Jenna opened the gate for him as Billy and Maria headed through the barn, talking nineteen to the dozen. Blue followed more slowly, Sugar at his side, and tied her to the hitching post.

Without asking, Jenna started to help him take off the tack. He was uncharacteristically quiet, his thoughts turned inward as they worked to get Sugar turned out.

"She did great."

"Yeah." Blue hefted the saddle into his arm and took it through into the tack room.

"Sugar's a great mount for her."

"Yeah." He clipped the halter on the horse and led her back into her stall.

Jenna waited until he locked the door. "So what's up?"

"She doesn't like me." He fiddled with the bridle. "She couldn't wait to get back to Billy."

"He's just easier for her to deal with right now."

"Apparently." He hung the bridle on its peg. "Hell, I even asked him to come and help me out today because I knew Maria wouldn't want to come with me. How sad is that?"

"Actually, I think that's very sensible of you."

"You do?"

"Yeah, why stress her out? If Billy is her security blanket, why take it away from her? She needs all the support she can get right now."

"But he's the last person on earth I would've imagined as a blanket for anyone."

"Because he messed up with you and your brothers?"

"Yeah."

She shrugged. "Then maybe he sees this as his chance to redeem himself with a girl that might well turn out to be his grandchild? People *can* change, you know."

He nodded, his expression thoughtful. "Hell, I know that. I just never figured he'd be one of them."

"I know how that feels." She turned toward the door, pushing away all the memories. "I've got to go and see that piglet."

"You want to ride down?"

"With you?"

"Yeah, Messi needs some exercise and Chase hasn't been on Nolly for a few days and he gets kind of squirrely if he isn't ridden."

"Chase or Nolly?"

His grin was way less strained. "I'm not saying." He leaned against the door frame, his body language relaxed. "You can ride, right?"

She gave him a look and marched back into the tack room. "Which saddle?"

"Have I roused your competitive instincts?" Blue called after her.

"I don't have any." She picked up the saddle he pointed out, staggering just a little at the weight. "I'll see you outside."

Blue kept an unobtrusive eye on Jenna as she saddled Nolly because Chase's favorite horse was a bit of a joker and liked to mess his riders around. But Jenna wasn't taking any shit and soon had Nolly ready to go. She mounted up, settled her baseball cap more firmly down on her head, and gathered the reins in her hand. She looked damn good on the back of a horse. Blue hurried to finish, shoving his gloves in the back pocket of his jeans and making one last check on Messi's reins.

He went to stand alongside Jenna, one hand on Nolly's bridle. "Watch out for his little tricks."

"Will do. I've heard all about him from January."

"Just be careful, all right?"

She blinked at him. "Don't worry about me. I'm a pretty good rider."

"I'm sure you are."

Her smile returned. "You don't believe me, do you?" With a sharp click to Nolly, she set off at a brisk trot, her body swaying from side to side in the approved Western fashion.

Blue hurried to get on board Messi and followed after her.

"How did it go at the Lymond place this morning?" Blue asked as they settled the horses into a walk to pick their way through the outlying boulders of the creek crossing.

"It was okay. The mare doesn't look well. She's super thin. Mark refused to accept that even when Dave agreed with me. We said we'd go back tonight, but Mark said he didn't want the expense and that he'd call us if there were any problems." She sighed. "I don't like it, Blue, but what can I do?"

"Nothing, I suppose." He angled Messi's head toward the curve of the uneven bank. "Ruth said Mark's wife has gone back to her folks in Modesto."

"Maybe that explains why he's so short-tempered."

Jenna leaned slightly back in the saddle to compensate for the pitch of the slope and then straightened as they waded carefully across the creek. The sun was out and catching sparks off the rushing water, which was as clear as crystal, having come straight off the peaks of the snow-capped mountains.

Blue took in a deep, uncomplicated breath. "I love it out here."

Jenna grinned at him. "You're certainly a lucky guy to have all this."

"I know." He settled deeper into the saddle. "I didn't appreciate it for years and couldn't wait to leave. Once I was gone, I kind of missed it. Even the bad part after Mom and Rachel disappeared and Dad took to guzzling alcohol like a champ."

"My birth parents were both addicts." She shivered despite the heat. "It's not a life I'd wish for any child."

"Hell, no. That's one of the reasons why I'm glad Maria isn't with Dan Lester. It sounds like he's heavily into the booze at the moment."

"Grief does weird things to people."

"Yeah, so everyone keeps telling me."

They reached the other side of the creek and let the horses pick their path through the tumbled rocks toward the more open pasture. Blue settled his Stetson more firmly on his head. "Want to go a bit faster?"

"Sure."

"But only if you feel safe."

She gave him a derisive look, clicked her teeth at Nolly, and took off like a rocket, crouching low over the horse's neck like a jockey.

"Hey!"

Blue went after her, but she was too far ahead of him.

Damn, he hated to lose. Just to rub things in, she came loping back toward him grinning like a loon. She didn't slow down or alter her course, so he pulled Messi up instead.

"Jenna?"

Hell, she was still coming straight for him, and then suddenly she wasn't there anymore and he bit back a yelp.

"Holy cow!" Blue briefly closed his eyes as she thundered past him, her body crouched low on one side of Nolly Indian hideaway–style before she settled back down into the saddle, whooping at the top of her voice.

He followed her down to Roy's place and tied Messi up in the shade of the small barn. She came in behind him and did a showy vaulting dismount.

"Okay, so you're a damned good rider. Where did you learn how to do that? You scared the crap out of me."

"My mom was a trick rider at the rodeo. I grew up watching her perform, and she taught me a couple of things. Apparently, I looked super cute riding alongside her."

"We're talking about your birth mom here?"

"Yeah." Her smile widened. "My adopted mom's in medicine. I hear from January that you and Chase have a couple of rodeo tricks up your sleeves as well."

"That was a one-off. If I hadn't wanted to outdo Chase, I would never have suggested it." He shuddered. "Never been so terrified in my life."

"You're a Marine. I'm sure that was a lot more scary."

"Not really."

She held his gaze, and he leaned in and kissed her.

"You're not supposed to do that."

"That's right."

"Then stop it."

He kissed her again. "Okay."

She stomped off toward the pigsty and he followed, smiling.

"When are you going to tell your pretend boyfriend it's all over between you?" he called after her.

"He's not my pretend boyfriend."

"Honey, he's a Turner, and you're not 'The One.'"

She turned. "How do you know?"

"Because if you were, Nate would've gotten you down that aisle five minutes after he'd met you. I worked it out after your first date with him." He strolled forward and propped one elbow up against the door of the barn. "Which means you haven't been going out with him for months."

She raised her chin at a challenging angle. "Maybe he's changed his mind and is giving it a try."

"Nah." He slowly shook his head. "Turners don't do that. My best guess is he's seeing you because he wants to mess with my head."

"So you think this is all about you, Blue Morgan?"

"Possibly."

"Well, you're wrong." She started walking again. "Maybe Nate *wanted* to marry me immediately, and I put the brakes on. Or don't you think anyone would want to marry me?"

He paused. That was one hell of a leading question, and one no prudent man would ever answer directly unless he wanted to be the one either walking up the aisle or being dumped on his ass.

"I don't think Nate *Turner* wants to marry you. But then, he's an idiot."

She leaned over the wall to count the piglets that had come running out to see what was going on. One of them had a patch of white tape over one ear, and she leaned in and competently scooped the piglet up. His little hooves scrabbled against her chest as she checked him over and them dumped him back in the sty. Her yellow T-shirt was now covered in pig shit, but she didn't seem to care.

What a woman.

Blue looked down into the angry eyes of the massive sow and hastily turned away. "How's the piglet?"

"Looking good." She turned away and walked toward the small barn. "I'm just going to wash my hands."

Not relishing the stench coming from the pigs, Blue followed her into the barn and waited by the door as she scrubbed away at her hands and arms. Roy's truck was missing from the front of his house, and so were his horse and dogs.

"Where's Roy?"

"Counting the herd with Ruth and then going to town to get some cash out of the bank. He'll be back around four." Jenna dried her hands. "I said I'd leave him a note about the piglet."

Blue turned toward the house. The back door was unlocked, and the coolness of the air inside was already welcome. He had no worries about invading Roy's space. He'd been running in and out of the house since he was a kid and had treated it like a second home. In fact, when things had gotten bad with his parents, he and his brothers had practically lived down here.

He opened the old refrigerator. "Want some lemonade?"

Jenna had come in behind him. "Won't Roy mind?"

"Nah. He'd be cross if we didn't help ourselves." He found two plastic glasses adorned with oranges and filled them with liquid. "I remember Roy getting these cups back in the 1990s. He saved up orange juice coupons or something. We helped him collect them."

Jenna was sitting at the table writing something on a pad. He put the glass beside her and took a seat.

"Thanks." She looked up briefly and took a long drink from the glass. "That's good. It's getting hot out there."

Blue rubbed his fingers through the condensation gathering on his glass and appreciated the quiet hum of the air-conditioning Chase had recently insisted on having installed for Roy. He glanced over at Jenna, but she was still contemplating the note she was writing.

"Hey, while you've got your pen out, write Nate a Dear John letter."

She met his gaze. "You are relentless, you know that? Like a tank."

"I'll take that as a compliment."

"Then go away and crush something else."

He sipped at his lemonade. "You don't look very crushed to me."

"Ha ha." She pointed her pen at him. "You are incorrigible."

"There you go with the big words again." He pretended to sigh. "I can only assume that means something bad."

"You scored over seven hundred on your SAT. Don't pretend to be a hick."

"Who told you that?"

"Guess." She returned her attention to the note and signed it. "Are you ready to go now, or do you have other stuff to do here?"

He stood up and walked around the table and held out his hand. "I'm good."

She looked up at him. "No, you are not good. You are a bad influence on me."

"Why?"

"Because you make me want . . ." She stopped and shook her head. "That's it, really."

"I make you want? What?"

"Things I can't have."

"You're going to have to be a bit more specific here, Jenna. Like what?"

She rose to her feet, but he didn't step back crowding her space a little. He wrinkled his nose.

"Damn, that's too bad."

"What?"

"I was going to kiss you, but . . ." He poked her in the sternum. "Your T-shirt stinks."

He'd never seen a bosom actually *heave* before, but Jenna's eyes flashed and the next second she was pulling her T-shirt right over her head, balling it up, and throwing it at his face.

"That better?"

When the T-shirt fell off his nose to the floor, he let his gaze travel slowly down from her face to her nice blue bra and then lower to her belly. "Yeah. Much."

She bent to pick up the T-shirt and brushed past him, heading for Roy's guest bathroom. "I've got a couple of shirts in the closet. I'll wash up and be out in a minute."

Blue finished his lemonade and contemplated the splashy noises coming from the bathroom. When Jenna reappeared and went into the room next door, he set his glass back down on the table and followed her.

"Knock, knock."

She gasped and crossed her hands over her chest. "What are you doing in here?"

"I thought you might like a second opinion on the state of your bra. You wouldn't want to put a clean shirt on over something that still stunk, would you?"

"My bra is fine, thank you."

He leaned back against the door frame. "I hate to disagree with you about anything, Jenna darlin', but how can you tell? You didn't even notice you smelled like pig shit."

"I washed up."

He took a step toward her and then another, but she didn't tell him to back off. He stopped an arm's length away and slowly raised his hand until his index finger rested right on the cute little bow at the center of her bra between her rounded breasts.

"Nice." His appreciative gaze traveled over her now tight nipples. "*Very* nice."

"And not smelling of anything but me, okay?"

He deliberately took a deep breath. "I like the way you smell."

She made a small despairing noise. "This is so unfair."

"You know, you're right. It is." Still holding her gaze he reached down, grabbed the hem of his T-shirt, and stripped it over his head. "Does this make it better?"

"Good Lord, yes . . ." Her hand came to her mouth. "I mean no, that's just—is that a tattoo?"

He flexed his right bicep. "Yeah."

"Semper fi."

"Always faithful."

She nodded. "It kind of suits you."

"Thanks." He took her hand and placed it on his arm right over the tat. "I have another one."

She scanned his chest and arms. "Is it on your back?"

He turned a full circle to let her check. "Nope."

"Then where?"

He raised an eyebrow. "I'm not telling. You have to write that letter to Nate first."

"That's so not happening." Her gaze dropped to his lower half. "Which is good, because I don't think I can take much more of you."

"See, I don't have that problem at all. You can shimmy out of those jeans and come and sit in my lap for as long as you want. You're beautiful." He glanced down at his groin. "Actually I wouldn't mind getting out of these jeans myself. Things are getting crowded down there."

"This is Roy's *house*!"

"It's better than your suggestion of the barn."

"I didn't—" She made another of those breathy frustrated sounds he was beginning to love and backed up until she was next to the closet. "Let me get a shirt."

"You quite sure you don't want to get naked? We're halfway there."

She flapped a hand at him. "Stop talking right now." Turning her back on him she rummaged in the closet, bringing out a red and white checked shirt on a hanger. "I left this here last time."

The hanger clattered to the floor when she turned and found him right up close to her again.

"Rats." She bent to pick it up almost bumping heads with him. "Double rats."

He placed the shirt on top of the dresser and put his hands on her shoulders.

"It's okay."

"No, it's not."

"Really?" He considered her for a long moment until she started to blush. "This is really not okay? Because if you don't want me to kiss you right now, you just have to say so."

"We agreed not to kiss."

"That's right."

"So this shouldn't even be an issue."

"Agreed."

"Then what are you trying to accomplish?"

He grinned at her. "Just testing your resolve."

Her brown eyes narrowed. "You conceited ass."

"Guilty." He stepped back and picked up his T-shirt. "You write that note to Nate and we'll talk again, okay?"

"Just so I can see your other tattoo? I don't think so."

He winked. "Honey, you know I'll show you a lot more than that."

He'd almost made it to the door before she seemed to recover the power of speech.

"Hold it right there. Have you changed your mind? Are you saying that if I wasn't going out with Nate, you'd ask me out instead?"

He looked back over his shoulder. "How about you ditch Nate and come and ask me again? I'll check the horses and wait for you outside."

Grinning to himself, Blue went out the door pulling on his T-shirt. So sue him, he had changed his mind, but he sure wasn't going to quite admit it. She'd laugh like a hyena, and he had some pride. He found his hat, made sure to clean up Roy's kitchen, and went out to see to the horses. God, had he ever had so much fun in a relationship before? Most of them had been just about sex, and he and Jenna still hadn't even done that.

Maybe that was the secret. Liking someone first and then realizing you wanted to make love to them made a lot more sense. Blue put on his hat. And he would be making love with Jenna, he was damned sure about that. Sometimes even a Marine had to reassess his priorities.

It took Jenna way too long to manage the buttons on her shirt because her fingers were trembling so much. Every time Blue showed some skin, she lost about a million brain cells and reverted back to basic "hit this man over the head with a club and drag him back to her cave" level of operating.

She found her cell in the back pocket of her jeans and

texted Nate, asking to see him. His reply flashed up almost immediately, saying he was heading up to the ranch to see Maria and Blue and would probably be there around dinnertime. It meant she'd have to stick around and put up with Blue Morgan, but there were plenty of things she could do to keep out of his way.

She texted Nate back that she'd be there, and put her cell away. She wasn't prepared to drag him further into her web of lies. He really did deserve better, and seeing as Blue had worked out what was going on from the start, it was unfair to keep pretending. Now came the difficult part. Walking out and pretending that nothing was wrong when all she wanted to do was drag Blue down to the nearest horizontal surface and climb on board.

But she had standards.

Didn't she?

She took her cell phone out again and checked the time before texting.

Yvonne, can I call u?

Her cell rang almost immediately. "What's up?"

"Blue Morgan."

"Ooh, what's happening?" Yvonne said. "Did you sleep with him?"

"No, I'm still going out with Nate, remember?"

"Like anyone believes that," Yvonne scoffed. "So what's up?"

"I almost gave into temptation."

"What stopped you?"

"Yvonne, you're supposed to be helping me resist him. I *knew* I should've called January. She's way more sensible than you are."

"Honey, Blue's single, right? And sinfully sexy."

"And he has tattoos," Jenna breathed.

"Damn, girl, you are so screwed. Apart from the non-issue of Nate, what's holding you back?"

"Blue's life is a little complicated right now."

"He told you that?"

"He keeps telling me that, and then he kisses me and makes me think he's changing his mind, and then I get all confused again. That's why I'm calling you. I can't let him win."

"So here's what you do."

Jenna clutched the phone tight to her ear. "Okay, shoot."

"Nothing."

"That's not really helping, Yvonne."

"Yes, it is. Sort things out with Nate so that you are both free, and then leave the rest in Blue's hands."

"Like give up control?"

"To fate, yes."

"I'm not sure if I can do that." Jenna frowned at her flustered reflection in the mirror.

"Why not? If he's meant to be yours, he will be."

"Maybe that kind of thing happens to you, Yvonne, but not to me. No man has ever looked at me twice, let alone chased after me."

"Then if Blue doesn't do that, you'll know he isn't the right man for you. Just let him have a chance to try, okay?"

Jenna took a deep breath. Okay, she was officially terrified now. Leaving things up to fate was *so* not her style. "I'll talk to Nate and leave the rest to fate. Hey, that rhymes."

"Great, you're a poet. Now get out there and get your man."

"I thought you just said I had to wait for him to come to me?"

"You know what I mean. I have to go, my break's over. Come and see me soon, okay?"

"Okay, and thanks." Jenna ended the call and put her cell away. Time to go and get back on her horse. Blue had cleared away their glasses and left her note to Roy on the table, so she picked up her cap and sunglasses and went out into the glare of the afternoon sun.

Blue was already mounted and walking Messi, so she was able to get on Nolly and just follow his lead. He waited at the bottom gate for her to go by and then dismounted to close it behind them.

"Wait up."

She tensed as he strolled over to her.

"What is it?"

He pointed at her shirt. "You've got it buttoned up all wrong."

"Maybe I like it like that."

"It would drive me nuts."

"That's because you're an overperfectionist."

"Or because I've been in the military for too long." He settled deeper into the saddle. "Could you fix it? It's giving me an eye twitch."

She sighed elaborately, took off her gloves, and redid the buttons. "Better now?"

"Thanks." He patted her knee. "Have you got time to sample our hot springs before you head out?"

"Hot springs?"

His grin was an invitation to sin. "Yeah. They are something of a family secret, but I'm happy to share it with you."

"I wish I had time, but I promised Ruth I'd check in with her this afternoon." There was no way she was stripping off a single sock near Blue Morgan again today. She smiled brightly at him. "But thanks for the invite. I might take you up on it one day. Have you taken Maria yet?"

"That's a good idea. I hadn't thought of it." His smile dimmed. "Not that she'd want to go anywhere with me."

"You've got to keep trying, Blue."

"Yeah, I know." He turned away, his hat shading his face. "It's just hard."

He mounted up and they were soon on their way back to the ranch. Jenna forgot all about Blue in the simple pleasure of riding through such glorious scenery. She couldn't imagine why Chase Morgan had ever considered selling the ranch. There was so much history here and so much *potential*. She was suddenly glad that January had been around to remind Chase of what he was throwing away. If she had roots in one place that went back over a hundred and fifty years? She'd be staying put.

As they neared the ranch, her cell buzzed, but as Nolly had decided to approach the barn at the speed of a race-horse, she had her hands too full to answer it. Cooling Nolly down and turning him out into the pasture took a while, so it wasn't until she was heading into the house that she took out her cell to check her messages.

"Damn." She slowed down to adjust her eyes to the interior light, and Blue bumped into her. "That was Dave. He's stuck with a calf delivery, and Mark Lymond called him to say his mare is in distress. I'll have to go right now."

Blue touched her shoulder. "Can't you call Big Mac?"

"He's out golfing. He'll never get here in time." She sighed. "It's going to have to be me whether Mark likes it or not."

"I'll come with you."

She looked up into his implacable face. "You don't have to do that."

"Yeah, I do. I'm not having you dealing with Mark if things go wrong."

"Okay."

He raised an eyebrow. "You're not going to argue with me?"

"Not this time."

"Good." He turned back to the door, suddenly all business. "We'll take your truck. I'll just go and tell Ruth where we'll be."

Chapter Eleven

"I'm sorry, Mr, Lymond." Jenna pushed her hair out of her eyes and held the enraged rancher's gaze. "There's nothing more I can do."

"There must be something! You get a proper qualified vet down here right now, missy, and quit pretending you know what the hell you're doing."

"Mr. Lymond. The mare was already weakened from lack of proper nutrition, which means that the foal was already compromised. We told you this earlier today when we suggested you bring the mare into our clinic where we could keep an eye on her."

"You said no such thing. You're just protecting your ass." Mark shoved a finger right in her face. "This is your fault!"

Blue stepped up alongside her. "Mark, she's right. Leave her alone."

"What the hell do you know, Morgan? Just because she's got a pretty face doesn't mean she's competent at her job. She killed that mare and foal."

"That's complete bullshit," Blue snapped. "Now, do you

want me to help bury the horses or are you going to send for Smedleys?"

"Get off my ranch, both of you." Mark threw his gloves onto the ground and stalked off, muttering obscenities.

Jenna exhaled. "The poor guy."

"He should've taken better care of his horses." Blue gripped her shoulder hard. "You're not the responsible one here."

"Thanks, Blue, but I still feel bad." She stripped off her gloves and turned wearily back to her truck. "If the mare had been at the clinic, we might have been able to do something about that blood loss, but here? I just couldn't stop it."

"Come on, grab your stuff. I'll drive you back to the ranch and you can take a shower there."

She could do little but nod and follow him out. To her amazement the sun was still shining and it wasn't that late. She'd thought she'd been in that stall for days fighting to keep the mare and foal alive, but time had passed slowly. Blue covered her passenger seat with an old rug, so she sat on that and let him drive her back to the ranch.

She looked out of the window as the sense of failure dragged her down. She hated losing an animal, and particularly a mother and foal. That just sucked so hard. One of the reasons she'd left the high-tech world of the horse racing stables was to work with a community who loved their horses and didn't just see them as financial assets to be destroyed on a whim. She'd forgotten that a lot of ranchers also had financial concerns, albeit different ones. Did it always come down to money? Did no one really care about their horses anymore?

As the truck bounced down the drive, she mentally reviewed every medical decision she'd made, and couldn't think what she would've changed. But that didn't mean that Dave or her uncle wouldn't have done a better job.

"You okay?"

"Not really." She didn't look round. "I need to write up my notes while everything is still fresh in my mind."

"Have your shower first."

She looked down at her bloodied jeans and shuddered. "Definitely."

There was no one in the ranch kitchen as Blue showed her the shower in the mudroom and provided her with pink shower gel, shampoo, and a towel that she was pretty sure belonged to January. She took her time under the spray, trying to ease some of the tension out of her muscles, and contemplated what she needed to do next.

When she emerged from the shower, she found some of January's shorts and a navy T-shirt with "Marines" on it that she suspected might belong to Blue. The rest of her clothes had gone.

In the kitchen, Blue had made coffee and was sitting at the table with his phone out texting someone.

"Hey, I put your stuff in to wash. I hope that was okay. Should be ready by the time you go home."

"Thanks." She took the seat opposite him, conscious that she wasn't wearing any underwear and that he knew it. "Is it okay if I write my notes?"

"Sure, I brought your bag in." He passed the heavy bag over the table to her one-handed without any apparent effort. "Dave texted me asking where you were, so I gave him the short version of what happened. He says he'll see you at home and you can run it by his dad."

Jenna groaned and buried her face in her hands. "Great."

"You did the best you could, right?"

"Yes."

"With the best of intentions and all your current knowledge?"

"Yes."

He sat back. "Then that's all anyone can ask of you."

She managed a wobbly smile. "Thanks, Gunnery Sergeant Morgan."

He gave her a casual salute. "You're welcome."

The back door opened, and several voices speaking over each other disturbing the peace of the kitchen made Blue smile. "The family's back."

Ruth came in with Maria, Chase, and January. From the look of them, they'd been to town and bought up the whole of Maureen's store.

Ruth smiled at Jenna. "You here for dinner? I saw Nate in town. He says he's coming out here, too."

"I'd love to stay."

"Good, because I've been practicing my nut loaf recipe."

Blue and Chase made identical gagging noises and Ruth scowled at them. "It's very good, isn't it, Maria?"

"Yes."

Blue winked at Maria. "Then I'll have to try it. Did you help Ruth?"

"Yes." Maria looked away at Ruth. "Can I take my things upstairs now?"

"Sure, and please hang everything up, okay?"

Maria gathered up most of the bags and went up the stairs.

"What exactly did you buy her?" Blue asked, his fingers tapping on the table.

Chase shrugged. "Just some riding gear and ranch clothes."

Blue stopped tapping. "That's my job, Chase."

"For God's sake, BB, it was just a fun thing to do with her."

"But I wanted to do it, and more importantly, I want to pay for her stuff. Let me know how much you spent, and I'll reimburse you."

Chase sighed. "Okay, maybe you've got a point. I'll total it up, all right?"

"Good." Blue nodded.

"Except for her hat." Ruth put on her apron and washed her hands. "I'm buying her that, so you can just suck it up."

Blue blinked. "Did you just say I should suck it up? Who's teaching you that language?"

Ruth rolled her eyes. "I watch TV. I get the lingo."

"What the hell does that mean?" Chase muttered, when Ruth turned her back. Blue grinned at his brother and the tense moment was over just like that. Things had gotten a lot better between him and Chase over the past few months—once he'd let go of the past and his brother had gotten rid of the stick up his ass.

"What's in the washer?" January asked as she came back in and dropped a kiss on Chase's head before sitting down. "And have you been using my shower gel again, Chase?"

"That was all me." Blue held up his hand. "Jenna needed a shower, and I put her clothes on to wash. She was at Mark Lymond's place attending to his mare in foal."

Ruth studied Jenna's downcast face. "I take it that didn't go well."

"I couldn't save them. He wasn't happy."

Blue reached over and squeezed Jenna's shoulder. "She did her best. He left it too late to get help."

"Still hurts to see an animal die, though," Ruth said gently.

Jenna nodded. "Would it be okay if I go into the parlor and write my notes? I want to make sure I get everything down correctly."

"Why?" Chase sat forward. "Do you think there might be a problem?"

She shrugged. "It's standard procedure to get as much information as possible, and I have to share what happened with Dave and Uncle Ron. They might want to go and follow up. I'm not a partner at the practice, so everything I do reflects on them and their reputation in the county."

"You go ahead, Jenna. Dinner will be ready in an hour," Ruth called out from her position by the stove. "I'll send Blue to let you know when it's time to sit down."

"Or send Nate," Blue suggested. "I know Jenna will want to speak to him."

She gave him an exasperated look, picked up her bag, and left the kitchen.

"Here you go." Chase turned his laptop around so Blue could see the screen. "Here's the total."

Blue blinked at the final column. "Jeez, Chase, next time remember we're not all loaded like you are, won't you?"

"You can pay me back in installments if you like."

Blue glanced at his brother and realized he wasn't joking. "Or you could start paying me a salary for my work here and take it out of that."

"I'm supposed to pay you now?"

"That was the general idea. I'm out of the military soon, which means I'm technically unemployed."

"Oh yeah, that's right." Chase frowned at his laptop. "I'll have to think about what you should earn."

"About half a million a year should cover it."

Chase gave a crack of laughter. "Dream on, brother, dream on."

Jenna typed up her final note and read through everything again, checking the information against the notes she'd scrawled at the time. The fragrant smell of something roasting had permeated under the door a while ago and her stomach was rumbling.

A knock on the door made her look up to see Nate framed in the doorway. He was out of uniform and into the other local uniform of jeans, cowboy boots, and a shirt.

"Hey." He grinned at her. "How's it going, fake girlfriend?"

"As to that." She patted the seat next to her. "I think it's time for us to break up."

"Cool. What did I do?" He ambled over toward her.

"Blue's onto us."

He high-fived her. "Awesome! That's just what you wanted, right?"

"He said he knew we weren't really going out because if I was The One, you would have married me already."

"Damn." Nate sighed. "He knows the Turner mode of operation too well." He took her hand. "You okay about this?"

"I'm fine." She gently disengaged her hand. "Did you come to see Maria?"

"Well, I came to see BB and Ruth *about* Maria. BB said he'd spoken to Daniel Lester and that he didn't think it would be in Maria's best interests to be returned to a drunk." Nate grimaced. "Social Services might have other ideas, but at the moment they are okay with Ruth looking after Maria while we wait for someone to interview Daniel Lester."

Jenna was intimately acquainted with both the CPS and Social Services and doubted they moved any faster than they had in her day. So Maria was safe at the ranch, at least for a little while longer.

Nate held out his hand. "I forgot—Ruth asked me to tell you that dinner's ready."

Jenna shut down her laptop, took his hand, and got to her feet. "Thanks for everything, Nate."

"You're welcome. Any time you need a fake boyfriend, I'm your man." He hesitated in the hallway. "Do you want to stage a big row over the dinner table? Maybe throw something at me?"

"I'm not doing that to Ruth's cooking. It's way too good to waste. Let's just be super polite to each other and let them work it out for themselves."

Chase belched behind his hand. "That was the best nut loaf I've ever had."

"That was the *only* nut loaf I've ever had, and it was awesome," Blue agreed.

"I told you so." Ruth gave them a complacent smile. "More peach cobbler, BB?"

He patted his stomach. "I'm good."

Ruth sat down and poured herself some coffee. "Is Jenna going to be okay?"

Jenna and Nate had left right after dinner, and January had taken Maria upstairs to paint her nails or something.

"She's worried about what Big Mac will say, but I was there. She did everything right. That poor horse wasn't healthy enough to be carrying a foal in the first place. Mark is the one who should be shot."

"He's certainly going to lose that ranch if he isn't careful." Ruth sighed. "Which is a terrible shame because it used to be such a thriving and happy place."

"If the worst comes to the worst and he decides to get out, we could always offer to buy it and add it onto our acreage." Chase pushed the plate of cookies away with a groan.

"You could afford that?"

Chase shrugged. "I should think so. It's not that big a place."

Blue wondered what it would be like to have that much money and found it impossible. He hadn't come across many multimillionaires in the military, and Chase's life in Silicon Valley was a complete unknown to him. But his brother was still remarkably down-to-earth in most ways, and he had eventually worked out where his roots were.

After a while, Chase became engrossed in some work on his laptop, Ruth went to put Maria to bed and then to watch TV, while Blue talked to January about ranch matters. Billy was in town at an AA meeting, which he attended with great regularity. It was all remarkably peaceful. Blue's only concern was how things were going for Jenna with her family, and he didn't feel he had the right to call and ask.

Eventually, everyone had gone to bed except Blue, who for some reason was still restless. Seeing all that blood and watching Jenna struggle to save the mare had awakened some of his less pleasant memories of his trips into the sandbox. He felt way too wired to sleep and decided to take a run around the property to use up some energy.

He loved being out at night with just the sound of his feet hitting the ground, surrounded by the crisp breeze coming off the mountains and the nocturnal creatures out hunting. A coyote howled somewhere in the distance and was answered by its pack, the yapping of young cubs eerily like screaming babies, which didn't help him get his mellow on at all.

He turned back and eventually came up the slope behind the barn where January was planning on putting the new guest cabins. Slowing down to a walk, he took in some deep breaths and prepared to go into his warm-down routine. Ruth's cooking was definitely affecting his weight, but hopefully all the riding was helping to even out the balance.

He bent to touch his toes and eased into a couple of lunges, relishing the pull on his hamstrings and quads before straightening up with a groan. A faint sound to his right had him freezing in place. He was fairly used to the noises of the barn, and that one hadn't registered with him before.

The faint mewling sound came again, and Blue forced himself to relax. One of the barn cats had been looking pretty plump for a while, which probably meant new kittens.

He jogged back toward the feed room and almost yelped when a small figure darted out in front of him. Instinctively he reached out and caught hold of the fleeing shape.

"Maria?"

She punched his chest. "Let me go!"

He eased up his grip. "Honey, it's me, Blue. There's nothing to worry about."

She looked up and the fear faded from her eyes. "You *scared* me."

"Not half as much as you scared me," he replied. "I nearly screamed like a baby."

"You'd never do that."

"Want to bet? Ask Chase what happened when he and the twins dressed up as ghosts one Halloween and scared the cra—I mean the bejeezus out of me." He relaxed his grip until he was just holding her shoulders. "You couldn't sleep either, eh?"

She shook her head. "I have . . . bad dreams sometimes."

"So do I."

She stared up into his face, her expression troubled. "I dream about my mom."

"Me, too."

Her nose crinkled. "What happened to your mom?"

"That's a really good question." He nodded in the direction of the feed store. "Do you want to come and see if we can find the new kittens first?"

"Kittens?"

"Yeah, come on." He held out his hand and she came with him. Her pink fluffy slippers weren't the best things to be walking around a barn in, but he wasn't going to spoil the moment and point it out. He'd make Chase buy her a new pair.

"Let's stand here by the door and keep quiet for a minute," he whispered to Maria. "Then we can work out exactly where the kittens are."

She moved closer toward him, her body leaning into his like it was the most natural thing in the world. Something tightened around his heart. Blue looked down at the top of her head and bent to brush a kiss on her black hair. God, despite everything, he hoped she was his kid. She deserved to be loved so badly.

"Over there."

He pointed toward the back left corner of the room and began to move, Maria at his side. He went down on his haunches and studied the lower shelving rack as his eyes adjusted to the dim light.

"Look." He breathed the word into Maria's ear and pointed out the squirming bunch of newborns on the old feed sack.

"Oh wow . . ." she squeaked. "There are six of them."

"Yeah, and just born, I should think. You see their eyes aren't open yet. We'll have to get Ms. Jenna out here to take a look at them and see if they are all healthy."

"Shall we call her now?"

"Tomorrow should be soon enough." Blue retreated, sat on the floor farthest away from the kittens, and patted his knee. "Want to sit here while we wait to see if the mama cat is going to come back? We might have scared her off."

"Oh no." Maria retreated and sat down on his lap with a thump that made him wince. "I hope we didn't."

"If she doesn't turn up soon, we can go and wait outside the barn. She'll come back."

Maria settled in, one hand braced on his bare knee. "Did you have a nightmare as well?"

"Sometimes."

"Billy said you were a soldier."

"A Marine, which means I was actually a sailor."

"On a ship?"

"Not really." He hesitated. "It's kind of complicated."

"Okay."

"Tonight I just couldn't sleep. How about you?"

"I dreamed my mom was dying and my dad—the man who I thought was my dad—was standing over her coffin screaming at her." She shivered.

"That must have been horrible."

"He didn't get angry at the real funeral. He was too drunk. Uncle Jim had to hold him up."

He hated the matter-of-fact way she accepted that. "Grief takes people in funny ways, Maria."

"That's what Billy says, too."

"Yeah, and he should know."

"Billy's stopped drinking now, though, hasn't he? He says my dad might come to his senses and do the same thing."

"I sure hope he does. He must've been a fool not to appreciate you."

She hunched her shoulders. "I'm not sure if he ever liked me much. I was always doing things wrong, you know? And the harder I tried, the worse it got. When Mom first got sick and he had to take care of me a lot, it was horrible. I didn't tell Mom, though."

"I can't think of a single reason why he wouldn't like you. You're awesome."

"You can't make people like you, though, can you?" Maria's breath hitched. "There was a boy at school I really liked, but he crushed on my friend Dayna."

"A boy? Aren't you a bit young for that?"

She elbowed him in the ribs. "I'm almost in *fifth grade*. I'm not a kindergartener."

Blue decided not to comment on that and mentally revised his future budget to include a private all-girls school.

"So what happened to *your* mom?"

He almost smiled. She was as tenacious as he was.

"Didn't Billy tell you?"

"No, he said it was something I should ask you."

Blue settled back against the wall. "A long time ago, she and my dad got into a fight and—"

"*Billy* did?"

"Yeah."

"Are you sure?" She frowned. "He's way too nice to fight with anyone."

"I was there, sweetheart. I heard them fighting. All us kids did. I was around your age at the time. My mom hadn't been doing too good since the birth of our baby sister, and she wasn't happy living at the ranch."

"Why not? Once you get used to the smell it's like super cool."

"She missed her family in the city, and she didn't like being out here in the middle of nowhere. Some people don't. So she and my dad had been fighting a lot."

She shivered and pressed closer to him. "I *hate* that."

"Chase and I would try and distract our little brothers when our parents went at it, but they knew things weren't right. One night my mom got really mad, and she tried to, um, hurt Billy. He managed to stop her but ended up unconscious. When he woke up, she'd gone and taken the baby with her."

"Gone where?"

"We don't know."

"How can you not know?" She turned around to stare at him, her arms folded across her chest in a way that reminded him of Ruth. "Can't you just look it up or *ask* someone?"

Ah, the Internet generation.

"We're trying. We thought she might be dead at first, and so did the cops, but after talking to Billy we realized she might have run away instead."

"Just like me."

He hugged her then, he couldn't stop himself. "You ran to the right place, honey."

A small black shape flitted through the shadows at the door, and the volume of noise coming from the kittens increased and then settled down again.

"The mama came back," Blue whispered. "Now we should go and leave them in peace."

He went still as she put her palm against his cheek, her blue gaze serious. "Maybe your mom will come back one day, too."

"Thanks. That would be awesome."

"I *know*."

He held her gaze. "You know I might be your dad, right?"

She nodded solemnly.

"And did you also know there are ways to find out if that's true."

"You mean like DNA tests?"

He nodded.

"My other dad said he was going to get one and prove I wasn't his kid."

"How would you feel about taking that test with me?"

She bit her lip. "It would be okay, I suppose." She suddenly scrambled off his lap. "I want to go in now."

"Sure." Blue didn't press her anymore. It was a lot for her to deal with already, and something had upset her. He wished he knew what it was or even how to ask. "You okay?"

"Can we come and see the kittens again tomorrow?"

He took her hand. "Absolutely. Now come on in and get back to bed."

She came with him willingly and he held the door into the house open for her, his finger to his lips to indicate she needed to keep quiet as she was near the parlor, where Ruth was watching TV. He pointed down at her ruined pink slippers.

"Leave them here."

She frowned down at her feet and kicked them off.

"Blue Boy Morgan, what are you doing creeping around at night?"

"She always did have ears on elastic." Blue cringed as

Ruth came out of the parlor. He tried to hide Maria behind his back.

"Sorry for disturbing you, Ruth. I went for a run, and now I'm going to shower and go to bed."

Ruth frowned and looked past him to the bottom of the stairs. "And why is Maria still up?"

"It was my fault." Blue turned fully toward Ruth. "There were new kittens in the barn, and I thought she might like to see them."

Ruth shook her head. "You haven't changed a bit. Always too impatient. You make sure Maria gets to bed right now, then."

"Yes, ma'am."

Ruth stomped back into the parlor and closed the door, leaving Blue staring down at Maria, who was fighting a smile.

"She told you off good."

"Yeah. She's had lots of practice." He started up the stairs and Maria followed him. "You use the bathroom, and I'll come and check up on you in a minute, okay?"

He went and washed up and returned to her door, knocking first and waiting until she gave him permission to come in. She was already in bed with only the night-light on and her music playing quietly in the background. Feeling rather out of place in the new flowery pink and orange décor, he perched uneasily on the side of the bed, dislodging several plushies.

"Thanks for not telling on me." Maria patted his knee.

"You're welcome. Do you think you'll be able to sleep now?"

"After seeing the kittens? Yes." Her smile was beautiful. "How about you?"

"I think I'll be fine." He leaned in and gently kissed the top of her head. "Night, sweetheart."

"Night, Blue." She hesitated. "If we do the test thing . . ."

"Yeah?"

"And I'm not your daughter either, will you kick me out?"

Blue reached out a hand to her. "Honey—"

She swallowed hard and looked away from him. "That was a silly thing to say. I know you can't answer it."

"I can't, but I understand why you asked. Having one dad bail on you means you don't want to have to go through it again with another one, right?"

She nodded. Suddenly her reluctance to interact with him made a whole lot more sense.

"All I can tell you is this. If you are my daughter, I'll be one hundred percent your dad. If you aren't, we'll find a way to make sure you get everything you need in this life to succeed anyway, okay?" He grimaced. "I'm not great with words, Maria, but if I say something you can guarantee I mean it."

"That's what Billy said about you, too." She yawned and covered her mouth. "I'm all sleepy."

"Then go to sleep, darlin'." He stood up. "I'll call Jenna in the morning and ask her to come and see if the kittens are okay."

"Okay."

She rolled onto her side and closed her eyes and was almost asleep before he even reached the door. She'd said more to him during the last hour than she had during the past weeks. But he got it now. She was guarding her heart against the potential disappointment of another father failure.

Blue went into his bedroom and contemplated a shower before deciding he'd be in more trouble with Ruth if he woke everyone up with gurgling Victorian plumbing at two in the morning. On impulse he got out his cell and typed a quick text to Jenna.

Hope all went well with Big Mac?

He was just about to get into bed when his phone buzzed and lit up.

They were awesome about everything. Thanks for checking in on me.

He smiled down at the screen like a besotted idiot. Who was he kidding? He *was* besotted. He wanted this woman. For the first time in his life he was willing to rearrange his schedule to make things right not just for Maria, but for Jenna as well.

You're welcome. Come up to ranch tomorrow?
We have new kittens in the barn.

Will do. I might as well live up there these days.
LOL

Hell, I wish you did.

Blue stared at what he'd typed and then across at his empty bed. He imagined Jenna spread out on it, her hair loose around her shoulders and her arms wrapped around him as he . . .

Yeah right, only because it would cut your vet bills if I was on staff.

True, but I was thinking about more personal things. He waited but there was no reply, so he typed again. Like you in my bed.

Still no reply.

You still there?

Yes. Just wondering if I have enough gas to make it out to the ranch right now. LOL

Blue slowly exhaled. I could come get you.
Again the wait felt like hours.

Blue . . .

He could almost hear the sigh in her text. He knew he wasn't being fair, but after his conversation with Maria and the nightmares he knew were waiting for him as soon as he closed his eyes, he wanted to be held by someone who cared for him.

Wow, he was not only arrogant but a complete wuss. He'd been telling her for weeks that having a relationship wasn't on his schedule, and now just because he was feeling vulnerable he expected her to come running. He typed fast, his thumbs flying.

It's okay. Just kidding. I know you've had a hell of a day. I'll see you tomorrow. Sleep tight.

He switched off his phone, stripped off his running gear, and climbed into his big, lonely bed. The cotton sheets smelled of lavender and the outdoors where they were hung to dry. He buried his nose in the pillow and inhaled the comforting scents of his childhood.

At least he'd made a connection with Maria, and he understood where she was coming from a lot better. He wasn't sure what he would've done if Billy had introduced a new mother to his kids. He suspected he would've reacted pretty much the same as Maria—convinced that this one might go away or stop loving him, too.

Poor little girl.

He closed his eyes and focused on how Maria's face had lit up when she'd seen the kittens and how it had felt to hold her in his arms. Those were good things. Hopefully they'd be enough to keep the nightmares away.

Jenna stared at Blue's last text until the letters danced around. Talk about a speedy retreat and shutdown. She couldn't complain that he hadn't picked up on her uncertainty and acted accordingly. Who would've thought he would be so considerate?

She texted him back.

Sure, see you tomorrow, night Blue.

Nothing came back, but she wasn't surprised. Blue Morgan was always decisive. So why was he up at two in the morning like she was? She at least had an excuse. Her uncle had listened quietly to everything she'd told him about Mark Lymond's mare and at the end said she'd done nothing wrong and that he was proud of her. She'd almost collapsed in a heap.

He'd also promised to forgo his daily game of golf and visit the Lymond place to talk to Mark the next day. She'd offered to go with him but he'd declined, saying he could handle Mark Lymond. She didn't doubt he could.

There was still no reply from Blue and she scrolled back to read his texts again. He wanted her in his bed . . .

"Rats."

Jenna lay down and stared up at the ceiling. Like she

was going to sleep now when Blue Morgan wanted her in his bed.

"He changed his mind, McDonald. He went to sleep like you should be doing. He doesn't have time for a *real* relationship." Jenna said the words aloud mainly to convince herself they were true. Her eyes refused to close. She did have enough gas to get to the ranch in the morning. Just about.

"Double rats."

She sat up and threw back the covers. The fact that he'd told her that he wanted her indicated he wasn't as hard-assed or as certain as he claimed. He'd been overseas. Maybe he was awake because his dreams were troubled. Heck, they'd seen enough blood today to give her nightmares, let alone him.

She put a fleece over her top, found her keys, and tiptoed down the stairs to the kitchen where her boots and socks sat by the back door alongside her medical bag. She wasn't really going to do this—was she? Her? Jenna McDonald, Miss Keep Out Of Trouble and Don't Disturb the Peace?

She fired up the engine of her truck and soon found herself approaching the circular drive in front of the Morgan ranch house. What if Ruth called the cops? Would Nate have to arrest her for breaking and entering?

"What the hell am I doing?" she whispered as she clambered out of the truck. "I'm really making a booty call on an ex-Marine who doesn't even know I'm coming?"

Her feet kept moving forward even as her brain objected. She went through into the hallway between the kitchen and the mudroom. All was quiet apart from the ticking of the big old clock in the parlor. The smell of peaches and sugar drifted in from the kitchen, and another qualm of doubt shook through her.

This was Ruth's *home*. She was behaving totally inappropriately.

She took off her boots and padded slowly up the stairs, pausing on the landing in a strip of silver moonlight to work out which door was Blue's. She knew which room belonged to January and Chase and which one was Maria's. That left three more, including a bathroom. It would certainly be embarrassing if she ended up climbing into bed with Ruth.

She walked slowly along the hallway, the old house creaking and settling around her, and studied each door as she passed. She smiled into the darkness when she read a plaque with Blue's name burned into the wood, which must have hung there since his childhood.

The door opened quietly under her hand and she went inside. Blue hadn't drawn the drapes and his bed was clearly visible, as was his shape sprawled out on the pillows. She hesitated, biting her lip. Something told her that walking up to a combat veteran and tapping him on the shoulder while he slept might not end well for either of them. Particularly her.

"Blue?"

"What the f—?" He sat up so fast she jumped and her back hit the door as he scrabbled for a weapon she hoped he didn't have.

After a few seconds he looked her way. She still couldn't see his face.

"Jenna?"

She briefly closed her eyes. This had been the most stupid idea of her entire life. Even more stupid than finding her birth parents. And potentially just as humiliating.

"Hey." She smiled even though she knew he probably couldn't see her properly. "I had enough gas. To get here, I mean, but—"

Oh God, he was coming toward her, moving like a big cat, and he smelled rumpled and delicious and he was completely naked and . . .

He put his hand beside her head on the door panel and leaned in to study her face.

"Am I dreaming this? Because you look damn real." His gaze dropped down to her torso. "Although if this was a dream I'm pretty sure you would be naked and not wearing fleece pants with ponies on them. What *is* it with those ponies? Maria loves them, too."

Her knees were threatening to give way just at the sound of his sleep-roughened voice. She reached out and cupped his jaw, feeling the brush of stubble against her palm, and almost died of lust.

"I know this isn't a good time, and—"

He kissed her very gently and she forgot how to form words as her arms went around his neck. With a soft sound, he gathered her close until she knew exactly how happy he was to see her.

"Come to bed, Jenna. Please."

She let him take her hand and lead her over to his bed, where the patchwork quilt had been pulled back to reveal the white sheets beneath. He laid her down, kissing each patch of skin he revealed as he slowly undressed her. When his mouth closed over her breast, she shuddered and threaded her fingers through his short hair to hold him exactly where she wanted him.

His hands roamed over her, touching and exploring as she moved against him and explored him herself. He was all hard lean muscle, so sleek and high performance that she could feel every sinuous stretch and curve of him flowing over and around her.

His hand slipped between her thighs and she moaned into his mouth as he discovered her slick welcome and slid one finger deep inside her.

"Beautiful Jenna," he murmured against her lips as his thumb settled over her as well, setting up a rhythm that made her rock into his touch seeking more. "Even better than my dreams."

She opened her eyes, wanting to see him, and found him waiting for her, his blue gaze narrowed and focused entirely on her and her pleasure.

"Do you want me, Jenna?"

"Yes."

He kissed her again, this time more possessively, while somehow managing to lean over, open his bedside drawer, and find protection. Her hand drifted down from the hardness of his ass around his hip to grasp his shaft, and he hissed a curse.

"Dammit, Jenna, keep doing that and it will be all over."

She grinned up at him. "You're a Marine. You're supposed to be one of the tough guys."

"Not when you're touching me." He sheathed himself and then slid home, both of them catching their breath as her body gave way to him. "God, I don't think I can . . ."

He started moving and she drew her feet up to clasp his hips as he rocked into her, one hand palming her ass, pressing her even closer into each thrust.

"Ah . . . Jenna, I'm . . ."

He thrust one last time and came, his arms braced on either side of her, his expression somewhere between desperate and horrified, which made her want to laugh. He remained over her, his breathing gradually returning to normal, and he looked her right in the eyes.

"I can't believe I did that."

She shrugged. "It's okay. A lot of guys can't manage more than a minute."

"I've never—" He stopped speaking and considered her. "Are you *laughing* at me?"

"I might be." She heaved a sigh. "I came all this way to see you and then I find I might not have bothered to come at all."

Silence and then he shifted slightly.

"Hold that thought."

She nodded as he pulled away and sorted himself out. She didn't make any attempt to move and just waited for his return.

He climbed onto the bed and straddled her, his blue eyes silver in the moonlight. "I can't have you coming all this way and being disappointed, can I?"

"Life is full of disappointments. Some men are just terrible in the sack. It's okay, you're still beautiful on the outside."

With a growl, he nipped her stomach and then moved lower, his wide shoulders spreading her thighs. And then his mouth was on her most precious parts, and God she was moaning and writhing as he added his fingers and everything dissolved into the kind of fiery bliss she'd only read about in romance novels.

After a while, when he'd reduced her to begging, he covered himself again and reintroduced her to his cock, and things got even better. This time when he eventually came she was with him, and that was the most extraordinary sensation of all.

With a deep groan, he rolled onto his back, and she draped herself bonelessly over him.

"Better?"

She managed a faint moan.

"Because we can try it again if it wasn't up to your exacting standards."

"Overachiever."

"Exactly." He kissed her throat and wrapped an arm low around her hips. "Thanks for coming."

She bit his shoulder and he pretended to groan and then she fell suddenly and unexpectedly asleep.

Chapter Twelve

Blue opened one eye and studied the curve of a very feminine throat and a tangle of reddish brown hair.

Not a dream, then.

Jenna McDonald was curled up beside him in his bed and he'd had the best night's sleep in months. Maybe even years. He figured from the extreme angle of the sun that it was just about dawn.

"Jenna," he murmured into her ear. "Are you awake?"

Which was a stupid question as she was snoring like one of Roy's piglets, but he was trying to be diplomatic.

Her eyes flew open and fixed on him.

"Oh God. I actually did it, didn't I?"

"You certainly did." He kissed her nose.

"I crept into your grandmother's house and ravished a serving member of the military." She pulled the sheet over her head. "You're a trained professional, right? Will you just kill me now?"

"And have all the trouble of having to explain why I have a dead body in my bed? It's not happening."

"Please?"

"Nope. I'd much rather you focused on serving that military member again."

She groaned. "No jokes. I can't even claim that I was drinking or anything. I just wanted to see you."

"Which I am totally okay about."

The sheet came down an inch. "You are? Because you have to know that this is totally out of character for me to do anything like this, I mean because I'm not normally the kind of girl who thinks she's the kind of girl any guy would want to turn up in his bed. Does that make sense?"

"No, but what do you want to do about it?"

She slowly disentangled herself from his arms and sat up. "You want me to go, don't you?"

"No, I want to know what *you* want to do next."

"About what?" She blinked at him like an owl.

Mornings obviously weren't her best time. Blue tried again. "Whether you want to come down and have breakfast with me, or whether you want to keep this to ourselves for a while longer."

"I can't go down with you. Ruth will think . . ." She made a face. "Ruth will think I sneaked into her house and had sex with you. Which is exactly what I did."

"She's more likely to think I smuggled you in, you can bet on that," Blue said. "I'm okay to take the blame if it makes things easier for you."

"You would?"

It was his turn to shrug. "I owe you."

She pleated the sheet between her fingers. "I've put you in a terrible position, haven't I?"

"No, you haven't." He patted her shoulder. "Look, how about I go use the bathroom. When I come back you can tell me what you've decided to do, okay?"

He pulled on his boxers and discarded running shorts and headed out to wash up. After the quickest shower of his life, he made his way back along the silent hallway to his room and went in.

"Coast is clear if you want to—" He stopped speaking and looked around the deserted room. "Where the hell did she go?"

Outside the cockerel crowed, which seemed fitting somehow. Blue dressed properly in jeans and a T-shirt before padding down the stairs in his socks to the kitchen, where he found a crockpot full of oatmeal and a note from Ruth telling them all to help themselves.

Moments later his grandma appeared and started cooking eggs and bacon, which always drew a crowd. Blue sat down and helped himself to oatmeal and then a plate of eggs and toast.

"BB, when you go down to the barn to start your chores, see if you can find Jenna and ask her if she wants to come up here for something to eat."

"Jenna?" Blue tried to sound surprised.

"Her truck's parked out front."

"You said she'd be coming to check out the new kittens," Maria added.

"Yeah." Blue carried on eating. Thank God for Maria inadvertently providing Jenna with an alibi. "I'll check her out as soon as I'm done."

"Can I come with you?" Maria asked.

"Sure." Blue looked up in surprise. To the best of his knowledge it was the first time Maria had ever asked to do anything with him. Billy winked at him.

Just as he reached for his napkin to wipe his mouth, the screen door banged and Jenna came in carrying her bag.

"Morning, everyone."

Ruth smiled at her. "Morning, darlin', now sit down and let me get you something to eat."

She took the seat opposite Blue, her gaze lowered and the color of her cheeks suspiciously high.

Blue sipped his coffee and contemplated her over the rim of his cup. "Jenna."

"Blue."

"You're out and about early."

"Yes."

"Did something come up?"

"Kind of." She shrugged. "You know how this job is."

She'd managed to comb her hair and tie it back, but if he looked closely he could still see the faint red mark where he'd bitten her throat.

"Were you up all night?"

"Part of it."

This time she did look right at him and he got the full "why don't you shut up" glare, but he wasn't giving up that easily. So she didn't want to be seen with him in public or acknowledge what had happened between them. That kind of stung.

She turned to thank Ruth for the plateful of food.

"Don't you just hate that when you can't sleep?" He shook his head. "I know I do."

Maria pointed her spoon at him. "Did you have bad dreams? I didn't. I dreamed about the kittens playing with my favorite ponies. It was *awesome*."

"Cool." Blue smiled at her. "I thought I had a really great dream, and when I woke up it had slipped away." He flinched as Jenna kicked him under the table. "Funny how that happens sometimes, isn't it?"

He picked up his empty plate and mug and stood up. "I've got chores to do. Maria, why don't you bring Jenna down to the barn when you've both finished eating and show her where the kittens are?"

"Okay."

Blue dropped his utensils in the dishwasher with a crash

that made Ruth complain and headed out, his good mood completely gone. He wasn't sure why he was surprised. Jenna probably didn't want Ruth to know she'd sneaked into the ranch house. He still couldn't believe she'd done it himself. It went against everything he thought he knew about her.

He picked up the bucket of kitchen scraps and put it on the counter in the feed room, trying to move quietly so as not to scare the kittens. A large scoop of chicken pellets mixed in with the scraps would make the free-range birds very happy indeed.

Outside the barn the sky was already set to clear blue, and the chickens were fretting to be released from their pen. As long as he had a stout pair of boots on, Blue didn't mind dealing with the birds at all. Chase still hated them. Blue had made lots of money as a kid doing Chase's chicken chores for him.

After releasing the chickens he fed the dogs and feral cats and then started on the horses in the barn. Shoveling soiled hay and horseshit sure kept his mind and body focused on anything but Jenna McDonald.

At some point he heard Maria's high-pitched voice and guessed she was bringing Jenna to see the kittens. He kept his head down and carried on with his work. If either of them wanted to talk to him, they knew where to find him.

Eventually he heard footsteps outside Nolly's stall.

"Jenna says the kittens look great."

"Yeah?"

He turned to smile at Maria, who was leaning over the half door of Nolly's stall feeding the horse a piece of apple.

"She said it would be really cool if I could keep an eye

on them and make sure the mama cat stayed around and to let her know if anything went wrong."

Blue straightened and leaned on the rake. "You can do that, right?"

Her face fell. "If I'm here."

"You will be if Ruth has anything to say about it."

"Ruth's awesome." Maria nodded. "And a bit scary at the same time."

"Exactly." Blue patted Nolly on the rump and eased past him. "You know how busy everyone gets around here? Having you taking on the responsibility of checking on the kittens would be super helpful."

"That's what Jenna said. I like her." Maria drew herself up to her full height. "Then I'll do my best." She looked up at Blue. "Can I go and tell Billy?"

"Sure. Maybe he could help you as well."

"He probably could." She skipped off in the direction of the house and Blue went across to the last stall where Sunflower, January's mare, resided.

"Blue? Can I talk to you for a minute?"

He turned to find Jenna behind him.

"What's up?"

She tugged at the end of her ponytail in a way Blue had come to recognize as a sign of discomfort. "I wanted to explain."

"There's nothing to explain. Actions speak louder than words, right?"

She took a hasty step closer. "I . . . panicked, okay? I tried to imagine how I was going to come down those stairs and look Ruth in the eye when I'd abused her hospitality and . . ."

"Shagged her grandson?"

"Well, I wasn't intending to admit that *out loud*, but I

assumed she'd work it out as soon as she saw me. It's just so unlike me to behave like that. It was so *unprofessional*."

"So you're going to pretend it didn't happen."

"That's not what I said."

"You ran away."

"I . . . made a tactical withdrawal in order to spare you, me, and your grandmother an embarrassing family moment."

He studied her for a long moment. "So which is it, Jenna?"

"I don't understand."

"Are you the woman who came to my bed, or are you just the family vet?"

"Can't I be both?"

"You tell me." He picked up the wheelbarrow handles. "Excuse me. I have to get this to the manure pile."

She didn't follow him, which was probably wise because he wanted to kiss her and throttle her at the same time. He wasn't going to do either of those things until she made a decision about who and what she wanted. Okay, he was pushing her, but she already knew he didn't deal in grays. If she wanted to have a relationship with him, they had to be completely on the same page. And seeing as she'd been the one to totally rewrite the verse and chapter they were currently on, surely he had a right to ask for some guarantees?

He dumped the manure and stood staring down at the steaming pile. Unless she'd really meant the bit about him just being a booty call . . .

Maybe he didn't know her at all.

* * *

Jenna turned back toward her truck, her footsteps slowing as she thought back through what Blue had said to her. Was she being a coward? That was what he'd implied. But it was all so easy for him. He knew who he was and never doubted his place in the world or that he could get what he wanted.

She'd never had that certainty. And every time she'd attempted to be brave and strike out by herself, she'd ended up worse off because she made stupid, reckless decisions.

Like sleeping with Blue Morgan.

She went to open the truck door and stopped. But did she regret that choice? She closed her eyes as her body remembered exactly how perfectly she and Blue had fit together and the pleasure he'd given her. Was she willing to give that up? Was she ready to stand up and declare they were a couple?

Jenna turned on her heel and headed back for the barn. There was no one around apart from Blue, who was busy in Sunflower's empty stall replacing the flattened straw with fresh sweet-smelling grasses.

"Hey."

He looked up at her, his blue gaze wary.

"You can't just go around making sweeping demands like that when I don't know where I stand with you."

He propped the rake against the wall and faced her. "You voluntarily came into my bed."

"That's where I stand. Or lie. But what about you?" She hesitated. "Maybe I forced the issue. I should've considered your perfectly legitimate objections to having a relationship with anyone at this point."

"I think we're beyond that now, don't you?"

"Not unless you want to be." She held his gaze. "I shouldn't have rushed you."

"I didn't exactly turn you away."

"You're a man. Of course you didn't."

He stiffened. "You're suggesting I would've been quite happy to see any woman turn up in my bed?"

Good Lord, now she'd offended him. "No, of course not. I just meant that I made a unilateral decision without adequately consulting with you first."

"Come again?"

She sighed. "I shouldn't have jumped you in your own bed."

He leaned one shoulder against the door frame and regarded her steadily. "Do you make a habit of it?"

"Jumping into men's beds? God, no."

"So you weren't just using me to scratch an itch."

The idea was so ludicrous that she actually gaped at him. "You're kidding, right?"

He shrugged. "Nope. Believe it or not, there are quite a few women who specialize in collecting men in uniform."

"Like a military buckle bunny?"

"Exactly."

"I'm not one of those." She held his gaze. "Is that how I made you feel?"

He half smiled. "Put it this way, leaving my bed without telling me was something of a clue. I suppose I should be glad I didn't find a twenty-buck note under the pillow."

"You're worth far more than twenty bucks."

"Yeah?" His smile this time was slower to come and more genuine.

"Not that I would've paid you because I don't think of you as a booty call—unless that's what you want me to think of you—because you aren't in the right place for a real relationship."

He stepped forward, stripped off his glove, and cupped her chin, his thumb tracing her lower lip.

"I've been meaning to tell you I changed my mind about that. Your preemptive strike last night kind of put me off my stride."

She grimaced. "I thought I'd pushed too hard and that you'd be glad to see me leave. I never meant to hurt you."

"Let's set a few things straight between us, shall we?" Blue said. "I know this isn't a good time for us to get together because I'm not at my best, but I don't want to be just a booty call."

"Okay."

"I want to be the only man in your bed, and I want us to be a couple. Is that clear enough for you?"

"Despite everything?"

"Yeah." He kissed her nose. "It's not going to be easy, and I think we need to keep it on the down-low until we sort out what's going on with Maria and get through Chase and January's wedding."

"Agreed."

"But I do want us to be together. Is that okay with you? Is that what you want?"

She nodded.

He searched her face. "I hate it when you go all quiet and acquiescent on me."

"It's only because you have overwhelmed me with your masterful logic."

"Masterful, eh?"

"Yes, please."

He kissed her properly this time, and within seconds she was pressed against the wall and his big body was covering her. His Stetson went flying when she wrapped her hand around his neck to hold him as close as she could.

"Ahem."

Jenna opened one eye and looked past Blue's shoulder to the door of the stall where Roy was watching them, a big grin on his face.

"So much for being discreet, Blue."

"You two should get a room." Roy chuckled. "Darn, I've *always* wanted to say that."

Blue bent to pick up his hat and then turned to Roy. "Keep this to yourself, okay?"

"You disrespecting Miss Jenna, BB Morgan?"

Jenna hastened to Roy's side. "No, there's just a lot going on at the moment and we don't want to make a big deal out of this until we see how we're getting along. I *have* just come out of a long relationship with Nate, so Blue might just be my rebound boyfriend."

Blue snorted.

Roy nodded as if she made perfect sense, which considering how much reality TV he and Ruth watched might actually be true.

"If he messes you around, young lady, you come and see me and I'll set him to rights."

"You going to put me over your knee and spank me, Roy?"

Roy looked Blue up and down. "If I have to."

"I'm sure it won't come to that," Jenna said hastily. "Now I have to get going. I promised January I'd meet with Yvonne in town to go over the menu for the wedding luncheon."

Blue caught her hand and reeled her back in for a kiss. "Come back here for dinner, okay?"

"I'll text you. I've got to help Uncle Ron with a surgical case this afternoon, and that could go on for a while."

She paused. "You could come over to my place. I can cook you dinner."

"You cook?"

"Sometimes."

He gave one of his decisive nods. "Then let's do that. Text me when you're ready and I'll come on over."

Chapter Thirteen

"So what was he like?"

Jenna frowned at Yvonne. "I'm not telling you that."

"Was he bad? Did he suck and not in a good way?"

"He was . . . everything I've ever wanted in a man."

Yvonne sat back, her muffin forgotten in her hand. "Wow."

Jenna shrugged as her cheeks heated. "We're keeping it quiet at the moment, so don't go telling everyone, okay?"

"Keeping what quiet?" January joined them at the table, holding a large white binder with the word "Wedding" on the front.

"Blue and Jenna."

"Oh that." January waved dismissively. "I called that weeks ago. In fact, you owe me ten bucks, Vonnie."

"You two were betting on me?" Jenna asked. "Your best *friend*?"

"Why not? There's not much else to do in a small town. And don't forget you called the January and Chase one and won ten bucks off me." Yvonne pushed the plate of cakes toward January. "How about I pay you off in éclairs?"

"Works for me." January happily helped herself. "Now

before we talk about the catering, can I ask you both something?"

Jenna nodded and so did Yvonne.

"Would you be my bridesmaids?"

"Really?" Jenna squeaked. "Oh my God, I'd *love* that. Thank you."

"So would I." Yvonne leaned in and the three of them had a big squishy girly hug.

"I thought you were never going to ask," Yvonne said and Jenna rolled her eyes at January, who was laughing. "Seeing as Chase is a billionaire, can we go for some McQueen like at the royal wedding?"

"We can talk about that after we decide on the catering," January said firmly.

Jenna sipped her cappuccino. "I'm not sure how much help I'm going to be. I've never organized a wedding, and I'm a vegetarian."

"Which is exactly why I want your input." January patted her arm. "I need to make sure that my non-meat-eating guests—and that includes half of the commune folk who are coming with my mom—get properly fed."

"Mrs. Hayes at the hotel is lending me her kitchen," Yvonne said, "and I've asked a good friend of mine from catering college who works in San Francisco to come and help me with the savory stuff, so we're all set. All we need is a menu and a budget."

January opened her file and took out some papers. "Here you go. What do you think of this?"

"Have you got a minute?"

Blue looked up from the form he was completing and beckoned Chase to come in. He was sitting at his old desk in his bedroom, enjoying the view out over the barn and the rolling foothills of the Sierras.

"I'm just finishing up some paperwork about pensions and stuff like that. I think I'm nearly done," Blue said. "I have to go back for one last week, and then I'm officially separated."

"Do you have to go into the reserve?" Chase asked.

"I could, but I don't have to. My name goes on the IRR list, the Individual Ready Reserve, for five years, but unless aliens wipe out our entire military I'm unlikely to be called in. And if that's happening, we'll have bigger problems than me being redeployed."

Chase came and sat on his bed. "Will you miss it?"

"The Marines? Some of it." Blue shrugged. "Some of it not so much. I lost some good friends, but I wouldn't be the man I am now if I hadn't joined up." He closed the paper file and swung his chair around to face his brother. "What can I do for you?"

"I've got a verified address for Big Mike. How do you want to deal with this? I can send someone from the agency to question him about what happened to Mom and Rachel, or we could do it ourselves."

"You're getting married. Don't you want to wait until after that?"

Chase looked down at the floor. "With our luck, I'm worried that he'll be gone before we get to see him."

"What about the other guy?"

"Red Williams?"

"Yeah. The one who was in prison in Sacramento."

"Well, I thought that if you were considering going to see Daniel Lester, you might consider talking to Red as well."

"I don't know if seeing Lester would be a good idea. At the moment, I'd still like to kill him."

"But if you did go . . ."

"I'll talk to Red."

"Thanks. If Red agrees to see you, I can arrange all the permissions with the state and the authorities."

"But that still leaves the problem of Big Mike. Do you want me to go see him as well?"

"I'd rather we did it together." Chase's blue eyes, which were so like his, met Blue's. "I have a gut feeling that Big Mike is the one who's going to tell us what we need to know. Red Williams is just a possibility to be discounted."

"I agree." Blue shifted in his seat. "So when do you want to go down there? I'll have to be free and clear of the Marines just in case I lose it and end up in jail."

Chase grinned at that. "Makes sense. I know we've waited a long time to solve this mystery. I just want it to be over. I want to know the truth."

"Yeah." Blue hesitated. "You know that not everything is always cut and dried? Sometimes when I was on a mission people didn't come back, and there was no way of piecing together exactly what had happened to them or why."

"Intellectually I understand that, but emotionally?" Chase grimaced. "I'm still a little boy who wants to know what happened to my mom and sister."

Blue had nothing to say to that.

Chase cleared his throat. "We're having the engagement party next week and the wedding a few months after that. We're having trouble settling on a date that works for everyone. I suggest we try and get down to San Diego sometime in between the two events and after you get out of the military."

"Sounds good to me."

"There is one more thing." Chase rubbed a hand over the back of his neck. "I wanted to ask if you'd be my best man."

"Me?"

"Yeah."

"What about Matt and Jake?"

Chase shrugged. "You're family."

"That's . . . really unexpected."

"It's okay, you don't have to do it." Chase stood. "I get that we've had our differences, and that you might not feel—"

"Hold up." Blue put up his hand. "I would be *honored* to stand up with you."

"Really?" Chase's grin was infectious.

"Yeah." Blue went forward and wrapped his arm around his brother, his throat suddenly tight. "Really, bro. I would be thrilled."

Chase's arm came around him and they hugged each other hard.

"Thanks, little Boy Blue."

"You're welcome, Trampas Chase Morgan." Blue stepped back. "Now all I have to do is persuade the twins to like you again, and we'll be a real family."

"Especially if we locate Mom and Rachel."

Blue slapped his brother on the back hard enough to make him rock in his boots. "When Billy turned up sober I decided miracles can happen, so dream on, brother, dream on."

"Dave?"

"Hey, what's up, Jenna?"

Jenna smiled sweetly at her big cousin, who was sitting at the kitchen table typing in some notes on his laptop while eating a handful of chips. She sat opposite him and his expression changed to wary.

"What?"

"I was wondering if you were planning on going out this evening?"

"Not really. Mom and Dad are staying at the golf place tonight, so I thought I could slob out in front of the TV and watch some horror flicks."

"I'd really appreciate it if you went out."

"Why?"

She raised her eyebrows. "Because I wanted to cook dinner for a friend?"

"Hey, is Yvonne coming over? Because I'll stick around for that. She's super hot."

"No, it's not Yvonne."

"Well, it can't be Nate because he says he dumped you."

"He did not dump *me*! I dumped him."

"Anyways"—Dave made a dismissive gesture—"so who is it?"

Jenna took a deep breath. "Blue Morgan."

"Hell."

"What's wrong with Blue?"

"Nothing. It's just that if you want to hang on to him, offering to cook probably wasn't your best idea."

"I can cook."

"Horrible piles of veggie burgers and stinking tofu."

"Actually, I was planning on liberating something from Aunt Amy's freezer and just adding my own little touches like bread and butter and salad."

"Sounds like a plan. And I bet you'll claim you cooked it all as well. Sweet."

"I wouldn't do that."

He gave her a skeptical look.

"I wouldn't because I know the moment my back was turned you'd tell him the truth."

Dave pressed a hand over his heart. "Cos, you wound me greatly. You're family. I wouldn't rat you out."

She fixed her gaze on him and fluttered her eyelashes. "So you'll do it? You'll go out?"

"Hell, no."

"Dave."

He grinned at her. "I will, however, take myself upstairs and promise not to intrude or notice what time Blue leaves the house, okay? I'm worn out, Jenna. I've been out on call three nights in a row. Another night out, even a good one, will kill me."

"Okay."

It was his family house, after all. She was still the interloper.

"I promise I won't tell the parents."

"Thanks."

"But you owe me."

"Definitely."

She checked the time and shot to her feet. "I'd better start cooking. There's vegetable lasagna in the freezer, which would do nicely. And Amy has that organic lettuce and stuff in the refrigerator. I can make a salad dressing."

"Cool." Dave returned to his typing. "Tell me when you want me to move, okay?"

She dropped a kiss on the top of his head. "Thanks, Dave, you're a star."

"You can thank me by introducing me to your friend Yvonne again."

"Will do."

"Not only is she great to look at, but she cooks like an angel."

"She's smart as a whip, too."

Dave sighed. "Don't say 'whip.'"

Jenna ruffled his hair and escaped into the pantry where

the large industrial freezer hummed away. Some of the vet's clients paid in kind, so they always had meat and vegetables to spare. She grimaced, as she had to move half a cow carcass out of the way to get to the lasagna. Amy had written clear instructions on the bag, so she was all set.

She had a feeling that Blue would prefer red meat, but she had no idea how to cook it. If in the future he wanted to indulge his carnivore instincts, he would have to sort it out himself.

Dave had turned the oven on, so she unwrapped the lasagna, checked the instructions again, and put it in to bake for an hour. The rest of it would have to wait until Dave left the table, which gave her plenty of time to take a shower.

Blue knocked on the back door of the fancy new log cabin–style McDonald home and waited and then waited some more. He'd showered and put on a new checked teal shirt and his most decent pair of jeans and boots. Eventually, he tried the handle and let himself in. The fragrant smell of browning cheese wafted along the hallway.

"Anyone home?" Blue called out.

"Dude!"

His heart sank as Dave strolled toward him wearing PJ bottoms with skulls on them and a vintage Star Wars T-shirt.

"Hey. What's up?"

Dave shook his hand. "It's all good. You coming for dinner? Jenna didn't say anything, but there's plenty of food." He put an arm around Blue's shoulder. "Come on in."

Blue glanced down at his new shirt. Maybe he'd misinterpreted Jenna's invitation and he was now going to be inspected by the whole of the McDonald clan. The vets vetting the vet. That was almost funny.

There was no sign of Jenna in the kitchen, but the table had been set for two with napkins and place mats and flowers in the middle. Blue turned back to Dave, who was grinning.

"You and Jenna always make this much fuss when you eat?"

"Yeah. We're real fancy, like royalty." Dave elbowed him in the side. "Nah. I'm off to bed. See you in the morning, lover boy."

Jenna came bursting into the kitchen from the pantry, two bottles of wine and a six-pack of beer clutched to her chest.

"What do you think he'll drink, Dave?"

"Ask him yourself." Dave backed out of the kitchen, his laptop in his hand. "Night, Jenna. Keep the noise down, kids, okay?"

Blue rushed over to rescue the beer from Jenna's faltering grasp and set it on the table.

"Hey."

She smiled up at him and suddenly everything was all right.

"Was Dave trolling you?"

He shrugged. "I wouldn't expect anything less."

"I tried to make him go out, but he was really tired, and it is his home."

He tucked a strand of errant brown hair behind her ear. "It's not a problem."

When she put the wine bottles down, he took a quick appreciative breath. "You look great. I think that's the first time I've seen you in a dress."

She smoothed a hand over her green patterned skirt. "I don't own many. They don't work very well with what

I do. But I'll have to wear one for January's wedding. She asked me and Yvonne to be her bridesmaids."

"Nice. Chase asked me to be his best man."

"That's awesome." She searched his face. "Isn't it?"

"I was shitty to him for a lot of years. I didn't expect him to forgive me so easily." He sighed. "He's a lot better at that forgiving thing than I am."

"You're just different people."

"But I always made such a big deal about being right about everything and refusing to change my mind. I'm starting to realize that there are a lot of grays in between those black and whites."

"Which means you can change." She held his gaze. "I always thought my birth mom would stay an addict, but you know what? She overcame that and went back to school to become a nurse and a trained counselor for substance abusers."

"Sounds like Billy. He's sober now and proving to be one heck of a grandfather to Maria." Blue shook his head. "I never in a million years thought he'd do that."

She stood on tiptoe and kissed his mouth. He took the invitation and kissed her back, wrapping one hand around her waist to keep her right where he wanted her.

Her stomach growled and he lifted his head.

"We should eat. You're going to need all your energy later."

"There's lasagna in the oven, so I've just got to make a salad and some dressing. Can you cut the bread?"

He did as she asked, appreciating her efficiency in the kitchen and the way she cleaned as she went along, meaning they wouldn't have to spend hours on cleanup when they could be doing far more interesting things.

"Do you want some beer?"

She glanced up from measuring the olive oil. "I'd rather

have a glass of red wine. Can you open the bottle and let it breathe a bit?"

"Don't have to worry about doing that for a beer." Blue demonstrated. "It just slides down fast and real nice."

The timer pinged. Blue was rewarded with the sight of Jenna's nice rounded ass as she bent down to take the lasagna out of the oven. Remembering his manners, he cleared a space for her on the countertop for the bubbling cheesy dish.

"That looks awesome. Did you make it?"

"It was Amy. I'm not a great cook, to be honest."

"I'm not bad." Blue picked up the large serving spoon. "Not that Ruth lets me try out my talents in her kitchen. She prefers to do it all herself."

"She is an amazing cook."

They loaded their plates with lasagna and headed for the table, where Blue lit the candles. Although the lasagna would've been improved with some meat, Blue still enjoyed it. Even better was the chance to sit and talk with Jenna without any ranch matters intruding. She was smart, funny, stubborn yet vulnerable and . . . jeez, he'd never met anyone like her.

"There's ice cream if you're still hungry?" Jenna said as she gathered the plates.

"I'm good. Tell Amy that lasagna was spectacular." He rose to his feet. "Let me do that."

"You can load the dishwasher while I make some coffee, okay?"

"God, I love dishwashers." Blue rinsed and stacked the plates and bowls. "When we were kids, doing the dishes was our job and I hated it."

He'd just about finished when his cell buzzed. "You okay if I check who this message is from?" he asked Jenna.

"Chase has just flown out of town, so I'm in charge at the ranch."

"Go ahead."

He wandered back into the den and fished out his cell. There was a voice mail sign flashing, so he held the phone to his ear to listen.

"Hey, it's Ry."

Frowning, Blue pressed Return Call and waited until his younger brother picked up.

"What's up?"

"Nothing much." His brother wasn't known for being talkative. He left that to his twin. "I'm coming to the engagement party."

"You are? That's awesome."

"HW won't come."

"Okay. Do you need a ride or some kind of ticket, because—"

"Nope. I'm good. I'll see you there. Later."

The connection went dead and Blue stared at his phone.

"Everything okay?" Jenna called from the kitchen as she brought in the coffee.

"Yeah, actually. Ry's coming to the engagement party."

"Ray? Is that one of your brothers?"

Blue sat on the couch and patted the seat next to him. "It's not Ray, it's an 'R' and a 'Y' from his initials and yeah, he's the ten-minute older and much quieter of the twins."

Jenna set the tray on the coffee table. "Does he have another of those weird TV cowboy names?"

"He does, which is why he goes by Ry. I can't believe he's decided to come out here for the party."

"I got the impression from January that the twins never visit."

"They took against Chase for a long while." Blue grimaced. "A lot of that was my fault, seeing as the reality was that he practically brought us up. Somehow we all ended up resenting him for that, which was totally unfair."

She curled up against his side and rested her head on his shoulder. "I know how that feels. I was the oldest, and when my mom wasn't . . . present, I had to try and bring up my siblings. They all hated me."

"I've been working on the twins for the last few months to get them to come back to the ranch, and I know Ruth has been, too. Ry was always the more thoughtful of the two, so I'm not surprised he's the one who's decided to check out the lay of the land."

"Does he look like you or Chase?"

"The twins are identical and are fair-haired like my grandfather, with a lot of reds and golds mixed in there like a field of wheat."

"Are they easy to tell apart?"

"Nope. They used to switch identities all the time. It drove everyone nuts."

He poured out two mugs of coffee and handed one to Jenna.

"What do they do now?"

"They both went into the rodeo business."

Jenna shuddered. "Ugh."

"Yeah, I know: injuries guaranteed both to the animals and the riders. I'm not sure exactly what they are doing right now, but HW used to ride saddle broncs and Ry the bulls."

"Both crazy, then."

"Exactly. But if we can convince Ry that Chase means him no harm, and that we all want to be a family again, maybe HW will come along to the wedding as well."

"Family's important to you, isn't it?"

"I suppose it is. I tried to get away from the ranch and my family when I went into the Marines, but all that did was make me realize how much I'd lost." He smiled at her. "The old clichés are always the best, aren't they? Despite everything that happened with my parents and all my resentment over Chase when I got back here none of it mattered. This place has a way of reminding you how small and insignificant you are in the big scheme of life."

"Maybe somewhere at your core you knew that the ranch and your family would always be here when you really needed them."

There was a wistful note in Jenna's voice that she couldn't quite disguise.

"I knew Ruth would never give up on me. My brothers? Not so much." He glanced down at her intent face. "Don't go around thinking I was the injured party in all this. I *caused* the rift with Chase, and I made sure the twins stayed right in line behind me. I tend to be inflexible."

"Really? I would never have guessed that."

He considered her for a long moment. "Are you going to put that mug down?"

"Why?"

He took it out of her hand and put it on the coffee table. "Because—" He rolled her over until she was on her back and he was straddling her waist. "I don't want to get coffee on that nice green dress of yours."

He bent his head and kissed her and murmured in satisfaction as she kissed him back.

"Beast." She nipped his lower lip.

"Grrr." He eased one hand over her shoulder to cup her breast. "Did you say something earlier about dessert?"

"I might have."

"Then can I take it upstairs?"

"You don't want to hang out in the den?"

"Not if Dave is going to walk in at any moment and start critiquing my style."

"Like Dave would know anything." She wrinkled her nose. "Not that I even want to t*hink* about that because . . . eew, gross."

"I'm fairly sure he'd feel the same way, but I'm not taking the chance that my naked ass will end up on the Internet courtesy of Dave's camera."

"That's just the kind of thing he would do. Like a 'whose ass is this?' contest or something. Mind you, with your tattoo of the eagle, globe, and anchor I don't think anyone would have any problem guessing who you were."

Blue rolled off the couch and drew Jenna to her feet. "Does your bedroom door have a lock on it?"

"Yes."

"Then let's go."

He followed her up the stairs as quietly as he could, ignoring the loud soundtrack of the movie Dave was watching that was making his door shake. He didn't think Jenna would scream too loud, but you never knew. She turned to him at the door.

"It's not really my room. It's Faith's, but I'm borrowing it until she decides whether she's coming back after completing college."

There it was again, that hint of uncertainty, as if Jenna always felt like she was on the outside looking in.

He framed her face with his hands and kissed her slow and deep. "I don't care about the room. I care about who's in it."

"That's a terribly sweet thing to say."

"That's me all over. Sweet. So lick me up."

She returned the kiss and he held her close, stealthily unzipping the back of her dress and sliding the straps off her shoulders to reveal the silky layer of her bra and panties. He wished she wore more dresses. It would make getting her naked so much faster and easier.

He kissed his way down her throat and nuzzled her breast. "Nice bra. Did you wear it for me?"

"Yes, I'm not really a silk and lace kind of person. Yvonne made me buy this set when we went shopping in the city."

He curved a hand over her hip and down over the softness of her silk-clad ass. "Remind me to thank Yvonne one day. You feel awesome."

He backed her up toward the bed and lowered her down onto the covers.

"Do you want me, Jenna?"

"Yes, please."

"So polite."

She pointed at his shirt. "I won't be polite if you don't start getting naked pretty soon."

"You threatening me?" He started on the buttons of his shirt, pulling it free of his jeans and tossing it over the nearest chair. She wiggled a little on the bed and he fumbled with his belt as he took in the sight of her waiting for him, one hand under her head, her auburn hair spread out over the pillow.

He wanted to keep that picture in his head forever . . .

"Blue?"

Now she sounded worried. Knowing her ability to leap to conclusions, he took off his belt and carefully undid his jeans, protecting his overenthusiastic cock from the perils of a hastily pulled zipper.

"You are so beautiful," she breathed.

"Me?" Blue looked down at himself. "I'm fit because I've worked hard at it, but—"

"Beautiful," she said firmly. "Now get down here and ravish me."

"Yes, ma'am."

That wouldn't be a hardship at all. There was something

about her combination of strength and vulnerability that ticked all the right boxes for him. He couldn't explain it to himself, and at that moment with a warm, willing woman ordering him to make love to her, his rational side was disappearing rapidly and he just wanted to be inside her.

He climbed onto the bed and gathered her in his arms. First he was going to see if he could make her scream louder than the soundtrack of Dave's horror flick.

Then he was going to make love to her for hours. He smiled against her mouth as he kissed her. She'd have no cause for complaints, he'd make sure of that. And if he lost himself in there with her? For the first time in his life, that was a chance he was more than willing to take.

Chapter Fourteen

"This was a stupid idea." January consulted her clipboard and ticked something else off the apparently endless list. They were down by the creek setting up the tables and chairs for the engagement party, and things were getting complicated.

"No, it's all good." Jenna hastened to reassure her friend. She'd gotten off work early and come to help with the setup. It was just after three, and the party was scheduled for six o'clock. "Once we've gotten all these major details ironed out, it will all proceed perfectly."

"I should've listened to Chase and let him bring proper caterers in."

"And spoil Ruth's fun cooking for you?" Jenna grinned at January. "She's in her element."

"True." They both looked over at Ruth, who was busy telling Chase and Blue what to do. Both men looked resigned to being nagged and more than willing to do their grandma's bidding. The amount of food Ruth had produced for the party was quite staggering.

"Do you want me to start putting the table coverings on?" Jenna asked. "Avery's coming from the hotel, Yvonne's closing up early, and will bring more desserts and fresh bread with her."

"Sure, go ahead. The cloths are in the back of Chase's truck, along with the place mats and the table decorations."

Jenna patted January's shoulder and made her way across to where all the trucks were parked. The sun was shining and the forecast hadn't mentioned rain, so she was fairly confident the party would go well.

Maria sat on the back of Blue's truck with Billy watching the proceedings, and Jenna called out to them.

"You two want to help set the tables?"

Billy lifted Maria down from the tailgate and they came over hand in hand.

"What can we do for you, Jenna?"

She handed Billy a stack of folded linen tablecloths that Ruth had borrowed from the Hayes family at the hotel. "Spread these out on the tables while Maria puts the place mats on, and I'll add the flowers."

"The flowers are so pretty." Maria gently touched the petals of a yellow rose. "Did Daisy at the flower shop do them?"

"She did."

"I'd like to do that when I grow up."

"That's a *great* idea. You could help out with all the weddings and stuff on the ranch."

Maria's smile wobbled. "If I'm still here."

Jenna sat on the bench so that her face was level with the little girl. "I think everyone here *wants* you to stay. That must make you feel good, right?"

"Sometimes." Maria sighed. "And then I get worried because what if things change again?"

Jenna held her gaze. "Yeah, I used to worry about that

a lot, too, even after I was adopted by the McDonalds, but things did work out in the end. There are still good people in this world who don't change their minds about the important stuff. I think the Morgan family are the good guys."

Maria nodded and looked away at the boxes Jenna had set on the tables. "Look! There are candles in there, too, so we can light them when it gets dark." She picked up a pile of place mats and danced after Billy, indicating the conversation was over. Jenna hoped she'd done some good as she attempted to pick up the shallow but large box containing a dozen flower arrangements.

"You okay with that?"

She looked up to find Blue behind her. He wore a gray Marine-related T-shirt and old jeans, and there was a smear of dirt on his cheek that made him look even hotter than usual. She found herself smiling at him like a besotted fool.

"I'm good."

He nodded and stepped back. "Need any help with anything else? Chase and I have just about finished setting up all the tables, chairs, and the awnings."

"I'm good. I've got Maria and Billy helping me out." She hesitated. "Is Maria okay?"

"In what way?" His gaze intensified. "Did she say anything to you?"

"She's just worried about her future. I tried to reassure her but—"

He cut across her. "I'll talk to her."

Jenna sighed. "Blue, this isn't something you can fix overnight. She's going to need time to learn to trust anyone again."

"I get that."

"Then don't go rushing in trying to make everything right, okay? The best thing you can do is provide her with a consistent and loving environment."

He nodded decisively. "I hear you."

He was about to turn away when she caught his hand. "I'm not trying to interfere or anything. It's just that—"

He squeezed her fingers hard. "Jenna, trust me. Anything you tell me at this point in time is golden. You understand what she's going through better than any of us."

"Okay then." She released her grip on him.

"Cool." He tipped his hat to her. "Then I'll start moving that mountain of beverages closer to the food tables. I'm not sure how many people were invited tonight, but I'm expecting the whole of Nor Cal."

She smiled and then realized if she didn't get moving fast, she was about to drop the entire box on his boots. Not wanting to look like a wuss, she gathered her strength and tottered after Billy, placing the box carefully on the first of the long trestle tables.

"Two flower things for each table, I think, Maria."

As she worked, she couldn't help the odd glance back at Blue, who was shifting packs of water and beer as if they weighed nothing. He really did understand her. It was a pleasure to watch him in motion—especially now, as she was well acquainted with all that strength up close and personal.

She stared at his back. She would have to be careful. He would be so easy to love . . . Sure, he was exasperating and bossy, but his heart was in the right place. It must be nice to be so sure of everything. She'd had to fight for every speck of confidence she had. She'd also had enough therapy to realize that no one could give her that sense of self-worth but herself, so she wasn't expecting some man to rescue her. Most days she was proud of what she'd achieved and knew that if it came down to it, she was a survivor.

The thing was . . . Blue Morgan made her want more than that. He made her want to be someone's number one priority. She had a sense that if he decided to love you, then you were set for life. But deserving that love, and living up to it? She got the feeling he wasn't very good at forgiving failure in himself or in anyone else. Would she want to risk all she had achieved in her life just for a shot at something even better? That was the million-dollar question, and it was one she wasn't ready to answer yet.

So she would enjoy what she had and maybe allow herself to hope things might get even better.

"What time is Ry showing up?" Chase asked.

"I've already told you about six times. I don't know. He's not exactly chatty."

"But he did say he was coming?"

Blue shot his brother an exasperated look as he stacked another case of water on top of the tower. "I know you like everything to be organized, but I can't help you. If he said he was coming, he'll turn up. That's it."

Chase grimaced. "Sorry. I'm just anxious about seeing him again."

"I get it." Blue bent to pick up another load of water. "The fact that he decided to come is a major indicator that he wants to make things better. I've been at him for months to get down here."

"Thanks." Chase hoisted a box of beer onto the table, making all the glass clink together, and split the cardboard open with his knife. "Ruth's been nagging them, too."

"And that usually works. You and I came back, didn't we?"

Chase smiled for the first time. "Yeah, we did. I'm glad about that and that we found a way to save the ranch." He put the beer into one of the waiting ice chests and closed the lid. "Maybe one day the twins will want to make the ranch their home as well. Plenty of places to build a house on Morgan land."

"Yeah, about that . . ." Blue straightened. "I'd like to have my own place one day."

"Sure. After the party, we can sit down as a family and work out where you want to put it."

"Really?"

Chase shrugged. "Hell, we're going to be constructing all those guest cottages in the next few months, so why not take advantage of that and get your own place started?"

"That would be awesome." Blue took off his gloves. "I kind of picked out a spot I liked a few weeks ago. I've never had my own house."

"Then it's about time that you did." Chase nodded and then looked over Blue's shoulder. "Who's that?"

An unfamiliar brown truck had drawn up alongside Blue's.

"No idea. Let's go and find out."

Blue led the way, watching carefully as a man got out of the driver's side and stood looking up at the menacing backdrop of the Sierra Nevada. He whistled and then turned to Blue, who had to look up at him. He was about an inch shorter than Chase, who topped out at six-foot-two.

"Dude. I'd forgotten that view."

"Ry?" Blue held out his hand.

"Yeah." Ry offered his own. "You're definitely BB, so this must be TC."

"Chase." Chase held out his hand. "It's good to see you."

Ry looked Chase over, his expression serious. "BB says you're okay, so I suppose I have to give you a chance."

"You don't have to, but I'd be glad if you would." Chase hesitated. "I should've reached out to you more often, but I got so busy with my own life that I let everything else go."

"It's okay." Ry shrugged. "Me and HW had each other."

"Will you stay for a few days?" Chase asked. "There's a lot to talk about."

"Sure." Ry looked over at the tables. "Is that Ruth over there? Cool." He strode away, leaving Blue staring at Chase.

"Is it really going to be that easy?" Chase grimaced. "I thought it would be like talking to you in those early days."

"Ry's nothing like me. He's deep."

"True, so I bet he's got a few things to say. We'll just have to wait him out."

Blue was just about to walk away when he thought of something. "I didn't tell him Billy was here. Did you?"

"How could I? Ry's not been communicating with me."

"Hell." Blue set off toward Ry and Ruth, but Billy and Maria were already on an intercept path heading back to Chase's truck. He heard Ruth call out to her son.

"Billy, come over and see who's here."

Blue picked up his pace as Billy slowly turned to look up at Ry.

"Good to see you, Dad."

To Blue's astonishment Ry enveloped Billy in a one-arm hug, which was warmly returned.

"You two are okay with each other?" Blue asked.

"Sure." Ry's golden gaze fastened on him. "We're cool. Dad came out and saw me and HW at the rodeo whenever he could."

"Did he?"

Billy's smile dimmed as he detached himself from Ry and faced Blue.

"BB—"

Blue opened his mouth and was distracted by a pull on his sleeve.

"Don't be mean to him."

He looked down at Maria. "I'm not going to be mean. I just asked a question."

Her eyes filled with tears. "But you made him sad."

"I . . . didn't mean to do that. I didn't know Billy was seeing my brothers when I wouldn't let him see me. So if anyone should be sad, it should be me for being a complete ass."

"Okay." She patted his arm. "Now, say sorry."

Blue looked up at his father and Ry. "She's right. I'm sorry."

Another tug brought his head down and Maria planted a kiss on his chin. "Now don't you feel so much better?"

He smiled at her. "Actually, I do. Where did you learn to be so smart?"

"My mom."

"She must have been a very special lady."

Maria nodded and then skipped after Ruth, who was busy with the exact placement of the food.

"Who's the little girl?" Ry asked.

"Her name's Maria." Blue met his gaze. "That's a story for another day. For now, just remember she's family, okay?"

He nodded at his younger brother and went back to finish sorting the beverages. No doubt Billy would fill Ry in on the details of Maria's parentage. His hand curled into a fist.

So he really had been the only one of Billy's sons to

completely repudiate his father? All the others had grown up and realized there were more sides to a story than you could ever imagine. Except he hadn't learned that. He was late to the party as usual, due to his inflexible nature.

"Are you okay?"

He was staring so hard at the ground that he almost walked into Jenna and had to catch her by the elbows to stop her from falling.

"Yeah, I'm good."

"You don't look it."

"I'm yet again realizing what an idiot I've been."

"What happened?"

"Just family stuff."

"Ah, okay." She took the hint and tried to ease out of his grasp, but for some reason he held on.

"I used to think that knowing right from wrong, and black from white, was the only way to live. I *thought* that if I stuck with those certainties, then I wouldn't go wrong or stray from the right path."

"And there's nothing wrong with that."

"But there is. You end up blinkered, and you hurt people."

She cupped his cheek. "Real bigots never realize that, Blue, so I think you're doing okay. There's nothing wrong with having standards and principles. Where would we be without them?"

He slowly exhaled. "When did you get so sensible?"

"Just lucky, I guess." Her mouth quirked up at the corner. "And about twenty thousand dollars of family therapy during my childhood. I'm very good at handing out advice."

"Do you know what Ruth's idea of family therapy was? Cleaning out the barn together. She had a theory that if she wore us all out, we wouldn't have the energy to fight or be miserable."

"Did it work?"

"Yeah. She and Chase somehow got the rest of us through our childhood. Maybe I need to work harder."

"I can think of one way for you to expend some energy."

"Right here and right now?" He waggled his eyebrows at her. "What was that about being discreet?"

"I meant you could help Chase with setting up the dais, idiot, but I see Ry is already helping him."

He kissed her on the nose. "Come on, I'll introduce you to my little brother. He's the quiet one of the family."

"Well, one of you had to be. He's tall. I can't believe he rode bulls."

"Yeah. I'll need to get a ladder if I want to get in his face."

"Or stand on a chair."

They'd reached his brothers, and he was still holding Jenna's hand.

"Ry. This is Jenna. She's one of the McDonalds."

Jenna smiled. "Nice to meet you."

"What's up?" Ry looked from her to Blue. "You're Dave's sister, right?"

"No, his cousin."

"She's from the prettier side of the family." Blue wrapped an arm around her shoulders and squeezed her tight. "And she's a damn fine vet."

"Nice."

"She's helping us get the horses ready for the guest ranch," Chase chimed in as he finished haphazardly banging in a nail Blue was fairly certain he was going to have to replace if he didn't want the dais to collapse.

"Cool."

As they walked away, Jenna looked up at Blue. "You're

right, he doesn't say much. I like him already, and he has such pretty eyes. They're almost as golden as his hair."

"Hmmph." Blue considered his younger brother. "I hadn't noticed."

"Don't worry, all the women will."

"Yeah, but five seconds of conversation with him, and they'll all be running for the hills."

Jenna cast a speculative glance back at Ry over her shoulder. "I dunno about that. Sometimes you don't want them to talk much."

"Jenna McDonald . . ."

She grinned at Blue and backed away. "Just kidding. Gotta go help January before she has a meltdown."

Blue slowly shook his head. Every time he was with her, she surprised him. It was like watching a tight flower bud unfurl into something glorious. He almost laughed at himself. Where had that come from? He sounded all romantic and shit. But he'd never had such strong feelings for anyone before in his life.

Ruth was beckoning imperiously and he knew better than to ignore her. There were lights to string around the trees and a parking lot to organize. Hopefully, after that he'd be able to get a shower and change into something clean. There was only an hour before the official start of the party, so he'd better get a move on.

"Do I look okay?"

Jenna turned from adding another layer of mascara to find January right behind her.

"You look *beautiful*."

January worried at her lip. "Really? Because I want to

look nice for Chase and I'm not used to wearing expensive clothing, and I'm worried I look like an imposter."

"Yvonne helped you choose this dress, right?"

"Yes."

"And is she ever wrong about anything concerning clothes?"

"No."

"Which is why you can be sure you look beautiful," Jenna said firmly. "And Chase wouldn't notice if you turned up in a feed sack. He's totally in love with you."

January finally smiled. "He is, isn't he? God knows why."

"Because you are awesome." Jenna patted January's shoulder. "Believe."

"It's hard sometimes because Kevin—"

"Kevin was and continues to be a first-class douche."

"True." January nodded. "Thanks for reminding me." She sat down at the vanity and smoothed moisturizer on her face. "You look great, too."

"Oh, this old thing." Jenna was wearing her favorite green dress. Blue had already seen it twice, but she didn't have the funds or the time to go shopping, and Yvonne wouldn't let her go on her own.

She took out her cell to check the time, as she had been given the responsibility of getting January to the party, and noticed a screen full of messages.

"Wow, Chase set up five-minute alerts to keep me on track."

"He would. The big nerd."

Jenna's smile died as she scrolled past Chase's texts to another set she'd missed while she was busy setting up the party.

"Oh dear God, no," Jenna breathed.

"What?" January swiveled around in her seat. "Is something wrong? Has Kevin turned up?"

"No, you're good . . . it's just that . . ." Jenna could barely form words. "My parents gave my sister my address, and apparently she's passing through, and . . ."

"Cool! You can invite her to the party." January paused. "Or tell her you have the plague, whatever works best for you."

"She knows about the party." Jenna sucked in a breath. "She's asking whether you'd mind if she and her boyfriend dropped by."

"If you don't want her here, I can always say no, and you can blame the bridezilla." January fixed her gaze on Jenna. "Is she a problem?"

"No, she's . . . gorgeous and successful, and self-confident, and I usually need a week to prepare myself to deal with her, you know? She's very fond of me and wants me to be happy, but she doesn't see any way but her way."

"Sounds a bit like the Morgans."

"I suppose she is." Jenna sat on the edge of the bed. "I'll have to see her. If I don't, she'll get worried and report back to Mom, and then my parents will come up here to see if I'm really okay and . . ." She waved her hand around in a spiraling gesture. "All hell will break loose."

"Then tell her she's welcome."

Jenna tapped in a reply, pressed Send, and held her breath.

"She's coming, She'll be here around six thirty."

Blue took a moment to walk around the perimeter of the parking lot and make sure the two Hayes boys he'd hired to direct traffic knew what they were doing. He had no doubt they'd do a good job. They were almost professionals after the spring branding season and their stints working the Morgantown festival. And he was paying them, which sometimes their parents didn't.

Looking back at the soft lights decorating the California oaks that reflected on the water in the creek made him smile. It was one hell of a place to hold a party. He must ask Chase and January if they'd decided to do weddings at the new guest ranch. He'd bet they'd make a killing.

It was good to be home, and these quiet moments before all the guests descended on the place were extra special. Being able to share this evening with his brothers, his grandma, and Maria made him more thankful than he could ever have imagined. And then there was Jenna. The frosting on his particular cake, the unexpected missing part of him that made sense of everything he was.

Bad timing—what with leaving the Marines, finding out he had a daughter, and starting a whole new adventure with the family ranch—but too good to let go. The roar of a V8 engine punctured the silence, and the familiar blue of Chase's massive truck turned into the parking area and drew up almost beside him.

Chase got out followed by Ry, who appeared to have exchanged one faded T-shirt for another one and possibly washed his hair in preparation for the event.

"Hey," Ry acknowledged him and then turned to open the door to help Ruth out. She was wearing a dress that he thought he recognized from his going-to-church days as a kid.

"Where's January?" Blue asked as Ruth started handing him stuff out of the truck and issuing orders nineteen to the dozen.

"She's coming with Jenna."

Chase's usual relaxed expression was absent as they walked toward the dais.

"You worried she won't turn up?" Blue teased.

"Yeah."

"It's not your wedding day." Blue punched his arm. "Dude, she loves you, anyone can see that."

"Yeah, but—"

"And then there's all your millions . . ."

Chase stopped moving. "January doesn't care about money."

"Exactly." Blue swung around and stared right into his brother's eyes. "So don't stress, okay?"

"Okay. But can you just text Jenna and make sure she's on schedule? She hasn't been replying to my one-minute alerts."

Blue rolled his eyes. "Really?"

Chase turned away, and Ry joined Blue on the dais where Ruth had started to light the candles.

"He's not like I remembered."

"Who, Chase?"

"Yeah."

"In what way?"

"He's a lot more . . . human, you know?"

"Thank January for that."

"She's cool."

"Yeah."

"So's Jenna."

"She's taken."

"Dude. Like I didn't notice." Ry winked at him and sauntered away, hands in his pockets, golden eyes gleaming with quiet amusement.

Blue heard another familiar engine and looked across to see January's old truck coming through the open gate.

Roy and the hands had moved the cattle and horses farther down the pasture so there was no danger of any runaways joining the party. Escaping behind Ruth's back, he walked down to meet the truck.

Jenna wore her green dress. She'd pinned her hair up in some kind of soft style on the top of her head, which immediately made him want to slide his fingers in there and mess it all up.

January looked . . .

"Wow." Blue grinned at her. "Look at you, beautiful lady. Chase is a lucky man."

Her smile was so hopeful it literally made him choke up. He immediately cleared his throat and offered both of them an arm.

"Can I escort you both to the party?"

"Now who's being all fancy?" January poked him in the ribs. "Is Chase okay? Jenna was threatening to shut off her cell if he didn't stop checking in on her."

"He was just being his usual overanxious self."

"I suppose I should be glad he didn't send a security team to escort me from my bedroom to the creek."

Blue chuckled as he spotted his older brother talking to Ruth.

"Hey, TC! Someone's here for you."

Chase's expression when he turned around and saw January was another of those moments that Blue would always remember. How his brother had overcome his fear of intimacy and let himself be loved was a lesson Blue was beginning to want to learn.

January walked toward Chase. He met her halfway and kissed the living daylights out of her.

Beside Blue Jenna sighed.

"That's *so* nice."

"Nice?" He looked down at her. "It's epic. I'm practically blubbing like a baby here."

"You are not." She searched his face. "You're a big bad Marine."

"And he's my big bro, and it's way cooler than I thought it would be to see him being happy for the first time in his life."

She stood on tiptoe and kissed him firmly on the mouth. "Blue Morgan a romantic. Who would've thought it?"

He kissed her back. "You?"

"Yeah, but that's our little secret."

"True."

A sharp poke in the back had him turning to see Ruth.

"When you've finished canoodling, can you talk to the band? They've just arrived and need help setting up."

"Canoodling?"

"You know what I mean." She gave him her best death glare.

"I can do that." Ry wandered over in the direction of the second raised dais.

Ruth pointed at Blue. "Then you can start setting out the water bottles and plastic cups."

"Yes, ma'am." Blue tipped his hat to his grandma and sighed. "Will you help me, Jenna?"

"Sure."

"She's going to help me finish sorting out the food." Jenna was led firmly away by Ruth in the other direction. She looked helplessly back over her shoulder and Blue winked at her. If he wasn't careful, he and Jenna would spend the entire night apart. But he was a Marine. Tactics were his forte, and he had no intention of allowing that to happen.

He checked his watch as a procession of trucks and

SUVs bounced their way down the dusty track toward the party area. Behind him the band was tuning up, and Ruth was in her element. It was going to be a great evening, and he was going to spend it with Jenna, Maria, and the rest of his ever-increasing family.

Life was good.

Chapter Fifteen

"Jenna?"

Blue snagged hold of Jenna's hand as she went by him and drew her close against the noise of the band and the chatter of the happy guests. Maria was being whirled around the dance floor by Billy, and the pair of them were laughing at each other. January was slow dancing with Chase, and they might as well have been the only people there. The party was a blast, and Chase and January were rocking it.

"What's wrong?"

She raised her face to his, her expression troubled. "My sister's here."

"Were you expecting her?"

"As of about two hours ago. January knows, and she said it was okay."

"Which sister?"

"Lily."

"The older one, right?"

"Correct. She's just arrived. I'm going down to find her." He took her hand.

"You don't have to come with me."

"I'd like to." Blue raised an eyebrow. "Unless you don't want her to know about me?"

"I'm fine about that, I just thought you might have better things to do with your time, like talk to Ry."

Blue glanced over to the tables where he could just about see his brother surrounded by a crowd of females. "I think he's busy."

"He's certainly popular."

She was walking easily with him now, her hand relaxed in his, their arms swinging in unison.

"She'll probably be near the exit if she just turned up. What's she driving?"

"I don't know."

He spotted an unfamiliar white Range Rover Sport. "I bet that's her."

"Yeah." Her fingers tightened within his. "I think it is."

A tall blonde dressed in a short white minidress and sky-high heels was standing by the car looking down at her phone and chatting to a guy who looked like he'd just stepped out of a magazine cover shoot. The pair of them looked completely out of place against the rural backdrop.

"Lily!" Jenna waved. "Over here."

The blonde smiled and picked her way through the uneven soil toward Jenna. "Jen! Darling!"

Blue stepped back as Jenna was enveloped in a hug and both of them were surrounded in a cloud of expensive scent and beauty products.

"Thanks so much for letting us come over. Daj offered me a lift back to LA in his private jet, so I was able to find some time to come out and see you."

Jenna gestured at Blue. "This is Blue Morgan. He's part owner of the ranch."

Blue tipped his hat, "Ma'am," and then held out his hand to Daj. "Welcome to Morgan Ranch. We're celebrating my brother's engagement tonight. You're more than welcome to join us."

"How sweet." Lily smiled at him. "I don't think I've ever been to a party at a ranch before." She slipped effortlessly between Blue and Jenna. "What exactly do you do here when you're not throwing parties?"

"Mainly cattle ranching, but we're expanding into the historical dude ranch business."

"How fascinating."

Jenna fell behind to talk to Daj, and Blue continued back up the slope with Lily chatting away at his side. At one point she stumbled, and he offered her his hand to help her over the more rocky terrain. Just as they reached the tables, Blue spotted Chase and beckoned him over.

"Chase, this is Jenna's sister, Lily, and her friend Daj."

"Nice to meet you guys, and thanks for coming to my party."

Lily looked up at his brother. "Oh my God, Chase *Morgan*? Cofounder of Give Me a Leg Up?"

"Yeah, that's me."

"I work for Heyer Biometrics! I met you a few years ago." She turned to Daj. "These guys were one of our initial backers."

"You seem to be doing pretty well now." Chase smiled. "I heard you were looking for round three funding."

"That's right, we—" She stopped. "I had no idea I'd meet you here in the back of beyond, but I have no intention of spoiling your engagement party talking business."

"Matt and Jake are around here somewhere, so feel free to go and reintroduce yourself to them. I bet they'd be delighted to hear your news."

"That's really sweet of you, but I *did* come to see my baby sister, so I'll try not to monopolize anyone's time."

"You go ahead," Jenna murmured. "Fine by me."

"Don't be silly, darling." Lily wrapped an arm around Jenna's waist. "I *want* to talk to you. Mom's very concerned about you, you know."

"You should come and say hi to Uncle Ron and Aunt Amy and meet Dave," Jenna said, which Blue recognized as a diversionary tactic.

"I'd *love* to. Come along, Daj."

Later, Blue was sitting at a table with Lily to his right. Jenna had gone off to help Ruth with something, and Daj was locked in conversation with Matt and Jake, the only people he had deigned to talk to the whole night.

Lily was tapping her foot to the music and drinking bottled water, a smile playing around her beautiful mouth. Close up her skin was flawless. She looked nothing like Jenna, but that wasn't a surprise seeing as they weren't actually related. Blue exerted himself to be polite.

"Jenna said you went to MIT."

"That's correct." She cast him a playful glance. "What else did she say?"

"Just that she was very fond of you."

"She's so adorable. I just wish she'd get over this desire to be totally independent, you know? Mom and Dad really miss her. She was the only one of us who stuck around near home for college and vet school, so they miss her a lot now that she's insisted on moving away."

"I suppose she felt she had as much right as the rest of you to get out there in the world." Blue took a swig of beer. "I can relate to that."

"Did you go out of California for college, then?"

"I didn't go to college. I went into the Marines."

"At eighteen?" She turned to face him, her gaze full of surprise. "But didn't you find lacking a degree hindered the advancement of your career?"

"I never wanted to advance. I just wanted to do my job, survive, and get paid. I *did* get to see the world, but not the places most people would want to visit."

"I don't wish to sound rude, but you're obviously smart if you have a brother like Chase, so—"

"I'm not like Chase. He's a genius. I'm a grunt. I'm okay with that."

She wrinkled her brow. "But education is the secret to everything. That's why I'm so concerned with Jenna wasting her talents out here. She should be living in LA and back in school specializing in some aspect of her profession. Mom and Dad even offered to fund her, but she refused." She sighed. "I'm worried about her."

"Worried about my what?"

Blue almost jumped as Jenna sat beside him, her gaze fixed on her sister. He'd never seen her look so tense before.

"I was just telling Blue that Mom and Dad wanted to fund your doctorate and that you refused their help."

"I'm kind of over school."

There was a flat note to Jenna's voice that made Blue want to give her a reassuring hug.

"But if you want to be successful, you need to get that next qualification."

"It's hard for me. I wasn't enjoying it anymore."

"Sometimes you just have to keep pushing through. You know what Dad always said, if it's worth having it's not usually easy."

"And I don't want to do it anymore. I'm not academic like you."

Lily patted Jenna's clenched fist. "Everyone needs a break sometimes. That's why Dad thought a year up here would be a good idea."

"Meaning what exactly?"

"That you'd soon realize what hard and boring work this was and want to come home." Lily chuckled. "Come on, Jenna. This is hardly worth your talents, is it? You graduated first in your class."

"And I love it out here."

Lily glanced uncertainly at Blue and then back at Jenna. "It's okay, I'm sure Blue won't mind if you tell the truth."

"I am. I have no intention of leaving general practice and going back to school."

Blue set his beer down on the table. "She's a really good vet, Lily, and we are proud to have her working with us on the ranch."

"I'm sure you are." Lily's smile was warm. "I know exactly how awesome she is—she's my sister."

"In fact, Chase is about to offer her a permanent job here on staff."

"Here?" Lily turned to Jenna. "You don't want to stay out in the middle of nowhere, do you, love? We want so much *more* for you."

"Lily—"

"There she is!"

The drunken shout behind him had Blue instantly on his feet facing the danger. People sitting at the nearby tables were all staring at Mark Lymond, who was weaving through the guests, his finger pointed straight at Jenna.

"She killed my mare and foal!"

Behind him Blue sensed Jenna stand up. He put his arm out to keep her exactly where he could see her.

"Go home, Mark. You're drunk," Blue said as quietly as he could.

Mark took another couple of stumbling steps forward. "She's incompetent. She doesn't know what she's doing, and she killed my stock!"

Jenna raised her chin and spoke out clearly. "I did everything I could to save your mare, Mr. Lymond. I swear it."

Around them the guests were beginning to murmur and point. Dave suddenly appeared at Jenna's other shoulder.

"The mare died because you didn't call us in soon enough, Mark. Don't blame Jenna."

"That's right," Mark sneered. "Stick up for the pretty little girl who shouldn't ever be allowed near a horse because she's incompetent." He rocked back and forth on his heels. "Or is it because you're afraid I'll sue your family? I bet you'd change your tune if you thought she was going to ruin you and admit she doesn't know what she's doing."

"That's enough, Mark." Blue closed the gap between them. "I'm going to take you home, now."

"You're not going to do—"

With a useful trick he'd learned in the Marines, Blue unobtrusively knocked Mark out and let the man slump into his arms. Ruth came up to him, her expression concerned.

"I'll take him back home and make sure he sobers up." Blue slung Mark over his shoulder. "Make sure Jenna's okay, will you?"

Jenna sat down, her knees trembling, and took several big deep breaths.

"You okay?" Dave touched her shoulder. "He was talking shit, you do know that, right?"

"Right." Jenna nodded, still looking down.

"Dad and I are right behind you on this one."

"Good to know."

"Cool." Dave wandered off toward the food.

"Jenna . . ."

That was Lily's voice. How typical that her sister had witnessed her humiliation. She could never get a break.

"Why on earth would you want to stick around here and put up with being treated like that? You are worth *so* much more."

"He's the only person I've had a problem with. Everyone else is great."

"Are you sure about that?" Lily hesitated. "Does your reluctance to return home and strive for excellence go back to you thinking you're not good enough? I thought we'd talked that out in family therapy."

"We did, and I know I'm good enough to do this job. I love it."

Lily sighed. "It is a beautiful place. I can see why Chase Morgan decided to work his magic on it and make it profitable."

"It's his home. That's why he loves it."

"Well, yes, but if that was true he would've just left it how it was and not invested all this money in upgrading it."

Jenna met her sister's eyes. "You don't get it, do you? He invested in this place so that he could continue a way of life and a tradition that had existed in his family since 1850. He did it for *love*, not for profit."

Lily bit her lip. "I'm not going to argue with you, Jenna. I just want you to be happy."

A familiar sense of hopelessness crawled over Jenna. Lily was super smart, and yet in some ways she seemed so out of touch with the realities of life. But she *did* love Jenna, and that made it even harder to say how she felt without hurting her sister's feelings.

After a short silence, Lily picked up her water bottle and took a dainty sip.

"Blue seems nice."

"I like him." Jenna realized she was getting tense again. "He's transitioning out of the Marines and into the role of manager for the new guest ranch. We've been working together selecting the horses."

"He seems to suit this place."

"It's his home. He grew up here."

Lily took Jenna's hand. "Is Blue the real reason you want to stick around?"

"He has nothing to do with it."

"Because you can't let a man hold you back, love. You know that."

"He is not holding me back. I am perfectly capable of managing my career and my love life without input from him, you, or our parents." Jenna sighed. Somehow Lily could always reduce her to her muddled confused twelve-year-old self. "Can you please just drop this? I'm really glad you came because it's great to see you, but can we talk about you for a while?"

Lily laughed. "But you're so much more *interesting*. I'm still working twenty hours a day in my lab and loving every minute of it."

Jenna found a smile somewhere. "Maybe you should get out more. Are you really going out with Daj? He's not exactly being very attentive to you."

"Daj knows my priorities. I asked him to talk business with Matt and Jake while I spent time with you. It was the best division of labor."

"Well, feel free to join him. I've got to go and help Ruth in a bit."

Lily looked around. "Why didn't they hire more staff? That poor lady must be worn out."

"Try telling her that. We all try and pitch in around here. It's called being part of a community."

Lily stuck out her tongue. "Funny. But you don't work for the Morgans, do you?"

"I might as well. I spend almost all my time up here dealing with their horses, cattle, and Roy's pigs."

"You aren't going to take that job, though, are you?"

"Why shouldn't I?"

"Because this wasn't supposed to be anything more than a brief helping out Uncle Ron kind of gig." Lily hesitated. "You do know Faith is coming back and she's going to want her job back?"

"All the more reason why I should take the job with the Morgans."

"Or come back home. We all miss you so much."

"Lily . . ."

Her sister grinned and stood up. "Okay, I'll stop. I'm going to talk to Daj. I'll come and find you before we leave and say a proper good-bye."

"I'll be over by the food helping Ruth pack up."

Jenna walked across the dance floor over toward Ruth's diminutive figure, her thoughts in turmoil. A couple of people looked at her funny and she heard the odd whisper about Mark Lymond as she passed. Great. Maybe she didn't need to worry about getting a job here because no one would trust her to treat their animals ever again. Maybe she should go home.

Nothing Lily said was wrong, and she wasn't trying to be mean, but she didn't seem to understand that there were different paths to happiness and fulfillment. And now she'd made Jenna doubt herself, and Mark Lymond's appearance hadn't helped either.

"You all right, Jenna?" Ruth gave her a cursory glance

as she handed her a large roll of aluminum foil. "Mark didn't upset you, did he?"

"Well, I wish he had better timing. Being bawled out in front of my other clients and my big sister was pretty sucky." Jenna tore off a strip of foil. "I hope January and Chase didn't notice."

"I don't think they did. Your sister is very pretty, but she doesn't look like you at all, does she?"

"We were both adopted. We're completely different in every way."

"Good thing, too," Ruth snorted. "I can't see her mucking out a stall somehow."

"She's a brilliant bioengineer."

"Which is all well and good in its place, and I'm sure she does wonderful things, but I'd much rather have you."

"That's really sweet."

Ruth patted her shoulder. "I saw you with her. You looked just like Blue when he and Chase brought home their report cards. I think half the reason Blue went into the Marines was to avoid having to compete academically with his brother—because he sure was smart enough."

"Lily thinks I need more qualifications." Jenna sighed. "I don't."

"It's hard to argue with people who love you and think they have your best interests at heart when they don't really, isn't it? But you know your own mind, my girl, and if being here makes you happy? Then I say you should do what's best for you."

"Thanks."

"And Blue would miss you if you left."

"Now who's using emotional blackmail?" Jenna smiled at Ruth.

"You make him happy. I appreciate that, but I'd no more tell you to stay here for his sake than I would tell him to stay for mine. People have to make up their own minds. Look at poor Annie. She felt trapped out here and ended up making some choices that hurt everyone."

Old hurt flashed in Ruth's eyes and was immediately blinked away. "But that's all in the past. I just want my boys to be happy, and seeing them all come back to the ranch? That makes my heart sing." She nudged Jenna in the ribs. "Now help me cover up this food before the flies get at it."

Blue returned from taking care of Mark Lymond to find the party was winding down. He stopped in the parking lot to speak to some of his neighbors. He was pretty sure everyone had enjoyed themselves and were now looking forward to the wedding, which was planned for later in the year.

Lily's white car was still there. As he looked up toward the dance floor, Jenna, Daj, and Lily were just coming down the path. He stayed where he was, aware that Jenna was looking strained and that Lily was talking her ear off—probably trying to persuade her around to her way of thinking again.

"Hey, Blue!" Lily saw him and waved. "We're just off."

She came toward him and surprised him by pulling him in for a hug. "Thanks for standing up for my sister against that drunk. She's not used to being treated like that."

"She's tougher than you think." Blue kept his voice low. Jenna was still talking to Daj, but she was close.

"She's my baby sister. I can't help but look out for her, I'm sure you understand." Lily paused. "Can I say one thing? If you really do care for her, will you make sure she thinks carefully about coming back to LA and continuing her career?"

"She's a grown woman. If she wants to talk things through with me that's fine, but I don't have the right or the need to tell her what to do." Blue smiled. "She'll work it out."

"So you won't help me." Lily sighed. "I suppose getting an education isn't a priority for you."

"From what I understand, Jenna's had enough, and if she wants to work as a regular vet, surely that's her choice?"

Lily opened her mouth to reply and then closed it again. Blue sensed that Jenna was right behind him.

"Bye, Jen." Lily swept past Blue and gave Jenna a big hug. "This was so much fun!"

"Thanks for coming, sis." Jenna returned the hug. "Safe trip home. Give my love to everyone, won't you?"

Daj nodded distantly at Blue and got in the car with Lily. Within moments the car turned around and headed out.

Blue glanced over at Jenna, who wasn't smiling. "Your sister is nice."

"Yes."

"Bossy, though."

"You think so?" Jenna twirled the end of her hair. "She's certainly got a one-track mind. Get an education, Jenna, no, that's not enough, do more, Jenna, climb higher, Jenna."

"I suppose she's just trying to do what she thinks best."

Jenna folded her arms across her chest. "And you agree with her?"

"I didn't say that."

"I heard you discussing me with her, Blue."

"Hang on a minute." So much for calming her down. "I was *defending* your choices."

"You were interfering!"

He held up his hand. "Look, just because you're mad at *her*, don't start in on me. She was trying to get me involved, and I was trying my best to keep out of it!"

"I'm not mad at her."

"If you aren't, then maybe you should be."

"What the hell is that supposed to mean?"

"Because you're better than that, Jenna. You let her talk and walk all over you."

"Because she's my *sister*. I can't stop her saying what's on her mind."

"Sure you can. You look her in the eye and you tell her straight to stop undermining you."

"She's not—"

"Then why are you upset?"

"Because *you* were agreeing with her!"

"That's just an excuse. If you don't like the way she's treating you, tell her to stop."

"You make it sound so easy."

"It is."

"If you don't care who you hurt."

He stiffened. "Is that some kind of dig at me because of what happened with my brothers?"

"You said it, Blue. The others worked it out with your father, and you didn't because of your inflexible nature. Maybe that's not an example I want to follow."

He shut his mouth on what he had been about to say and contemplated her angry face.

"Ma'am." He touched the brim of his Stetson in a formal salute. "When you work out who you're angry with, let me know, okay? Have a great night."

Turning on his heel, he walked back up the slope and started helping with the clean up shoving paper plates and cups into black sacks with the speed of a maniac. That was why he didn't open up to people, because it gave them the opportunity to stab him in the back.

He tossed a full bag onto the growing pile and started

on another. Hell, he'd expected better of Jenna. Sure, there was a line you shouldn't cross with your family and he'd jumped all over that, but he'd learned from his mistakes, hadn't he? And he would never let anyone walk all over him.

"You okay, BB?"

He looked up to see Ry leaning against one of the tables, a beer in his hand.

"I'm good, why?"

"Because you look like you're going to rip someone's head off."

"Are you offering?"

Ry grinned and finished his beer, tossing the bottle toward Blue's half-filled sack.

"Jenna's pretty furious as well. Her sister was pretty."

"Yeah." Blue met Ry's gaze. "Anything useful to say, or is this just a fishing expedition?"

"Depends on whether you're taking the bait." He shrugged. "Maybe I should go talk to Jenna instead. She looks like she could do with a shoulder to cry on."

"She has January and Yvonne for that. No doubt she'll feel better after she's told them what a scumbag I am."

"What did you do?"

"Nothing." Blue scowled. "I was being sarcastic. I did nothing except exist and be in the wrong place at the wrong time. Oh, and I tried to offer some advice."

"That was your first mistake."

"Tell me about it. I forgot the golden rule. Never get between a woman and her siblings. They can talk shit about them all they like, but God help you if you join in. Suddenly you're the bad guy."

Even as he said the words Blue realized the truth of them. "Hell."

Ry straightened and picked up about four of the bags. "I'll put these in the back of my truck, okay?"

"Thanks."

Blue continued to clean up until all the tables were clear. On the other side of the makeshift dais, Jenna and Ruth were working together on covering the remaining food. His grandma looked tired, and Jenna's attempts to keep a smile on her face were obvious.

He straightened his spine and went over.

"Ruth, why don't you call it a night and hitch a ride back with Ry? Jenna and I can finish up here."

"We're almost done." Ruth stacked another box full of leftovers.

"Then go." He took the box out of her hands.

She heaved a sigh. "Okay. I am a little tired."

The fact that she was admitting that made Blue instantly worried. He turned to see Ry coming toward them.

"Will you take Ruth home?"

"Sure." Ry's gaze swept over Jenna. "You coming, too, Jenna?"

"No, I'll get the rest of it done. It won't take more than half an hour."

Ruth patted Jenna's arm. "Then come and stay at the ranch when you're done. I'm sure you can put up with Blue's snoring for a night."

Jenna still didn't look at Blue. "That's very kind of you, but I probably should get home. I have to handle morning surgery."

"I'll make sure she gets home safely, Ruth." Blue hugged his grandma and then turned her gently to face Ry. "Now go, and sweet dreams."

* * *

Jenna kept her head down and concentrated on the task at hand. She should've gone with Ruth, but she hadn't felt right leaving Blue all alone. Now it was just awkward. He worked silently beside her, loading the back of his truck with the boxes, which were destined for an overnight stay in the industrial-sized refrigerator in the mudroom and then distribution to the Morgantown retirement community luncheon the next day.

What was left to say? He'd been his usual interfering, overdecisive self and she'd told him to back off. Getting stuck between his and Lily's powerful personalities hadn't been a pleasant experience. And then hearing the pair of them discussing her like she was a problem to be solved? That had sucked.

"I think we're done."

It was the first time Blue had spoken since he'd walked away in the parking lot. He closed the tailgate of his truck and went around to the driver's side. A moment later the engine started up loud in the silence. Jenna contemplated her options. Her vehicle was parked at the barn, so technically she could walk back to it, but she was exhausted. Blue seemed as reluctant to talk to her as she was to him, so surely she could stand ten silent minutes in his truck?

With a sigh she got into the passenger seat and settled in. His familiar scent with an added hint of beer and barbecue surrounded her and she closed her eyes. The truck bumped up the incline through the darkness, rocking back and forth, and she fought not to fall asleep.

She wasn't sure if she'd succeeded because the next thing she knew, the truck had stopped. Blue was getting out and getting on with the business of unloading the truck. She stumbled down and had to steady herself against the door. He gave her a brief glance.

"I've got this. You go on home."

She stared at his retreating back as he propped open the door and carried a stack of boxes into the mudroom. It felt wrong not talking to him, but what the heck was she supposed to say? At some level she was still mad, but she was too tired to have it out with him, and too confused.

"Jenna, it's okay. I've really got this." He paused. "Unless you are too tired to drive? If that's the case, go on up and take my bed."

"I can't . . . do that."

"Because we're fighting?" He shrugged. "Then hang in my truck for a few minutes, and I'll take you home. You can pick up your vehicle tomorrow."

She nodded and he carried on lifting out boxes and taking them inside. She managed to walk over to her truck and then hesitated. How much had she drunk? After Lily left and Blue stormed off she'd had a couple of beers.

"Jenna?"

Blue was back and staring down at her.

"I think I've had too much to drink to drive home."

"Then it's your call. Either go up to my bed or I'll drive you home." He grimaced. "Hell, you already think the worst of me, so why don't I make the decision easier for you?"

She yelped as he picked her up and headed into the house. His breathing remained even as they mounted the stairs and he kicked open the door to his room. He placed her gently on the bed and stood over her.

"Night, Jenna. You know where the bathroom is."

She blinked up at him and then he was gone. Lying in the dark she could hear him working outside and then it all went quiet. She held her breath as the screen door closed, but then there was nothing. He wasn't going to join her. She knew that in her bones. Despite everything, he'd still put her first. Shame washed over her. He deserved an apology. She'd lashed out at him because he'd gotten in the middle of the long-running saga of her relationship with Lily. Even as her eyes closed, she vowed to set things right with him in the morning.

Chapter Sixteen

"I'm done? I'm out?" Blue stared at Carly Hughes. "You sure?"

"Absolutely." She grinned and offered him her hand. "Welcome to the real world. Mr. Morgan."

He shook her hand and smiled right back at her. The last few days had been busier than he'd anticipated with friends to have a last beer with and his replacement to get up to speed. But it was done. He was finally free.

"There is one thing we'd like you to consider before we lose you completely." Hang on. Carly was still talking.

"What's that?"

"We occasionally run a horsemanship course for when special ops have to move through terrain that can't be navigated by motor vehicles. We don't run it regularly, and we do have one guy on staff who usually takes care of it, but we'd appreciate knowing you could act as backup if necessary." She paused. "You did say you were a cowboy, right?"

"Do I get paid?"

"Yes." She handed him a sealed envelope. "The details are in here. Let me know what you decide."

"Thanks, I'll certainly consider it."

"I'll miss you." She sat back down.

"I'll miss everyone here. I really will."

She crossed her world-class legs. "When are you leaving?"

"Today if I can manage it."

She pouted. "No time to take me out for a drink, then."

"I wouldn't want to waste your valuable time." He hesitated. "I'm kind of involved with someone back home."

Well, he thought he was. Not that he'd contacted Jenna after leaving her sleeping alone in his bed.

"Of course you are. Men like you aren't allowed to run free for long."

He snorted. "As she's the local vet, I worry what she'd do to me if she actually caught me and held me down." He nodded at Carly. "Thanks for everything, though. I really do appreciate it."

"Off with you." She made a shooing gesture with her hand. "Have a great life, cowboy."

"Will do, ma'am." He tipped his imaginary hat to her.

She sighed theatrically and clutched her hands to her chest. "Oh Lordy. Don't *do* that."

His smile faded as he left the HR offices and made his way back to his old desk. The new guy had already spread his stuff all over it, including a picture of his two kids and his wife. Blue's possessions sat in a box on the floor.

"You off, dude?" Mel called out to him from across the room.

"Yeah." Blue went over to give his old buddy a fist bump. "You're going to come and see me this fall, right? Bring the kids?"

"It's on my schedule." Mel stood up and slapped him on the back. "Good luck, Gunny, we'll miss your ugly face around here."

A chorus of agreement rose from the rest of the team.

Blue made a somewhat less-than-polite gesture as he left to a round of applause and good wishes for his future. Damn, his throat was tight. He loaded up his truck with all his remaining possessions and remembered to stop at security to hand in his badge and all the other crap he would no longer need.

It felt . . . weird.

He put on his sunglasses, started the truck, and headed home.

"He doesn't want me to operate on his calf, does he?" Jenna faced Dave across the surgery table. "He doesn't trust me."

"It's not that. He's just used to me and Dad, and—"

Jenna stripped off her mask and started on her gloves. "Fine. Go ahead."

"Don't get all mad."

"I'm not."

Dave held up his hands. "You said fine. You're a woman, therefore you're mad."

"I'm more worried about treating this calf. And if Adam wants you to do it, then get on with it."

"Jenna—dude."

She backed out of the room. Her hands were shaking and she wanted to cry, but she wasn't going to give anyone the satisfaction of seeing she was upset. Meg raised her eyebrows as Jenna continued to take off her scrubs.

"You okay? I thought you were operating on that calf. I was just coming in to assist."

"Dave's doing it."

Meg frowned. "But you were scheduled for surgical cases today."

Jenna balled up her gloves and threw them in the general

direction of the trash can. "And apparently, Adam Breton doesn't want me touching his calf."

"He's an idiot."

Jenna let out her breath. "No. He thinks I'm incompetent."

"Mark Lymond has a lot to answer for." Meg offered her a one-armed hug. "Don't get upset, okay? We all know you're perfectly capable. This is a one-off."

"It's the second time this week," Jenna said flatly. "I don't want to sink the practice."

"You won't. Really. Those two guys are good friends of Mark's and they're just out to cause trouble. No one else cares." Meg reluctantly released Jenna. "I'd better get in there and do my job."

"You go ahead. I'll check and see if anyone actually wants my veterinary skills around here, and if not, I'll head up to the Morgans'. They have a lame horse."

"Okay. Tell Lucille up front your schedule before you leave."

"Will do."

Jenna sat at the small table and found herself eye to eye with some kind of bird in a cage. The bird put its head to one side and observed Jenna through round yellow eyes.

"Loser."

Jenna looked at the bird. "Yes, exactly." There was a note attached to the cage that identified the owner as one of the Hayes family, who had more pets between them than the zoo. No wonder the bird was up on its insults. She dragged her hands over her face and stared down at the table.

Her week had only gotten worse. She'd woken up the day after the party to find that Blue had returned to his military base, and she hadn't heard a peep out of him since. And now this . . .

Maybe she should just give up and go home to LA. She'd ruined things with Blue so the job at Morgan Ranch was off the table, and Dave and her uncle weren't going to want her to hang around if their clients started objecting to her presence. What happened if there was an emergency and she was the only vet around, and someone refused to let her treat an animal? How would that feel?

With a groan, she got to her feet, grabbed her bag and her coat. At least Roy would be pleased to see her, and with Blue away, at least the ranch was a safe place for her to do what she loved, which was working with animals.

"Hey, Roy." Jenna dumped her bag on the barn floor and looked around the stalls. All of them were now filled, and the ranch had a dozen good horses ready to be ridden by the incoming guests. The plan was to add to that if the ranch took off. She was proud of her input on that, at least.

"Jenna." Roy's head popped up over one of the doors. "I'm in here. Blocky's not putting any weight on his rear left hoof."

"Do you want to walk him out for me?" Jenna moved to one side.

"Sure."

She watched carefully as Roy coaxed the gelding out of the stall and paraded him up and down.

"Yeah, definitely lame. Any idea what might have caused it? Any injuries to the other horses?"

"Not that I've noticed."

"Was he let out this morning?"

"He was out with the others yesterday afternoon. We brought them all in around sunset. Ry noticed he was standing awkwardly when he went to feed him this morning."

"Can you hold Blocky still for me, or do you want to tie him up?"

"I've got him. You go ahead."

Jenna approached Blocky from the front, made eye contact, and gently ran her hand down the gelding's neck along the sleek line of his body and then down his leg until she had to crouch to see what she was looking at.

"It doesn't look like he got kicked or nipped. There's some swelling here. I wonder if he was bitten? Seen any snakes around?"

"Good question." Roy frowned. "It's possible, I suppose."

Jenna resumed her examination. "I'll clean out the wound and give him a shot of antivenin just to make sure he'll be okay." She looked up. "His tetanus shot's up to date, right? We just did all those."

"Yeah. He's good."

Jenna cleaned out the wound and gave the shot. "He should be fine, but keep an eye out for any extreme reaction over the next few hours."

"Will do, and I'll get Ry and Miguel to take a look around that field." Roy took off his hat and scratched his head. "I can't say I've seen many snakes up this close to the house, but you never know. It's been really dry."

Jenna heard the sound of a horse coming in and turned to see Ry Morgan easing Nolly down into a walk. Like all the Morgan brothers, he rode like a dream.

"Hey, Jenna." He gave her a casual salute as he dismounted and patted his horse's neck. "Did you take a look at Blocky?"

"She thinks it might be a snakebite." Roy undid the saddle cinch, his fingers flying over the leather as he talked. "I said we'd take a look in that field."

"Not that you're going to see a snake sitting out there

in the open," Jenna said gloomily. "If you do, we might have a bigger problem than we realized."

"Snakes in a barn." Ry took off the bridle and hung it over his shoulder. "I'd watch that movie."

Jenna repressed a shudder. "I'll talk to Uncle Ron and see whether he has any other suggestions as to treatment."

Ry paused to look thoughtfully at her. "Why do you need to ask him?"

She shrugged. "Just making sure I've covered all my bases."

"I thought you were the one with the most up-to-date veterinary degree in the practice?"

She met his gaze. "I don't know much about snakebites and their effect on horses. That's all."

He nodded but still looked skeptical and went into the tack room, emerging a moment later to pick up the saddle and blanket and put them away as well. It wasn't surprising Ry was looking at her funny. She hated the way Mark Lymond had made her doubt herself and obsess over every decision she made.

Roy put Blocky back in his stall and closed the door. "Chase and January are back today."

"Nice." Jenna crouched down to pack up her bag. "January's already been texting me about wedding details— not that I know anything about all of that stuff."

"All women know something about it." Roy chuckled. "It's in their blood."

"Sexist much, Roy?" Ry raised his eyebrows.

Roy snorted. "I watch *Say Yes To The Dress*, and I don't see many men on there. It's usually a big gaggle of females who all have very strong opinions. Sometimes I feel sorry for the poor bride."

Ry's amused gaze met Jenna's. "He does have a point."

"Maybe." Jenna picked up her bag. "Is it okay if I come inside and call the clinic?"

"Sure, you come on in." Roy patted her shoulder. "Ry and I will finish up here. Ruth's been wondering where you've been."

Jenna hesitated. Did that sound more ominous than it was? Had Ruth noticed something was up between her and Blue? She hadn't said anything when Jenna had come down into the kitchen still in her crumpled green dress except to ask her how many eggs she wanted in her omelet. And Jenna didn't think she'd let on how disappointed she'd been to hear that Blue had already left for the Marine base.

She pushed open the screen door and went inside, relishing the cool air and the shade.

"Hey, Ruth."

"Morning, Jenna. I thought you were coming out here after morning surgery?" Ruth wiped her hands on her apron and put her rolling pin down.

"Dave ended up doing that, so I was free to come earlier."

Ruth pointed at a chair. "Take a seat. I'll get you a nice glass of iced tea."

"It's okay, I can get it."

"Sit."

Jenna did what she was told.

"I'm making you pancakes, so settle in."

Eventually even Ruth finished feeding her and took the chair opposite while they both sipped at their coffee.

"So Meg says Dave did the surgery because someone objected to you doing it."

There was no point in asking how Ruth knew this so fast. She knew everything.

"Yeah. Adam Breton. He's not the first either." She sighed. "Maybe I should talk to Chase about letting Dave do the work up here instead of me. Maybe I *should* go home."

"To Los Angeles? To do what?"

"Go back to school and work with toy breeds and pampered pooches?" She groaned. "That would suck so hard."

"My, you are feeling sorry for yourself today."

Jenna raised an eyebrow. "Is that your idea of a sympathetic and motivational remark?"

Ruth held her stare. "You're letting three crabby old ranchers derail your plans?"

"It's more than that. I don't want to damage the practice's reputation. Faith is coming back next year anyway, and they probably won't need me."

"What about the job Chase offered you up here?"

Jenna had nothing to say to that.

"What about BB?"

"He's not talking to me right now."

"And whose fault is that?" Ruth shook her head. "Actually, that one is probably on him. He has a tendency to run off his mouth like a fool."

"It was me." Jenna cleared her throat. "I owe him an apology."

Ruth sat back. "Well, wonders will never cease. If he accepts your apology—and he will—will you reconsider your options?"

"It's not about him, Ruth. It's about me. I have to work out what I want and whether there still is a place here for me as a vet. That's all I've ever wanted to be."

"One thing I've learned in life is that you can't please everyone." Ruth reached across the table and took Jenna's hand. "Have faith in yourself. If you want this life—with or without my grandson in it—then maybe it's time for you to fight for it."

* * *

Blue pulled up in front of the barn and smiled. The sun was setting behind the Sierras, plunging everything into complex shadows. Lights shone in the house, and from the barn came the sound of happy, settled horses. His new life. Now all he had to do was persuade a certain female veterinarian to share it with him. He'd had lots of time to think on the way home.

Jenna was a strong woman. She'd already made choices that had run contrary to her family's wishes, and she was still dealing with the fallout. He had to give her time and resist the temptation to set her straight. It was his worst sin. Just because he *thought* he was right about everything didn't mean that he was. Who would've thought he'd slip up and have a ten-year-old daughter? Not the old BB. He would've been quick to condemn anyone in that situation. The new one was learning to allow for some gray areas in between those blacks and whites.

He got out of the truck and stretched out the kinks in his spine. Chase's F-450 sat between January's and Roy's trucks, dwarfing them. And Ry was apparently still here, which was an unexpected bonus. Maybe tonight would be a good time to talk about the future. Ry seemed interested in what they were doing and had simply fit right back in, taking on his share of the chores without a word.

Blue opened the screen door and called out, "Honey, I'm home!"

The heavenly scent of Ruth's beef stew tantalized his nostrils. The whole family—including Roy, Maria, and Billy—sat around the kitchen table smiling a welcome at him. It was just like one of the dreams he'd had while overseas, far away from those he loved and in a constant state of alertness.

He threw his arms wide. "I'm free!"

"Awesome." Chase grinned at him. "And about time, too."

"Come and sit down. I'll get you a plate." Ruth got another plate down from the cupboard and passed it across to him. "We only just said grace. You always did have a good nose on you."

Blue dug in, and for a while there was no conversation. Working outside meant they needed a lot of calories to keep going. Eventually Maria was yawning, and Blue handed her his napkin to wipe the peach juice off her chin.

"Time for bed, young lady," Ruth said. "BB, will you take her up and make sure she's settled?"

"Sure." Blue smiled down at Maria. "Come on, then. Race you."

She was off like a whippet and Blue followed a lot more slowly, considering the load of food he'd eaten. When she was all set and tucked up in bed, Blue sat on the quilt beside her.

"You okay?"

"Yes. Billy took me swimming in the hot springs today. It was awesome. You should come next time."

"I will. How are the kittens?"

"They are getting bigger every day. Roy thinks they'll be good rat catchers 'cause their mama is."

"Awesome. I'm done with the military now, so I'll be here full-time. Maybe we can do more stuff together?"

"I'd like that." Her smile faded. "Although I suppose I'll have to go somewhere else soon."

He tensed. "Why would you think that?"

She scrunched the sheet in her fingers and wouldn't look at him. "I heard Ruth talking on the phone. They want to take me into the foster care system or something. Do you think we could do that DNA thing now?"

"If that's what you want."

"I'd like to try. Billy says whatever happens, I'll still have a place here."

"Billy's right." He held her gaze. "I have the DNA kits. Do you want to do it right now?"

She raised her chin. "Yes."

"Then give me a minute to fetch them."

He returned with the kits, his heart thumping hard. "It's not difficult to do or anything. We just gently swab the inside of our cheeks to collect our buccal cells and send the swabs off to the lab to be analyzed."

She was far calmer than he was as they did the tests and sealed the results up in the bag Chase had given him.

"How long will it take?" Maria asked.

"About a week."

"That's good." She nodded and patted his knee. "It's okay."

Blue kissed the top of her head. "Then we're good. You get some sleep and I'll see you in the morning, okay? We'll go for a ride or something."

"Night, then."

"Night, Maria."

It was only when he was on his way downstairs that it occurred to him that she never called him anything. Everyone had a name but him. Either she didn't like the name Blue, or she was afraid to slip up and call him Dad. He kind of understood that. He tended to avoid calling Billy Dad as well.

Walking through into the kitchen, he held up the bag to Chase.

"We did the tests. Maria wanted to."

Chase picked up his cell. "Then I'll contact the company and arrange for pickup."

Blue sat at the table. "I think they can go in the regular mail."

"No, let's make sure they get there in the best condition possible." Chase glanced back at his cell. "Someone will be here to pick them up in the morning."

"Fast work, bro," Ry commented.

Blue grinned at him. "Our oldest brother is a very well-connected man."

"So Maria might be your kid, BB?"

"Yeah. I only found out she existed a few weeks ago. We've been keeping her here while we try to work out what's going on."

"Did the mother finally contact you?"

"Nope. And before you start expressing your opinion about that, you should also know she died about six months ago. It was the guy Maria thought was her dad who suddenly kicked her out."

"Damn," Ry said quietly. "Poor Maria."

Blue let his gaze roam around the assembled faces. "I'd like to put something on the table. Even if Maria isn't officially my daughter, if she agrees, I think we should try and keep her with us."

Billy was the first to nod. "I'd certainly like that. She's a good kid."

Blue turned to his father. "And you've been awesome with her. I might not have said that to you before, but I certainly should have."

"She's easy to love."

"Yeah, but you really put yourself out there for her and . . ." Blue braced himself. "I didn't really expect you to do that seeing as I've been nothing but a complete ass to you since you came back here."

"You're still my son, BB, and it was a way to help out without getting in your face, you know?"

"Well, thanks." Blue reached over and covered Billy's hand with his own. "I appreciate it, Dad."

For a moment there was silence and then Billy squeezed Blue's fingers. "Thanks, son."

Ry cleared his throat. "Damn, I think I'm going to cry."

Blue glared at him and then turned to his older brother. "What do you and January feel about Maria staying on regardless?"

"Fine by me," Chase said and January nodded. "The person you need to run it by is Ruth. It's her ranch."

Blue turned to his grandma, who had been listening quietly. "Ruth?"

"I'd love her to stay. I don't know quite how we're going to manage it if she isn't your daughter, BB, but I'm sure we'll find a way."

"Chase will." January poked her fiancé in the ribs. "He's good at getting things done and he has the best lawyers."

"Then that's settled. I'll have to talk to Daniel Lester again, but I'll wait until we hear back about the DNA." Blue straightened in his seat. "Now what else do we need to talk about?"

"Well, there is the matter of what Ry's planning on doing with his life." Chase directed his gaze at their younger brother. "Are you set on returning to the rodeo?"

"I think I'm done. I'm getting too old."

"Thank God for that," Blue muttered. "So come back here and work with us. Roy could do with a good second-in-command."

"I could." Roy settled his hands over his round stomach and rocked back in his chair. "And Ry is easy to work with. He keeps his mouth shut. I appreciate that."

"Then if you want to come back, there's a place for you

here, and a regular paycheck," Chase said. "And the offer applies to HW as well."

"I'll ask him." Ry looked from Chase to Blue. "Can't guarantee what he'll say, mind."

"That's okay." Blue looked around the table. "Anything else?"

"Jenna."

He brought his attention back to Ruth. "What about her?"

"I'm worried she won't take the job Chase offered her."

"Why not?" Blue sat up straight. "Hell, this isn't about me, is it?"

Ruth sighed. "Not everything is about you, BB. Since Mark Lymond started going around telling everyone she was incompetent, some of the veterinary clients have refused to let her treat their animals."

"What?" Blue just about managed not to curse. "When did that happen?"

"This last week when you were away. Meg told me. Jenna's starting to think she's bringing her uncle's practice down. Which is nonsense, of course, but—"

"Jenna would think that," Blue said slowly. "She always feels like an outsider."

January blinked at him. "You get that, too? Like she's always worried that she hasn't really been invited to the party?"

Blue nodded.

Just like Maria, as well. No wonder Jenna got along so well with her.

"Jenna's thinking that with Faith coming back next year, she should leave before they lose any more clients."

"Leave?" Blue almost shouted. "She's not leaving. She's going to take the job here!"

"She wasn't the last time I talked to her. But maybe you

and Chase can change her mind. I'd really like her to work up here with us. She's really good with the animals."

"Agreed." Roy finished his coffee. "Maybe if you boys talk to her and offer her a decent salary, she'll step up."

Chase caught Blue's eye. "We'll both go and see her tomorrow, okay? Now can we talk about one last thing?"

"What's that?" Blue wasn't really in the mood to discuss anything else. He wanted to be out that door and driving as fast as he could over to Jenna's place to ask her what the hell was going on.

"Big Mike."

"Who's he?" Ry asked.

"The man we think helped Mom get away from the ranch twenty years ago."

Ry's jaw dropped. "You think Mom and Rachel are still *alive*?"

"That's what we're trying to find out. I've arranged to meet Big Mike next week in San Diego. I want you to come with me, BB."

"Sure."

"I'll get Daizee to add the details to our shared calendar and book the flights and everything, okay?"

"Sure. Thanks."

Chase sighed. "You're welcome."

"I have to go out." Blue stood up.

"Really?" Chase rolled his eyes at January. "That's a surprise. Are you sure you don't want to wait until tomorrow when I can chaperone you?"

"Nah." Blue was already halfway out the door. "Some things are better said in private."

He only just caught Chase's shouted reply as he opened the back door.

"And don't forget, some things are better left unsaid!"

Chapter Seventeen

"Your boyfriend's here," Dave said in a singsong voice as he looked out of the kitchen window. "And he's looking pretty damn determined."

"One, I don't have a boyfriend; and two, if Blue Morgan *is* here it's probably because there's something up at the ranch and he needs a vet." Jenna was quite proud of how calm she sounded.

"Tell him to come in and have dinner with us," Amy called from the kitchen. "I haven't seen BB for ages."

"Will do."

Dave deftly body-checked Jenna out of the way and went to open the back door.

"Hey, BB! Come on in. Ma wants to see you."

Jenna scuttled back to the safety of the kitchen and started laying the table. Blue came in and took off his Stetson, smoothing down his short brown hair.

"Evening, all."

"BB!" Amy came to hug him. "I hear you're back for good now. Ruth will be so happy." She kissed his cheek and pointed at the table. "Now sit down and tell us all your news."

Blue looked over at Jenna, who gave him a quick smile and then avoided his gaze. Ron ambled in from his study and immediately started talking horses with Blue.

"Here you go, Jenna, put this mac and cheese on the table while I dish up the real food."

Jenna went to help her aunt. She had to squeeze behind Blue's chair, and just the sight of his strong tanned neck made her knees go weak. Which was both weird and wrong, considering he wasn't talking to her.

"Sorry, am I in your way?" Blue looked up and she just stared at him, forgetting everything but how pretty his eyes were and how lush the slight curve of his lower lip and . . .

"Jenna?" Amy called her name and she jumped like a rabbit.

"Coming."

Eventually, they were all seated and Amy and Ron talked to Blue, leaving Jenna to pick at her mac and cheese and Dave to stuff as much in his face as he could before the others got around to having seconds. Blue answered all the questions easily, only fielding a couple about Maria and January and offering no real information. She admired his skill, which considering how blunt he preferred to be was commendable.

She doubted he'd intended to come and have dinner with them, but he didn't betray any impatience to talk ranch business. He didn't even seem particularly anxious to talk to her, which served her right.

"So why did you come over, BB?" Dave finally asked the question Jenna had been longing to ask all night. "Something up at the ranch?"

Blue smiled. "Nope, it's all good. I came to see Jenna."

"Jenna?" Ron and Amy gave each other one of those concerned looks Jenna had been seeing a lot of recently.

"Is there something wrong with how she's handling things up at your place?"

Dave snorted with laughter. "It's okay, parents. I don't think BB's come to say Jenna's incompetent or anything."

"She's an excellent vet," Blue agreed. "I hope she's going to stick around."

Jenna slowly met his gaze. "You do?"

He smiled at her. "You want to come and take a walk in the moonlight with me and talk about that?"

"Right now?"

"No better time." He rose to his feet and nodded at Amy. "I won't keep her long."

Jenna automatically stood, too, and Dave scooted his chair out of her way. "Behave yourself, now." He winked.

"As well as you would, which gives me lots of scope." Jenna narrowed her eyes at him. "No peeping, okay?"

"Why, what you gonna do?"

Ignoring her cousin, Jenna walked around to Blue's side, and they exited the kitchen together. Even before they made it through the back door, Jenna heard an excited babble of voices and Dave whooping.

Blue kept hold of her hand, and he started walking around the edge of the flower garden and artificial putting green Ron had insisted on placing on the flat side of the lot. Down below them, close to the creek, was the original homestead that now functioned as the veterinary hospital.

"Blue." Jenna tugged at his hand until he came to a stop. "I want to apologize."

"For what?"

"I was angry and frustrated about how to deal with Lily, and I turned that on you when you tried to help."

He scuffed the toe of his boot in the soft ground. "But you're forgetting something."

"What?"

"Rule number one of dating someone with siblings. Never get between them even if asked for an opinion. I was out of line."

"You're always out of line. That's part of your charm."

"And the reason why I mess up all my relationships. You were right about that, too." He sighed. "You find dealing with Lily frustrating? I sometimes feel the same way when I'm dealing with you."

"Why?"

He looked down at her. "You're such an amazing person, Jenna. Sometimes it feels like the only person who doesn't believe that is you."

"I want to believe it."

He cupped her jaw, his fingers warm and gentle. "Then what's stopping you?"

"Fear, I suppose."

"Yeah?"

"Fear of being found . . . lacking."

"I'd never do that."

"Not by you, but by myself."

He considered her for a long moment. "Then I can't fix that, can I?"

She mutely shook her head. With a soft sound his arms closed around her and she rested her cheek against his chest. They stood like that for what seemed like hours, and then he cleared his throat.

"I'm done with the Marines."

"Welcome back to civilian life."

"And we did the DNA tests tonight. Maria's decision."

She raised her head to look at him. "Are you worried?"

"Yeah." His smile was crooked. "Not for the reasons you might think. I've already started to think of Maria as part of the family, so whatever happens we've all agreed that we'd like to keep her."

She stiffened. "She's not a pet."

"And the ultimate decision is of course, hers."

Jenna wrinkled her nose. "Sorry, I get twitchy when people talk about adopting or fostering children."

"Totally understandable."

She put her hand on his chest. "You're being remarkably amenable this evening."

"You mean I'm being nice?" He raised his eyebrows. "I'm always nice."

She let that slide. "So, is there anything else you needed to talk to me about?"

"No, I think we're good."

She desperately wanted to ask him exactly what that meant, and what exactly *was* good, but didn't want to give him the satisfaction.

"Okay, then. Shall I see you tomorrow at the ranch?"

She half turned back toward the house, and he caught her hand.

"I didn't say I was *finished*."

He twirled her back into his arms and kissed her hard. With a breathy moan she kissed him back, her hands all over him.

When he finally came up for air she was clinging to him like bindweed, her body plastered over his from knee to shoulder. He pushed a few strands of her hair behind her ear and kissed her nose.

"I told you we were good."

"You showed me even better."

He studied her intently. "Is there anything you want to tell me?"

"Like what?"

His blue gaze darkened. "Like about certain ranchers not letting you work with their animals?"

She stamped her foot. "Oh, *Blue*, why do you have to go and spoil everything? I thought you said we were done?"

"I said *I* was done. I'm still waiting for a full report from you." Suddenly he was all business again. "You know those guys don't represent the whole valley, right?"

"How would I know that? They are all long-term clients of my uncle's who are threatening to pull their business because of me. That's not acceptable. I came here to help out, not to ruin the practice."

She took three steps back so that she could see his expression more clearly and then wished she hadn't.

"So come and work for us."

"I haven't received an official job offer yet, and I'd still be working with all the locals. What if they refuse to help out at Morgan Ranch because I'm there? That would be even worse than the situation I'm in now."

Blue just looked at her.

"What?"

"I'll get Chase to put something in writing, okay?"

"And what about the rest of it?"

He shrugged. "That's up to you."

Jenna opened and then closed her mouth. What the heck was she supposed to do now?

"Time I took you in. Don't want you getting cold." Blue took her hand and set off purposefully toward the house. "I've got to get back. I drove down from Bridgeport today, and I'm dead on my feet."

"You shouldn't have come all this way out here to see me."

He stopped walking. "Hell, yes, I should. Sometimes things can't wait, Jenna."

"I was planning on apologizing to you the moment I saw you," Jenna confided.

"Good to know." His expression softened. "I'll sleep better knowing we're on the same page."

"Are we?"

He lowered his head until his lips brushed hers. "Jenna, darling, if we weren't at your uncle's house and I hadn't just eaten my second dinner of the night, I would be stripping you naked and making love to you."

"You ate *two* dinners?"

His eyebrows shot up. "That's the only thing that jumped out at you in that romantic speech?"

She started to laugh and after a moment he joined in. The back door of the house opened and light streamed out catching them cackling like two schoolkids.

"Oy," Dave shouted. "Keep it down out there, you're scaring the dogs."

Blue kissed Jenna one last time. "I'll see you tomorrow, okay?"

She watched him drive away still grinning, Dave by her side.

Only after she'd reached the sanctuary of her room did her smile disappear. As usual, Blue made everything seem easy. She sank down onto the side of her bed and studied her linked fingers. Could she do it? Could she finally reach out, take what she wanted, and be happy?

At least she hadn't told him about her craven plans to return home, but she hadn't told anyone but Ruth . . .

"Darn it!" Jenna sat bolt upright.

She couldn't imagine Ruth *not* telling Blue anything she thought would affect him. But he hadn't mentioned her leaving, and had only offered her an opportunity to stay. Did he know her better than she knew herself? Did he truly see beyond her fears to what she really wanted? That was both the most terrifying and the most exhilarating thought she'd ever had.

Blue drove back slowly, appreciating both the silence and the sense of freedom. For the first time in twelve years he wasn't serving his country, being shot at, or being bawled out by an officer. The offer to go on the roster at the Mountain Warfare Training Center for the horse-riding course intrigued him. He'd probably sign up, but that was the extent of his desire to go back into the military again. He was lucky. He'd survived relatively unscathed and had a job and a family to come home to. A lot of soldiers didn't, and the transition to civilian life was often painful.

He stopped the truck to let himself through two sets of gates and arrived back at the ranch, driving as slowly as possible to minimize the noise. Jenna hadn't said anything about leaving Morgantown. Should he have pressed her on that? He'd been so damned relieved to find her willing to accept his apology and offer one in return that he hadn't wanted to spoil their reunion with more questions.

Maybe this was one of these occasions when he was going to have to try trusting her to make the right decision. Nagging her into something would probably backfire. She really did have to make up her own mind and make a stand. He sighed as he turned off the engine. She should've gone into the Marines. He couldn't even count the number of times when only blind faith in his colleagues had kept him up and running, and alive.

Stepping out of the cab, he noticed a shadow moving by the barn and instantly went still. He walked around the truck and down the slope away from the house. As he entered the barn he caught the murmur of a low voice and relaxed.

"Ry?"

His brother turned his head and nodded to him. "BB. I'm just saying good-bye to the horses."

"You're leaving?"

"First thing in the morning. Gotta go talk to HW."

Blue leaned against the stall door and patted Nolly, who was busily guzzling carrots out of Ry's palm. "But you'll be back?"

"Yeah."

"Will HW come with you?"

"I don't know."

Blue frowned. "But you two have always done everything together."

"Maybe not this time."

"What's he up to?"

"Hanging out with some real losers." Ry sighed. "Thinks he's in love."

"Damn."

"I'll tell him what Chase said, but I don't think he'll come."

"I'm sorry, bro. It was hard enough when I broke things off with Chase. I can't imagine how it must feel to be fighting with your twin."

Ry didn't say anything for a long while as he continued to pet the horse. "We're not fighting. We're just not in sync anymore. It's kind of like losing half your soul."

Blue thought that was the longest and most personal speech Ry had made since returning to the ranch. "Maybe when you get back he'll have missed you and had an attitude adjustment."

"Yeah."

Ry didn't sound very hopeful.

"Do you want me to go down there and talk to him?"

"He wouldn't listen." Ry stepped back and stared up at the sky. "Man, look at all those stars up there. You just don't see them in the city."

Realizing the subject was now closed, Blue wrapped an arm around his brother's shoulders and walked him back up to the ranch, telling him about his unavoidable second dinner of the night until Ry was smiling again.

He needed to sleep well because he was going to have a busy week. Jenna might not believe that her neighbors in Morgantown were more than happy for her to stay, but Blue knew it was true. All he had to do was find a way to let her know it as well.

Chapter Eighteen

"What do you mean you can't make it? I've got my bag packed and I'm sitting here waiting for the taxi to take me to the airport. You were supposed to meet me at LAX." Blue paced up and down the worn rug in his bedroom, his cell clamped to his ear.

At the other end of the call, Chase sighed. "Jake was in a car crash."

"Damn. Is he okay?"

"They're not telling us anything yet. I can't get away until his family arrives from Washington."

"What about Matt?"

"He's with me. We both need to be here."

"I understand. Are we going to reschedule?"

"I'd rather not do that. I had to pay Big Mike to even agree to see us. I only know where he is right now because the detective agency is keeping a twenty-four-hour tail on him." Chase hesitated. "Could you get Billy or Jenna to go with you?"

"I'm not taking Billy."

"Okay, that was a stupid suggestion. Take Jenna. I'll

get the tickets changed right now. Call me back when you're on your way."

"Chase—"

But his brother was already gone. Blue stared at his packed bag for a long, frustrated minute and then picked it up and stomped down the stairs.

"Ruth!"

"There's no need to bellow like a bull. I'm in the parlor."

Blue poked his head around the door and eyeballed his grandma. "Chase can't make the trip. Jake was in an accident. Is Jenna around?"

"She's out with Roy and the pigs."

"Okay." He came in and kissed the top of her head. "Look after Maria for me."

"Will do. Have a safe trip." She grabbed hold of his hand. "I hope you find out what you want to hear, BB, but don't be surprised if you don't."

"Got it." He kissed her again. "Love you. Tell the taxi to hang out if I'm not back in a few, okay?"

He left his bag on the front step, jumped into his truck, and drove down toward Roy's place and the pigsty next to it.

"Jenna!" He was already talking before he got out of the truck. "I need you."

"What's wrong?" She was up to her elbows in pig shit and on the wrong side of the pigsty wall. "Is it one of the horses? Is it Ruth?"

"No, I need you to come to San Diego with me right now. Chase can't make it, and it's our only chance to get to see Big Mike."

"Me?" She glanced uncertainly between Roy and Blue.

"Chase has already changed the tickets. You've got

about fifteen minutes. You only need an overnight bag. We'll be back tomorrow."

"But—"

Blue held her gaze. "Please? I could really do with the company."

She sighed. "Okay, but I need to shower and change my clothes."

Roy bowed with a flourish. "*Mi casa* is your *casa,* lady."

"Thanks, Roy. I have an overnight bag in my truck. Could you grab it for me, Blue?"

"What, are you psychic or something?"

She was running for the house now, the sweet smell of pig wafting behind her. "No, I often end up covered in unmentionable stuff and need to change. It's the nature of the job."

To his astonishment, in fifteen minutes she was showered, freshly clothed, and sitting beside him in the cab as it headed for the local airport. His cell buzzed and it was Chase's admin confirming the new ticket assignments. His brother was nothing but efficient even in a crisis.

Blue typed a thank-you and an inquiry about Jake, but there was no update. Jenna was also busy texting, presumably settling things with her family.

He touched her arm. "Thanks for doing this."

"You didn't give me much choice."

"Chase thinks that if we don't speak to Big Mike now, we'll never find him again."

"Then let's go and talk to him."

The taxi pulled up at the small local airport, and a man dressed in some kind of uniform opened the door.

"Mr. Morgan? Ms. McDonald? There's been a slight change of plan. Mr. Chase Morgan has chartered a private jet for you to complete your journey to San Diego in one hop."

"Nice." Blue grinned at Jenna.

"I've never been in a private plane," Jenna whispered as they were whisked along a series of hallways to a secure lounge.

"Neither have I," Blue confessed. "Unless you count a military transport."

"I'll just check you in." The man retreated behind a desk, leaving them alone.

Beyond the door Blue could already hear the rumble of an idling engine. It made his heart rate increase, although he hoped his current mission wouldn't be quite so stress inducing as his last.

"Mr. Morgan? We're ready to go."

Blue took hold of Jenna's hand and marched forward into the unknown. Sometimes that was all you could do.

Time hadn't been kind to Big Mike. He'd piled on the weight, and even on his massive frame it was starting to show. His vibrant red hair was faded to sand and his weathered face bore the expression of a man who'd let life beat him down.

He glanced up as Blue and Jenna filed into the seats opposite him in the coffee bar he'd chosen as the meeting place. It was near the sea, but at the less touristy end of the commercial dock.

"You look familiar."

"I'm BB Morgan. You worked on our ranch near Bridgeport a while back. This is Jenna McDonald."

Big Mike screwed up his bloodshot eyes. "There was a vet called McDonald, right?"

"Same family."

"Seems not a lot changes out there." Big Mike sipped his coffee. "So what did you want to talk to me about?"

Blue contemplated the man sitting opposite him. "Don't you know?"

"I don't remember much." Mike shrugged his massive shoulders. "Too much booze and too many blows to the head, so they tell me at the clinic."

"Okay, then I'll just put it out there. Do you remember my mother Annie?"

"Sure I do. She was a nice lady."

"I remember she liked you a lot."

Big Mike smiled for the first time. "I was popular with the ladies back then."

Blue kept quiet, but Big Mike didn't say anything else, so he tried again. "Annie left the ranch around the same time you did."

"Did she now." His smile disappeared.

"In fact, we think she left the same night. Can you confirm that?"

"Maybe she did, maybe she didn't. I can't quite recall. After that bastard Roy fired me, I got good and drunk before I packed up my stuff and left."

Blue took a careful breath. "And when you left? Did Annie and my baby sister come with you?"

"What does it matter? What are you trying to do?" Big Mike glared at Blue. "Convict me of something? Because I've had enough shit from the cops to last me several lifetimes, and I won't be dragged back into something that happened so long ago any decent folk would have forgotten it!"

Blue kept his voice level and pleasant. "You're talking about the disappearance of my mother and sister. It's still very important to my family and me. We just want to know the truth."

"And I'm telling you I don't really remember that night

at all. I woke up a couple of days later in a motel and was kind of surprised to find myself there."

"Were you alone when you woke up?"

"Yeah."

Blue exhaled. "You sure about that?"

"Yeah."

"Then there isn't really a lot left for me to say, is there?" Blue slid twenty bucks under the coffeepot and stood up.

"Hold on, where's the rest of my money?" Big Mike held out his hand.

"What money?"

"The five grand I was offered if I would meet with you."

"You'll have to take that up with my older brother. He's the one with the cash, and I'm going to make sure he knows the 'information' you passed on amounted to diddly-squat." He tipped his hat to Big Mike. "Nice meeting you again. Come on, Jenna."

Outside the shop he took deep breaths of the fresh sea air, but nothing could stop the frustration and rage of decades of loss bubbling up inside him.

"Blue . . ."

"What?"

Jenna was biting her lip. "I think you should go back in there."

"What the hell for? He doesn't know anything. He's just using us for some sick purpose of his own."

"I don't think that's true. If you could just calm down—"

He rounded on her. "I've waited twenty years to find out what happened to my mother and sister. Don't you think I have a right to be angry when that loser is messing with us?"

He slammed his hand against the brick wall. "I am so fucking done with all this." He swung around again in time to see her flinch away from him. "*Shit,* Jenna, I didn't mean—"

She started speaking fast, as if she was afraid of him cutting her off, or worse. "Perhaps he knows more than he maybe realizes. Think about it. If he really was that drunk, who drove him away from the ranch?"

Blue stared at her for a long time. "I . . . don't know."

"Would you let me talk to him?"

"You think you'll do better?"

"I tracked down my birth parents and had to deal with a lot of denial before they'd admit to even *being* my parents." She raised her chin. "You can stay out here if you'd rather."

"You mean if I can't control my temper."

Her cheeks reddened but she didn't need to say anything. He already knew how much she hated violence. What a great time for him to lose his cool and scare his favorite woman in the universe.

"It's better if I do it. I'm not involved."

"I'm not going to hurt him."

She held his gaze a faint question in her eyes that made him feel like hitting the wall again, which would just confirm her opinion that he was out of control. She also looked poised to run away, which made him feel like a heel. He took a slow breath.

"Did your dad hit you?"

She stilled. "What did you say?"

"You heard me."

She blinked and looked away from him. "That has nothing to do with the problem in hand. Do you want me to try and talk to Big Mike or not?"

He nodded.

"Sometimes you have to put your personal feelings aside and concentrate on the goal, Blue."

"You think I don't know that? I'm a goddamn Marine."

"Then act like one and stop jumping to conclusions," she snapped. "Maybe you could call Chase and get some information about how the money is supposed to be delivered to Big Mike, and then come and join me."

She opened the door into the coffee shop and went back inside, leaving him staring after her in shock.

Jenna was aware that she was trembling. Violence or rage always made her feel sick, but she didn't let that stop her from reaching her target. Luckily for her, Big Mike was still sitting in the booth, getting his money's worth out of his carafe of coffee.

She slid into the booth opposite him and summoned a smile.

"Blue's upset. He really wants to find out what happened to his mother and sister. I'm sure you can understand that."

"Sure, but there's no need to try and double-cross a man."

"He was telling the truth about the money. His older brother is the one who arranged this meeting, and then wasn't able to be here. Any financial arrangement you made will have to go through your contact with him." She tried to sound sympathetic. "Blue's out there right now trying to contact his brother and see what the situation is, okay?"

"Okay."

A waitress came by and Jenna ordered a glass of lemonade, a refill for Big Mike's coffee, and an extra cup for Blue.

"The night you left the ranch, you said you were really drunk, right?"

"Yeah. With good reason."

"So how did you manage to drive?"

Big Mike sat back and contemplated Jenna before shaking his head. "I dunno."

"Is it possible that Annie took advantage of your drunkenness and stole a ride with you?"

"I suppose she could've done that." Big Mike appeared to like that idea. "Yeah, that's probably what she did. There's no good those Morgans saying I stole her away or blaming me or anything."

"I don't think they want to blame you. They just want to understand what happened." Jenna thanked the waitress and took a sip of her lemonade. "When you woke up in the motel, was there any sign that Annie might have been with you at any time? Somebody must have cared enough to make sure you were in a safe place, so it might have been her way of thanking you for the ride."

Big Mike stared off into space for so long that Jenna began to worry. Eventually he sighed and looked across the table at her.

"Diaper stink."

"What?"

"In the bathroom trash. I almost puked when I went in there." He shook his head. "I only just remembered that."

"Do you remember the name of the motel you stayed in or which town you were in?"

Big Mike's gaze hardened as he looked past her to the door. "Your boyfriend's coming back."

Talk about bad timing. "Do you remember the town?"

"I'll have to think about that."

Blue sat down beside her. "Sorry I took so long. I had trouble getting hold of Chase." He held Jenna's gaze. "Chase said we are authorized to pay him up to five thousand dollars, depending on the usefulness of his information." Big Mike started to interrupt, and Blue held up his hand. "Chase *also* says that Big Mike has already been paid five grand to even grace us with his presence, so he's talking shit if he says he hasn't."

"Good to know," Jenna said. "Blue can you confirm that your family has no intention of involving the police in this matter, and that Big Mike is not being held accountable for kidnapping or stealing Annie away from the ranch?"

"I can confirm that."

"See?" She turned back to Big Mike. "Now if you want to earn some more of that 5K, perhaps you might try and remember the name of that hotel and the town?"

By the time the taxi was almost at the San Diego airport, Jenna was running on fumes. After she'd filled him in with the relevant new details, Blue had remained uncharacteristically silent. He was still distracted now as he picked up her backpack.

"I just texted Chase. We're staying here tonight. He's got us a hotel room." He leaned forward to talk to the driver. "Can you take us to the Fairmont Grand Delmar?"

Jenna sat back and closed her eyes against the beginnings of a headache. It had been a stressful day. Far worse than she had anticipated. She hadn't even realized Blue had a temper. He was usually so in control . . .

"Jenna? We're here. Give me your bag."

Someone opened the door of the cab and she was bowed into the lobby of the hotel like a visiting celebrity, Blue at her side. The suite they were shown into was huge and faced the ocean. After using the bathroom and washing her face, Jenna stared longingly at the huge California king–sized bed.

"Want to take a nap before dinner?" Blue emerged from the second bathroom wearing just his unzipped jeans.

He suddenly stopped about six feet away from her. "By yourself, I mean."

She was too tired to work out what that meant and simply climbed onto the bed, rolled onto her front, and buried her face in the pillow. Within seconds she was asleep.

When she woke up she opened her eyes to a room in half darkness. The drapes remained open, giving her a fine view of the ocean and the lights dancing along the seafront. Blue sat in one of the easy chairs, his legs stretched out in front of him as he contemplated the view. The pillow next to hers hadn't been touched.

"I'm just going to shower."

Jenna escaped into the bathroom and spent quite a while using all the lotions and potions that were heaped in a basket beside the bath. When she came out wrapped in a velvety soft white bathrobe, Blue had disappeared. She wandered out onto the balcony and admired the view. Having a multimillionaire for a brother was obviously a useful thing. She wasn't sure how she was going to deal with going economy again.

Her cell buzzed and she took it out of her pocket.

Why didn't you tell us you were in San Diego, darling?

Jenna pulled a face and texted back. Sorry, Mom. It was a totally unplanned trip.

Understand you are staying the night. We will be at your hotel to take you for breakfast tomorrow morning. No excuses! x

"What's up?"

Jenna looked up as Blue came toward her. He'd obviously been in the shower as well.

"My mom thinks I'm close enough to take out to breakfast. What time does our flight leave?"

He looked amused. "I think that's up to us. What time do you need it to leave?"

"I'd better see her. It means she's less likely to hunt me down at the ranch."

"Go ahead. There's no rush to get back."

Sure! We're at the Fairmont Grand. Ask for Blue Morgan's suite.

We'll be there at seven thirty sharp. Can't wait to see you!! xxx Bring your young man.

Jenna put down her phone. "You're invited as well, by the way. Seven thirty."

He sat opposite her. "Do you want me to come?"

"It's up to you."

He held her gaze. "You impressed me today."

"Really? I thought I just annoyed you." She kept her tone civil and light.

"I was angry with Big Mike, not with you."

"I get that." She hesitated. "I didn't know you had a temper."

His hand tightened on the chair rest. "I don't."

Jenna just looked at him.

"I mean I try really hard not to lose it, okay? Today was just . . ." He shook his head. "So frustrating. I had this stupid idea that we'd meet Big Mike and he'd take us to his home and there would be Mom and Rachel and . . . Ruth told me not to get my hopes up."

"But we did learn something. Annie definitely left with Big Mike, whether he realized it or not, and left him somewhere near Humboldt. Maybe Chase's detectives can find out who paid for that room and trace your mom from there."

"It was twenty years ago. What's the chance of that? Maybe we should just let it go."

Jenna studied him carefully. "Maybe you should."

"You didn't." He suddenly looked up at her. "You found your birth parents."

"Which is why I'm suggesting you don't make the same mistake. They weren't how I pictured them at all. And neither of them wanted anything to do with me."

"That sucks."

"Yeah." She forced a smile. "But at least I knew, and it helped me appreciate how lucky I was to be given a new family."

"Jenna, darling, they were lucky to have *you*." He stretched out his legs and yawned so hard his jaw cracked. "I just want to know whether they are alive. I'd even sacrifice seeing them again if I knew that."

"Blue Morgan, you are such a liar. If you found them you'd be knocking on their door in a heartbeat."

"Chase wouldn't let me."

"Like you've ever let anyone stop you doing whatever you've wanted in your entire life."

"Okay. So maybe I'd check up on them, but I can be discreet." He frowned at her. "Why are you smiling?"

"'Discreet' is not a word I associate with you."

He grinned and rose slowly from his chair like the big predator he was. She shrank back in hers. "What are you doing?"

"Closing the drapes and checking the doors are all locked."

"Why?"

"Because I'm taking you to bed." He raised an eyebrow. "Is that discreet enough for you?"

When he returned to her side he had already discarded his jeans and was naked. He ran his fingers over her shoulders and down to the sash at her waist.

"You want me?"

She met his gaze. "You know I do."

He cupped her chin. "I'd never hurt you, Jenna. I'll do my damndest not to lose my temper, but I can't promise it won't ever happen again."

"That's honest of you."

"I don't want to be that man—a mean-tempered drunk who thinks it's okay to take his rage out on those he should be protecting. If I ever laid a finger on you or any kids of mine, I'd kick *myself* out."

"Did Billy hit you?"

"No, but after Mom disappeared he drowned himself in whiskey. It was frightening, you know? Because my dad was the most awesome person in my life and then suddenly he wasn't, and he'd get drunk and lose his temper and . . ." He shrugged. "You know how it goes."

"Yes."

"So I'd never do that."

"Okay."

His thumb traced the curve of her jaw. "So please tell me you're not scared of me."

She kissed his mouth, and with a sigh, he kissed her back, his hands sliding beneath her robe to caress her bare skin and make her shiver. He backed her toward the bed, his mouth never leaving hers, and she allowed him to lay her down on the crisp cotton sheets and straddle her hips.

"God, I'm sorry, Jenna." He bent to kiss her breast, his breath hot, his stubble rough against her sensitive skin.

"It's okay." She wrapped one arm around his neck, holding him as close as she could. "You'll find them. I know it in my soul."

And then all she could do was make love to him, and hope that his experience went better than hers and didn't make the pain even harder to bear.

By the time Blue got out of the shower and dressed in the clothes he'd worn the previous day, Jenna was already up and pacing the suite, her high ponytail swinging back and forth. He paused to button his jeans and kept a wary eye on her.

"You okay?"

"Sure! Why wouldn't I be?"

"I don't have to come with you."

She stopped walking. "You don't have to come if you don't want to."

For a moment they locked gazes until Blue sighed. "This is stupid. I want to come, but not if it's going to make things awkward for you."

"Things will be awkward anyway. They don't understand what I'm doing out in Morgantown, and Lily will have just made everything worse." She puffed out a breath. "Come with me. We might as well get it over with."

"How about I just call Chase and give him the details of our chat with Big Mike and then I'll text you to see if you want me to join you?"

"Blue . . ."

She looked way too vulnerable. He turned away to unplug his phone from the recharger they'd borrowed from the front desk. Apparently guests left them behind all the time.

"You'd better go. I'll catch up with you later, okay?"

She bit her lip and he resisted the urge to go to her, hold her in his arms, and make everything right for her. He was learning that sometimes he had to let other people work shit out for themselves. And this was definitely one of the occasions when she needed to face her fears without him butting in.

She slammed the door on her way out, so he guessed she didn't feel quite the same way. He called Chase, who was also on California time, and gave him the bullet points about the meeting with Big Mike. In return he found out that Jake was doing okay and was out of intensive care, so that was good.

Reassured that Chase would get on tracing the hotel records, Blue sent Jenna a text and quickly received a reply.

We're at the breakfast buffet. Come and join us.

Blue went down in the elevator and into the crowded restaurant. He soon spotted Jenna's burnished hair and made his way through the packed tables to her side. She shot to her feet when he approached.

"Mom, Dad, this is Blue Morgan."

Blue studied Jenna's adoptive parents. Mr. McDonald looked very like his brother Ron and wore a polite smile as he held out his hand to shake Blue's. Mrs. McDonald was blond and petite and radiated positivity and energy. She went on tiptoe to kiss his cheek and then patted his arm.

"It's good to meet you, Blue. Lily told us all about your lovely family ranch."

She waved him to the seat beside Jenna and they spent

the next few minutes ordering drinks and getting up to check out the offerings on the buffet, which turned out to be excellent. It wasn't until everyone was seated again and tucking in that Blue answered her.

"It's not my ranch. It still belongs to my grandma, but we all take an active part in helping it prosper." He smiled. "It's our family business. Jenna's been a real godsend these past few months."

Mr. McDonald smiled. "So I hear from my brother. It was kind of her to step in and help out for a few months."

Ah, the first salvo had been fired. Blue forked up a sausage. "Well, we're hoping to persuade Jenna to stay on much longer than that."

Beside him Jenna cleared her throat. "Chase, Blue's brother, offered me the job of full-time vet on the guest ranch."

"How super sweet of him," Mrs. McDonald exclaimed. "I'm not surprised, though, you must be the most educated person in that neck of the woods."

"I'm certainly the most recently qualified vet around, but as I keep telling you, there's nothing like the knowledge you gain on the job, and that only happens with experience."

Blue nodded slowly. "You know, Jenna's got a point. There's no denying she's as smart as a whip, but Big Mac's been practicing in our valley for over forty years. He knows everything a man needs to know about doctoring cattle, and Dave's almost as good with the horses."

Jenna stared at him, her fork frozen midway to her mouth.

"And Faith's coming back next year, so we'll have someone with an even more up-to-date degree around, won't we?" Blue smiled at the McDonalds. "And with my multimillionaire Stanford-educated brother Chase at the helm, there's no shortage of brainpower or experience in *our* valley."

Mrs. McDonald put down her knife. "Are you suggesting that Jenna wouldn't be the best person for the job?"

Blue shrugged. "I thought I was just agreeing with you."

"Jenna is an amazing and talented vet."

"Sure she is."

"Any veterinary practice or ranch should be glad to have her!"

Blue took a sip of coffee. "Exactly."

"Including yours."

"I couldn't agree more." Point made, Blue rose to get more food and took his time before returning to the table.

Jenna was refusing to look at him. Blue smiled at Mr. McDonald.

"So what do you do with your time, sir?"

"I'm a professor of theology at UCLA."

"Which means you do what, exactly?"

"I study the theory and history of religion."

"Oh right." Blue considered what to say next and realized he had nothing. "And how about you, Mrs. McDonald?"

"I have a doctorate in psychiatry and run a large medical practice treating mainly adolescents with mental health issues."

"Useful." Blue nodded.

"I understand you were in the Marines."

She made it sound like he'd been part of a terrorist organization rather than one of the few and the proud.

"Yeah, I just came out."

"Were you ever stationed in Afghanistan or Iraq?"

"A few times."

"What was it like?"

"Hot and dusty." He shrugged. "Boring most of the time."

"I doubt that," Mr. McDonald murmured.

"Lily said you enlisted."

Jenna stirred. "Mom . . ."

Blue kept his attention on Mrs. McDonald. "That's correct. At eighteen."

"Did you ever attempt to become an officer?"

"Why would I want to do that? I made gunnery sergeant, and that was good enough for me."

The McDonalds were looking at him as if he came from a different planet. He didn't care. He felt the same way about them.

"Blue served with honor and came back in one piece. Maybe instead of questioning his choices, Mom, you should be thanking him for his service."

At that moment, Blue wanted to kiss Jenna very badly. It was interesting that she'd happily stand up for him and not for herself.

"We're grateful for everything our military does to protect us, but—"

"But nothing, Mom. If he'd wanted to be an officer, he would have done so. He sure is smart enough. He scored higher than me on his APs and SAT." Jenna turned to Blue. "I apologize for my parents, okay?"

"There's no need. It's nothing I haven't heard before. My grandmother was furious when I chose not to take up any of my scholarship offers, and went down to the local recruiting office."

"You turned down scholarships?" Mrs. McDonald said faintly.

"Yeah, sports ones mainly for UCLA, Berkeley, and Stanford." He grinned at Mr. McDonald. "Hey, you could have been one of my professors."

Mr. McDonald finally smiled back at him. "So tell me more about your family ranch."

"You done yet?"

Jenna glanced across at Blue as he sat beside her in the taxi, which was taking them back to the ranch. It was early evening and the sun was just dipping down toward the horizon. It was still hot outside and the air-con was set to high.

"Done with what?"

"Sulking. You haven't said a word to me for hours," Blue said.

"I am *not* sulking. I've been thinking."

"Yeah? Looked more like you were planning how to end my existence."

She stared at the back of the taxi driver's head. "I *was* going to kill you, but then I worked it out."

He draped one arm along the back of the seat, his long fingers curving around her shoulder.

"You somehow managed to get my mom to agree that me working at the ranch would be a good thing."

"I know." He grinned at her. "Your face was a picture, by the way."

"I still don't understand how you did it."

He shrugged. "How do you think I survived the Marines?"

She rolled her eyes at him. "Not by using your brains."

He pouted. "I think I'm hurt."

She poked him in the ribs.

"Ouch."

"You deserved that."

He rubbed the spot. "Especially when you defended my military service."

"Yes, I *did*, didn't I?"

"I wanted to lean over that table and kiss you stupid."

"I wish you had."

He held her gaze. "Really? Damn. I was trying to make a good impression on your parents."

"My dad liked you."

"Don't worry. I'll bring your mom around."

"To me working at the ranch?"

His smile deepened. "And the rest."

She hurriedly looked out of the window. He shifted closer, his hand closing over hers.

"What's up?"

"I want to stay here."

"Good."

She waited, but he didn't say anything else. The taxi pulled up at the exterior gate of the ranch. Blue got out to unlock the gate and let them through. When he came back inside, he spoke to the driver.

"Can you take the second road on the left instead of going up to the main house?"

The driver nodded, and soon they drew up outside Roy's home. His truck was missing, and there were no lights on inside the house.

Blue paid the driver, and gave him instructions about how to get out of the gate while Jenna found her keys and put her bag in her truck. There was a light breeze blowing off the mountain range, which was refreshing. She turned her face into it, gathering her hair off her neck. After the taxi drove away, the ranch settled down again into relative silence apart from the occasional grunting pig.

She went to speak, but Blue beat her to it. "Have you got time to do one more thing with me?"

She rolled her eyes. "Didn't we do that enough at the hotel?"

"Not *that*." He grinned. "I want to take you somewhere."

"On the ranch?"

"Yeah. It's not far." He cocked his head in the direction of her truck. "Will you come with me?"

Ten minutes later, after his easy-to-follow directions, she pulled up and turned off the engine. It was quiet outside; only the wind rustled the treetops and dry grasses.

"This won't take long."

Puzzled, but willing to follow him, Jenna got out of the truck to find him waiting for her. He took her hand and drew her over some flat but rocky ground toward a line of bushes.

"Wow, nice view," Jenna breathed. From their position she could see down across the creek and over to the foothills of the Sierra Nevada.

Beside her Blue cleared his throat. "I'm thinking this would be a great place to build a house."

"Yeah, it would be *awesome*."

He glanced down at her. "So you approve?"

She tried to smile. "Well, it's not up to me, but yeah."

After a long moment while they both stared at the view, Blue started talking again. "Thanks for coming to San Diego. If it had been left to me we would've found out nothing, and I'd probably be in jail right now for starting a fight."

"You would've worked it out."

"No." He slid a hand around her neck. "You were the brave one, not me."

"It's easier to be brave when you're not emotionally involved in the issue."

"Who said I was emotional?"

Jenna raised her eyebrows. "Blue, you had every right to be frustrated and upset."

"But not to scare you." He hesitated. "Were you this calm when you met your birth parents?"

"I was terrified."

"Were they . . . aggressive toward you?"

"Not really. They just didn't care about me at all."

"Their loss." He bent his head and kissed her gently on the lips.

As soon as he lifted his head she blurted out, "I thought you'd be mad at me for not confronting my parents and telling them I want to stay here."

"It's not my place to tell you what to say or how to deal with your parents."

"You're right." Great. Now she looked stupid and needy. "It's not as if we're in a committed relationship or anything."

He went still. "Aren't we?"

Surprise held her silent.

"We're sleeping together—we spend most of our working days together, and you know all my secrets." He paused. "That's not a relationship?"

"I wasn't sure . . ."

He sighed and took a step back. "Jenna, it's all yours, you know, the ranch, the job, this house I'm planning on building, *and* me. All you have to do is reach out and take it." He touched his hat to her and started walking back to the truck. "Let's get you home."

She drove back to Roy's. Blue got out, came around to her open window, and smiled at her. "Night, darlin'. Drive safely."

"Don't you want a lift back to the house?"

He shook his head. "Nah, I could do with a walk. I do my best thinking when I'm on the move."

She managed to nod and mumble a good-bye. He made it sound easy, but he'd also made sure that she knew he wasn't going to do everything for her. Part of her wished he'd sweep her into his arms and solve all her problems. She knew he could if he wanted. He *loved* telling her what to do. But what he wanted was far more dangerous.

It required a leap of faith.

She'd have to admit she loved him, which she somehow did, and that she wanted to be with him forever. She'd have to face her family's disappointment and possible rejection. And what if everything went wrong, and she abandoned her family, and then lost Blue? She'd almost lost her family when she'd gone after the dream of her birth parents. Sure, they hadn't outwardly *rejected* her when she'd come back, but their confusion and hurt had been obvious and her sisters had been furious at her for being so *ungrateful*.

She stared up at Blue's retreating figure as he walked up the hill to the main house.

What if she jumped, and he wasn't there to catch her?

Chapter Nineteen

Blue rode Messi in a slow circle and then clicked his tongue, applied the smallest amount of pressure with his knees, and kicked into a lope. He loved riding fast, and Messi had the smoothest gait. He'd spent the morning with the new horses, trying out their paces and writing notes about what kind of rider would work best with each horse.

He knew from experience that sometimes you just had to sit someone on the back of a horse before you could see if it was a match. The relationship between a horse and rider was more complex than an amateur might imagine, and it would be his job to match each guest with the best horse.

It was a beautiful crisp day and he'd been up early after a restless night disrupted by dreams of Jenna and nightmares about his mom—sometimes both at the same time. He sensed Jenna was beginning to believe he meant what he said, and he was determined to stand back and let her make her choice without input from him. Anyone who committed to a life out in the middle of nowhere on an isolated ranch needed to make that decision with eyes wide open. His mom had hated it, and he couldn't bear the thought of Jenna feeling like that.

He eased Messi back down to a walk and let him cool off as they approached the rear of the pastureland bordering the barn and house. He'd also spent some time thinking about his new house and even jotted down some ideas about the style and interior, which had been far more interesting to do than he'd anticipated. By his reckoning, the property was far enough away from the new construction of the guest cottages, but close enough to get back to the main ranch house when he was needed.

He dismounted outside the barn and spent a while brushing Messi down and making sure he had enough water before putting him back in his stall. After lunch he'd type his notes into the database Chase had constructed for each horse so that everyone had access to the same information. He'd laughed at his brother for suggesting it, but he was secretly super impressed.

He walked up to the house, where he found Ruth, January, and Chase sharing a pot of coffee around the kitchen table. They were all looking remarkably serious, and he paused in the doorway to take off his hat.

"What's up?"

Chase held up an envelope. "I got them to speed up your DNA results."

Blue took the envelope and sat down heavily on the nearest chair. "Where's Maria?"

"She's out riding with Billy and Roy," Ruth volunteered, her blue gaze steady but anxious. "They won't be back for a while."

Chase cleared his throat. "Do you want some privacy?"

Blue shook his head, his fingers already easing under the envelope flap. He took out the single sheet and slowly read through the contents twice before looking up.

"She's my daughter."

"Well, thank the Lord." Ruth pressed a hand to her chest.

"You okay?" Chase asked.

Blue nodded. "Yeah. I'm . . . kind of relieved, you know? We can keep her safe here and love her as much as she deserves." He blew out his breath. "I suppose I should go to Sacramento and sort things out with Daniel Lester."

"I don't think you have a choice. Maybe he'll let you have some of Maria's things."

"He's probably gotten rid of them all by now." Blue rubbed a hand over his jaw. "I'll just turn up on his doorstep so he can't refuse to see me."

"Maybe you could check in with Red Williams while you're up that way. He's given his permission for us to visit him in prison."

Blue looked at Chase. "Do you think it's worth it? After all, we know Mom and the baby left with Big Mike."

"It can't hurt." Chase shrugged. "I'd like to investigate all the angles and close this one down."

"Sure—unless you want to come with me and see him while I tackle Daniel Lester."

Chase grimaced. "I've got to get back to the office. With Jake out of action, the workload is crushing us."

"At least he's getting better. You should get him out here. A few weeks of peace and quiet and Ruth's cooking would do him a world of good."

"I've already suggested it." Chase hesitated. "When are you going to tell Maria?"

"And do you need any help?" Ruth reached for his hand and squeezed it hard. "I can tell her if you'd prefer it."

"I need to do this myself." Blue kissed his grandmother's work-roughened fingers and released them. "I'll catch her when she gets back from her ride."

Ruth got to her feet and put on her apron. "Then I'd better start cooking a celebratory dinner. Seeing as you boys refuse to give me great-grandchildren, it's not often we *get* to welcome a new member of the family."

Chase rolled his eyes at Blue. "I'm going back to the city tomorrow. You can catch a ride with me if you like?"

"Private jet?"

"Yeah, so what?"

"Then I'll definitely come."

Voices echoed in the hallway and Blue tensed as Roy and Billy came into the kitchen.

"Maria's gone upstairs to wash. She'll be down in a minute," Billy said, his gaze moving around the kitchen and finally settling on Blue. "Is everything all right?"

Blue nodded as he headed for the stairs. "Talk to Chase. I'll be back in a minute."

As he reached the top of the stairs, he heard Maria singing to herself as she skipped along the landing, her braids bouncing.

"Hey." Blue smiled at her. At his *daughter,* and something inside him curled tight and solidified right next to his heart. "You got a moment?"

Her smile faltered and she backed up and went into her bedroom. By the time Blue reached her she was sitting on her bed, her arms folded across her chest.

He shut the door and crouched on the floor in front of her.

"The DNA results came in. You're my daughter."

"Okay."

He met her worried gaze. "I just want you to know that I'm proud to be your father, and that if it's okay with you I'm going to do my best to always be there and never ever let you down again."

She studied him for a long while.

"You can't promise things like that. What happens if you change your mind?"

"I won't."

"You might."

"I will do everything in my power not to." He hesitated. "Maria, I can't predict what will happen in the future, but I do know that you will always have a home and a family here. We love you, honey."

Her lip trembled, and with an inarticulate sound she flung herself into his arms. He held her tight and dropped a kiss onto her black hair. He wished he could hold her like this forever and keep the world from ever hurting her again.

"I know it's been horrible for you lately," he murmured. "But we'll sort everything out, I promise."

"Even with my other dad?"

"Especially with him." She raised her head and he loosened his grip on her shoulders. "Do you want to come down and see Ruth and Billy? I'm sure they'd love to welcome you into the family."

Her expression lightened. "Is Billy my *granddad*?"

"Yeah, and Ruth is your great-grandmother, and Chase is your uncle, as are Ry and HW, and January is going to be your aunt."

She tugged on his arm, hauling him to his feet, and started for the door. "What about Roy?"

"Roy's like an extra-grumpy great-uncle."

"How about Jenna?"

Blue winked at her. "You never know what might happen there, kiddo."

They started down the stairs hand in hand and went into the kitchen, where everyone still congregated. Maria went straight to Billy, who gathered her into a hug.

"So I understand I have a new granddaughter. Any idea who that is?"

Maria buried her face in his shoulder and wrapped her arms around him. "Me?"

Billy met Blue's gaze over Maria's head and smiled. "You sure?"

"Blue said so."

"And he's quite correct. We have the science to prove it." He drew Maria onto his lap. "Now all we have to decide is what you're going to call me instead of Billy. How about Gramps?"

Blue turned away and went outside, gulping in the clean mountain air. He'd thought about Maria being his daughter, but the actual reality of it—the science, as Billy had put it—was overwhelming. He'd missed out on so much, and he wanted to give her *everything*—fight for her, die for her, kill anyone who so much as made her cry . . .

His hands clenched into fists and he stared out over the ranch. He'd never felt like this about anything before in his life, so out of control and so *vulnerable*. He didn't like it one bit.

"Are you all right, Blue?"

He looked down onto the driveway where Jenna was standing, looking up at him. He'd been so distracted he hadn't even heard her truck pull up. She took a step forward.

"Is Jake okay? Is Maria—?"

He walked down the steps to her. "She's my daughter."

She searched his face. "And you're okay with that?"

"It just hit me hard."

"In a good way or a bad way?"

"In a 'what the hell am I supposed to do now? I know nothing about being a parent' way."

She patted his arm. "You'll work it out."

"You think so?" He groaned. "I just want to wrap her up in cotton wool and keep her safe."

"That's good."

"I bet she won't think so."

She smiled. "Maybe you're overreacting just a tad, but that's to be expected. Finding out you have a ten-year-old daughter can't be easy."

He groaned. "Don't keep *saying* that."

She cupped his chin. "Blue, you will be a great dad. I know it in my bones. Trust me on this, I've had plenty of experience."

"Okay." He took a deep breath. One of the things he loved most about Jenna was her ability to keep her head and to share that calm optimism with him. "I think I'm ready to go back in now."

She kissed his mouth. "Good man."

Reflecting back on his moment of sheer panic the next day as he parked his rental near the correctional facility, Blue couldn't help but be glad Jenna had turned up when she did. He hoped he would've gotten his shit together and gone back inside, but he wasn't 100 percent certain. She just made things right for him. She added the parts he missed and made him whole.

"Sir? You need to go through our security systems."

He looked up to see the walls of the prison rising above him and hastily found his ID. "Good morning, I have an appointment."

Almost an hour later he was inside the prison and sitting in a stark interview room at a table bisected by a bulletproof screen that stretched the entire length of the room and up to the ceiling. After a long wait, a prisoner in an orange jumpsuit was escorted into the other side of the room and maneuvered into the chair opposite.

Red Williams still looked like the sweetest man alive with dimples, bright brown eyes, and a friendly smile. But that probably explained his unfortunate success rate with women and the scattering of irate exes and babies he'd left behind him.

Blue picked up the phone, and the other man did as well.

"Is that you, BB Morgan? You sure grew a bit."

"Hi, Red. Yeah, I suppose I did." He wanted to ask how Red was doing, but it seemed a stupid thing to say when the guy was stuck in prison for the next five years.

"Your brother said you wanted to talk to me about your mother and baby sister."

"That's right." Blue collected his thoughts. "We're trying to find out what happened to her the night my father was arrested. Do you remember anything from back then?"

"Son, the older you get, the more clear the past becomes. I do remember that night. That's why I agreed to speak with you." Red settled into his chair, his expression focused inward, softening the harsher lines of his face.

"I remember coming out of the bunkhouse and seeing your mama getting into Big Mike's truck. I only noticed because she climbed in the driver's seat, and Big Mike, who'd been fired by Roy earlier that day and had just come to get his belongings, was slumped in the passenger seat. I suspect he was drunk as usual, which was why he got fired in the first place."

Blue nodded. "That's Big Mike's take on that night as well. He claims he didn't know who drove him away and that he woke up in a motel all alone."

"It's possible. He was a horrible drunk."

"The thing is, we don't know what happened to my mother after that."

Red scratched his ear. "Well, maybe I can help you with that. A couple of years after I left your place I happened to stop at a diner near Eureka, and guess who was working there?" He smiled. "Yeah, your mom. She wasn't real happy to see me, and she tried to pretend she didn't know who I was, but I soon calmed her down."

He winked at Blue. "I was always good with the ladies—which is why I ended up with three wives, seven kids, and in jail. She'd changed her name to Betty or something like that according to her name tag, and she begged me not to tell anyone I'd seen her. Now, I was able to do that because I had no intention of going back to Morgantown, seeing as one of those embarrassing situations concerning paternity rights and stealing had come up right there."

"Did she ask about us?"

"No, she was more concerned about me not ratting her out. Poor woman."

"Did she look . . . healthy?"

"A bit on the scrawny side, but she always was affected by her nerves."

"Did she mention my baby sister?"

Red blinked at him. "No, come to think of it, she didn't."

Blue sat and stared at the man opposite him for way too long before recollecting that his time would soon be up. "Is there anything else you want to tell me?"

"I think that's it."

"You've been really helpful."

Red shrugged his bony shoulders. "Got nothing else to do in here except think about the past and wish I'd done things differently. Glad to help. She was a nice lady."

"Is there anything I can do for you to say thank you?"

Red grinned. "Get me out of here? Nah, I'm just kidding. It was a pleasure seeing what a fine man you've grown into, BB. How's Ruth?"

"Still alive and bossing us all around."

"Figures." Red glanced around as one of the guards moved purposefully toward him. "Time's up."

"Thank you."

"I hope you find your mom. She was a handsome woman." He winked. "Too faithful to your daddy, unfortunately, but a man could always hope."

Red put down the phone and was helped to his feet by the guard. He nodded at Blue and then turned and shuffled away.

Blue stayed put for a while, processing what he'd heard before getting to his feet and retracing his steps through the slow-moving security and out into the parking lot. He took out his cell and called Chase. He didn't bother with small talk.

"Red saw Mom two years after she left the ranch."

"What?"

"In Eureka."

"That's only about eight hours away from the damn ranch."

"Yeah, hiding in plain sight, although Red said she was calling herself Betty and working in a diner."

"Damn . . ."

"My feelings exactly. She asked him not to tell anyone, and due to him having to leave Morgantown under suspicious circumstances, he promised her he would never go back."

"Did she ask about us?"

There was the same hopeful note in Chase's question as there had been in his.

"Apparently not."

"Did he see Rachel?"

"She didn't mention her, either."

There was a long silence. "It's all new information for the investigators. Thanks for doing that, BB."

"You're welcome."

Chase sighed. "You okay?"

"I'm feeling about the same as you probably are. She really didn't want to come home, did she?"

"She probably had her reasons."

Blue had nothing to say to that. "Look, I'm driving back to Sacramento to find Daniel Lester. Do you have any more information about where he works?"

"I'll text it to you as soon as I have it."

"Okay. Thanks, bro."

Blue ended the call and put his cell away. It *hurt*. The fact that his mother hadn't asked after them rankled even after all this time. What kind of person forgot their kids like that? His dad had stumbled away in a drunken stupor, but even he had found the guts to come back after twenty years. Why hadn't his mother?

He turned the engine on and punched in Dan Lester's home address. If Chase didn't come up with another place to find the man, he'd wait him out until he turned up at home.

By the time Chase came through with Daniel Lester's business address it was almost five, and Blue decided to stay put at the house. There was a car parked in the driveway of the modest ranch house and the drapes were all drawn. Blue wondered whether Daniel had even gotten to work that day. If he was still drinking heavily, he might not have a job anymore. A light came on in the hallway and Blue made his decision, climbing out of his rental car and going up to the front door.

He was surprised when it opened, and almost recoiled

from the blast of stale air, sweat, and alcohol that streamed past the disheveled figure.

"You're not the pizza guy?"

"No, I'm Blue Morgan. I need to talk to you about Maria."

Daniel started to close the door, but Blue stuck his foot in the way.

"We need to talk at some point. I'd rather do it face-to-face and man-to-man than get the lawyers involved. It's up to you."

Daniel sighed and stepped back. "If you're anything like my brother you're not going to leave quietly, so you might as well come in."

"We Marines are like that." Blue stepped inside and then halted as he saw a set of framed photographs lining the hallway. "Wow, that's Angel, right? And Maria when she was a baby?"

"Meant to take them down. You can have them if you want." Daniel walked away and Blue followed him, his fascinated gaze fixed on the images of his daughter as she grew from a baby into a toddler and then a little girl.

The kitchen was a mess, and from the pile of boxes and plastic containers littering the countertops, it appeared that Daniel lived on takeout. His pasty gray complexion confirmed that he wasn't doing too well, and the slight tremor in his hands as he attempted to clear a space on the table confirmed Blue's suspicions that he was still drinking. Memories of Billy in a similar state flashed through his head.

"Take a seat."

Blue removed an empty vodka bottle from the chair Daniel indicated and sat opposite him at the grimy table.

"I wanted you to know that the DNA testing confirmed that Maria is my daughter."

Daniel's shoulders sagged even further. "Yeah, well, that's a surprise."

"I'm willing to take full responsibility for her, but I wanted to get some feedback from you first."

"What about? She's not my kid."

"She thought she was for ten years. She misses you, and she doesn't understand why you kicked her out."

"So what? She'll get over it. I got over her mother cheating on me with you."

Blue kept a tight rein on his temper. "For what it's worth, I didn't know she was married when I met her. I would never have—"

Daniel held up his hand. "I'm not interested in your excuses, okay? I'm also not interested in discussing my late wife, or her kid."

"I can't believe that."

"Believe it, sonny. Angel's dead and Maria's . . ." He hesitated. "Not my problem. If you want her stuff? Take it, or leave me your address, and I'll send the whole damn lot in the mail."

Blue sat back and studied Daniel's resolute expression. "Then you don't intend to contest my taking full responsibility for her?"

"Nope. I'm done. In fact, maybe you should be paying me for her upkeep for the last ten years."

"I suspect you have some legal rights to see her if you wish, and I'm more than willing to work with you—"

Daniel stood up. "I don't want to see her! Don't you get that? Now get out of my house and don't come back."

Blue rose too, more slowly. "You're making a terrible mistake, you know? That little girl loves you."

Daniel pushed away from the table so hard his chair fell over and he lurched toward the refrigerator. He retrieved a half-empty bottle of vodka and started for the door.

"Get out."

The doorbell rang and he disappeared, staggering down the hallway. Blue took a moment to write out the address of the ranch and stuck it on the refrigerator under a magnet with Angel and Maria's smiling faces on it.

When he reached the front door, Daniel was searching haphazardly through his pockets, and the teenager holding the pizza box was looking terminally embarrassed.

"Wait a sec, I have it right here," Daniel mumbled.

Blue reached over his shoulder and handed the delivery guy forty bucks. "Here you go. Have a nice day."

He eased past Daniel, took the pizza, and placed it in his hands. "Enjoy. I'll be in touch through my lawyers."

He stomped back to his car, the pizza guy's thanks ringing in his ears, and just sat in the driver's seat trying to calm down. What a *fool*. How could Daniel not want to be part of Maria's life? Blue shook his head and started the engine. He had to return the car to the airport and get home. Concentrating on those necessary tasks would prevent him from going back into that house and shaking some sense into Daniel Lester.

But he'd done his best to be honest and up front. If the man was too stupid to deal with him face-to-face, he'd get Chase's team of crack lawyers on the case and make sure that Daniel could never take his daughter away from him again.

Chapter Twenty

"Okay, you can do this."

"Is it a long way?" Maria still looked anxious.

Blue made sure her boot was positioned correctly in the stirrup before mounting up himself.

"Not really. We're just going to ride down to the boundary near the county road and check the fence line, okay? You got sunscreen on?"

She rolled her eyes at him. "Yes."

"Then let's go."

He set off slow, watching her out of the corner of his eye. She was turning into a good little rider. It was true that the younger you started, the better you were. Her confidence and lack of fear constantly amazed him. Billy had done a fine job with her over the summer.

He'd spoken to Chase about the legal issues attached to Maria being his daughter and the possibility of Daniel making things difficult. He was fairly confident it would all work out. He checked his cell again, but there was nothing from Jenna. He'd hardly seen her in the week he'd been back, and he was beginning to think she was avoiding him.

Which was a pity as there were things he wanted to say to her—life-changing things that had ripped up his previous orderly plans and made him as nervous as hell. But he needed some sign from her that she was on board, and so far she'd not given him one. It was killing him not acting on his feelings, but this was too big an issue to mess up.

"Look! It's the mailman."

Maria pointed down to the lower gate, where a white-and-blue vehicle had just pulled off on the side of the road.

"Why don't you go on down and get the mail?" Blue suggested. "It'll save Brian a trip up to the house. Shout if there's anything big, okay?"

He checked his phone again, squinting against the sun, and saw he had a message. Putting the phone to his ear, he allowed Messi to amble down the side of the hill behind Maria as he listened to Daniel's quiet voice.

"I'm sending Maria's stuff to you. You should get it in a week or so. I . . . guess I should apologize for my behavior last time. I was a complete dick. I just miss Angel so much, and I just can't get my head around loving her, and hating her and—God, Maria—the thought of her. I can't deal with it, you know? I just can't."

There was a long silence and a stifled sob.

"So, yeah, I apologize, and maybe you're right and I should try and see Maria or something. I'll call you again, okay?"

Blue sat up in the saddle and looked down the slope to where Maria was chatting to the mailman and smiling. Crap, he didn't want that drunken idiot within a hundred miles of Maria. What the hell had he been thinking?

He'd call Chase, insist that Daniel only dealt with them through the lawyers, keep him tied up in legalese until . . .

"I got the mail!"

Blue waved to Brian as he got back in his vehicle. "Need any help?"

"No, I put it all in my saddlebag."

"Smart girl. We'll take it up to Ruth, and she can sort it out. You ready to ride the fence line?" He forced himself to smile at her. "It's about time you started earning your keep around here."

She made a face at him, and this time he smiled for real. Whatever it took to keep her safe? He was 100 percent committed to doing it.

Dinner at the ranch was noisier than usual, as everyone was present including Roy, and there was some major discussion going on about a party to celebrate Maria's upcoming eleventh birthday and her becoming part of the family. Blue was only half paying attention, his mind stuck in a loop about what Daniel intended to do and what *he* would have to do to protect Maria.

"And Dave said the pig was fine, but I reckon Jenna would've said differently. She's got a real *way* with those animals, you know?"

Blue looked up. "Why is Dave looking at the pigs?"

Roy shrugged. "I dunno. Maybe Jenna is busy."

"But it's her job to deal with Morgan Ranch."

"Not her official job. She hasn't accepted my offer yet," Chase chimed in.

"You made one?"

"Yeah, last week. Didn't she tell you?"

"She's not telling me a lot at the moment." Blue wiped his mouth with his napkin. "She's still around, right?"

"How the hell would I know?" Chase smiled at January. "I have my own woman to take care of. Why don't *you* know?"

"Because I'm an idiot?"

"True." Chase nodded solemnly.

"She's still here, Blue," January said. "I saw her at Yvonne's yesterday." She hesitated. "She seemed okay."

"Great. So it's just me she's avoiding."

"I wouldn't say *avoiding*, more like keeping busy doing her own stuff."

Blue raised a skeptical eyebrow. "Yeah, stuff that doesn't involve being around me."

"No, I really think she's trying to work through some personal issues before she has to deal with you. Give her some space, Blue. I'm sure she'll work it out."

He nodded, his gaze drawn to Maria, who was looking downright miserable.

"You okay, honey?"

She jumped and looked away. "I'm just a bit tired."

"You did a lot of riding today. Maybe you need an early night. Want me to come up and say good night when you're settled?"

"Okay."

She slid out of her chair, kissed Billy, and was gone. Blue frowned after her. She'd been quiet ever since they'd returned from their ride together, and he had no idea why. He gave her another half an hour to get settled and then went up the stairs, knocking gently on her door until she told him to come in.

She'd braided her hair and wore one of her favorite rainbow pony T-shirts. The ponies looked nothing like a real horse. Blue was getting used to them, but he had no intention of learning all their stupid names.

"You did good today." He sat on the side of her bed. "We'll make a real rancher out of you yet."

"Marigold is the best horse ever. Much better than Sugar."

"She's perfect for you right now. When you get a bit older we'll choose something with a bit more fire in her."

"But what if I'm not still here?"

"Honey, I thought we'd settled all that. You're here for as long as you want to be because we all love you and you're part of our family."

She bit her lip. "But what if my other dad wants me back?"

Blue went still. "I went and saw him, Maria. All I can say is that if you want to stay here, I'll make sure he can *never* take you back. Don't worry about it."

She stared at him. "But what if he says he's sorry?"

"Do you think he'll do that?" Blue asked as gently as he could.

"He might."

"If he does then we'll talk to him, okay? But I won't let him take you. This is your home now, and you don't have to have anything to do with him ever again. Period."

"Okay."

He kissed the top of her head. "Try and get some sleep. It's your birthday in a few days, so you've got to save your energy for that."

"Night, Blue." She reached up and hugged him hard. "I had a lovely day."

He went down the stairs with a sense of something still not being right, of something he'd missed, but he couldn't pinpoint what it was. He poked his head into the kitchen and focused on Ruth.

"I'm going out. Can you check in on Maria later? She's worrying about something."

"Sure I will." Ruth nodded. "I thought she was quieter than usual."

"I think she's worried about Daniel snatching her back. I told her it wasn't going to happen on my watch."

"I'll make certain she's settled. You going to see Jenna?"

"I might be."

"Give her my love, won't you, and don't forget to invite all the McDonalds to Maria's party."

"Will do."

"And, BB? Sort things out with her. She's way too perfect for you to lose."

"Yes, ma'am." Blue saluted smartly and left the house. He figured if he just turned up at the McDonalds', Jenna wouldn't be able to avoid him for long.

"So when will you be coming out here?" Jenna walked back and forth in her bedroom, one finger stuck in her ear as she tried to concentrate on what her mother was talking about. "No, that's fine. I wanted to see you both anyway, so that weekend works perfectly. Yeah, you can stay here with Ron and Amy."

Her mother talked on and she half listened as the gleam of headlights swept around the drive and a truck rumbled to a stop in front of the house.

"Okay, then. I have to go. Let me know your exact arrival time, and we'll take it from there. Love you both."

She peered closer at the truck and her heart gave a little bump as she recognized the lean-muscled shape of Blue Morgan striding up to the front door. She clutched her cell to her chest so hard that it slipped out of her grasp and clattered to the floor.

She wasn't ready to see him yet. She had a plan and everything and—dear God, was that him knocking at her bedroom door? Had he just walked right on in and up the stairs like he owned the place?

She opened the door. *"What?"*

His eyebrows rose. "Can I come in?"

"It depends."

"On what?"

"Whether this is a social call, which means we should be downstairs in the den with Dave and my uncle and aunt."

"There's nobody down there. I checked."

"And came up here *anyway*?"

"Says the woman who broke into my grandmother's house and got into my bed."

She felt her cheeks heat. "That was an aberration."

"It was a good one. I liked waking up finding you wanting me."

"It was a terrible infringement on your personal space."

His smile was slow and so intimate her knees weakened. "I *like* you in my space. Can I come in? I promise to behave myself."

She sighed and stepped back, letting him close the door behind him. He wore his usual well-fitting faded jeans and a gray T-shirt that somehow made his eyes look even bluer.

"So what's up?" she said brightly.

"We're going to be social?"

"What else were you planning?"

His gaze ran down over her long nightshirt to her bare feet. "Getting you naked and getting inside you as fast as humanly possible."

She folded her arms across her chest. "You said you'd behave."

"You don't want to do that?"

"Fast is not necessarily what every girl wants, you know."

Still holding her gaze, he reached out and ran his thumb

over her lower lip. "I'll start fast because I'm desperate, but I promise I'll slow down for round two."

A small whimper escaped her lips. "This isn't a good idea."

"Why not?"

"Because I'm still thinking."

"Can't you think and make love at the same time? I thought women were supposed to be the multitaskers of this world."

She shook her head. "When I'm with you, all rational thought goes out the window."

"That works for me. You don't think, and you count this time spent with me as one of your 'aberrations' and pretend it never happened."

"But that's not fair to you."

He shrugged. "I'll be okay. I'm a tough guy."

She inhaled his warmth and the subtle pine scent of his shower gel. He was so beautiful . . .

"I'm scared, Blue."

"Of me?"

"Of how I feel."

He cupped her face in his hands. "Then that makes two of us." He bent his head and kissed her gently on the lips. "Maybe we could try and work this out together?"

She couldn't help but kiss him back. When he was close and when he touched her, she forgot everything except her desire for more of him, more kisses, more skin, more . . .

His hand slid up inside her T-shirt, and he groaned into her mouth. "God, I missed you so much."

He went back to kissing her, walking backward to sit on the edge of her bed. She followed him down, straddling his lap, the thin barrier of her panties the only thing keeping her away from the hard ridge of his jeans-covered erection. She rocked into him and his hand fisted in her hair.

"I want to be inside you right now, I want . . ."

She carefully unzipped him, cupping the heat and stretch of his cotton-clad shaft, rubbing her thumb over the wetness dampening the fabric. He groaned, pushing himself into her palm as she covered him, wiggled out of her panties, and slid down, taking him deep and hard.

He wrapped one arm low around her hips, controlling her motion, and drove upward in quick urgent thrusts, one thumb sliding over her most sensitive flesh until she came hard, startling her and making him curse and follow her over the edge.

His breathing was as ragged as hers as they remained locked together, his face buried against her shoulder as she gulped in some much-needed air. A strange buzzing sound reverberated against her thigh and she looked down to see Blue's pocket vibrating.

"Your phone."

"If it's important they'll leave a message or call back." He eased her away from him and she fell back on the bed. He rolled on top of her, his smile lazy, but also determined. "Round two?"

His phone buzzed again and then there was the ping of a text. Across the room where she'd plugged it in for the night, Jenna's phone started to ring as well.

"What the hell—?" Blue delved into his pocket and took out his cell. Jenna leapt off the bed to get to hers.

Downstairs a door banged, and there was the sound of booted feet running up the stairs.

"BB, are you there?" Dave yelled. "Ruth's desperate to get hold of you."

Jenna put on some clean panties and wiggled into her jeans as Blue set himself to rights.

"What's wrong?" Jenna asked Blue.

"I've got to get back, Maria's not in her bed."

Jenna opened the door to Dave. "He got the message. He's coming, okay?"

Dave made a face. "I could make a terrible joke about that, but considering what's going on, I won't." He looked over her head at Blue. "Do you want me to come and help?"

"I'll let you know." His eyes were blazing and his mouth hard. "Thanks for the offer." He nodded at Dave and moved past him.

Jenna followed down the stairs. "I'm coming with you."

He gave her a brief glance but didn't try and stop her. She put on her boots and went out to his truck. Within seconds they were moving off, and she held fast to the sides of the seat.

He thumped the steering wheel with his fist. "I *knew* something was up. I should've stayed there and made her tell me what was wrong."

"There's no point beating yourself up about that now," Jenna reminded him. "I shouldn't have been such a coward and made you come and find me. You would've been at home right now."

He flicked his gaze her way. "I'm not blaming you."

"Maybe you should."

"I'm her father. Something happened today to make her doubt everything, and I don't know what it was." He groaned. "I can't deal with this again, Jenna—someone I love disappearing on me—I just *can't*."

She put her hand on his knee. "We'll find her, Blue."

He didn't answer, his attention on the rugged terrain as

they left the McDonald property and headed back toward the ranch.

Ruth wasn't downstairs, so Blue raced up to Maria's bedroom, where he found his entire family awaiting him.

"BB, I'm so sorry." Ruth came toward him. "She must have slipped out when I was watching TV."

He gathered her into a hug, acutely aware of how small she was and how hard she was shaking. "It's okay. It's my fault. I should've stayed here and got to the bottom of what was worrying her."

"This might have something to do with it. I didn't read beyond the first sentence." Ruth handed him a folded sheet of paper. "She must have gotten this in the mail, but I didn't see it come in, did you?"

Blue took the letter and sat on the side of the bed. "It's from Daniel. How the hell—?" He smacked a hand down on the quilt. "She picked up the mail from Brian today at the lower gate. It must have been in there."

"Talk about bad timing," Chase muttered. He was sitting in the window seat, January perched on his knee. "What did he say?"

Blue read out loud.

"Dear Maria, I know you must be thinking all kinds of bad things about me right now. I want to say that I am sorry for how I behaved. When your mom got sick, I was so worried and upset that I kind of lost myself for a while. You know that better than anyone because you had to live with me. I'm so sorry, sweetheart. I miss you, and I hope one day you will forgive me and let me see you again to apologize in person. With all my love, Dad."

Dad. Blue slowly exhaled. "Well, that certainly puts things in a different light. Maybe she decided to go back home?"

"She wouldn't just up and leave in the middle of the night, would she?" Ruth demanded.

"She might if her *new* dad had just told her that he'd do everything in his power to keep her away from her old dad." Blue groaned and rubbed a hand over his unshaven jaw. "I thought she was scared he'd take her away. I didn't realize she was having second thoughts."

"You don't know that, and we have no evidence that she's decided to go back to Daniel Lester," Ruth said. "She's probably just confused and wanted time to think things through."

"So she gets out of bed and wanders off in the dark in the middle of nowhere?" Blue cleared his throat. "Yeah, we all know what happens with that scenario."

"Not necessarily, son." Billy's voice was gentle. "We'll find her. She has a few special places on the ranch where she likes to go. If we split up we can easily cover them all."

"You didn't see her on the main trail down to the gate, right?" Chase asked.

"No." Jenna shook her head. "I looked the whole way."

"Then she's probably in one of the places Billy knows." Chase stood up. "Did anyone check the barn to see if she took a horse?"

"Roy's out there looking right now." Ruth stood, too, and straightened her spine. "She's a smart girl. We'll find her."

Blue went straight to the barn and Roy came to find him, his expression concerned.

"Marigold's not in her stall."

"So Maria might have gotten farther than we thought." Blue patted the older man on the back. "Why don't you keep Ruth company up at the house while the rest of us search? She'd probably appreciate it even if she'd never admit it."

"I'll do that." Roy stomped off toward the main house. "I know she's feeling pretty bad right now."

"Blue."

He spun around to see Jenna at the door of the feed store. She had something in her hand.

"Is this Maria's?"

He took the rainbow hairband from her and swallowed hard. "Yeah. It's covered in those stupid ponies she loves, but she might have dropped it at any time because she's always in there with those darn kittens."

"What kittens?"

"There should be a basket of them right . . ." Blue went into the room and stared at the empty shelf. "Where'd they go?" He turned a slow circle in the room. "Is it just me, or does it look like there was a fight in here?"

"It's certainly a mess."

"And Chase doesn't let us make a mess anywhere, so what happened?" Blue frowned. "Maybe she thought she had to save the kittens from something?"

"And take them where? Why not up to the main house?" Jenna asked. "She must have known Ruth wouldn't mind."

"Maybe they weren't her priority," Blue said slowly. "Maybe she just decided to take them with her when she left."

"But she'd soon find out that dealing with a bunch of kittens and managing a horse was harder than she'd anticipated."

"So where would she drop them off?"

Their eyes met. "Roy's place?"

He ran back to his truck, Jenna at his side, and then they were off into the darkness. Billy had gone to the hot springs, and Chase was searching around the old silver

mine. Blue was supposed to go toward the ghost town of
Morganville, but a detour to Roy's place wouldn't hurt.

When they reached Roy's house, it all looked quiet.
Blue cut the engine. As he got out of the truck, he heard
the whiny of a horse and went still.

"Could be Marigold," Jenna whispered. "Let's check
out the barn."

Blue put a hand on her arm. "Listen. Do you hear that?"

She turned her face up to his and breathed. "Kittens."

Blue made his way past Roy's two horses, and toward
the open door of the last stall in the row.

"Maria?"

A stifled sob made him speed up. In the corner of the
stall, well away from Marigold's bulk, was Maria. She had
the basket of kittens in her lap and looked as if she had been
crying for quite a while.

Just as his knees gave way with relief, Blue sank onto
his haunches in the straw.

"You okay, darlin'?"

Maria rubbed a hand across her nose and shook her
head.

"Did something happen to the kittens?"

"Their mama's dead . . ." She gulped. "There was a
coyote, and she was trying to stop it getting near the kittens
and . . ."

"Oh, sweetheart." Blue sighed. "So you decided to save
the kittens?" He wanted to point out that the damn coyote
could've taken her out as well, but even he knew there was
a time and a place for that discussion. "That was a brave
thing to do."

"But then I had to figure out where to put them, and I
couldn't go back to the house . . ."

"So you came here. That was a good decision." He hesitated. "Jenna's outside. Do you want her to take a look at

these little guys while you and I talk? You know she'll take good care of them."

"Okay."

He handed the basket of kittens over to Jenna and she disappeared out the door, leaving him and Maria in the peace and quiet of the night. Blue sat on the floor and patted his knee.

"You want to come and tell me what's up? I promise I won't be mad."

She eyed him carefully and then with a sigh came to sit on his knee. "I'm sorry."

"Well, you did scare us all half to death wandering off in the middle of the night like that."

"I didn't know what to do."

"Because of that letter from your dad?"

She sat bolt upright on his knee, her knees together and her hands twisted in her lap. "You said you'd make sure I couldn't see him again."

"Yeah. I thought you didn't *want* to see him."

"So did I until I read the letter and he said sorry. Then I felt all confused. I thought maybe if I said I wanted to see him you'd get mad and kick me out, and then what if he didn't really like me again or got drunk and I had no place to go?"

Blue took a long moment before he answered. "Number one, I'd never kick you out. I promised you'd always have a home here if you wanted it. And number two, next time you have a problem like this, please talk to me. I will always listen."

"And you'll let me see him?"

He kissed the top of her head, avoiding her direct gaze and the question. "We can talk about that tomorrow, okay? It's late, we're all tired, and I don't want to make any promises I can't keep."

"Okay." She sagged against his chest. "I didn't want to go. I thought my heart was going to break in two. I know my dad did some bad things, but I still love him."

"Yeah. I totally get that. I felt the same way about Billy." He stood up with her in his arms. "I'm going to put you in my truck and call Ruth to let her know you're safe."

He placed her on the backseat and covered her up with an old blanket. "Sit tight. I'll go and check on the kittens and put Marigold to bed. Roy can bring her back in the morning."

A couple of hours later, Jenna sat with Blue in the ranch house kitchen cradling a mug of hot chocolate as the old house settled around them. Blue looked exhausted, and no wonder. Reliving another unexpected disappearance at the ranch must have been traumatic.

"Will you come to bed with me?" He reached across the table to take her hand.

"Sure." She smothered a yawn. "To sleep."

"Don't think I can manage much more than that," he murmured as they walked up the stairs. "But I'll keep you informed."

In a relatively short space of time they were cuddled up together in his bed. He lay on his back and she curled against his side.

"That was one of the worst nights of my life." Blue exhaled. "I thought being sent overseas was terrifying, but it's nothing compared to this."

"That's because she's family."

He sighed against her hair. "What am I going to do, Jenna? She wants to see her father. She's relying on me to sort that out for her, and all I want to do is tell that idiot never to come within a hundred miles of her. I know what it's like to live with a drunk—to not know whether you're going to have to deal with abuse, or maudlin tears, or them puking their guts up—it sucks."

"But Billy managed to get it together."

"Eventually."

"Who says that Daniel won't manage it either?" She spread her fingers over his chest. "Even my parents got their shit together eventually and remarried."

"Yeah?" He paused. "I thought you said they didn't want anything to do with you."

"They didn't."

"Hang on." His fingers stole into her hair and went still. "They got it together, and they still didn't want *you*?"

Even though it was dark and she couldn't see his face clearly, she still closed her eyes. "They had two more kids and were living in a respectable neighborhood and they just weren't interested in having a constant reminder of their past." She sighed. "I invested so much time and effort in finding them that I almost alienated my adopted family and then . . . my parents didn't want me, Blue. They flat out didn't want me."

She buried her face against his chest, and his arms closed around her.

"It was the most humiliating experience of my life, you know? It's almost okay when your birth parents reject you because they are still troubled individuals, but when your parents work things out and *you* become the embarrassment? That sucks."

She let out her breath. "I've never told anyone about this before. Even my adoptive parents. I wanted to tell you because I know it's going to be hard, but I really think you should let Daniel be a part of Maria's life, warts and all."

"But what if he wants to claim custody of her?"

"He's in no fit state to look after her at the moment, any

judge will see that, and you have rights as well *and* a stable home environment."

"What if she wants to go back to him?"

The uncertainty and pain behind his question made her want to hold him tight and not let anything near him again. Her big bad Marine was hurting, and that was unacceptable.

"Then you think of what's best for Maria, and work something out."

"You're right. I've still got to get my head around that." He sighed. "I've got to put her first."

Jenna swallowed hard, but the tears still came. "You will. You're a good man."

"Hey." He suddenly rolled her onto her back and rose over her. "Don't cry, honey."

"I'm not."

He kissed her slowly, taking each tear away, his gaze solemn.

"Thank you, Jenna."

"For what?" She tried to smile. "For crying about myself when you're the one with the problem? How selfish is that?"

"Don't say that." She blinked up at his suddenly ferocious expression. "Don't you dare put yourself down. Your birth parents were assholes." He kissed her hard. "I'm not going to be like them, I can promise you that."

"Good."

"And if you ever care to share their address, I'll go and tell them to their faces that they are assholes."

"Er. Thanks, but I think I'm over it."

He drew her into his arms and they lay quietly together until exhaustion overcame her and she fell asleep.

* * *

Blue smoothed Jenna's hair away from her face and contemplated her serene expression. How much had it cost her to share that parental rejection with him just to help him decide what to do about his own daughter? No wonder she didn't trust anyone. No one had ever put her needs first. Unable to sleep, Blue pulled on his jeans and headed barefoot down to the kitchen.

He almost screeched when a figure appeared in the darkness.

"BB."

"Dad?" He sat at the table opposite his father. "You okay?"

"I couldn't sleep. All the worry about Maria brought everything back to me."

"I know how you feel."

"It was the worst night of my life."

"Yeah." Blue put his elbows on the table and held his head in his hands.

"The first of many." Billy's dry laugh held little humor in it. "After that I just lost the plot completely."

"But you made it back here eventually." Blue hesitated. "Daniel Lester's a drunk."

"Like your father. I guess that scares you, huh?"

"It scares me for Maria's sake. I don't want her to have to grow up like that. I want to keep her here with me where it's safe, but what if she hates me for that and goes looking for him? What if she finds him, and he treats her badly?"

"Chase has good lawyers, right?"

"The best."

"They could probably keep Daniel away from Maria until she's an adult."

"Possibly."

"But eventually, she'd still want to see him because she's like you—a determined kid who never forgets anything.

So how about you find a way to make this work? Let her see him, let her make her own judgment about who and what he means to her. *Trust* her."

"It's hard."

"Because me and your mother broke that trust. I get it. I damn well caused it. But you're gonna have to find a way to make Maria happy, and I know in my heart you're going to do it. You're a good man, BB, a *fine* man, and you did it all by yourself." Blue reached out to find his father's hand waiting for him. "Just keep on loving her, BB. In the long run that's all that you can do."

Chapter Twenty-One

Jenna consulted the list January had handed her. Pink and blue balloons dancing on strings in the breeze, check; ponies everywhere, both real and fake, check; a rainbow pony birthday cake and a huge banner wishing Maria a happy eleventh birthday, check. Jenna surveyed the party site and smiled despite her nervousness.

Maria was dancing around between Billy, Ruth, and Blue, hindering the preparations rather than helping, but no one minded. She had rainbow ribbons in her dark hair and a pony dress with net skirts and sparkles, which she had assured Jenna, who'd bought it for her, was the best thing ever. Maria seemed to accept her as Blue's girlfriend and sometimes even asked her about stuff. When Jenna consulted with Blue about whether this was okay, he'd told her to be honest—that no one else could empathize quite so well with Maria and that he was grateful for everything she did.

Jenna smiled at the excited little girl. Whatever happened in the future, she would always make a point of being available. She hoped she'd be far more involved than that . . . The first guests were arriving, and Jenna sensed Ruth was about to call everyone to order.

As usual, most of the town had been invited because Ruth was determined that Maria would be accepted by the community the Morgan family hoped she would choose to belong to. Jenna had kept away from the ranch during the last week or so, aware that Blue needed time with his daughter and to sort out some legal issues with his lawyers. She hadn't asked him what he'd decided to do, but she had faith he would make the right decisions.

She looked over at him and noticed his smile disappeared whenever Maria turned away from him. He looked stressed, which made her want to go over and hold him tight. Hopefully if things turned out how she'd planned, he'd never doubt her feelings for him ever again.

He caught her gaze and tipped his hat to her, but he didn't come over. She was okay about that because she had a tendency to babble when she was trying to hide something, and he'd pick up on that way too quick. She smiled brightly back and busied herself sticking the paper tablecloth to the corner of the table.

There was a little stage at the front where the cake had been set out and a fancy table for Maria and some of the kids she'd been starting to get to know over the summer. If she stayed she'd be seeing more of them at the local middle school in Morgantown, which went up to eighth grade, giving her three more years before being bussed to high school.

If she stayed.

A flash of movement down in the parking lot had Jenna looking around as a procession of trucks parked. There was no sign of her parents yet. Her mom had texted to say they were on their way. Her parents would be easy to spot—the lone rental car amongst a sea of trucks and SUVs.

Soon Maria was standing with Ruth, Billy, and Blue and greeting guests and their families with her usual smile and enthusiasm. She'd certainly grown in confidence in the past few weeks. She reminded Jenna of herself at that age—cautiously coming to terms with her new family and starting to understand that they meant to let her stay forever.

A lone figure came up the path, and Jenna didn't recognize him. She glanced across at Blue and saw him stiffen before he bent down to draw Maria's attention to the approaching man.

"Daddy!" Maria shrieked and ran down the slope. She was caught in a fierce embrace and swung around. Jenna looked back at Blue and instinctively went over to him. By the time she got there, Maria had the man by the hand and was dragging him up to the reception committee at the top of the field.

"Welcome to Morgan Ranch, Daniel," Blue said quietly and held out his hand. "I'm glad you could make it."

Maria's smile was blinding as she grabbed Blue's hand as well.

"This is so *cool*! Now, Daddy, come and meet my grampa Billy, and this is Ruth and . . ."

Blue half turned away and Jenna stepped close to him.

"That was a really nice thing to do."

He shrugged. "Possibly the most stupid thing I've ever done in my life. But at least he's on my land. If he starts getting antsy, I'll drop him down one of the abandoned shafts at the silver mine."

"Good thinking, Marine." She went up on tiptoe and

kissed him even as he grimaced. "It's always best to be prepared. Did I tell you my parents were coming today?"

He held her gaze. "No, you didn't mention it. Any particular reason?"

It was her turn to shrug. "My mom's found me a new job in LA. She wants to talk to me about it."

"Jenna . . ."

She pointed over his shoulder. "I think that's them now. I'd better go and make sure they get settled down."

Blue had never expected to be sitting on one side of an eleven-year-old girl eating birthday cake, which was so full of sugar his teeth hurt, while on the other side sat the man who had raised his daughter for ten years. Maria seemed to think it was the best idea in the world—in fact, she'd insisted, saying she wanted both her dads sitting with her. The fact that she'd acknowledged him as her father while Daniel was sitting right there had made Blue feel a lot better. Now all he had to worry about was what happened at the end of the evening.

Would Maria want to leave with Daniel? Would he let her go? In the few weeks he'd known her, she'd made a space for herself in his heart that would never disappear. Maybe that was what Billy had been talking about. If she went back to Daniel, he wouldn't stop loving her, he'd just bide his time and hope that one day she'd want to have a relationship with him. Billy was proof that even the worst relationship could be mended if both parties were willing.

"Blue, have you got a minute?" Daniel leaned over behind Maria's chair and spoke softly in Blue's ear.

"Sure. Come over by the present table while they finish their cake and ice cream."

He didn't want to talk to Daniel, but he was pretending to be a civilized adult, and apparently in today's complex modern families that was what you had to do.

"Thanks for inviting me," Daniel said as he turned to survey the majesty of the Sierra Nevada range. "It's beautiful out here. What an amazing place to grow up and what great history."

Blue jammed one hand in his pocket and nodded.

"Maria seems to love it."

"Yeah. She's fit in really well."

Daniel sighed. "She sure looks happier."

Blue had nothing to say to that.

"I heard from your lawyers. I gather you'd like her to live here at the ranch full-time?" Daniel swallowed hard. "I don't think I'm in a good place to have her at home right now. I . . . lost my job and I'm having to move into a smaller place and . . . I'm going into counseling to address my issues with alcohol and all the rest of it."

Blue finally looked him in the eye. "That's a lot of stuff to deal with at once, and it's good of you to admit Maria needs a more stable home. I can give her that—if she wants it."

"Yeah, and a ready-made family. That's kind of awesome." Daniel awkwardly rubbed the back of his neck. "When Angel told me about you . . . I just kind of lost it. I'd been told it was unlikely that I'd ever have kids because I had mumps when I was a teen. I never told Angel that. I kind of married her under false pretenses. She was getting desperate to have a baby and was threatening to leave me. When she came back from visiting her sister and then was suddenly pregnant, I was just so damned ecstatic that I convinced myself it was a miracle."

His mouth twisted. "Stupid, eh? It wasn't until she was being tested when she got sick that the subject somehow came up again, and eventually . . . just before she died she told me what she'd done. Of course I didn't say anything to her—how could I? But I knew then that I'd been fooling myself and that you must be Maria's father."

Blue just nodded. What the hell could he say? He almost felt sorry for the guy.

"And then there was just me, Maria, and a bottle of vodka left in the house and I was just so angry and so furious at Angel for dying and leaving me and . . ." He groaned. "I lost it. I scared Maria, and at some point I realized that if I wasn't careful I'd say or do something inexcusable, so putting her on the bus to you? That felt like the safest thing to do for her."

Blue kicked a stone. He still wanted to punch the man, but he had to give him credit for trying to be honest. "My dad always says that grief does funny things to a person's head, and he should know. It took him a lot longer to get help with his drinking than you."

Daniel let out a long slow breath. "So, do you think I could still see her? Once I've gotten my shit sorted out, obviously."

"It's up to her, but from the expression on her face when she saw you, I'd say she'd be more than happy to see you again."

"You think so? I feel like such a loser right now."

Privately Blue agreed with that statement, but he wasn't going to say anything. One thing he was learning was that those gray areas between the blacks and the whites sometimes made a whole lot of sense. He patted Daniel awkwardly on the back.

"Let's sit down together with Maria and ask her what she wants, okay? You can stay the night. We can talk it through tomorrow."

"Okay. I'd like that."

Blue managed a smile. "Now there's a piñata full of candy waiting to be batted to pieces, so we'd better get with the schedule before Ruth starts complaining."

Daniel wandered off and Blue stayed put, his gaze on the smiling face of his daughter. He had a good sense that he and Daniel would work things out. Now, if he could only do the same thing with Jenna. Maybe it was time to stop waiting on her and make some decisions for both of them. Maybe it was time to let her know she would always come first with him. He spotted her at one of the tables gesticulating to her parents, her auburn hair in a high ponytail that bobbed as she talked.

He loved her.

It was as simple as that—a single black-and-white moment that had no shade to it at all.

So he'd wait for her.

As he watched she got up and went over to Chase and whispered something in his ear. Blue stiffened as she mounted the small stage and grinned down at the assembled guests.

Chase cupped his hands around his mouth.

"Listen up, everyone! Jenna has something to say."

"Firstly, the piñata is ready to be whacked, so after I finish speaking please go down to the oak grove and form a line—birthday girl gets first hit. Little kids before the big kids, okay?"

Everyone laughed.

"Secondly, I wanted to share some news with you." She paused to take a deep breath. "From the end of this month, I will no longer be working for my uncle's veterinary practice."

Blue's gut tightened and he took a step forward only

to be blocked by one of the local ranchers, who wagged a finger at Jenna on the stage.

"Don't you go leaving because of that Mark Lymond, now, Jenna. You're a good veterinarian."

Two other ranchers stood up as well. "Hear, hear."

Jenna's cheeks went pink and she pressed one hand to her face. "That's . . . so nice of you guys, but—"

"You want us to talk to Big Mac? There's no need for you to leave." That was Maureen from the store. "Because I'll tell him how great you were with Missy's horse."

"No, it's all good." She searched the crowd and her gaze fell on Blue. "I'm going to stay. Chase Morgan has offered me a job as the new vet for the guest ranch, and I've accepted."

Blue started to smile.

She looked down. "Sorry, Mom and Dad, but I love it here, and I never want to leave."

Dave whooped and punched the air as Blue walked toward the stage.

"There is one more thing," Jenna called out above the applause.

"What's that?" Blue spoke up.

"It's kind of about you, actually." She smiled right down into his eyes. "I wanted to tell you that I'm ready to believe in myself."

"Yeah? And what else?" He'd reached the stage now and only had to look up a little to see her clearly.

"I love you and I want to be with you."

He took a long slow breath, reached up, and wrapped her in his arms. "That's my girl." He kissed her slowly. The crowd started to clap and holler again.

A persistent tugging on his elbow made Blue look down.

"So, can I be a flower girl?" Maria asked.

Blue raised an eyebrow. "I haven't had a chance to ask her to marry me yet."

"But you're going to, aren't you? Ruth says she's perfect for you."

"Ruth's right."

Maria's smile widened. "She told me to tell you she always is."

For Blue Morgan

Grandma duPont's Peaches and Cream Cake
(Courtesy of the Mentink Family)

¾ c. flour
½ tsp. salt
½ c. sugar
1 tsp. baking powder
3 oz. package of vanilla pudding mix
3½ Tbsp. butter, softened
1 egg
½ c. milk
1 29 oz. can drained peaches or apricots in heavy
    syrup (reserve 3 Tbsp. of the syrup)
1 8 oz. cream cheese, softened
½ Tbsp.–1 Tbsp. sugar
1 tsp. cinnamon

Preheat oven to 350 degrees. Butter sides and bottom of a 10" deep pie plate.

Mix flour, salt, baking powder, and pudding mix. Blend in butter, egg, and milk. Mix until smooth. Spread in pie pan. Arrange fruit on top of batter.

Beat cream cheese with ½ c. sugar and 3 Tbsp. reserved juice. Spoon over peaches. Mix ½–1 Tbsp. sugar with cinnamon and sprinkle over the top. Bake for 40 minutes until brown. Serve room temp or cold with vanilla ice cream or whipped cream.

For more recipes check out:
www.themorgansranch.com

The Morgan Ranch has seen its share of bad times. But as the four Morgan brothers are drawn back to their childhood home, the nightmares of their past give way to the promise of a new beginning . . .

Ry Morgan has always had a thing for Avery Hayes— one more hope his twin wrecked for him, pretending to be Ry to kiss her at the high school prom. Eight years later, Ry has had enough: he's quitting the pro rodeo circuit, moving home to California to mend fences, and letting his brother clean up his own messes for a change. Reclaiming Avery's stolen kiss is at the top of his agenda . . .

But Avery has changed. Her rodeo career ended with a fall that left her lucky to be alive, let alone walking. She hasn't been on a horse since, and between surgeries and fighting off everybody's pity, she hasn't done much else either. Ry is strong, confident, and sexy as hell— exactly what she thought she wanted at seventeen. Now she'll have to protect the safe space she's made for herself—or risk it all for a dream she thought would never come again . . .

Please turn the page for an exciting sneak peek of Kate Pearce's

THE LAST GOOD COWBOY,

coming soon wherever print and eBooks are sold!

Sacramento, California

Before he even left the parking lot, Ry Morgan heard the bass booming through the walls and the sound of heavy partying from the third-floor apartment. When he turned the corner, he almost walked into a squad car flashing blue lights and a small crowd of agitated neighbors gathered around the door.

"Hell, not again," he breathed as one of the helpful neighbors pointed him out to the cop.

He held his ground as she came toward him and the noise from above suddenly shut off.

"Can I help you, Officer?"

She jabbed her thumb in the direction of the apartment block. "You live here?"

"I used to. I just stopped by to pick up my stuff."

"Are you HW Morgan?"

"Nope, I'm his brother, Ry."

"You sure about that?"

Used to being mistaken for his identical twin, he

cautiously reached inside his jacket, took out his wallet, and handed over his driver's license.

"Thanks." She studied it, made the usual face at his given name, and then handed it back. "Have you seen your brother recently?"

"Not for about three weeks. What's up?"

He asked even though it was obvious. The last time HW had thrown a party, the police had been called. Maybe HW had learned something by not sticking around long enough to get caught in the aftermath. Ry's gut tightened.

"Is it okay to go up there? I just want to get my stuff and head out again in the morning."

"Wise decision." The officer looked at him steadily. "Maybe you can make sure the party doesn't start again."

"I'll do my best." He tipped his Stetson to her. "Thanks."

"And tell your brother that if he keeps this up, he'll be spending the rest of his evening with the Sacramento Police Department."

Ry nodded as he turned away and headed for the front entrance of the building. A police officer was escorting a group of partygoers down the stairs. There were others emerging from the two elevators, still complaining loudly about the abrupt end to their evening. Ry ignored them all. They weren't his kind of people. They stunk of booze, cheap perfume, and other substances he hoped the police hadn't noticed.

Wearily, he climbed the stairs, spoke to the building security guy who had lingered on the landing to make sure everyone had left, and went inside. The place was a mess. He shut the door and leaned against it, letting his backpack slide to the floor.

"Well, look who's turned up."

He raised his head to see Lally Goldstein glaring at him from his brother's bedroom doorway. She wore a halter top that had silver spangled bits on it and tiny blue shorts. Her blond hair was piled up on top of her head in a messy ponytail.

"You still here?" Ry asked. "I thought the cops cleared everyone out."

"I live here now."

"First I've heard about it."

She tossed her head. "You left. Someone had to look after your brother."

"HW knew where I was." He glanced around the wrecked apartment. "Where is he, by the way?"

"What's it to you?"

Ry didn't even bother to answer that and stared her down. Eventually she gave an elaborate sigh. "He should be back soon. Randy and Araz took him down the stairs when the cops turned up."

"Protecting their assets, right?"

She crossed her arms over her chest making her fake boobs jut out. "They've done more for him than you ever did—bringing him down, making him feel bad about himself—having to hold himself back for *years* because he felt sorry for you not being as good a rider as he was."

"Yeah?" Ry wanted to turn around and walk away from all the shit that was coming out of her mouth, but he refused to leave first. He hoisted his backpack onto his shoulder. "I'm going to bed."

"You can't—"

He spun around so fast she took a step back. "HW and I rent this place. Until I hear differently, I'm going to bed."

He unlocked the padlock he'd installed on his bedroom door and went inside. Nothing looked as if it had been touched, which made a change. His twin tended to think that what was Ry's was his, but not vice versa. Not that Ry wanted anything his brother had.

With a groan he placed his hat on the desk and shoved a hand through his short blond hair. His stomach growled, but he wasn't going out there again to face Lally. If HW came back, he could knock on the door and be polite. Maybe Ry would talk to him.

Maybe.

He stripped off his shirt and jeans and took a quick shower in the tiny bathroom attached to his bedroom. There was no more partying, but whether HW would come back Ry no longer knew. Sometimes his twin would stay away for days and return so shitfaced he'd sleep for a week and be as grumpy as hell if Ry tried to talk to him about anything.

He wasn't sure he cared anymore. Hunkering down on the rug beside his bed, he delved into his backpack where his grandma Ruth had deposited enough food to feed an army. Just the thought of her lightened Ry's dark mood and gave him strength. He pictured his family at the ranch—his older brothers, Chase and Blue, and his father, Billy. They liked him for who he was. They *loved* him.

A knock on the door made him go still.

"Ry? You in there?"

He took out the bundle of food and placed it on the desk before slowly turning to the door and opening it. His twin stood there grinning like a loon and swaying slightly in his fancy cowboy boots. They were identical, so it was like looking at a drunk version of himself.

"Dude! You're back!"

Ry stepped aside and let HW in.

"Something smells good. Did you bring stuff back from the ranch?" HW wandered over to the desk and went to grab the container of food. Ry, who was stone cold sober, moved faster and blocked his twin's hand.

"What do you want, HW?"

His brother blinked big golden eyes at him. "That's harsh, Ry. What the hell is wrong with you?"

Ry leaned against the edge of the desk, folded his arms over his chest, and repeated, "What do you want?"

HW retreated to the bed and sank down on it, his expression disgruntled. "Some of Ruth's good cooking, but it looks like you've decided to hog it all for yourself."

"I'll gladly share the food with you after you've told me what's going on."

"You mean about the party?" HW hiccupped a laugh. "That was so sick, man. Those cops have no sense of humor."

"Those cops told me to tell you that if you host a party again, they'll be taking you in and charging you."

"Not unless they catch me first."

"I think they'll manage it, especially if you keep drinking."

HW sighed. "Gawd, when did you become such a boring Dudley Do-Right, bro? I'm just having some fun."

"Yeah." Ry studied his twin. HW's pupils were too large, his eyes were bloodshot, and his whole body was shaking. "You should go to bed. I'll talk to you in the morning, okay?"

"What's wrong with talking now?"

"Because you're too drunk or high or whatever the stimulant of the day is to talk much sense."

HW rose unsteadily to his feet. "Don't preach at me."

Ry set his jaw. "I'm tired. I've got a lot to do tomorrow."

His twin took three lurching steps forward that brought him right in Ry's face. "Screw you. Talk to me about wussing out on me."

Ry straightened, almost overbalancing his twin. "I am not talking to a belligerent drunk! Get out of my space, or I'll be the one calling the cops."

For one frozen second, Ry couldn't believe what he'd said, and then he realized he meant every word.

"Get out, HW. I'll speak to you in the morning."

His twin mumbled something obscene and stumbled away, slamming the bedroom door behind him. In the stillness Ry waited until he heard his brother's girlfriend start in on him, and then there was comparative silence. He slowly let out his breath.

No regrets. He'd promised himself that he'd make a clean break, so tomorrow he'd tell HW what was happening and leave. His hand clenched into a fist, and he sat down heavily on the desk chair. Now all he had to do was follow through with his plan, and this time make sure he stuck the landing.

It was almost eleven in the morning, and Ry had made good inroads into packing up the stuff in his bedroom. He had to fit everything in his old pickup truck and was determined to make only one trip. He'd already decided not to take any of the furniture—most of it had come with the apartment anyway or had been chosen by HW.

He stuffed four pairs of socks in his open duffel bag. Chase had offered him his pick of the ranch land to build his own place on, which was kind of cool. Not that he needed all that space yet, but it was good to dream.

"Ry, what the hell are you doing?"

He turned to see HW propping up the doorway wearing nothing but a pair of boxers that barely hung on to his narrow hips. He was also shading his eyes against the glare of the sun.

"I'm packing my stuff."

"What the heck for?"

Ry looked his twin right in the eye. "Because I'm leaving."

HW frowned. "We always fight, bro. You know I don't mean anything. That's just the way we are."

"No, it's the way we've become. I don't like it, HW, and I'm not going to play that game anymore."

"So, what? You're walking out on me?"

"I barely see you these days. You're either training, going to extra events, or . . ." Ry paused. "Doing other stuff I don't enjoy."

"I've been working my ass off to qualify for the national finals, you *know* that."

"Yeah. I really hope you'll get there."

"But you're sulking because I haven't been spending enough time with you? Hell, Ry, that's half your problem. If you don't train hard and compete often, you won't qualify."

"I get that."

"So don't blame me if you haven't been dedicated enough to achieve what I have."

"I don't." Ry added another drawer full of underwear to the bag. "I'm just not cut out for this life."

HW sat on the bed, his bloodshot gaze fixed on the filled and labeled boxes. "We're identical twins. If I can do it, you can."

"But maybe I don't want to."

"So you're going to disappear and leave me here by myself?"

Ry faked a smile. "You're hardly by yourself. You've got Lally all moved in, a potential agent, and a promotional exec hanging around to protect your ass."

"But they're not you."

Ry zipped up the bag and sat on the chair by the desk, swiveling to face his brother. "You'll be fine."

"Where are you going?"

"Back to the ranch."

"For good?" HW frowned. "You're seriously not coming back?"

"Nope."

He scratched his unshaven jaw. "We said we'd never do that."

"Things change. Chase is not as bad as BB painted him—hell, even BB agrees he was wrong, and that's saying something."

"But we've always been together."

Ry took a deep breath. "Yeah, I know."

"You and me against the world."

"As I said, things change. You're going forward into a successful career riding saddle broncs, and I'm . . ."

"Yeah, what exactly *are* you going to do stuck in the middle of nowhere?"

"Help Chase and Blue rebuild the ranch and make it into something special. I might not be a great rodeo guy, but I'm a damned good hand."

"Help *them*? What about me?"

"I don't think you need me at the moment, bro," Ry said as gently as he could. "You're doing great."

HW shot to his feet and took a short turn around the room. "This is because I've done better than you—isn't it? Lally said you were jealous, but I didn't believe her. But now? Maybe she was right all along."

Ry stood as well. It felt like his heart was actually trying to punch its way out of his chest. "Maybe I just want different things in my life right now."

"Because you're not good enough to have what I have?" There was a combative note in HW's voice Ry had learned to dread.

"I'm not as good a rider as you are. I never will be."

"True, but only because you won't take it seriously."

"Which is the whole point, HW. Can't you at least see that? I don't care about winning as much as you do. I just don't."

"Because you know you can't beat me." HW came closer. "Admit it."

"Sure, if it makes you happy." Ry shrugged. He really didn't need to argue about something that meant so little to him. They weren't in high school anymore. Sometimes HW seemed to forget that. "It doesn't change the fact that I'm leaving."

"Abandoning me right when I need you most."

Ry blinked. *What?*

"That's why you're doing it now, isn't it?" HW nodded. "Yeah, you're probably hoping I'll fail when you aren't around."

His twin was probably the only person on earth who knew Ry had a temper and exactly how to make him lose it.

"That's utter *bullshit*, and you know it. I'm leaving because you have surrounded yourself with a group of people I despise, *okay*? Is that straight enough talk for you?"

HW swung around and poked a finger way too close to Ry's face. "Those people are looking out for me and my career. They *care* about me. You're just pulling this stunt because you're jealous."

"You've been talking to Lally too much. You're my *twin*. I've spent my whole life supporting you. Trouble is, you're not interested in what I have to say anymore, and that's fine because, trust me, I'm sick and tired of saying it."

HW took a step back and a deep shuddering breath. "Look. At least stay until I find out whether I qualify or not."

"I can't. I promised Chase I'd be back this week."

"You promised Mom you'd always be there for me."

Ry met his twin's gaze head-on. "How about just for once, you let something be about *me*?"

HW looked down at his feet. "Do you need money? Can I pay you to stay?"

Ry marched over to the door. "Get out."

"What the hell's wrong now?"

"If that's what you've become—if that's how you think you keep a man's loyalty, then go back to that bunch of losers you surround yourself with, and see what happens when you can't pay them anymore."

"Screw you." HW walked out.

"Right back at you, bro," Ry muttered under his breath, and then turned to survey his pile of boxes.

He'd said things he hadn't meant to say out loud, and HW had . . . changed beyond recognition. His brother was still caught up in being a rising star, and the better he did, the more hangers-on he'd acquire. He didn't need Ry. That was certain, but it still hurt.

They'd never spent more than a month apart in their entire lives, and now HW would be off competing in Texas next week and he'd be back on the ranch working with Roy. Unless HW followed through on his promise to attend Chase and January's wedding in a couple of months, he might never see his twin again.

He couldn't let himself think like that or he'd be chasing after his brother, begging to tag along for another few months. It was up to HW to get his shit together. He was *not* Ry's responsibility.

"Yeah, right. Thanks for loading that on me, Mom."

He checked all the drawers, picked up his hat, and propped open the bedroom door with his backpack. There was no sound of HW or his girlfriend in the apartment. HW tended to storm out when he lost an argument, so there was no surprise there. He hadn't even had a chance to tell his twin that their mom and baby sister might still be alive twenty years after disappearing from the ranch.

Ry picked up a stack of boxes, set off for the front door, leaving that ajar as well, and used his elbow to call the elevator. It wasn't too busy in the complex during the day, as most people worked, so he had no trouble getting the boxes and bags down to his truck.

On his last trip upstairs he paused in the kitchen to grab a couple of cold water bottles from the refrigerator and contemplated the silence. Neither Lally nor HW had made any effort to clean up yet. They were probably too used to him doing it. Not anymore. He checked his room again, making sure he hadn't forgotten anything, and then sat at the kitchen table to write HW a note.

> *Rent is paid until the end of the lease, which is up next month. I've contacted the leasing company about taking my name off, so I'm sure you'll be hearing from them when you renegotiate.*

Ry sat back and contemplated what to say next. He wasn't going to drop the bombshell about their mom in a letter. That was something HW needed to hear in person. Ry still couldn't believe it himself.

> *Good luck in the saddle bronc events, and hope you make it to the finals in Vegas. Call me when you get a chance—you know where I am. Ry*

He anchored the note under the salt and pepper shakers and slowly stood up. There was so much he wanted to say, and so little his twin currently wanted to hear . . . He had to remember that inside HW there was a good, kind, and amazing guy—the guy he'd grown up with and loved with all his heart. Someday that HW would resurface, Ry had to believe that.

He unhooked his front door key from his chain, laid it on top of the letter, and walked out, his throat tight and his emotions all over the place. Part of him felt like he was abandoning his twin, but the rest of him?

Suddenly felt free.